# The Wife and the Ward

**Edward Money**

# The Wife and the Ward

Reprint of the original, first published in 1859.

1st Edition 2022 | ISBN: 978-3-37513-066-4

Verlag (Publisher): Salzwasser Verlag GmbH, Zeilweg 44, 60439 Frankfurt, Deutschland
Vertretungsberechtigt (Authorized to represent): E. Roepke, Zeilweg 44, 60439 Frankfurt, Deutschland
Druck (Print): Books on Demand GmbH, In de Tarpen 42, 22848 Norderstedt, Deutschland

# THE

# WIFE AND THE WARD;

OR,

## A Life's Error.

BY

LIEUT.-COL. EDWARD MONEY,

TURKISH SERVICE (LATE BENGAL ARMY),

AUTHOR OF "TWELVE MONTHS WITH THE BASHI-BAZOUKS."

LONDON:

ROUTLEDGE, WARNES, & ROUTLEDGE,

FARRINGDON STREET;

NEW YORK: 56, WALKER STREET.

1859.

The Cawnpore Ball.

Page 271.

TO

## THE RIGHT HON. LORD STANLEY,

### Secretary of State for India.

My Lord,

The following Tale, of fiction founded on fact, in which an attempt has been made to depict in a familiar style English social life in Hindostan, as also the saddest scene in the late Bengal Mutinies, will owe much of its success, if it has any, to your kindness in allowing the same to be dedicated to you.

That under your Lordship's government India will prosper, and that your name will henceforth be connected with the new and happy era now dawning o'er our great Empire in the East, is the belief,

My Lord,

Of your most obedient humble Servant,

EDWARD MONEY.

East-India United Service Club.

*February 15th*, 1859.

# CONTENTS.

## CHAPTER I.



## CHAPTER II.



## CHAPTER III.



## CHAPTER IV.



## CHAPTER V.



## CHAPTER VI.

## CHAPTER VII.



## CHAPTER VIII.



## CHAPTER IX.



## CHAPTER X.



## CHAPTER XI.



## CHAPTER XII.



## CHAPTER XIII.



## CHAPTER XIV.

## CHAPTER XV.



## CHAPTER XVI.



## CHAPTER XVII.



## CHAPTER XVIII.



## CHAPTER XIX.



## CHAPTER XX.



## CHAPTER XXI.



## CHAPTER XXII.

## CHAPTER XXIII.



## CHAPTER XXIV.



## CHAPTER XXV.



## CHAPTER XXVI.

# THE WIFE AND THE WARD;

OR,

# A LIFE'S ERROR.

## CHAPTER I.

### THE MESS—WHAT'S IN A NAME?

The cloth was removed from the long table in the mess-room of the 99th regiment of Bengal Native Infantry at Dinapore, and the stout "khansamah," or mess-man, having completed his evening duties, had retired, followed by the crowd of dusky table-attendants, who are always to be seen round dinner-tables in India.

It was the height of the hot weather, so that the officers seated around the board were dressed in cool white uniform, while over their heads the "punkah," or large fan, dependent from the ceiling, waved to and fro with a steady and noiseless motion, and rendered less unbearable the sultry and oppressive atmosphere.

This was the weekly guest-night, when the married officers of a regiment generally desert their own domestic circle for the mess-table, and the party was consequently larger than usual, consisting of, perhaps, a dozen of the officers of the regiment, with four or five guests. At the time we introduce them to the reader, the dinner was just finished, and those who wished had lit their cheroots, while a few inhaled the fumes of fragrant and perfumed tobacco through bubbling water and the long snake-pipes called "hookahs."

The last subject discussed had come to an end, and

there was a temporary lull in the conversation, as each and every one around the board settled himself comfortably in his chair, and in some cases undid the upper and lower buttons of his white waistcoat, as he muttered his opinion that it was "awfully hot."

"Come, Edgington, start a new topic," said the jolly lieutenant-colonel who commanded the regiment to a captain who sat opposite, and who had been rather silent all dinner-time—"something that will make us all talk, and forget that the thermometer stands at 98°."

"Well, I was thinking of the new arrival, sir, we saw on the course to-night," replied Edgington. "I was told her name, but forget it;—she is certainly a very pretty girl."

"Oh, Miss Plane, I suppose you mean," joined in a six-foot ensign, named Earnest, at the bottom of the table; "I met her at the general's at dinner yesterday—she's staying there. Yes, she's very handsome, but rather cold, I should think."

"An advantage, this weather, at all events," added, in a drawling tone, Lieutenant Percy, a thin, pale, and somewhat effeminate-looking young officer: "but what an unfortunate name for her!"

"Not at all, I think," said Captain Edgington; "the absence of beauty implied in it rather enhances her charms."

"Well, there's something in what you say," Lieutenant Percy again drawled out: "but what's her christian name?"

"Ah! if you could tell us *that*," remarked Hoby, the senior ensign in the regiment, "we should know something more about her."

"You certainly would, for you'd know her name in full, *et voilà tout*," Percy replied; "but I see not what further insight the information could give you," he continued, as he lit a fresh cheroot.

"Of course you don't," replied Ensign Hoby; "for every one knows *you* are not an imaginative character,

Percy; but tell *me* her christian name, and I'll tell you what she's like."

"How do you mean?" asked Major Bruce, the second in command; "do you think characters and names assimilate, and the knowledge of the latter proclaims the former?"

"Not exactly, perhaps," replied Hoby; "but everybody knows—or, at least, I know—that names *are* characteristic. Who ever saw a pretty Martha? who ever met an ugly Julia? The former, I would swear, was a round, moon-faced, healthy-looking, strapping girl, with no intelligence to make up for her want of personal charms, and no refinement of manner to compensate for her masculine appearance and large red hands: the latter, every one feels without seeing her, is more or less of a beauty, 'soft, languishing, and lazy;' possibly bestowing greater care on the adornment of her person than the culture of her mind; but, in spite of this or other defects, a most desirable companion for a moonlight stroll, more especially as the peculiar softness of her person and attributes, also indicated by her name, would well harmonize with such a scene and such a time."

"Upon my word, Hoby," laughingly replied the major, "you seem to hold a curious theory in the matter; and as you certainly have ideas in your head which sometimes repay for the trouble of extracting them, suppose you tell us a little more of this crotchet, and what you think of other names."

"If you'll mention any, I'll try," Hoby replied.

"Well, let me see,—I must be careful, however, not to select the names of any ladies in the regiment,—Emma, there's no one of that name in the 99th, or in Dinapore, that I know of. What do you think of Emma?"

"Oh, Emma is a loveable creature; one *I* would not marry unless I loved her very much, for no ordinary affection would satisfy her. She might be pretty or not, though I think the mass of Emmas are good-looking; but anyhow, she would be very affectionate, and very exacting. Yes, Emma is a tender name—decidedly tender, and should be avoided by all men not very tenderly inclined."

"Very good, very good," called out the colonel, amidst the laugh that went round the mess-table. "Let's try you again. Let me see, now,—what name shall we give? Fanny—yes, Fanny; tell us what she ought to be—that is, if no one has any objection," he added, looking inquiringly round the table. "If so, let him speak." No one did speak, and Hoby continued,—

"Fanny, strange to say, begets more the idea of a sister than a wife; a useful and industrious sister, too, who works hard with her thimble, her pen, or head, for anybody in the family she can benefit. I should not at all mind marrying a Fanny; for, *when* they marry, they make very good wives; but I, and everybody else, know ten sister Fannies for one Fanny a wife. So it is as a sister we must discuss her. He's a lucky fellow who has a Fanny for a sister! In my mind the name is connected with the kindest and most sisterly actions: playthings and the morning tub of cold water bestowed on a child, plum-cakes on a boy at school, loving letters and worsted slippers for the brother at college, with an affectionate endurance of tobacco-smoke during the vacations; and, in short, Fanny-like actions at all periods of life. There's another peculiarity in Fannies—though few of them marry, there are no old maids of that name. I never could account for this: the fact, I'm sure, all will allow; the solution has yet to be given."

"Devilish good, upon my word," laughed out the colonel. "Come, this is amusing enough," he added, filling his glass, and pushing the wine round; "let somebody else give him a name; eh, Edgington, its your turn, I think—come, what name shall it be?"

"I really don't know, sir; I'm not interested in any particular name, as many at the table, I doubt not, are. I see one or two who are not long from England, and surely they have sufficient interest in some fair ones they left behind to wish to hear Hoby detail their virtues."

"Well, I'll give a name," called out the junior ensign in the regiment, named Merton, who, with the matrimonial rashness peculiar to India, had taken to himself a wife—in whose veins dark blood mingled—six weeks after he had joined.

"You, you!" called out several of his brother officers. "Why, hang it, you're married, and *can* care about no particular name."

"And what if I am married," he replied, laughingly; "hang it, does a man, when he marries, become dead to all without his own domestic circle? It is true I cannot have the same kind of interest in a name as the bachelors around; but, as I happened to know a girl before I left England, who puzzled me a good deal, I shall be glad to hear what Hoby has to say about her, on hearing her name. At one time I thought her all perfection; at another, I—I was never in love with her, major, so don't smile—but, to cut the matter short, her name was Edith; and I want Hoby to tell us what Ediths are like."

"A very good name, too, for an opinion," said Major Bruce, "as it is an uncommon one. Now, Hoby, are you ready?"

"I had a very old aunt of that name," interposed Lieutenant Percy; "but she has been dead many years, and will, I am sure, not be disturbed by anything Hoby can say; so fire away, old fellow, and I'll smoke your hookah in the meantime," he added, taking the snake out of his hand, as he sat next to him.

"If I'd known of all this, I would have prepared myself," said Hoby; "as it is, I can but give you my crude impressions; however, such as they are, you are welcome to them."

"I like Edith better than any other name; in fact, it's my favourite name. I know not if among our Saxon ancestors it was a common one; but the present generation certainly shows a great want of taste in allowing it to be so rare;—or is it that the name combines so much excellence, that few, now-a-days, deserve to bear it; and *ergo*, few get it? This may be, for certain it is, that all Ediths are very charming, loveable creatures; and I am sure, if Percy had known his old aunt in her young days, he would allow it to be true. Ediths are always quiet beauties: by which I mean, that they owe their charms to no extraneous adornments, or elaborate toilets; for in their case, generally, 'beauty unadorned is adorned the most.' An Edith is never the belle of a ball-room; hers is not the flashing beauty which gains that distinction for its owner; and in a crowd she will often pass unnoticed. She is content with this, however, as she cares not for the idle homage paid to mere beauty; and she is too sensitive, too truly modest, to derive pleasure therefrom. See Edith, however, at home, by her own fireside, if you would see her in her proper element; and if by that hearth sits one to whom she has given her heart, watch well how love, deep and sincere, pervades her every action; and how she will then accept with gratitude, with heartfelt pleasure, that admiration which would but have caused a blush of anger, if offered by one whom she had not first learnt to regard and esteem. I should weary you, did I detail all her qualities; but I cannot omit one which governs all her thoughts and deeds, and which, argue as we may, must, in its extended sense, be the foundation of all that is good and noble—I mean charity. She possesses that virtue to perfection: it influences her every thought and action; and I know not how I can better express my admiration of her, and of her paramount virtues, than by closing my short and imperfect description with the statement, that charity makes her an Edith!"

"Well, you've evidently studied the subject of names," said the colonel; "and this is great fun; I should like to hear more of your opinions regarding them. Let me see, now,—what other name shall we give him? Oh! we all know the pretty Mary in the square; it shall be her name this time. By the bye, though, Edgington, isn't that the name of the little girl you were left guardian to, some years ago, and sent home when we were in Calcutta?"

"Oh no, sir," Edgington replied; "her name is Marion."

"All right, then," added the colonel; "and I suppose Hoby may abuse the name, if he likes. So come, arouse thyself, thou mysterious oracle, and tell us what a Mary should be."

"Everything, sir, and nothing;—'tis the only name, I think, which is not characteristic. If it has any character, it is that of extremes. A pretty Mary is very pretty; nay, beautiful;—an ugly Mary cannot be mistaken. Avoid a clever girl of that name; her talent, however charming in an acquaintance or friend, would be painful in a wife. I have known industrious Maries and lazy Maries; the former worked themselves to death in whatever they undertook; the latter would have died rather than exert themselves at all. If a Mary is good, she is a perfect angel; if bad, she is a perfect—— you can guess what! In short, in virtue as in vice, in all corporeal and mental qualities, Maries run to extremes. I never knew but one exception, and that exception proved the rule. She was an amiable Mary, and though her virtues did not run to the excess I have described, the absence of all evil made her character a very charming one; and thus she too supported my theory."

"Well, it is altogether an odd idea," drawled out the thin and pale lieutenant named Percy; "but you don't suppose any one will adopt your theory, as you call it?"

"I don't suppose he cares if they do or not," added the colonel; "but I think the idea is amusing enough, and I should be glad to see its soundness put to the test. Now, there's this Miss What's-her-name, who has just arrived. You know whom I mean," he continued, addressing Captain Edgington; "the girl you said you had been thinking about."

"I said I'd been thinking about? You mistake, sir."

"No I don't; you were the first who mentioned her after dinner. What's her name? You told us, I think."

"Miss Ugly, isn't it?" suggested Lieutenant Percy, with his usual drawl.

"No, no; not so bad as that," Hoby remarked laughingly. "Her name, Earnest says, is Miss Plane, and it's *plain* enough, Percy, your imagination is improving; in fact, that you are getting quite witty."

"I would I could return the compliment on your pun, but I can't," answered Percy, good-humouredly; "for, to tell the truth, it's a very *Plane* one."

"A truce to punning!" called out the colonel. "I want to put this theory of names to the test. There's this girl, now, Miss Plane, who's just arrived; it's very certain we none of us know anything about her, and it's equally certain a month hence we shall all know a great deal. Who knows her christian name? Let's give it to Hoby, and get his opinion of her character, and then we'll see how far he's right, in her case at all events."

"I know it," said the tall ensign, named Earnest, who had given her other name. "I saw it in a book on the general's table last night. But what am I to get for all the information regarding this angel which you are dragging out of me?" he added laughingly.

"Mercenary wretch! out with it!" playfully added the colonel.

"What, in goodness' name, should you get?" drawled out Percy.

"Well, I don't know," returned Earnest, laughing; "but it's a nuisance giving it gratis: however, you shall have it. Now prepare, Hoby, to give it a character," he continued seriously; "and if, when you have heard it, you feel you can't give it a good one, or rather, that you must invent a bad one, acknowledge the fact like a man, and let's pass on to something else."

"Yes," said Captain Edgington, who seemed much interested; "for goodness' sake, don't slander the poor girl; discuss names that affect no one, but not hers."

"Ah! Edgington, I shall begin to suspect something," laughingly added the colonel; "if the discussion does not affect *you*, I'm sure it affects no one else here."

"Nonsense, sir; but consider the poor girl herself, and, moreover, consider——"

"The name! the name!" was now called out by many, and Captain Edgington's further remarks were lost.

"Well, Edgington looks so wretched about it, I've half a mind to hold my peace," answered Earnest, thus appealed to. "But, I really don't see what harm it can do, so you shall have it; it is—it is," he added, speaking very slowly, and enjoying their impatience, "—it is Beatrice."

"Beatrice! Well, Hoby, what do you say to *that* name?" was eagerly asked by more than one voice.

"Give him time—give him time," called out the colonel; "never press a willing horse. But, Edgington, what on earth's the matter with you?—you are staring at Hoby as if he were going to pronounce your own fate."

"Was I?—I mean, did I stare? I didn't mean to do

so," replied Edgington confusedly, while the warm blood coloured his cheek in a manner seldom seen at the age of thirty. "But stop; before Hoby gives us the character," he added, "let's drink a glass to a toast I'll give you on the subject, and 'twill give time to our prophet."

"A toast!" called out the mess president at the head of the table. "Come, charge your glasses, all of you."

The glasses were soon filled—not all with wine, for many men in India drink nothing but bitter ale, and no one there thinks it wrong to drink healths in this beverage.

When all was ready, Captain Edgington stood up. He was a very popular man in the regiment, and as he was especially remarkable for the utter want of humbug apparent in his actions and words, every one waited with interest to hear the toast he was about to give, for they felt that whatever he did say would be said in all sincerity and truth.

We cannot resist the opportunity, as he stands before his brother-officers with a slight but not painful shyness, to describe his appearance. We do so the more readily as the outward man in his case was very indicative of the character within—not that we are going now to dwell on the latter; we would rather it should gradually speak for itself as the tale proceeds.

He was not a handsome man, and we are very sorry for it, but we cannot alter the fact. We would that we could, for he is the hero of our tale, and the admission will probably seal its fate with many who will forgive anything in a hero but this want. Do not, however, gentle reader, if you are of this class, shut up the book here; read on a little further, and see if you cannot, in spite of this unpleasant admission, still interest yourself in Arthur Edgington and his fortunes.

Well, he was not handsome; but a close student of physiognomy would have seen, nevertheless, much to admire in his face—its prevailing expression was frankness, openness if you will, and this quality might be seen in each and every feature. The mouth, especially, told of its possession by the owner; there was no unnatural straining of the lips, which is always indicative of a desire to prevent that tell-tale organ from making public the inward feelings. With Edgington, when his eyes laughed, his mouth laughed; when anger was depicted on his forehead and eyebrows, his mouth told the same tale—not, as in so many individuals one sees, *in spite of itself*, but boldly, and in a manner that proclaimed as plainly as spoken words, "Anger stirs the spirit within, know it and see it who will." By the bye, he had a beautiful mouth, a mouth which you loved for the honesty it bespoke. He was rather tall, and his well-knit frame, telling of strength more by the absence of all superfluous flesh than by the enlarged development of muscle, had the effect of somewhat increasing his stature.

Yet he was not handsome; in fact very far from it; the outline of his face, the shape of his head, each would have prevented it, and the whole countenance was one which neither he nor any one else had ever thought above par.

He seemed, as he stood there, half to regret the task he had taken on himself, and which task he doubtless undertook to divert attention from the notice which the colonel had drawn upon him.

He spoke at last, and said: "We have been discussing a new-comer in the small society which Dinapore boasts,—a lady who has just arrived from England's happy shores,—a lady of whom we know nothing, except that she is young, and—and—handsome. I am sure no one amongst us would wish to speak of her in an uncharitable spirit; and the fact that she has neither father nor brother, nor male protector that we know of, can only, I think, make us all the more careful in our discussions. It has been proposed that one of us, who appears to have made names his study, should divine her character from her Christian name, which appears to be Beatrice. I know my friend Hoby too well to suppose that he will be uncharitable in so doing; and much less do I fear that, for the sake of supporting the curious theory he has started, he will resort to invention for the sake of our amusement. With this conviction on my mind, and joining in the feeling which I am sure all of us have, that it is merely a joke—a new subject to while away the time, I await as anxiously as any of you the dictum of our oracle, and propose, that ere, through his means, we become better acquainted with the fair lady in question, we shall all drink her health with due honour, and, in doing so, hope for the verification, in so fair a shrine, of the latent virtues which, I feel convinced, will now be detailed. Mr. President, I beg to propose the health of our new-comer, Miss Plane, and success to the prophecies of our oracle!"

The din of jingling glasses, as the table vibrated with the loudly-expressed plaudits of the company, was so great that for a time nothing else could be heard. Edgington sat down in the midst of the noise, and pouring out half a tumbler of wine, drank it off without drawing breath. The speech he had just made went sorely against the grain; he did not at all approve of Miss Plane being made the subject of conversation at a mess-table, and nothing could have induced him to make her the object of a toast, had he not thereby thought to predispose Hoby to give her name a good character.

When the din had somewhat subsided, the president said,—

"Gentlemen, you hear the toast that has been proposed. I hope you will all drink it standing, and with the honours which I feel sure none will refuse. Are you all ready? Very good. Now, take the time from me. It shall be three times three, and yet another cheer. Steady, steady; let's do it with a will, keep time, and show the world how the 99th *can* cheer, with such a toast. Gentlemen, Our new-comer, Miss Plane, and success to our oracle!

"Hip, hip, hip, hurrah! Hip, hip, hip, hurrah! Hip, hip, hip, hurrah! Once more, and a good cheer—all together, mind—Hip, hip, hip, hu-r-r-a-h!"

The walls of that mess-room had not often echoed such vociferous shouts. The sound felt cramped in the building, and, purely for relief, rushed outside right around the square, awakening many from their first sleep, and causing the commandant of the European regiment to run out into his verandah, in his night-clothes, to ascertain the cause of the deafening uproar.

When the glasses had been drained of their contents, and silence ordered by the president, to enable the oracle to speak, all eyes were turned expectantly on Hoby. He was evidently not comfortable; he moved restlessly from side to side; he flung away a cheroot but recently lighted, and ignited another; he took his cap, which hung on the back of his chair, and seemed to meditate an abrupt retreat; at last, with a great effort, he arose and said hurriedly,—

"I thank you all for drinking my health, or rather Miss Plane's, and success to my predictions; but I think the joke has gone far enough, and, with your leave, I will change the subject, which I do by calling on our worthy vice-president for one of his capital songs."

"No, no!" was vociferated by all but Major Bruce, Captain Edgington, and Ensign Earnest,—"The prediction! the prediction! let's hear it; after all this parlance we'll be in at the death, anyhow; come, fire along; you don't get off so easily—fair play's a jewel."

These and similar sentiments, in loud voices, from all parts of the table, showed Hoby that he could not easily stem the current which he had himself caused.

"But I really had rather not," he pleaded seriously.

"And we had much rather you did," was the rejoinder.

Hoby looked entreatingly round the table. Nowhere could he see any inclination to bear him out in his wishes. He looked at Edgington, for instinct told him he should be supported there; that officer, with both elbows on the table, had shaded his eyes with his hands, and saw not the mute demand for assistance; Major Bruce, however, interfered in his favour.

"I agree with Hoby; I think we've had enough of names: what do you say, Colonel?"

"I say nothing, one way or the other," replied the colonel, who evidently wanted the oracular character, but would not directly sanction it. This kind of negative consent was, however, taken advantage of, and the calls on Hoby to make good his promise became louder and more frequent; many whom the subject had not much interested previously were drawn into the general excitement, and longed to hear what Hoby so evidently thought had better be untold. The noise became great, and still he hesitated. At last Lieutenant Percy said to him,—

"It's the character appertaining to the name, my dear fellow, not the character of the girl, you are to tell us."

"Is that well understood, then?" said Hoby, apparently much relieved by the suggested distinction.

"Of course, of course, it is," was echoed all round the table.

"Well, then, remember, I give you, according to my theory, the character of a Beatrice, not that of Miss Plane. I've nothing to do with her; it may, possibly, not be her name at all. No one knows it is for certain. Do you all understand it in that light?"

"Yes, any way you like!"

"Once more, will you let me off, and take another name instead, or even two."

"No, no,—such nonsense, after all your pretended wisdom!"

"Then listen," he replied, with a half-savage expression, like a bull driven to bay by its tormentors. "In the same way as I've sketched to you an Emma, a Mary, an Edith, and a Fanny, I'll now tell you what a Beatrice is like: Proud to excess; hers is not the pride that apes humility, but rather the pride that feeds on the failings of others, and holds itself more erect each time a fresh sin in any of her neighbours is made known. Not exposed to the many temptations to which those of a warm and generous nature are subject, she does not consider this fact, but blames without charity any backslidings arising therefrom, and values herself highly, inasmuch as she can truly say, 'Their ways are not my ways!' Would you ask a Beatrice if she is religious, she will scarcely deign to answer, so evident does she think the fact must be to all; but if you seek information on this point elsewhere, you will encounter many doubts whether such exclusive religion as hers, made up of form and ceremony, devoid of charity, and which certainly has never touched her heart, can be true religion. Ice is generally thought cold, but inasmuch as the thermometer shows us many degrees lower temperature than the freezing point, so does the temperament of a Beatrice, in its frigid and self-wrapped nature, set at defiance all comparison with any material substance. Hers is not the character that ever forgives, much less forgets, an injury; for she lives in an ideal world of her own, and under the conviction to which she has attained, and which she truly believes, that she is all excellent, any injury to herself assumes magnified proportions, on the principle that cruelty is greater when exercised towards an innocent and virtuous lamb, than its mother. She believes woman to be superior to man, simply because she is herself a woman; and she cannot understand,—though she cares not to make this avowal,—why obedience in marriage should be demanded from the latter.

"With all this array against her, Beatrice has some

redeeming qualities. The birth of a child calls forth in her affections of a nature so strong, as to astonish those who had known her before but through her frigid nature; she is an affectionate daughter, to her mother especially, for her theory of man and woman extends to her parents. She is generally spoilt, for she has imbued her mother with the idea of her excellence; and her father's authority she does not submit to. A Beatrice is clever, and she reasons well on most points, for enthusiasm never warps her judgment. She is natural, also, for her proud nature is far above concealing what she believes to be her perfect attributes; but this natural manner, which extends to the intercourse of every-day life, must not be mistaken for frankness; for, on the contrary, she is peculiarly reserved, and is thus not easily read by a casual observer. The pride which I have stated her to possess, differs much from vanity, for of the latter failing she has none; the force of the former passion pervades too much her every thought and action to allow the latter to creep in. For the same reason she is neither a coquette nor a flirt; nay, she has the most supercilious contempt for girls who try in any way to court the admiration of man. She is ladylike, of course,—vulgarity could not well exist in the character I have painted; and her appearance and carriage bears the stamp of proud and haughty beauty. In short, to sum up all in a few words, whether she be more beautiful than proud, more proud than cold, more cold than reserved, more reserved than haughty, more haughty than uncharitable, neither I nor any one else would like to determine."

"An extraordinary character, certainly," said the major, after a short pause.

"An impossible character," said Earnest.

"Make a devilish bad wife," drawled out Percy.

"Not as amusing as I thought it would be," said the colonel, filling his glass again; "the character has not got devil enough in it."

"Well, I hope we've done with names for to-night," added Major Bruce, seriously. "So far, no harm's done,—at least, I hope not; but let it stop here."

Captain Edgington did not speak—his eyes were on the ceiling, and he seemed in deep thought.

"A penny for your thoughts, Edgington," called out the officer who filled the president's chair.

"I will give them without the bribe," he quickly replied. "I was thinking on what Hoby has been telling us. He has certainly a very persuasive way of reciting his opinions, and the character he has painted may or may not suit Beatrices in general. But one thing I'll swear, it does not apply to Miss Plane, be her name Beatrice or not. You'll ask me why? I would simply answer, it is my *conviction* it does not; and Hoby can give you no better reason for the opinions he holds regarding names. Besides," he added, "irrespective of the theory being all nonsense, utter nonsense, which every one who thinks a moment must allow, the character just now painted is a most improbable, if not, as Earnest said, an impossible one. Did anybody at the table ever see a character at all resembling it? and yet I'll be bound any real character would come within the ken of some of us. No, no, Hoby, you have given us an ideal shape of your own; one, perhaps, you've met with in your dreams, but never in this sober, every-day working world. You did it well, however, I'll allow; and if you have no other reward, you have my thanks for killing time so successfully to-night. Why" (looking at his watch), "its half-past ten o'clock, I declare, and I have to be at target-practice at five to-morrow morning: so good night to you all; good night, colonel—I shall come up to your quarters when I've done my work in the morning."

So saying, Edgington left the mess-room. He was discussed after he left: some thought he was "spoony" on Miss Plane; others that he was not likely ever to marry; but they all agreed he was a devilish good fellow, and that if he ever did marry, they should be sorry to lose him at the mess.

No one stopped long after him. In India early hours are necessarily kept, and eleven o'clock saw most of the inhabitants of Dinapore getting such sleep as the musquitoes and the stifling atmosphere would permit.

We have now brought forward such of the officers of the 99th Native Infantry as will figure in our history. There were, of course, others in the regiment; but it is not necessary the reader should know them by name, as only those already mentioned will individually appear in the following narrative.

## CHAPTER II.

AN INDIAN MORNING—BEATRICE PLANE—FIRST IMPRESSIONS.

INDIA! how little art thou known to the mass of the English public, and yet who can doubt that thy loss would rob Britain of the brightest jewel in her crown. Nay, more; that when England's flag shall cease to wave o'er the peninsula of Hindostan, our island home will no longer occupy her prominent position among the nations of the earth, but sink irretrievably from that day into the rank of a second-rate power.

'Tis strange, this apathy, this ignorance on all Indian subjects; for how many thousands have family ties that interest them in those sunny lands, and yet truly how little is known in England of every-day life in India. The cadet who arrives in the country where he will probably pass the greater part of his life; the young English girl who goes out to her parents or friends, and who knows that, in the natural course of things, India will be her future home; neither of these have any idea, when they first behold the land of the Mussulman and the Hindu, what the country is like in which they are coming to reside. They know, indeed, that it differs from England; but wherein it differs, that they know not; and thus many find, after casting their lot on its shores, that the climate, the habits, and customs are repugnant to them, and wish, when too late, their previous knowledge had been more extended.

Such thoughts, or something like them, passed through Captain Edgington's mind, when, the morning after the scene described in the last chapter, he met, looking pale and wan, riding on the course, a little before five in the morning, Miss Plane, accompanied only by a syce, or groom, on foot, who walked by her side, and brushed away, with a long horse-hair fan, the flies, which settled in dozens upon her thin-skinned steed, and annoyed him not a little.

It was an Indian morning, following on a truly Indian night. At no period since the sun, in all his oppressive and fiery splendour, had sunk in the west the evening before, until the hour of which we write, when the increasing and vivid streaks on the Eastern horizon announced his speedy return, had there been a moment of freshness, much less coolness, in the air. As each hour of the night had passed away, the suffocating heat and painful stillness of the atmosphere had increased, as if both air and earth had drunk in so much of the solar rays on the previous day, that the hours of darkness were insufficient to dispel them.

It was evident to Captain Edgington, as he met the fair lady on his way to target-practice, that she had been and was suffering from the consequences of such a night, as also that her object in thus seeking refreshment from the early morning air would be frustrated, on account of the still high temperature that prevailed. As we have said before, it was an Indian morning; perhaps we ought to have said it was a hot Indian morning, for all mornings in India, even in the hot months, are not as bad as this one, the cool air, if any exists during the twenty-four hours, being generally prevalent at this time. On the day in question, however, the air was not only perfectly still, but very, very warm, and Captain Edgington could not wonder at the look of despair depicted on that beautiful face, as its owner moved uneasily in her saddle, and put back the massive braids of her dark brown hair from her forehead, in trying vainly to court the lightest zephyr.

Edgington had not been introduced to her, so would, of course, have passed on without speaking; but she reined in her horse as he came up, and, with a degree of self-possession which astonished him, said,—

"Excuse my stopping you, but I am very thirsty and faint, and have been endeavouring for the last ten minutes, without success, to make this man understand what I want. Will you interpret for me, and tell him to bring me some water?"

"Certainly—of course: he can get some in the lines of that regiment," replied Edgington, pointing to long rows of huts on one side of the road or course. "Get some drinking-water for your mistress," he added in Hindostanee to the syce. "Allow me," he continued, addressing the fair horsewoman, and springing from his saddle as he spoke, "to hold your horse's head in the mean time; the flies make him restless."

"Thank you. Is not this an unusually hot morning?"

"Rather so; but the mornings are usually hot at this time of the year."

"What a detestable place India must be, if the heat of the last twenty-four hours is a sample of what I may expect."

"I hope you will find it better than you anticipate. Many new-comers, who dislike it much at first, think very differently later. India has many advantages."

"This burning thirst, for example, under which I'm suffering, and this frightful atmosphere at five o'clock in the morning."

"No; but you would scarcely appreciate the said advantages at this moment, did I enumerate them. Keep quiet, will you," he exclaimed, trying to pacify the horse, who, irritated by the flies, and missing the attendance of his syce, moved restlessly from side to side.

"He will stand better alone, I think," she said, reining him back almost rudely; "besides, you'd better look after your own horse," she added, "for he seems inclined to go home without you."

Edgington dropped her rein, and turned to look after his steed, which, in his hurry to assist Miss Plane, he had quite forgotten, and which, out of revenge for being deserted, was now trotting away towards his stable.

"Never mind, he knows his way home, and my syce will bring him to me later," he continued. "Ah, here's the water; I know not how you'll drink out of that awkward vessel," he added, as her Hindu servant appeared with a large-mouthed earthenware pot, called a ghurrah, which could not be held but with two hands.

"I'll get off to drink," she said, springing lightly to the ground without assistance, and giving Edgington the rein, which she drew over the horse's head, to hold; "the syce, as you call him, can help me to lift this curious water-pot."

"She's not shy, at all events," thought our hero, as he took the rein, which she held out to him with a commanding air, and then watched how she would succeed in quenching her thirst. He almost laughed as she directed her attendant by signs to lift the large goblet to her mouth, and essayed to drink therefrom, at the imminent risk of receiving its contents over her person. The effort, as he knew it would be, was unsuccessful, and he proffered his advice.

"You'll find it easier, I think, if you bend your head and drink without lifting up the ghurrah."

She did not answer, but followed his advice, and succeeded better. As she stooped over the earthenware pot, which was held by the syce, and quenched her thirst, one of the braids of her hair, which was loosely fastened up under her riding-hat, fell down, and almost enveloped the vessel in its profusion. She did not remark it; her whole being seemed wrapped in the enjoyment the cold water imparted to her heated frame, and it was not till she had drunk enough, and looked up, that she became conscious of the accident. As she did so, she perceived the ardent look of admiration with which Edgington regarded her; and while her cheeks were suffused with a blush, to which, however, the expression assumed by the mouth gave more the indication of anger than modesty, she hastily gathered up her pendent tresses, and advanced towards her horse.

"Let me assist you to mount," said Edgington, longing to touch, however slightly, the fair form which had already made sad inroads into his heart.

"I want no help," she replied, with a haughty look, "beyond what the syce can give me, but shall feel obliged if you'll hold the horse's head while I get up."

Poor Edgington!—he fell back to make room for the Hindu, who went down on all-fours to make a stepping-stone for his mistress.

"Now, pray don't let him start," she said, as she gathered up her riding-dress; "perhaps you'd better put your hand over his eye, that he may not see me—that's right. These Arab horses are easier to get on," she added, when a moment later she was seated in her saddle, "than the large creatures we have in England; perhaps that's one of the advantages of India," she continued with a half-smile.

"I know not—perhaps it is," Edgington replied, scarcely knowing what he said.

"I'm afraid I've kept you from your duties," she remarked, looking at the sword at his side. "I thank you for your help, and I trust you'll not be late. Good morning," she added, making him a formal bow, and striking her horse sharply on the flank with her whip as she spoke.

The blood Arab that bore her started off at the stroke at a good hand-gallop, and bore his mistress—who was evidently a capital horsewoman—away at a speed which set at defiance the efforts of her dusky attendant to keep up with her.

Edgington stood in the middle of the road, staring at their receding figures. He felt that more than Miss Plane, her horse, and her syce, had gone away: he was painfully conscious that something belonging to himself had gone with them. In short, Edgington was in love —love at first sight, too, it was; for he had seen her but for a minute or two the evening before. 'Tis a strange thing, love; but love at first sight is stranger. Philosophers may moralize, Reason may argue with all her powers, but love at first sight, when it exists in some natures, is a strong passion—not lasting, perhaps, if it be not sustained by subsequent events, but all-powerful at the time; and so it was with Edgington, as he recalled all the personal charms of the fair being who had just left him.

"What an idiot I am!" he exclaimed, stamping his foot on the ground; "I am sure she was not so very agreeable, that I should feel as—as—I do feel towards her. At the same time, her very hauteur has something fascinating in it. What pleasure it would be to bend that haughty will; to infuse into that cold heart the affection which, when once it had entered, would break up the icy nature that enthralls it, and burn all the more brightly, and with the more force, from the virgin soil on which it was planted, and the totally new aim it would give to her being! What delight to teach——"

A bugle calling out one of the native regiments to parade sounded within a few yards of where he stood, and cut short his soliloquy, as it also brought him suddenly down from the fanciful love-region to which he had attained.

"You are a fool, Edgington," he pursued, after a moment's pause; "and as if that was not enough, you'll be late for your target-practice. Why, hang it, the very bugler looks at me, as if he thought I was mad; and truly I think he'd be right, if I allowed my thoughts to dwell much longer on Be-a-trice Plane" —The Christian appellation seemed to stick in his throat—"I wonder if that's her real name. She *can't* be all that Hoby painted last night; and yet——

"Ah, well! it's no use fancying evils; I feel sad enough without that."

He gave a deep sigh, and wended his way across the parade-ground, to the "butts," where his company already awaited his coming to commence their target-practice.

## CHAPTER III.

TEA IN THE COLONEL'S VERANDAH—AN OLD INDIAN'S VIEWS OF ENGLAND, WOMEN, AND MARRIAGE—STEEPLE-CHASE ARRANGEMENTS.

"Well, Edgington, did you make good practice this morning?" asked the colonel, as our hero came into his commandant's verandah an hour later, where the teapoys (small three-legged tables) covered with tea-things, showed the usual preparation for, generally, the pleasantest hour of the day in India.

"Pretty well, sir, though not so good as I could wish; still, if they'd fire before the enemy as well as they did at the target this morning, John Company would have no cause to complain."

"Ah, *that* they'll never do; they always fire too high in action, and the devil himself can't prevent it. Come, sit down, and have a cup of tea;—rather tepid this morning."

"Yes, but I think it is cooler than it was two hours ago; however, that's often the case after a sultry night; the morning sun brings a little wind. If you'll allow me, I'll undo my shell-jacket, for it's rather suffocating."

"Of course. Here, bearer, take the sahib's sword, and tell the khitmudgar* to bring the tea. I say, Edgington, they've no milk like this in England") pointing to a jug of frothy goats' milk)—"at least, I can remember nothing like it; but, then, it's a long time since I came out."

"I don't think they use goats' milk much at home; in India it is certainly better than that of cows. How long is it, colonel, since you left England?"

* Table-servant.

"Two-and-twenty years next month. I was eighteen then, I'm now forty."

"Don't you often long to see the old country again?"

"Well no; I can't say I do. Most probably I shouldn't like England. Having been so long in India, I've become a regular old 'Qui-Hi,' and the formal stiffness of English society wouldn't suit me at all. Hang it, there's no real hospitality there now; they always want a *quid pro quo* for everything; if you can return dinners and parties, you'll get invitations, not otherwise. Then, again, people in England live so much for appearances: Mrs. B. is wretched because Mrs. A., who lives next door, has a brougham, and she hasn't; while Mrs. A., in her turn, envies Lady Thingumbob the powdered lacqueys behind her carriage. No, no; we've no nonsense of that kind out here; there's a little of it in Calcutta, perhaps; but Calcutta's not India. Here, bearer!"

"Sahib!"

"Give me a cheroot. You don't smoke in the morning? I wish I didn't." (Cheroot duly lighted.) "No, Edgington, if I went home, I should do as many have done already—come out again as quickly as possible, with the determination never to return."

"It seems to me, sir, that a long-continued residence in India often brings about this state of feeling, and that is why I am so anxious to take my furlough, and renew all my English associations and ideas; to say nothing of the desire I have to see the little girl I am guardian to, and sent home in forty-seven, when we were in Calcutta. She's grown up, I hear, into a perfect beauty."

"Indeed! She was a nice child; I remember her well. Her father, they said, was immensely rich. He was some relation of yours, was he not, and left you a lot of money at his death?"

"Hardly a relation—at least, a very distant one.

There were two families of Edgington, though we both originally came from one stock, and he, poor fellow, was the last surviving member of that branch. His name, as you remember, was Paris; but he took it as the condition of inheriting a large fortune left him by a relation of his wife's."

"I didn't know that," the colonel observed; "for, in fact, I never knew him intimately. He shut himself up after the death of his wife, which occurred shortly after I first met them. She was certainly a lovable creature: I'm not, as you know, an admirer of women generally, but I certainly never met with her equal."

"I never saw her," remarked Edgington; "but every one spoke of her in the same way. You, of course, know she was a Greek? Mr. Paris met her at Athens. Little Marion, he used to say, was very like her."

"May-be; she had, if I remember right, the same perfect Grecian profile. Every one remarked how Paris, after his wife's death, appeared to adore the child. Who has charge of her in England?" asked the colonel.

"My mother," Edgington replied; "and she has brought her up entirely at home. Marion is now sixteen years old. Strange, is it not? It seems to me but yesterday she was with us in Calcutta, a playful thing in short petticoats, and yet it was eight years ago last month. Well, as I was saying, I hope to take my furlough next year, and see her; besides, I want another peep at the old country, to renew all my English associations."

"Ah, you're younger than I am, and it's perhaps as well you should do so. You'll come out a married man if you do, Edgington."

"That is not a necessary consequence, sir."

"No, not exactly; but you *are* a marrying man, I expect, and such generally get caught when they go home. To tell you the truth, that was partly the reason why I never went."

"Girls in England don't ask you to marry them, colonel," added Edgington, laughing.

"Very nearly, if not quite. Go into any country town, and live there six months, and see how many traps will be laid for you by intriguing mothers and calculating fathers. A man must be always on his guard. Here, in India, the male sex preponderate, and so a man 's pretty safe, unless he knowingly rushes into danger; it's not so in England."

"You've been so long away, sir, I don't think you judge England fairly: besides, you speak of marriage as if it should be carefully avoided; surely, a married man is often happier than a bachelor."

"I doubt it. Look at Mason, in the European regiment, for example, who married last month. He has all the novelty of the thing to recommend it, and I'm sure *he* doesn't look happy."

"What! do you think he regrets his marriage?"

"I think, between ourselves, there are very few married men who do not do so."

"Come, come, colonel, that's a dreadful idea, and you'll find few to believe it besides yourself. I could quote fifty instances to the contrary; but it's no use discussing the point. I know of old your aversion to marriage. It is, pardon me, almost a monomania with you, and I think it often makes you judge woman harshly."

"No, not at all; I love the dear creatures—at a distance; but I'll resign my liberty to none of them. By the bye, talking of women, how well Hoby did that last night!"

"Did what?"

"Why, his characters from names. He's a clever fellow enough; one would think, however, he must have studied the subject,—he had it all so pat."

"Yes; but I think the characters were overdrawn, and there can necessarily be no truth in his theory."

"I don't know that," replied the colonel. "The names he dwelt on were certainly characteristic of the characters he gave them."

"Because, perhaps, in one or two cases they happened to accord with your experience, sir. Another who heard him, and who had known a disagreeable Edith, or an amiable Beatrice, would have come away with a different opinion."

"Very likely. I suppose it's fancy, after all; but it was a funny idea. I shall laugh at him if that girl's name turns out to be really Beatrice, and we find she is not the dreadful creature he painted. Somebody said she was staying with the general, I think."

"Yes, I believe so."

"Plane, Plane—there's a man in the civil service of that name. Why, hang it, of course; how stupid I am—she must be a daughter or relative of the new collector coming to Patna. I saw it in the *Gazette* yesterday, and I'm almost sure the name was Plane. However, we'll soon see. Wait a minute," he added, as he went into the house.

Edgington awaited his return with impatience, although he was not long absent. "Just as I thought," called out Colonel Carstairs, as he returned into the verandah with the *Gazette*, and laid it on the table,—"here it is,—'Mr. J. Plane to be Collector at Patna.' Depend upon it, she's his daughter."

"Did you ever meet him?" asked Edgington.

"No; but I've heard he is a great booby. He'd just left Berhampore when I went to that station, five years ago. He had made no enemies there, but also no friends. At the same time, he kept open house, and gave no end of parties; but everybody said it was absurd to see the way in which Mrs. Plane ruled him."

"Oh, then, Mrs. Plane is with him?"

"I don't know if she is now; she was then. A masculine, strong-willed, hard woman, was the character she had there; so, if she comes to Patna, she'll be no acquisition, after all, nor her daughter either, if Hoby's portrait was a true one."

Edgington sat lost in thought, while the colonel puffed away at his cheroot. He remembered what Hoby had said of the parents a Beatrice often has, and he was pained and surprised to find how well what he had just heard accorded therewith.

A step on the gravel walk announced another arrival, and Major Bruce appeared.

"I came to say, colonel, I think it would be much better if you put Ensign Earnest as superintending officer on the court-martial to-day to try that sepoy. It is a serious case, and that young lad Merton is too inexperienced for it. Ah, Edgington, I didn't see you behind the pillar. What do you think, colonel,—am I right?"

"Oh yes; settle it as you will. Issue a morning order, making the alteration; you'll find pen and paper in that room, and one of the orderlies can take it to the adjutant."

While Major Bruce is writing we should like to say a few words about him. He was of that happy compound between the old and new Indian school, which certainly makes the best public servants and the most agreeable men in India. The said happy compound, as we have designated it, can best be described by negatives. He did not, like the old school, drink or smoke from morning till night, or sleep three or four hours in the daytime, or fancy a Hindu the most perfect character in creation, except a Mussulman; or the Indian climate perfection, or the mode of life in India superior to any in Europe; or rail at any innovation by the younger generation; or, in a few words, make himself as disagreeable as he could to any one who was not, by habit and consent, the same dried-up old specimen of a hookah-smoking, curry-eating, yellow-skinned, exclusive old Indian, such as the old school so often are. On the other hand, Bruce did not, like "young India," swear with or without occasion, or beat his servants; or think good billiard-playing the highest art attainable; or live in his stable; or class all the natives under the one head of "niggers;" or vote the service a horrid bore, and India a brutal hole only fit for the niggers aforesaid. These, and many other things characteristic of the new school, he eschewed; avoiding, at the same time, the errors of the old, and thus forming his judgment of India and the natives in that spirit of moderation which alone enables a man, in that strange land, to appreciate rightly the good qualities of both Mussulman and Hindu, while he cannot also but perceive their equally numerous national defects. In a word, the natives of Hindostan were, he believed, neither to be set down as angels nor devils.

Bruce had also many high and rare qualities which were peculiarly his own, by which we mean that they were significative of no particular school or type. He was a gentleman in every sense of the word; he never knowingly and needlessly hurt the feelings of another; and if at any time he had acted in a manner which after-consideration did not approve, no one was more ready or willing to admit it than himself, and make reparation in whatever way lay in his power. He was a *just* man,—and how much is comprised in that one little word! This it was that made him bear with and make allowances for failings in others, even when they militated most against all his preconceived notions and prejudices, and caused him to use the great power he had in the regiment in such a manner that all recognized what he did as the actions of a man who had the good of the body at heart, and sacrificed all petty feelings, ay, even friendships and animosities, to the welfare of the whole.

Bruce was a soldier, and a soldier with firmness, judgment, and tact. None questioned his orders, for all knew they must be obeyed; yet none could mix on more friendly and equal terms with those below him than himself, for there was ever that in him which forbad his authority being thereby lessened, or made him less the commanding officer when he returned to that character. We say the commanding officer, for he was truly little less in the 99th; of a much higher order of intellect and ability than Colonel Carstairs, and possessing, as he did in an eminent degree, the moral firmness so necessary for those in command, the colonel had for a long time deferred to him, or rather, we should say, leant upon him and his judgment. To whatever extent the fact was known in the 99th, it was only from the colonel's own unguarded expressions or actions, for, with happy tact and good sense, the major allowed no one to see how often he held the reins of power. In fact, he was extremely sensitive and jealous on this point, and nothing annoyed him more than any remark which inferred such to be the case; for though he could not be blind to the fact that Colonel Carstairs was not of the metal to make a good commandant, he at all times tried to prevent this truth from oozing out; and with such success were his efforts attended, that the colonel continually got the credit, both from seniors and juniors, of acts with which he truly had had little to do.

Our major had married, early in life, the daughter of an indigo-planter. Young as he was at the time, for he was just of age, his bride was much younger, having only completed her seventeenth year. She had therefore grown up to womanhood as his wife; and being much inferior to him in force of character, and of a very loveable and confiding disposition, all her ideas had been formed by him. Mrs. Bruce was in truth, if such an expression is allowable, "Bruce a little compressed." You could not be in her society many hours without seeing this; and though of course it did away with any originality of character, the resemblance of Bruce was so softened down in his wife's nature, and combined with such ladylike gentleness, that the possessor, even with her borrowed plumes, had many charms. Bruce, though a major, and consequently in receipt of good allowances, was a poor man. He had been somewhat extravagant, when, a little more than a boy, he arrived in India; had borrowed money at a high percentage from one of those scourges of the Indian army, the banks for loans, and had never recovered from the effects of that unwise step.

One word on the subject of debt—of Indian debt, so little understood in England. A father sends out his son as a cadet to India, with perhaps twenty-five pounds in his pocket when he lands, and looks on him as well set up in the world—nay, thinks him, with the splendid Indian allowances, a reprobate if, five years later, he turns out to be in debt. But there are excuses for the Indian sucking soldier. Once in debt, and it is most easily contracted, we know no country where it is harder to get out of it. A young man, or rather a boy (for cadets are little more when they go out), *can* live on his pay from the moment he arrives; but to do so he must deny himself much which others around him have, and which the facility of borrowing money in India will, if he persists in his rigid economy, leave him alone in its exercise.

There are some ingenious institutions, arrogating to themselves the name of banks, in India, which have devised a safe and certain method of drawing into their coffers the surplus increase of officers' pay. By surplus increase, we mean the increase of pay accorded to each rising grade; or rather the amount in excess of what an officer requires to live on in each rank.

The *modus operandi* is simple enough: these learned institutions, knowing the exact sum every officer receives monthly, as also the exact sum he *can* live upon, they, with a wild generosity, will lend whatever money an officer applies for, provided its amount does not exceed the difference, in the three coming years, of the pay he will receive and the sum on which he can exist. The borrower must, however, provide himself with two sureties, also officers in the service, who hold themselves responsible for the due fulfilment of the contract he then enters into. This is, to refund such a sum out of his monthly pay as shall, in three years, repay the capital borrowed, plus the very large interest charged upon it. In case of an officer retiring from the service in debt to the bank, or in case of expulsion by sentence of court martial, the two sureties, by the papers they execute, render themselves liable for whatever may then be the remaining portion of the debt. There remains, therefore, but one contingency by which the office that grants the loan can lose, and that is the death of the borrower; he is consequently required to insure his life for the amount necessary, in favour of the bank, for the said three years, and the premium for this insurance is at once deducted out of the sum advanced, as these banks have, with sagacity, discovered the advantage of being their own insurance offices.

Now, all this business on the part of these huge loan offices—for surely they deserve not to be known as banks—is legitimate enough *for* loan associations to conduct; and if they will designate their institutions rightly, we can find no fault; but what we do find fault with is, that the Government did, if it does not now, indirectly lend itself to the transaction, inasmuch as the paymaster,—on receipt of a written request from the borrower, executed at the time of contracting the loan,—deducted from his monthly pay the sum specified, and remitted it to the so-called banking institution, which, well aware of the great power this gave them, granted no loan without such a request on the paymaster being executed.

It does not in India follow, like it would in England, from the difficulty of finding such obliging friends, that *because* the loan has to be protected by two sureties, few would be contracted. On the contrary, on all money points, people in India act differently to what they do at home; money has not apparently so much value;

our countrymen out there are more lavish than in England; salaries are higher; the mass are richer, more careless, and more generous too. A borrower can, therefore, almost always find two sureties, even in his own regiment; and when the transaction is considered in its details, the securities really take upon themselves very little risk, for as long as the officer they oblige keeps clear of dismissal, they are pretty safe.

The consequences of this borrowing system, now so general among, at all events, the junior branches of the army, is very disastrous. Young men, as we have said, *can* live on their pay when they go out; but they are not likely to do this when they have only to ask for money to obtain it: and we feel confident that, in thousands of cases, the first loan contracted, and the later ones it has necessitated, have hung like a dead weight for life round the neck of the borrower, rendered him a less valuable soldier, and hastened his death, inasmuch as it has prevented him seeking a renewed lease of health in England.

Can the system be stopped? We think it might be, to a very great extent, by the following simple means:—Let paymasters attend to no requisitions of officers regarding the disposal of any portion of their allowances, but simply in each case pay the amount to its proper recipient; and let certain rules be framed for Courts of Requests (the courts to which officers are liable for debt), which would place such loan obligations behind claims of other kinds.

If this borrowing system did not exist, none who know India can doubt that officers in the East would be richer men; debt amongst them the exception, not the rule; and that, therefore, their services would be more valuable to the State.

Major Bruce had been a victim to this borrowing system. He was very young, and somewhat extravagant when he came out to India, and contracted his first loan shortly after his arrival. By the time he had repaid it, he was obliged to contract another; this, with its heavy interest, his early marriage, and young family, necessitated a third; and so he had gone on ever since; for though after the first two years he had always been economical, he never could get rid of the millstone, in shape of debt, which hung round his neck.

A cup of hot tea, with an extra supply of the aforesaid rich goat's milk, evinced the khitmudgar's desire that the Major Sahib should stay awhile. He did not disappoint the wish, for he sat down when he returned into the verandah; and an instance of the regard which Bruce inspired in all, might be seen in the manner the turbaned attendant placed a chair for him, and smiling a welcome, waited deferentially with folded arms to see if he had succeeded in making the tea as the major liked it.

"We were talking as you came in, Bruce," said the colonel, "of our new arrival, Miss Plane. I've found out who she is. See here," pointing to the *Gazette* on the table, "there's a civilian, named Plane, coming to Patna as collector, and I suppose she's his daughter."

"Very likely," answered the major. "I heard the name the other day; she's staying with the general, I suppose, till her father comes. I met her out riding his morning—at least I suppose so, as it was a young and handsome girl whom I had not seen before."

"Is she, then, very pretty?" asked the colonel—"in short, as pretty as, by Hoby's account, a Beatrice ought to be?"

"Yes, I thought her very handsome—a face not easily forgotten. But I am sorry her name was dragged into last night's discussion. I know not with whom the fault lay, but it would certainly have been better avoided."

"Oh, it was only a joke, and no harm can come of it," the colonel replied. "So many other names were freely discussed, that no one could think it personal.

Hoby did it well—didn't he? What do you think of the theory, as he called it?"

"A whimsical one; certain, however, to make thoughtless proselytes—not from any excellence in itself, but because the author takes care to paint by far the majority of names in agreeable colours, and all whose experience in any one case tallies with his descriptions will, at all events, be pleased with the idea. Besides, in spite of what we are told regarding sin being the natural state of man, I am sure we like better to discover virtues than failings in our acquaintances; and, with one exception, in all Hoby's descriptions last night the good much preponderated. I therefore think it an idea that would please many, particularly that class who accept anything new and amusing without caring to examine too closely into its foundations."

"Yes, what you say is very true," replied the colonel; "and I certainly think there's a charm in a name."

"So there is," added Bruce; "for however true it may be that 'A rose by any other name would smell as sweet,' it is very certain any new floral name would not be so suggestive to us of pleasant odours, and the rose would, however unjustly, lose something of its reputation by the change. But this in no way either bears out or militates against Hoby's theory. What do you think of it all, Edgington?"

"I think you've taken a very good view of the case, and I certainly am not one of Hoby's proselytes."

"Ah, then you never knew a loveable Julia or a charming Edith," replied the major, laughing; "but never mind, you'll meet lots of them when you go home, and then you'll call to mind Hoby's description. You take your furlough next cold weather, don't you?"

"Well, yes—I'm not sure—probably I shall."

"You bachelors have, at all events, the pleasures of freedom; but we married men don't envy you, for it's the only pleasure you have Eh, colonel?—though you are not married, I'm sure you'll agree with me," added the major in his light-hearted and joking way.

"Liberty goes a long way, though," replied the commandant; "and a man ought to have many pleasures to make up for its loss. 'I think I'll keep the good I have, rather than fly to pleasures that I know not of.' That's not the right quotation, but it will do to express what I mean."

"Very well indeed," replied Bruce, "and I won't quarrel with it. Why, Edgington, you're not half merry this morning; what's the matter with you?"

"You and the colonel talk so fast, you don't give me a chance to get in a word; and now I fear it's too late, for I must be wending my way homeward," he replied, getting up as he spoke. "By the bye, Bruce, I hope you haven't forgotten the steeple-chase that comes off next week; you are one of the stewards, remember. I wish you would enter your mare Bessie, and let me ride her; for the only horse I have fit for a steeple-chase is lame, and I'm sure Bessie would have an excellent chance, if well ridden; besides, I could just get up the right weight."

"Earnest asked me the same thing yesterday, and I said no, for he's too heavy, and I defy a man to ride a steeple-chase well in a seven-pound saddle. But the objection doesn't apply to you; and if you like, we'll enter her together. I think with you she ought to have a chance."

"Then Earnest shall beat you both, for I'll lend him my big Cape horse," added the colonel, laughing; "and if he doesn't walk away from Bessie, in spite of the extra stone, over the heavy ploughed land, I'll eat him; that is to say, the horse, not Earnest, for I suppose he'd object to that conclusion."

"You couldn't have a better rider," said Edgington, "and the race will be great fun. I'll tell him as I pass his bungalow—may I? I know he's most anxious to ride."

"Do," replied the colonel; "and tell him he had better try to get the horse in wind, and begin at once. I'll send the syce over by-and-by, and he can give him orders."

"Ah, you'd better do the same with Bessie, Edgington," added the major, "for she is too fat by half; suppose you begin this evening. There were one or two training on the racecourse this morning, and we must bring the mare out in as good condition as we can, for she'll have some awkward customers to deal with, to say nothing of the colonel's Cape."

"Yes, the Cape will do the trick," called out Colonel Carstairs laughingly, as he went into the house. "Good-bye; we shall meet, I dare say, on the course in the evening. Will you stop to breakfast, Bruce?"

"No, thank you; I must go home at once, for this is the last day of the overland mail," he replied; and so saying, he and Edgington walked off together.

They parted at the compound gate, and Edgington walked thoughtfully homewards. What did he think of? Beatrice Plane? Yes, of her, and the steeplechase; he hoped she would be there to see it. Edgington was a splendid rider; and there are few things a young man in love, and confident in his powers across country, likes better than the opportunity a steeplechase gives him to show his "ladye faire" what he can do in the saddle. Occupied with these ideas, he forgot all Hoby had said the previous night. The gloomy thoughts which had that morning stolen over him gradually vanished; he saw not the glaring barrack-square, as he walked through it, the dusty natives he met, or the creaking hackerys he passed; for a lovely pale face, shaded by rich tresses of dark-brown hair, occupied his vision, and somehow it appeared to smile upon him!

Edgington went home happier than he had felt for some hours. Ah! youth, youth! how many blessings are thine! Not the least is the power thou possessest of never dwelling long on the gloomy side of a picture. If 'tis true that "hope springs eternal in the human breast," how much more is it the case in those young hearts which have not learned, by sad experience, that in all our aspirations in life, failure is the doom of the many, success the lot of the few.

## CHAPTER IV.

### MR. AND MRS. PLANE—HOT WINDS—CONJUGAL CONVERSE.

We change the scene, though scarcely the time; for it was on the same morning, at about ten o'clock, that a gentleman and lady sat down to breakfast, in one of the largest rooms of one of the largest houses in Benares,—a town or station, we may mention for the information of our non-Indian readers, about 150 miles farther up the country than Dinapore.

The gentleman was an old gentleman; at least, he had all the appearance of one at first sight: if, however, you looked closely into his face, you saw what induced you to modify the opinion previously arrived at. Age was not written in its lines; in fact, the more you looked the more you wondered to see such a young head on such old shoulders—that *they* were old was beyond doubt; and their somewhat bent form accorded with the rest of the body, which, both from appearance, as also from a restless, undecided manner of movement, denoted fidgety old age. In short, the body and face were in contrast, for time appeared to have favoured the latter; but still the head altogether had no great advantage in the way of youth, for it was garnished, with the exception of a small bald spot, with snow-white hair, which quite bore out the tale of years bespoken by the senile bearing of the body. The countenance, as we have said, was comparatively youthful in appearance; but it was singularly deficient in expression. You could swear, when you looked at it, that the owner was famous for nothing, except the art of getting through life with but little exercise of the mental powers. There was no evil expression in the face; on the contrary, what did exist was rather the reverse, and denoted a mild and weak, but good man; a fact which the eye fully bore out, for it was soft, and evidently of that genus which quickly fills with tears. The mouth told also the same tale; for it wore a weak, unmeaning smile, which did not appear to arise from any passing incident, but to be, in fact, its normal character. The old gentleman had just begun breakfast at the time we describe him; and he smiled at his egg, as he broke it over his Indian dish of fish and rice, as if he wished to atone, as far as lay in his power, for the violence he perpetrated on it.

The lady who sat opposite to him was ten years his junior in reality, but would have looked even his senior, could you have seen the two faces alone, set in picture-frames. She was a marked contrast to him, in every way. She looked her age, which was about forty; but she bore her years well, as the strong and regular proportions of her well-knit frame testified. Her face was a hard one; in youth it must have been handsome, for the features were very regular, but it must always have lacked gentleness of expression. It was evidently the countenance of a strong-minded woman, who had never learnt in life to defer to another, but had always had her own way, and was now likely to have it to the end. There was great character in the face; it spoke plainly of the strong will, and the deep thoughts within; for the owner in no way lacked intellect: but the cold, gray eye, and the thin, compressed upper lip, denoted also a character which would sternly employ the will and talent at command to accomplish her views, treading down without remorse all opposing obstacles. She, too, broke an egg over her rice, but she did it with a frown and a compression of the lips: trifling points these, but those who study character know all such minute traits have weight.

The room in which they sat was large, and boasted but little furniture. There were no curtains to the windows, as is usual in England, but green jalousie blinds, outside, extended, as the windows themselves did, to the floor. The room was a bow one, and the centre window, or door, in the bow—for no one could say which it was—had been removed, and its place was occupied with a large kuskus tattee. And what is a "kuskus tattee?" A little patience and we will explain.

At a certain season of the year, in certain parts of India, blow hot winds. These generally commence about eight in the morning, and puff away their hot blasts till sunset. In *more favoured* spots, they blow away till ten, eleven, and twelve at night, or even sometimes till they begin again next morning. The degree of heat which is contained in these sultry winds exceeds the comprehension of the European reader. They vary in intensity in different localities, but in all is the temperature as if the blast were fresh from the mouth of a furnace. The wind itself is also strong, generally increasing in force as the day gets older, till it declines with the declining sun. When at its height, towards mid-day, it blows half a gale, and the atmosphere is charged with clouds of dust and fine sand, so that it is often difficult to see fifty yards ahead.

This phenomenon is not general in India, for it is mostly met with in what are called the North-West provinces. It does not exist in Bengal proper; the damp nature of the climate there preventing it; besides which, it is, we believe, an admitted fact, that this great heat is imparted to the winds in the sandy deserts of Arabia and Persia, and that the parts of Hindostan farthest removed therefrom do not feel its effects. However that may be, it is very certain that the farther north-west you go in India, the stronger and hotter do you find these winds to be. At Ferozepore, for instance, one of the most north-westerly stations, they blow night and day for months; while Meerut, Delhi, Cawnpore, Allahabad, and Benares all get their share. Dinapore has them only by fits and starts; while below, or rather to the east of that point, they cannot be said to blow regularly.

In the north-west of India these hot winds blow between two and three months, with little or no intermission. The months are those immediately preceding the rainy season, which commences in June. The climate in this part of Hindostan is, however, generally thought preferable to that of Bengal, for these fiery blasts themselves are less enervating than the damp heat of the lower provinces. Again, in the upper part of India, the cold weather lasts three months; during which time no portion of the earth's surface boasts a more delightful and invigorating climate in every way. This is not the case in Bengal; there the winter,—if so it may be called,—does not continue more than six weeks, and even during that short period the mid-day sun is often oppressive.

All this, however, does not explain "kuskus tattees," and we have wandered widely from our subject. In a few words, they are mats or screens, formed from a peculiar spongy grass, and bound together by light bamboo frames; they are placed before an open door or window, during these hot winds, and kept continually wet; the hot air is cooled in a wonderful way in passing through them, and enters the house not only deprived of all its strong and fervent heat, but bears also with it the peculiar and delightful odour of the kuskus grass. By these means a house, during the hot winds, may be kept at a comparatively delightful temperature, and the only being who does not profit thereby is the agent of this beneficial change; in other words, the poor fellow who, standing outside in the verandah, exposed to all the force of the wind, is continually employed in dashing water, by means of a small leathern jug, over the "tattee." Without "kuskus tattees," in the north-west of India, Europeans could scarcely exist during the hot winds; and they are in truth almost as necessary to life as is fire to ice-bound navigators at the North Pole.

Gentle reader, you probably are one of the denizens of the temperate English climate, and, if so, can scarcely realize such a state of things. Think of such facts when you hear the climate of Britain abused; think of Europeans in India shut up in their houses from sunrise to sunset; think of the "brick-fielders" or dust-storms, with the high summer temperature, in Australia; of the more than frequent high winds, storms, and earthquakes in New Zealand; of the weeks upon weeks of continual drought, and then the months of incessant rain, common in many parts of the tropics; of the numberless crawling vermin common throughout the East; of the frightful winter in the extreme North of Europe; of the mosquitos which, in those northern regions, make life, during the short summer, unbearable; of the long and dreary nights, and the no less endless, dreary summer days in those high latitudes. Think of all this, and of fifty other things which we could enumerate, and believe, for it truly is the case, that no other country in the world is so free from the annoyances of excessive heat and cold, the curse of vermin, the pest of crawling and flying insects, as your island home. If, therefore, you *have* a little more fog than you like, if the climate *is* changeable and uncertain, learn to bear these minor evils; perfection belongs not to earth, and we must doubt whether, could you transfer any known climate to England's shores, the mass of the population would not in a very short time regret, and regret with reason, the change.

Well, the hot wind puffed and blew, almost drying up the already shrivelled carcass of the old man, or "bheestie,"* outside, who continued indefatigably to water the tattee. He was dressed as all bheesties in India are—that is, not dressed at all; a piece

* Water-carrier.

of coarse red stuff bound round his loins, and a light turban of the same colour, constituted his whole toilet, which, at all events, had the advantage of simplicity. In spite of the hot blast and clouds of fine dust in the verandah, we will venture out and watch him. Swich—swich—swich—he has just dashed three small leather jugs full of water over the tattie, which always produces the above sound as it is thrown against the spongy grass; it will not be necessary to repeat the dose for three or four minutes, so our bheestie sits, or rather squats, down on the heated floor of the verandah in the manner common to Orientals. It is a peculiar position, so we will endeavour to describe it. We have never seen human beings in Europe assume the attitude—perhaps they lose much by their ignorance thereof; though we must allow the position itself is not comfortable, at least to a beginner, and we have never proceeded beyond that stage. No more of our friend the bheestie touched the ground while squatting than when he stood; his feet, and his feet alone, in both cases were in contact with the floor, but there all similarity between the two positions ceased. As he squatted, his legs were bent double at the knees, that part of the leg above the knee rested on the part below; or, in other words, the under part of the thigh lay touching the calf, forming, if we may use the term, a "point d'appui" for the rest of his body, which was somewhat bent forward, to preserve the equilibrium which the squatting position otherwise destroys. But the most singular feature in the squatting attitude is the use, or rather disuse, made of the hands and arms: the latter are thrown forward at an angle of forty-five from the shoulders, and rest on the knees; the forearms are in no way bent, but preserve the same rigid straight line to the wrists, which, however, disclaim any control over the hands, for these hang down as if they were tied on, and somehow or another invariably manage to look as if they did not properly belong to the wearer. Such was the squatting position assumed by the bheestie as he rested from his labours, as it is also the position the lower-class natives of Hindostan invariably take when they have five minutes to spare.

As the bheestie, Ramadan by name, took his ease as described, it struck him that he had now been watering the tattee two hours, and had smoked but one pipe, or hubble-bubble, during that period. This was quite against his principles; and as he rose to take up the pipe, which lay at the foot of one of the verandah pillars, he turned up his eyes into his head in such a manner as to show nothing but the white balls, his usual way of expressing anticipated pleasure, the opportunities of which, in his case, poor fellow, were few enough.

A small piece of live charcoal,—some stood in a pan at the end of the verandah,—having been placed over the composition of tobacco, sugar, and spices smoked in these pipes, and swich, swich, swich, over the tattee again, down squatted the bheestie once more to enjoy a smoke. This time the left arm alone, with the hand dependent, was placed on the knee; for the right hand held the small water-pipe, which consisted of a cocoanut-shell as the receptacle for water, and a small stem and bowl above it. There was no mouth-piece, the lips being placed to a small hole in the shell when smoked.

Bubble, bubble, bubble, goes the water in the pipe, and Ramadan rolls about his eyes in the most frightful way, as indicative of the pleasure he derives. Thus he soliloquizes between the inhalations: "Master and mistress are at breakfast inside; I know that, for I saw the khitmudgar take in the fish just now. Well, it's cooler inside there than it is here; but the mem sahib* scolds so, it takes a good deal to make it cool where *she* is. Never mind, the sahib is good enough—too good for her; she's no feeling, not a bit of it; she cut eight

* Mistress.

annas * off my pay last month, because I fell asleep here one day at the tattee. How she laughed when she did it—ah, dear! it wasn't much for her, with two thousand five hundred rupees a month, to gain eight annas, but it's a good deal for me to lose, with but four rupees for everything and eight balbuchas † to support —bubble, bubble, bubble. Well, the servants say master and mistress are going to Patna soon, and wages are there better for bheesties—bubble, bubble, bubble—ah, this *is* nice tobacco!" A smack of the lips; and a most diabolical rolling of the eyes is brought up very short by a shrill, masculine, hard voice within, calling out in Hindostanee—

"Bheestie, fling more water on the tattee, you lazy rascal—it's nearly dry; you think more of your hubble-bubble—for I can hear it plain enough—than anything else, and you are a faithless servant."

The bheestie answered not, but swich—swich—swich went the water, and the pipe was left for a more favourable opportunity.

We have been out in the verandah long enough—too long in such overpowering heat—and had better hasten in again. You can scarcely see when you first enter, the contrast of the darkened room to the flaring day outside is so great; but on getting accustomed to the light, the same lady and gentleman are discovered at the breakfast-table whom we so unceremoniously deserted to explain "kuskus tattees," "bheesties," and what not. They have finished breakfast, however, now; and as Mr. Plane—for he it is—smokes his hookah, the lady says,—

"Dear Beatrice is not pleased with her first impressions of India; in her letter this morning she complains sadly of the heat at Dinapore. Poor child, I wish I were with her."

"Well, you will be in another fortnight, and the heat won't kill her in the interval."

* Half a rupee, or one shilling. † Children.

"Ah, sufferings from the heat never excite *your* pity, James. You've got accustomed to it yourself, and think others don't feel it. See how *I* suffered when I returned from England last year."

"Well, my dear, I pitied you then, and I pity Beatrice now; I can do no more."

"Yes, you can, James; you can write to-day to the general at Dinapore, and ask him to be very careful to give the dear girl a cool room."

"No, no; I can't do that, Elizabeth. It's very kind of him to give Beatrice a home till we arrive at Patna; and its quite unnecessary to tell him of such things."

"There, again, *because* I suggest a thing, you at once think it quite unnecessary. That's so like you, James."

"How, my dear? May I not differ with you?"

"Not on such points. I must know better than you what is good for our daughter."

"But she'll get the good without my writing for it."

"No, she won't. Now, James, you know I yield to you in many points, and you must do so to me in all connected with Beatrice," answered Mrs. Plane, decisively.

"Well, my dear, as you have often told me, I should defer to you in all matters connected with the house, in all connected with the society we keep, in all pecuniary points, in the official matters in which you choose to interfere, and many other things; if to this long string is to be added all connected with our daughter, it strikes me forcibly that, beyond the management of my stable, my dogs, and my hookah, I am not allowed to have any opinion whatever."

"Now, James, you know I was feverish last night, and you surely do not suppose this continual opposition to my slightest wishes will make me better."

"We have now been married three-and-twenty years, Elizabeth; and it is a singular coincidence, that whenever, during that period, I have differed from you, you either had lately been, were then, or shortly would be, '*feverish.*' I say it's a singular coincidence, for, from your appearance, no one would suppose you were a prey to such bad health."

"A more singular circumstance, Mr. Plane, I think, is the fact that, whenever during the said three-and-twenty years we have had a discussion on any point, so much have you believed in the fever and its effects that you have invariably yielded!"

"I grant the fact," replied Mr. Plane, "but not the premises. I *have* always yielded, 'tis true. At first I did so from kindness, afterwards from habit; never, I think, because I believed in the fever. I dare say I shall yield now; in fact, I'm sure I shall; but as I know you never awoke once last night, and have eaten a capital breakfast this morning, my doing so cannot be attributed to pity for the past or fear for the coming malady.—Here, khitmudgar!"

"Sahib!"

"Order my buggy. I'll write the letter at kutcherry,* Elizabeth. I'll do anything for a quiet life; and I yield all the more readily this time, as I know it's your love alone for dear Beatrice that prompts the request. I shall be so glad to see her, a little minx—ah, she's a big minx now; but she was a tiny thing enough when I last saw her. Do you remember when I put you both on board at Calcutta, twelve years ago, what a pretty child she was, and how unlike most children in her reserved and quiet manner? You say she has that still."

"She's a daughter we may be proud of, James, in every way. She was by far the prettiest girl at Cheltenham, when I left home eighteen months ago; and as for her reserve, she has none with me."

"No; with you, I remember, she had none as a child: but it was different with papa. Ah well, I

* Office.

dare say she's more sensible now; at least, I'll hope so, for I remember her cold manner often pained me formerly."

"Girls look naturally to their mother, James; but I dare say, after me, Beatrice will love you, and be as frank with you as girls can be with their father."

"Hem! I see not why papa is to be number two, or what is to prevent the utmost candour between daughters and fathers; but we will not discuss the point, for fear the feverish symptoms should return."

So saying, Mr. Plane left to go to kutcherry. Mrs. Plane leant back in her chair, and twiddled her thumbs, while a gleam of satisfaction stole over her face. "He's easy enough to manage now," she said, half aloud; "but it was not so the first few years of our marriage; many women would have given up the attempt in despair, but I felt all through confident of final victory. I have often thought and wondered whether the result would have been the same, had I married a more intellectual or a more determined man. I believe it would, but the treatment or tactics must have varied to suit the case. Well, poor James, he has nothing to complain of, I'm sure; for under my directions all has gone on swimmingly. He holds a first-rate position in the service, we are fast getting rich, our daughter is all I could desire, and I'm sure our married life has as few clouds as the most favoured. It's all nonsense talking of husband and wife giving in to each other, *one* must be master; and with all deference to the generally-received opinion, I think the woman makes the best head. If calmly considered, it stands to reason it must be so. A woman is naturally quicker, has more intuitive tact than a man; sees farther into consequences; is a better judge of character; has more patience, endurance, and fortitude. What absurd nonsense it is, then, to speak of us as the weaker sex. It may be true in a physical, certainly in no other sense. No, no; let the man, as intended by nature, do the work of life, produce the wherewithal to carry it on, but let him not interfere further; the rest belongs to woman; and I think the day will come, and that shortly, when what I think will be generally recognized and allowed. Ah, Beatrice! I hope you will think and act as your mother. I think you will, for you inherit much of my nature, and in some points are superior to me. You are more self-relying, more calculating than I was at your age; and these qualities must all tend to produce the only happiness a sensible woman should know in marriage—the control and management, for his good, and the good of the family, of the being facetiously termed her lord and master."

The above cogitations somewhat softened Mrs. Plane's naturally austere and hard face; and she proceeded about her household duties with a sense of the vastly superior attributes of woman, and the insignificance of man, which was highly edifying to behold.

Fair reader! are you a wife, or are you about to enter that state? Abjure Mrs. Plane's theory—believe her not; but believe what any happy married woman of your acquaintance will tell you; viz., that happiness in wedded life consists in *neither* being master, in Mrs. Plane's acceptation of the term, but in the mutual forbearance, the deference to each other's wishes, the exercise of that cardinal virtue charity to one another, which, when joined to love and affection, renders the relation of husband and wife the most beautiful, as well as the most enjoyable, under heaven.

## CHAPTER V.

THE RACE-STAND—THE LADIES' LOTTERY—THE STEEPLE-CHASE.

The day and afternoon on which the Dinapore steeple-chase was to be run had now arrived, and by four o'clock the station presented an unusually lively appearance. Horses, with and without saddles, were being led out by their syces to the steeple-chase ground, or awaited their masters at the doors of the bungalows, or else at the officers' quarters in the barrack-square. Every now and then sallied forth mysterious beings enveloped in most absurdly thick great-coats, considering the sun shone bright, and the thermometer stood at ninety-six in the shade; but then they were the riders in the coming combat, and under these coats they wore their racing-jackets of party-coloured silk, which, as every body knows, according to all recognized and received racing etiquette, must not be seen until, in front of the stand, the upper coats are doffed, the saddle and bridle taken in hand, and the suddenly transformed green, red, or yellow aspirant steps into the scales to adjust the weight his horse is to carry.

But led horses were not the only signs of life at Dinapore on that afternoon; many buggies, some dog-carts, a few phaetons, and a couple of curricles, enlivened the scene; while opposite one door might be seen a tremendous high-wheeled dog-cart, to which was yoked a tandem team, perfect enough as far as the horses went, when taken separately, but absurdly matched in every way; for the wheeler, one of those high-stepping, big sixteen-hand New South Wales horses, of a bright bay colour, with a short dock tail, seemed, when trotting his twelve miles an hour, as if he was hunting, like some ferocious ogre, the small gray fourteen-hand Arab in front of him, which had never trotted in his life, and was necessarily obliged to keep up a long gallop to escape being run over by his gaunt pursuer. However, tandems were rare at Dinapore; many there had never seen one; so that such imperfections did not attract much attention; and even if they had, it would not have signified much, for the owner thereof, Ensign Earnest (who, the reader may remember, was to ride the colonel's Cape horse in the steeple-chase), was sensible enough to drive the said tandem solely for his own amusement, and cared not if others found fault or pronounced it an imperfect turn-out.

But we must hasten to the steeple-chase ground, whither already numbers are wending their way. We must take care not to get run over, however; for the hot wind still blows in fitful puffs, and there is so much fine dust along the road that it is difficult to see far.

"Edgington," says somebody, whom we cannot see, but who cannot be far off, "I fear we shan't have many of the ladies on the ground, and that the stand we have built will be so much labour lost. This cursed wind is quite enough to keep them away!"

"Oh no! they'll all be there by the time the race comes off. The wind will go down with the sun; and even if it did not, they have not so much amusement that they can afford to miss the only bit of fun they've seen for weeks."

"I hope there *will* be a good muster of petticoats. Somehow, I think one rides better, certainly bolder, when woman looks on—eh?"

"Yes, it's an advantage."

"Do you think Bruce's mare, Bessie, that you ride, is going to win?"

"I can't say," replied Edgington. "She fences very well, but she is not so powerful as some of the others, and there is a lot of heavy land. I shouldn't wonder if one of the large horses were to win."

"Yes, Colonel Carstairs's Cape, for example, which Earnest, of your regiment, rides. The horse is well up to the work, and a better man than Earnest could not be on his back. I think he's the best rider in Dinapore; at all events, you and he are the two best."

"Do you think so," replied Edgington, laughing. "Well, I hope we shall merit the opinion by our riding to-day. I'm sure Earnest will, for a cooler and more determined man on the pig-skin I never saw."

"Yes, he's bold enough. Do you know, I doubt there being many together at the last jump, for the last but one is a regular teaser."

"What, the double ditch and bank? Yes, there's only one way to get over, and that is by going at it railroad speed," remarked Edgington.

"True; *if* your horse will rise going that pace, it's all very well; but *if* he doesn't, what then?"

"Why, you must get an awful purl," replied Edgington laughingly, "and no one should ride a steeple-chase who is not quite prepared for that contingency."

"Ah, well, we shall be wiser as to the race in another hour, for there's the course; and, by jingo, there's the first bugle for weighing."

They put spurs to their horses with this last remark, and cantered up to the stand. We are there before them; for in spirit we can travel faster than they. It is astonishing how many bonnets and ladies' hats grace it, in spite of the heat. Why, the small temporary bamboo-built shed is nearly full, and still ladies make their appearance in dog-carts, in buggies, and on horseback, while the continually recurring grunt of palankeen-bearers, as palkee after palkee arrives, shows that the course will not be quite destitute of the better class of natives. Many of these, however, come also in carriages and on horseback. A large fat, and evidently rich, native has just made his appearance in a buggy; let us examine both him and his turn-out.

Taking the human portion firstly into consideration, what a contrast between the fat and oily-looking baboo inside the buggy, and the syces, or grooms, outside: the former looks as if he never had run a mile in his life (he certainly could not run the hundredth part of one, fat as he now is); the latter look as if they had been running all their lives, and were fit now to run any distance for ever so small a sum. Look! as they approach the stand,—the large, sleek, and shiny chestnut horse flinging his head into the air, as if proud of the large brass knobs and crimson throat-lash with which it is decorated,—how the baboo inside the buggy leans against the softly-padded crimson back, as if sitting up were too much of an exertion, and how the syces, one on each side, with one hand on the open hood, run lightly along, their bare feet taking no heed of stones or other impediments in the way; and from long practice, though stepping within six inches of the fast-revolving wheels, never looking down to see that they even preserve that short distance. But they have arrived at the entrance of the stand; the baboo pulls up the horse very short, which the sharp bit in his mouth enables him to do; and at the same moment one syce rushes to his head and holds the rein; the other darts forward with a long party-coloured horse-hair tail or brush, set in a silver handle, and standing on the opposite side, immediately commences to brush off the flies which have already settled, or are anxious to regale themselves, on the shiny and glossy coat of the well-fed horse. Our baboo drops the reins, heaves a deep sigh, the invariable prelude to exertion, and descends. Hark! do you hear that short and hurried breathing? Of course; 'tis the syces panting after their sharp run, for our fat friend drove up to the stand at a great pace. But there's only *one* of them panting—we hear it distinctly, and can only hear *one*. See again—how strange! the syces are talking quietly together; it can't be them at all; and yet, hearken! the panting continues. Is it the horse? A horse breathes very differently. Let's come nearer, and see what it really is. Ha! ha! well how absurd; it's the fat baboo after all, blowing like any grampus with the exertion of getting down from the buggy. Oh, had he, in this respect, one particle of sense, how he would envy the condition of his syces, who show no signs of distress from their hard run; but he hasn't, so we will leave him to waddle up the stairs as best he may, and recover himself when he arrives at the summit as best he can.

Let us turn to a more active part of creation. Fresh arrivals are taking place every instant, and the temporary race-stand boasts many a pretty English face, somewhat pale, 'tis true; but who could have a colour in such weather? And, then, pale faces are so much the rule in India, those with colour so much the exception, that at all events the force of contrast does not there exist to make the fair owners dissatisfied with their complexions. So they are satisfied with themselves, the male portion in and around the stand are satisfied with them; nay more, thankful that they honour the coming steeple-chase with their presence on such a blazing hot afternoon, and the consequence of all this satisfaction is a profusion of pleasant smiles, under bonnets and riding-hats, which certainly assist, in no small degree, to set the owners off to advantage. So thinks our fat Baboo, who, having at last recovered the exertion of the ascent, is regaling himself with a small and richly-ornamented hookah; and who, being a Mahommedan, is calculating the chances of the true believers' heaven being peopled with such "houris" as now surround him.

Ah! there is the second bugle for weighing, and all the riders may now be seen around the weighing-scales. Many of their servants are also there with them. Syces with saddles; bearers with shot-weights; khitmudgars with leather-covered bottles, containing lemonade, brandy pawnee,* and what not. What in England would be done by one person, is always in India done by six; and consequently the crowd of white-turbaned attendants here and everywhere, without whom nothing is executed. Now the weighing is going to begin in earnest: the iron weights are already in the scale; one of the stewards stands by to superintend the operation; the before-mentioned great-coats and wrappers are taken off, and the various-coloured silk racing-jackets thus brought to view enliven still further the already lively scene.

One word as to weighing for races, addressed to the fair reader, who probably has never understood its importance. People ignorant of such matters will scarcely believe the great difference a little extra weight makes to a horse in a race. It is an old saying amongst racing men, that "seven pounds is a distance;" or, in other words, that a horse who would generally run even, or neck and neck with another for a mile and a half race, will, if he have an extra seven pounds put on his back, be a whole distance behind. This is, perhaps, a little exaggerated; but it is still astonishing how nearly in practice the result comes up to the saying, and how even one or two pounds will cause a horse to lose a race he would otherwise have won. To make the case still more clear to those who, having nothing to do with weights in any shape, scarcely realize how little one pound is. Suppose two horses to run a dead heat of a mile race at any given weights, and after half an hour's interval the same race, with the same horses and riders, is run again; but in the meantime one of the riders, ignorant of the effect of weight, and being both hungry and thirsty, takes a good luncheon. He may almost spare himself the trouble of getting into his saddle, so certain is he, barring accidents, to lose; and

* Brandy and water.

that purely because his horse has to carry so much more, by the luncheon aforesaid, than he had before.

It is not, then, to be wondered at, if weight is an all-important thing in horse-racing; and as riders are always weighed after running, as well as before, both to insure the winner having carried the given weight and to prevent the losers having carried extra weight with a view to deceive the public as to the powers of their horses; and as the exertion of riding a race, particularly in hot weather, causes a loss in weight to the rider from perspiration; and as no winner is allowed to win if he does not come up to the full weight after the race; it is necessary from all these causes that the weighing should be very carefully executed.

In such a race as the Dinapore steeple-chase, for example,—*id est*, a race amongst gentlemen, where the owners are all well known to each other, and there is no idea of foul play with a view to deceive the public as to the powers of any losing horse,—the ceremony of weighing all the riders after the race is not gone through; but the winner is still weighed, as he has not won the race unless his horse has carried and comes to the winning-post with the proper weight on his back. In steeple-chases, where the distance is often considerable, the ground heavy, and the jumps severe, weight is of even more importance than in flat races; and as there are different breeds of horses in India, which vary much in size and strength, the weight in such a race as we are now about to describe is generally graduated to suit the powers of these different breeds.

We will here describe, in a few words, the different kinds of horses that are found in India. Firstly, we have the imported English horse, always a good weight-carrier, for none but strong and serviceable beasts are sent out such a long journey. Secondly, the Cape horse—that is, horses bred at the Cape of Good Hope from English, Dutch, and other stock in that colony. They are also generally large and handsome animals, for none but the best are sent over to India. Thirdly, we have the New South Wales horses, or "Walers," as they are called in India. Before the gold discoveries in those colonies, many of the best Australian horses were sent to the Calcutta market; they were generally beasts of great bone and strength, and able to carry great weights.

The above three breeds are the largest and strongest found in India, and they generally carry extra weight in races.

Next on the list, as far as size goes, are the stud-bred horses of India,—that is to say, horses bred at the Government studs in different parts of the country, with a view to horse the European and regular native cavalry regiments. These are not generally so large as either the English, Cape, or Australian horses; besides which, the best are never sold, but kept for Government purposes.

We now have, further, the country-bred horses of India. These are of all sizes and shapes; some are very good animals, some are very bad, but, as a general rule, they lack blood, and are often vicious.

Last, but far, far from least, unless, indeed, in size, is the Arab. He is, as all the world knows, a small horse; his general height is fourteen hands, and an Arab of 14—3 is considered very large. The world-wide fame of these "sons of the desert" renders any praise from our pen superfluous, besides which we are not writing a treatise on horseflesh; but as their good qualities, viz., their endurance, spirit, courage, temper, and tractability are known everywhere, we may mention the only faults the race possess: they never trot well, they seldom are good jumpers. The last failing is, however, not invariable, for there have been several good Arab steeple-chase horses in India; and *when* an Arab can fence at all, he can generally do it remarkably well.

We must apologize for this long digression on weights

and horses, and return to our tale; for the riders are all impatient for the coming contest. While they are weighing, however, let us read the terms of the race as shown in the "correct cards," one of which has been given to each and every lady in the stand. The said cards are not printed, but are the produce of the laborious penmanship of a native writer, hired expressly by the race stewards for the occasion. We would we could transfer his flourishes to this page—but that is impossible.

## DINAPORE STEEPLE CHASE.

A purse of 50 gold* mohurs from the race fund, for all horses *bonâ fide* the property of officers and civilians stationed at Dinapoor and Patna; over one and a half mile of fair steeple-chase ground, to be selected by the stewards.

English, Cape, and Australian horses, 12 st. 7 lbs.

Arab, stud, and country-bred, 11 st. 7 lbs.

Mares and geldings allowed 7 lbs.

Entrance, 5 gold mohurs; half forfeit.

Second horse to save his stake.

Nominations to be sent in to the secretary by 12 o'clock the day before the race, and the riders to be declared at the same time, or at the Ordinary the same evening.

Colonel Carstair's brown Cape gelding, Prince, 12 st.—Mr. Earnest, *red and white.*

Mr. Walker's black English horse, Sultan, 12 st. 7 lbs.—Owner, *black.*

Captain Mason's gray country-bred mare, Whistle, 11 st.—Owner, *orange.*

Major Bruce's gray Australian mare, Bessie, 12 st. — Captain Edgington, *green and white.*

Mr. Hardman's bay Arab horse, Pluto, 11 st. 7 lbs.—Peer Bux (native), *yellow.*

Captain Fellow's white Arab horse, Snowdrift, 11 st. 7 lbs.—Owner, *blue.*

Mr. Peter's dun stud-bred horse, Chance, 11 st. 7 lbs.—Owner, *crimson.*

By order of the Stewards.

WM. WILLIAMS, *Secretary.*

No less than seven horses in all. Really it's a very grand affair, as far as the card goes; we hope the race will bear it out. So Major Bruce's mare, Bessie, is an Australian. Well, it's all in her favour; capital horses, many of the Australian, across country; and Bessie, — only look at her as the syce girths up her saddle,—is a likely-looking creature enough. See her

* A gold coin not now in general use; but the term is, nevertheless, used for all sporting purposes: its value is equal to sixteen rupees, or one pound twelve shillings.

sloping shoulders and high withers, rendered more prominent as she stretches out her neck, and, with ears laid back, makes believe that she would bite any one within her reach. It's not really viciousness though, for you might stand before her with safety; but she's ticklish, and the girths, as they are tightened, somewhat bully her. Ah! though you'd be safe in front, you'd not be safe behind; that near hind-leg, as just thrown out, would have smashed any bone ever contained in mortal body. It's very evident she can kick if she likes. She's quiet now, however, for the saddle is taut, and she curves her beautiful neck as she takes from Edgington's hand the bit of bread he put in his pocket at tiffin for her. Really they are well matched —Bessie and her rider; the latter has just been weighed (the saddle and bridle on Bessie weighed just one stone of the twelve), and now stands forth in his racing costume of black jack-boots and striped green and white silk jacket and cap. See, there's no superfluous flesh on either, but in both man and horse it's all bone and muscle. Perhaps Edgington is somewhat too tall to suit all fancies as a steeple-chase rider,—his jack-boots make him look taller than he really is;—but he has a riding-figure in spite thereof. When he sits in his saddle there's nearly as much length and weight below as above, and that's the great point after all. The boots hide much of his leg; but from the size above the knee (the thin and white close-fitting cashmere breeches enable you to see it) you may judge of the size below, and that the strength wherewith to hold on and clasp his horse firmly, as he forces him at a jump, is not wanting. Ah, he's about to mount! He rides short, and Bessie being 15-2 in height, he does not easily get his foot in the stirrup. Back go the ears again as the syce holds her head, and Edgington springs up. Now he's safe on the pig-skin, whence it's no easy job for either man or horse to dislodge him; and, with pardonable vanity, he rides out of the inclosure and gives his mare a breathing gallop opposite the stand. Does she not move beautifully? and is she not really a perfect steeple-chasing shape? He does not go far, for Major Bruce is on the course awaiting his return; and as Bessie pulls up, and stands motionless, with quivering flank, distended nostrils, and flashing eyes, her owner comes up and fondly pats her shoulder.

"Well, how does she feel, Edgington,—at all like a winner?"

"Yes, all I could wish; but there are others as good in the field, and I can say no more than that both she and I will do our best. I'm sure I may answer for her," he added, as, leaning forward, he fondly stroked her glossy neck.

"I'm sure you will both do well," replied Bruce. "I should certainly like to win, for irrespective of half the eighty gold mohurs which I should then pocket, and which, with my large family, I want as much as any one; I should like to succeed for both your and her sake. Isn't she a nice beast, Edgington?" he continued, as Bessie poked her muzzle into his hand, thinking perhaps she might find another bit of bread there. "But tell me," he added, "which of your opponents do you fear the most?"

"The colonel's Cape, with Earnest on his back. Sultan, the black English horse, is a queer customer also; but his rider, Walker, the civilian, is not equal to Earnest. The truth is, however, they are a good lot altogether, and no one can say who'll win. There's the stud-bred Chance, for example, he jumps beautifully; and Peters, the magistrate from Patna, who rides, knows well what he's about. Ah, here he is, coming out from the inclosure. Has he not a beautiful seat?"

"Never mind him, Edgington,—we have not much time. Tell me how do you intend to ride the race?"

"I don't understand you."

"Shall you take the lead and keep it if you can, or lag behind and wait your time?"

"It all depends how the others ride at the first jump. Its an awkward one, as you know,—a wattle hurdle with bamboo stakes, nearer four than three feet high. It won't give an inch, and to touch it is to fall: there's not very much run to it from the starting-post, so if the others will go quietly I shall do so too, and then try hard to get over first; but if they gallop from the post, I shall keep behind all, and as some are sure to refuse, I hope to find myself in a better position after the jump. The fact is, it's a fence I'd rather not ride at too fast—at a moderate pace I feel sure I can force Bessie over, even if one or two refuse before her."

"Quite right; I agree with you in all that," replied Bruce; "but *if* you get over that jump first, for goodness' sake let her go, and try to prevent being ever *collared* again. I'm sure, with you on her back, she can do everything in the race easily; but, as you know to your cost, when she fell last cold weather and broke your arm, she does not jump so steadily with another horse racing by her side."

"I'll not forget it, Bruce, but others know it too; Earnest mentioned it laughingly last night, and you may be sure he'll make the most of it."

"Do you think the two Arabs have any chance?"

"Oh yes, some chance of course; especially the bay horse, Pluto. I saw him run very well in a hurdle-race at Sonepore last year. The native rider he has now rode him then. The horse is a good jumper, and the man is a good rider; but the jumps are large for such a small horse, and I think Peer Bux, his native rider, has yet to learn the difference between a hurdle-race and steeple-chase."

"I say, Edgington, remember when you come to the last jump but one, I mean the double ditch and bank, that you let Bessie go at her——"

"Excuse my interrupting you, Bruce; but has the

general come?" asked Edgington, who had been scanning the faces in the stand very closely for the last two or three minutes.

"No, but I saw his syce just now, and he said the general sahib would be here directly. Anyhow, we must wait till he arrives."

"Yes! he's been so liberal to the race-fund," said Edgington, "it would be a shame if he lost the race."

"I think so too," Bruce answered, with half a smile on his face; "besides which, all the ladies in the stand are dying to see the new beauty, Miss Plane, who is with him."

"I wish you'd take up Bessie's check-strap one hole," said Edgington, somewhat hurriedly, "the snaffle hangs looser in the mouth than I like it. Oh, well, perhaps it's a pity to change it; it's as she's always had it, and I don't think, after all, it *does* look loose. See, here comes the colonel's Cape, with Earnest on him. By jingo! the weighing is nearly over. Well, Earnest, going to win to-day?"

"I may ask you the same," Earnest good-humouredly replied from his mountain of horse-flesh, for the Cape was a tower for size and strength, "and expect the same answer which I'll give you now—I'll try. When once the word 'Off' is given, Edgington, it's every one for himself; and it's not a little thing will stop some of those who ride to-day."

"Do, like a good fellow, Earnest," said the major laughingly, "take that elephant of a horse *through* instead of over the first jump; he'll make a hole large enough for all to follow, and its the fence regarding which I'm most nervous about Bessie."

"Sorry I can't oblige you, major; but as I shall probably go either over or through it after Bessie, it would not avail, unless, indeed, two of us run a dead heat and had to run over again. But I must breathe my horse," he said, closing his legs and touching the flanks sharply with the spurs as he did so; for the Cape, never too ready to move, was not over brisk this afternoon.

"Did you see that?" said the major, as Earnest cantered off. "I mean the way he spurred his horse: he knows well what he's got under him; and from what he said about the first jump, I strongly expect he means to wait upon Bessie, and try to destroy her chance by racing with her. I know he fears her more than any other horse; and Earnest has ridden too many of these races not to take every fair advantage."

"Well, well! we shall all be wiser half an hour hence," Edgington replied, "for here comes the general with his staff, and the race will, after all, take place at five exactly."

"Good-bye, and good luck to you, then!" replied the major, "for I must go up in the stand and conduct the ladies' lottery. Its a funny idea, but they've got up a lottery amongst themselves alone: they've each put in two rupees to buy a ladies' riding-whip; in fact, the whip is bought already, and is now in the stand. The winner of the race is to present it to the lady who draws his horse. Quite romantic, is it not?"

"Quite! When does the lottery come off?"

"Now, at once; there's still one——"

"Major Bruce! Major Bruce!" called out several ladies' voices from the race-stand, "come up and settle the lottery; we can't get on without you."

He was with them before they had done calling him, and in another two minutes he had written the horses' names on separate pieces of paper—folded them up like the blanks—and all was ready.

"Stop, stop, Major Bruce!" said one of the prettiest ladies there, a married woman lately arrived from England; "tell me, are all the tickets taken?"

"Enough, and more than enough, to pay for the whip; but any surplus goes to the expenses of building this stand, and, according to the list drawn up, there are still two numbers vacant. Will you take another?"

"No, but my little girl here will—eh, Annie, would you like to try and win the whip?"

"Of course I should, mamma dear. Oh, what a splendid whip! Is that all real ivory?" said little Annie, a sweet child of seven years old, taking the whip off the table; "but won't it be too big for me?"

"Yes, but you can keep it till you get older. Put down Annie's name, Major Bruce, for one of the spare tickets. There, dearie, I hope you'll win," she said, fondly kissing her daughter.

"Now, what enterprising lady will take the last ticket?" called out Major Bruce, after writing down Annie's name in the list; "you all know, of course, the last ticket is a lucky one."

As he finished speaking, an old, but still manly, voice was heard on the rough stairs leading into the stand—

"Now, Miss Planc, gather up that dreadful long riding-dress, or you'll trip me up; and I can't stand a fall now as well as I could thirty years ago. That's right; the stairs are too narrow for me to give you my arm, though, in truth, I think if they were broader you ought to assist me."

All eyes were turned to see the new-comer, whom, as is generally the case in a small society, they had all heard of, while the few who had seen her only further excited the curiosity of the rest.

A buzz of admiration would have gone round the stand as she appeared, had not the society there been much too well bred for any such display. In truth, she looked very lovely—a plain but well-cut brown-holland habit showed to perfection her exquisite form, while a riding-hat of brown and white straw, with a long drooping feather on one side, seemed as if the maker must have invented it expressly to suit the beautiful face it overshadowed. Her rich brown hair, almost too long and copious for such a head-dress, was plaited both down the sides of her face and at the back of the neck; and the intuitive knowledge which woman always has when she is the observed of all observers, mantled her cheeks, as she stepped on the platform, with a crimson glow which made her at the moment quite bewitching.

"Ye gods, how lovely!" was Colonel Carstairs' involuntary remark, as he sat on the front rail of the stand, so loud that many heard it—Beatrice Plane also, it may be; for the blush left her cheeks as suddenly as it came, and she drew herself up to her full height and looked with supreme hauteur on the assembled throng.

"*Now* I can help you, general," she said, stretching out her hand to assist him up the last two or three steps, "for all here are too much engaged to notice you. So, now, where am I to sit?"

"Stop a minute," the general said, as he hastily returned the salute which greeted his arrival from all the officers present; "I must introduce you first to some of my friends. How do you do, Mrs. Bruce?—very glad to see you gracing our sports with your presence; let me introduce to you Miss Plane, staying with me till her father arrives at Patna. Ah, Major Bruce, I'll kill two birds with one stone, and introduce you at the same time; you can chat together presently—no time now, for here's another lady, Miss Plane, you must know, a very dear ally of mine, and then I shall leave you to make your own way while I look at the horses. Ah, Mrs. Peters, now that's really good of you, saving me the walk along these rickety boards; please know Miss Plane, the daughter of an old friend of mine, destined to be a near neighbour of yours at Patna when her father arrives. Patna is rich already in ladies, I know, but still you will greet another, I'm sure. Now I shall leave her under your care for a few minutes, for I know but little of the horses and riders in this break-neck race, and steeple-chasing always interests me, for I broke a collar-bone myself at it when I was young. Who'll give me a race-card?"

He had one soon, and was soon conning it with his

spectacles as he leaned over the rail, while one of his aides-de-camp pointed out the different horses and riders as they passed below.

"Once more, ladies," called out Major Bruce, ("not ladies and gentlemen, for in this lottery none but the fair sex are admitted;) there's still one ticket going begging—who'll have it? I'm *sure* it will win, and if nobody speaks quick I shall give my wife a conjugal wink, and she'll put down her name. Going—going—third and last time——"

"*Do* you take it, Miss Plane," urged Mrs. Peters; "I have a ticket already, and see, it's only two rupees, and such a love of a whip. Hold it up, Major Bruce, as a temptation. Now can you resist the chance of possessing it?"

"I don't understand it—I mean, what a race-lottery is; besides, I have a whip, though in truth it's nearly worn out," she replied, holding up her own.

"What's that—what's that about a spare ticket?—a ladies' lottery, eh!" called out the general, "and a lady's whip, too!—the very thing to make Miss Plane take an interest in the race. Put down her name, Mrs. Peters;—come, no objections—what a capital idea! Who got up the lottery?"

"*May* I write down your name, Miss Plane?" said Major Bruce; "and then we will draw it at once."

"Oh yes, as the general insists on it. It certainly is a very pretty whip," she added as she took it from Major Bruce, who handed it to her, "and if I win it, I'll discard my old one."

"Better still to give it, out of gratitude, to the rider who wins you this," said Mrs. Peters, laughing.

"That's not in the terms of the lottery," added Major Bruce, "but, doubtless, the winner of the steeple-chase would prize it as much, if not more, than the stakes he runs for. Now then, all is ready—a hat is the approved receptacle for lottery-tickets, but nothing masculine is admitted in this affair, so we will put them into this little work-basket which my wife has sagaciously brought with her. You shall all draw as the names stand on the list; there are seven horses, or prizes, and only three blanks, so every one may fairly *hope* to get a prize, though, alas! all can't. You are first, Mrs. Peters; now try and draw the winner—remember, no one is to open their ticket till all have drawn. You are second, Mrs. Bruce; be sure and take only one ticket—sometimes they catch in one another, and then it's a false lottery, and has to be drawn all over again."

But we will leave them to finish the lottery alone, for the bugle calling the horses to the starting-post has just sounded; and as it has apparently awoke Colonel Carstairs from the dreamy state he had fallen into since Miss Plane's arrival, and he is going down to take a final look at his Cape horse, we will accompany him. At the bottom of the stairs he met Ensign Hoby, chuckling over his good fortune in having effected what he considered a really good bet on the race, he having taken two to one, and backed the horses of his own regiment against the field. He was smoking a cheroot in high glee; and as soon as he saw the colonel, he commenced to recount to him what he had done, when, to his astonishment, his commandant interrupted him, and, clutching his arm so tight that the expounder of characters winced, hissed out,—

"Curse the horses! Hoby, you are a villain—a perfect villain—a demoniacal villain. Do you remember the character you drew at mess last week of Miss Plane or 'Beatrice,' for you put it on the name. Now go up-stairs and see the subject of your sketch, and then fall down on your knees, eat the dust at her feet, and plead for forgiveness."

"I can do nothing, sir, as long as you hold me so tight and squeeze me so hard; besides, you hurt most infernally. That's right; now I can talk quietly, though I shan't be able to hold my sword for some days, my arm is so sore. Well, what am I to do all this penance for?"

"Go up-stairs, see for yourself, and you will not ask the question."

"But I have seen her already."

"What, seen her!—seen her with your own eyes, and you are standing here; nay, more, smoking, at peace with yourself?"

"And why not? I've recovered the shock, colonel, which seems to have been too much for you. Time, that great mollifier of all things, has had its effect with me, for it was the day before yesterday that I saw her."

"No excuse at all—I cannot admit it; but tell me, have you not acknowledged the error of your sketch ever since?"

"By no means, sir; I painted her beautiful—my injured arm is evidence that she is so; haughty—I saw no reason to alter my opinion; cold—the expression of her mouth bears me out fully; uncharitable—it needed no——"

"Hold! hold!—I'll hear no more: you are even worse than I thought you, Hoby; but there is still a chance for you to retrieve yourself in my opinion," added Colonel Carstairs, while a smile forced itself on his lips. "You saw her in a gown and a bonnet, perhaps even at home in a morning dress. Tell me, oh tell me it was so, and let me still call you my dear Hoby," he continued in a half tragical tone, while the absurdity of his words and his inclination to laugh made him blow his nose very suddenly.

"No sir," replied Hoby, laughing; "but perhaps the way I did see her will do as well: it was on the river-side, where the steamer was lying; and she had ridden there to look at it. We even spoke together."

"Worse and worse—things look very dark; but tell me, had she a riding-dress on?"

"Yes; how else could she ride?"

"I mean, had she that plain, simple dress, which sits so close to her figure, and makes her look like—like—I'm at a loss for a comparison."

"I'll help you. Like a girl riding who, whatever her faults, is too sensible to smother herself in a cloth habit during the hot weather;—yes, she had, for I remarked how cool it looked."

"*Your* coolness will drive me mad! She had not, however, that love of a riding-hat she has to-day—a brown and white straw one."

"The very same. I thought it pretty enough."

"What, and that long, drooping feather? Answer quickly."

"Let me get on the fourth step first, so as to have a fair start in case of need. Now I think I'm safe. Alas, yes, I remember it perfectly, for I thought it a shade *too* long."

"I'm quiet now, Hoby," the colonel said, with a deep-drawn sigh; "but I give you up—yes, give you up finally. You must be more or less than man, as far as woman is concerned. Ah! well, well, it's very sad," he continued, as he looked at his watch; "but after all, my dear fellow, it's not your fault, but your misfortune; so instead of *giving you up*, I'll only *pity* you. Come down, then, and give me a cheroot; and as we've had enough of this folly, let's come and look at the horses. We've only just time, for some are already on their way to the starting-post."

They were not too late, however, to catch Earnest on the colonel's Cape, ere he followed the others, many of whom were far on their way.

"The nag looks well, Earnest, to-day. I hope he'll do well," said the colonel. "Remember and push the others over the heavy land. The old beast is the strongest in the field; and we know his wind is good. Don't forget, also, to keep your eye on Edgington, and to race with Bessie, if at any time she looks like a winner. You must be off, however, for you must ride quietly down; and you'll be late unless you go at once. Good luck to you."

"Remember, I've backed the horses of our regiment!" called out Hoby, as Earnest trotted quietly off; "so win, for my sake."

"I'll do it for my own also, old fellow, if I can. I'm the last, by the bye, to leave this place; I hope I shall be the first to pass it again."

The colonel and Hoby returned to the stand. On arrival, they found the ladies' lottery over, and they were at once assailed with a multitude of questions regarding the merits of different horses.

"Who has drawn my Cape horse, Prince?" asked the colonel.

"I have, sir," answered little Annie; "see, here's the ticket."

"You dear little thing! I'm glad of it, for I think you've a good chance of winning the whip."

"And I've got the English horse, Sultan, said Annie's mother; "do you think he's any chance?"

"A very good one; but truly no one can say who'll win, for many of the horses are very evenly matched. Who drew Bessie, the Australian mare Captain Edgington rides?"

"Oh, Miss Plane did," answered the general, who was near; "and we all tell her she'll win the whip."

"Well, she has certainly one of the favourites; and I'm not sure that she has not the best rider in the field. Will you not introduce me, general,—you have not done so yet."

"Of course; certainly. I beg your pardon for not doing so before. Miss Plane," he added, turning round to where she was sitting, "let me introduce to you my friend Colonel Carstairs."

The colonel was saluted with a frigid bow.

"I was congratulating the general, Miss Plane, on your success in the lottery; you've drawn one of the best horses, and perhaps the best rider in the field."

"So they tell me: who is this famous rider?"

"Captain Edgington, of my regiment. You will see his name on your card. His colours are green and white, so in the race you will easily distinguish him."

"Colonel Carstairs," said Mrs. Peters, coming up, "I hear you've been telling every one that Captain Edgington is the best rider in the race; now I cannot allow you to deceive Miss Plane on this point, and thus raise her hopes too high. My husband, Miss Plane, rides quite as well," she added, laughingly.

"Tell me your husband's colours, please, that I may judge for myself," answered Miss Plane.

"Crimson. Which do you think is really the best rider, general?" asked Mrs. Peters.

"I know not; but you must all come to the front of the stand, if you want to see the race," said the general; "for the horses are nearly at the post."

The ladies were all given chairs close to the rail, while such of the gentlemen as could not find room by their sides, stood behind them.

"Miss Plane, take my glass," said Colonel Carstairs, "and you will easily distinguish all the horses at the starting-point. I think that is a good focus. Are you far-sighted?"

"Yes, I am; fortunately, I both see and hear well."

"Devil take it," thought the colonel; "what does she mean by that?—could she have heard what I said when she came into the stand? Well, never mind; if she did, she can't mind it, or she's the first woman I ever met who——"

His further thoughts were interrupted by Miss Plane, who was looking through his glass:—

"I can make out my champion, the green and white one, Colonel Carstairs; his horse seems very fidgety and anxious to start. I can see your husband, too,

Mrs. Peters; he has dismounted, and is walking up and down by the side of his horse."

"They'll soon be off," said the general, who was looking through another telescope; "who's going to time them?"

"Hoby, you have a stop-watch," said the colonel; "will you do it, and do it carefully?"

All was now expectation and excitement; questions and answers followed each other so quickly; it was a perfect Babel of tongues. We shall leave the noise, and fly with the speed of thought to the starting-post, for we had rather run the race with the riders than have an indistinct view of it from the stand.

Already we are there, and not out of breath with our rapid flight. At the post is one of the stewards to start the horses; they have drawn lots for places, some preferring the near, some the off side, and are now ranged up in a line, about twenty yards beyond the starting-point. Many of the horses are very restless, and it is no easy matter to keep their noses in a line. "Now, gentlemen," calls out the steward in a loud voice, "you will advance at a foot pace to the post, and on arrival I will give the word 'Off!' Are you all ready?" No answer was returned. "Then advance!—back, back, Mr. Peters; keep the line!—that's right; come on steady all of you." A pause as the line advances, many stroking their horses' necks to keep them quiet. They are at the post now; and, hark! there's the word; "Off!" is bawled out by the steward in a stentorian key, and off they are with a vengeance, in a cloud of dust.

With our capacity for rapid flight, let us await them at the first jump, the stiff hurdle with bamboo stakes, described before. See, we have time to examine it before even the foremost reaches us; it's not a bad jump, is it?—three feet nine if it's an inch, and not likely to give, either. The sides or wings on the take-off side are a good idea—the horses will not so readily refuse. But, here they come; now for it! Peters's stud-bred Chance is leading, and going as if he meant to jump. Peters holds him well, both hands to the reins, and well down on the withers. Ah, Chance doesn't like it; he swerves. No, he *can't;* his rider screws him to the point, and, putting in both spurs, rushes at it. "Up!" he roars out, with a voice of thunder, when he thinks his horse is near enough to rise, and Chance makes a noble spring, while Peters throws himself back in the saddle, but sits so close that you cannot see daylight under him. Well done, by Jove! splendidly cleared! Now run, Chance, for your life; you'll not be long alone!

Look! look! there's another over: which is it? The English horse Sultan, ridden by its owner, Mr. Walker. See, though, he goes off, after the jump, at racing speed; he has already caught up, nay, he has passed Chance; and his rider has lost all power over him. Well, *he'll* not win, unless he sobers down.

Now come the others. There are three together—the two Arabs and the country-bred mare, Whistle. There's a frightful crash! it's the Arab horse Snowdrift; he never rose an inch, the hurdle did not give, and God save the rider, poor Captain Fellows, as he lies motionless on the ground, some fifteen feet from the hurdle on the landing side! The other Arab, Pluto, has refused, and Whistle has followed his example. They both turn, and ride back fifty yards for another attempt. In the meantime come the two last, Bessie and the Cape. What is that we hear?

"Who shall go first?" mutters Edgington, with closed lips. "Both together," answers Earnest, with a shrill laugh, and at it they both come. See, how the big Cape lashes his tail, as Earnest puts in the spurs. We really know not which is first; never mind, they both clear it, and clear it well too, side by side, almost knee to knee. But, good Heaven! they will run over poor Captain Fellows; they see him not, and he lies just in front. No; each diverges, and they pass him between them; but neither has a foot to spare. Poor fellow! he knows nothing of it. He is stunned, senseless; and his horse, frightened to death by the fall and the pain, is limping away as quickly as a dislocated shoulder will permit. But they've no time to stop; a steeple-chase is like a cavalry charge in this respect—one may pity the fallen, but no one can stop to help them.

Well, we must get on; for we also have no time, if we would see the race, either to assist Captain Fellows or see how and when the last two horses get over. We soon catch, and are with the leaders once more. Look! Chance is again first, for Sultan has now fairly run away, and gone off nearly at right angles to the steeple-chase course. He is *hors de combat* for he'll not stop in a hurry.

Thus, of seven who started, but three now seem to have any chance; for, besides Sultan, one has fallen, and two have refused at the first jump. The field has been quickly thinned, that's certain; but the hurdle, —not an English, but an Indian hurdle, remember,—was a trying thing to begin with.

There is now a long, clear space, but the ground is heavy—it is ploughed land—and the pace tells on all three. Chance is not more than fifty yards ahead, and as Peters feels the necessity of easing him, he looks back to see his opponents. They are still side by side, but they are also now riding slowly, for they know they could not hope to do what yet remains to be done with their horses blown. In this order they advance. Now they have left the heavy ground, and are picking their way carefully over the baked soil, in which, however, are the innumerable cracks or fissures common in many parts of India; and they cannot with prudence ride quickly over it. Again, the ground improves, for they are riding through short rahur kates,* and the pace improves also.

They near the next jump: it is a plain artificial ditch or trench, and a baulking one, for there is no enclosure at the ends where the small flags, to mark out the course, are placed. It is twelve feet wide and three and a half deep; but the ground, both on the take-off and landing side, is good. Chance arrives first, but he swerves just as he is about to jump, though too late to stop his impetus, and he falls into it. Before either he or his rider have recovered their legs, and got out of the ditch, for neither are hurt, Edgington and Earnest have cleared it, again side by side, and are riding quickly forward.

"If we go on like this," quoth Earnest, for they were so close together they could easily converse, "the fastest horse in the run home will win the race, for I expect we shall see no more of the others."

"We shall see Peters again, or I'm mistaken."

"He'll have a job to get out of that ditch; but, perhaps, he'll do it. By Jupiter, he's done it already!" exclaimed Earnest, as he looked back; "see, he's now mounting!"

Edgington did not answer, but touched Bessie slightly with the spur; she was comparatively fresh again, and darted forward at the hint some distance ahead.

"It will never do to let him go on alone," thought Earnest; "and I must catch him at all costs."

"I'll leave him behind if I can," thought Edgington; "my mare will go as well again by herself."

"They've got a devil of a start," thought Peters, who was once more in the saddle; "I must make up for lost time."

The pace perceptibly increased; but they preserved their relative distances, which was about sixty yards between the two first, and three hundred between the

* Fields with shrubs bearing a kind of pea. The word "kates" is used indiscriminately to all fields with crops.

second and third. Hitherto the race had been through an entirely open country; but they were now approaching enclosures, divided from each other, and from the plain, by banks and ditches. In some of these grew crops, and in all were trees here and there, so that the horses, when going through at a quick pace, required careful guiding. This part of the race, on account of the foliage in the enclosures, could not be so well seen from the stand, though from the whole course being in a segment of a circle, it had not impeded a good view of the first portion.

"The banks and ditches before me are all easy enough," thought Edgington, as he steamed along at a rattling pace; "but it must be 'steady' through the trees, or I shall come to grief there. Tally-ho! hie along, Bessie! run and win the race without a mistake, and your fame will spread from Calcutta to Lahore! Let's show them what we can do, Bessie," he cried, as he felt her spring under him, animated by his cheers; "for bright eyes look on us, Bessie; so away, away, old girl!" A bright gloam of pleasure passed over his face, as he remembered one particular pair, under a riding-hat (he had caught a glimpse of them as he rode in front of the stand), and he positively yelled to his mare in encouragement, as she bore him along at a pace that, for the moment, made Earnest, who was watching him closely behind, have serious doubts of his sanity.

"Why, hang it, the man's mad—gruelling along in such a way. What does he mean by it?"

Echo answered, "What?" for no one was by to respond to Earnest's query; and at that moment Edgington before him cleared the first ditch and bank into the enclosure.

"We've run a good mile of the mile and a half," thought Earnest; "and unless Bessie gets blown, or makes a mistake, she's safe to win. Come along, then, old fellow," he said aloud, as he dug his spur-rowels deep into the lethargic Cape; "let's make one good effort."

They jumped the said ditch and bank before Edgington was half-way across the first enclosure, and the next jump to it, a similar one, was passed by Edgington but a few strides ahead of his opponent.

Once more they are side by side; but the comparative nearness of the goal, and the necessity of husbanding all their strength for what yet remains, precludes further conversation. At this point of the race, Earnest saw that Bessie was certainly the fresher of the two, and that therefore, in all probability, barring accidents, he should lose the race. He did not despair, however; he knew well the "glorious uncertainty" of the turf, especially in steeple-chasing, and was prepared for every contingency.

The enclosure they had now reached was a long one, with many trees in it, and narrowed much towards the end, where was an open space, with a prickly-pear* hedge on either side, and the jump at the extremity.

This differed from the two last, inasmuch as it was a *double* ditch and bank; or, in other words, a bank with a ditch both on the take-off and landing side. The ditches were wide and the bank was high, so that it was a most formidable affair, and it was also a leap which, from the great space it covered, must necessarily be ridden at, full speed.

The said open space, or neck, converged to where it joined the jump, and was there so narrow, that more than one horse could not well pass at the same time; and it was therefore evident that whichever arrived first at the clear space would have a considerable advantage, inasmuch as his opponent could not proceed till he was well over, and any mistake made by the first horse

* The prickly-pear is, we believe, of the genus "cactus;" it is very common in India, and the long, formidable thorns on its leaves renders it, as a hedge, quite impenetrable.

could not be taken advantage of by the second for the same reason.

These objections—for objections they were—had been fully seen by the stewards when they marked out the course; but in truth they had not much choice of ground in the open country around Dinapore, and the jump itself being a first-rate one, with the prickly-pear bushes on either side, as wings to prevent a horse shying, they overlooked its faults and included it.

It was supposed to be, as it doubtless was, the most trying jump in the race, and being at no great distance from the stand, and therefore easily discernible from there, much anxiety was manifested by the spectators to see how the horses would get over it.

The advantages to be gained by being first at the commencement of the neck, or narrow open strip, were fully appreciated by both Edgington and Earnest, and never had either of them ridden at greater speed through a "tope,"* than they did on this occasion. Both of them, moreover, had doubts, up to the last moment, which would succeed in his efforts, when a mango-tree with somewhat low boughs, round which the latter had to make a detour, decided the contest in favour of Edgington, who emerged into the narrow open spot a few seconds before Earnest.

The said narrow portion was not more than sixty yards long, and as this was none too much as a run for the formidable jump at the end, Edgington at once gathered up his reins, and laying hold of his mare in a manner to show her obedience was expected, touched her sharply with the spurs, and rode at a hard gallop towards the bank and two ditches, which seemed to increase in size as he advanced, until they attained such a magnitude that it appeared to him next to impossible for his horse to clear them.

Bessie, however, was as true as her rider. Nothing

* The name given in India to a number of trees together.

daunted at their size, she rushed on, until within twenty yards of the object, when she, of her own accord, gave an extra impetus to her course, and sprung into the air, forming, with Edgington, who looked as if he were part and parcel of her, a beautiful picture for the moment. The next instant, however, man and horse rolled on the ground, on the landing side; the latter, falling on her nose, formed a half-somerset, while Edgington was thrown some feet in advance.

Poor Bessie! she had touched the bank with her forelegs; perhaps her pace had been too great to allow her to rise properly, and though the momentum attained broke the top of it, and carried both her and Edgington clear of the second ditch, the backers of Bessie in the race-stand despaired when they saw the catastrophe.

For a moment Edgington lay still, apparently stunned, while blood flowed from a deep cut over the eyebrow; the next instant, however, to the astonishment of all, he was on his feet, and by the side of his horse, which had sprung up immediately. Seeing that he was in the way of Earnest, who, at the end of the narrow strip, called out to "clear the way," he at once generously led his horse on one side, and attained the saddle just in time to see the "Cape" clear the jump, taking advantage, however, of the large gap he had made in the bank.

On, on—once more on, and once more side by side. Earnest looked at Edgington, and saw with pain that his face was much disfigured with blood, and that he was very pale. Not a word, however, was spoken as they rode forward to the last jump,—an artificial stone wall in front of the stand, a hundred and fifty yards beyond which stood the winning-post.

Already can they hear the voices in the stand encouraging them. "Well done, Edgington!" "Bravo, Earnest!" They heed them not, however, for they are both preparing for the final struggle,—the stone wall and the rush home.

Had Edgington then known that Miss Plane had drawn his horse in the lottery, that she was at that moment watching him with anxiety, and hoping he would win, perhaps the knowledge would have made him unsteady, would have destroyed the nerve so necessary to success; and so we really are glad he did not; for though Earnest and he equally deserve success, we would not have either attain an undue advantage.

On, on—still on! Those few hundred yards since the last jump have appeared immeasurably long to both riders and spectators. Well, indeed, have you run, both good and true steeds, and bravely have ye ridden them, ye two champions! Would that ye could both win!

But now they near the stone wall—the last jump of the race. The excitement in the stand has reached its climax, the horses are neck and neck,—the riders are knee to knee,—at the end as at the commencement. Once more are the reins gathered up—once more are the spurs pressed to the flanks; a rush,—we know not which is first,—see, they are both in the air! Hurrah; hurrah! they have both cleared it, and press on for the winning-post!

"They'll run a dead heat!" "Bessie is the fastest!" "Now the weight will tell!" These and similar exclamations come from the stand, mixed up with much cheering, as they rush past in the final struggle. Both coursers' sides are covered with blood, and yet do the spurs again and again kiss the flanks,—the right hands release the reins, the whip arms are raised,—swish, swish, swish! both spring to the cutting strokes; but two or three more strides and the goal is attained; the horses seem to rush in positively *lifted* by their riders, and Bessie wins by half a neck!

## CHAPTER VI.

### A BACHELOR'S BREAKFAST—PAY-DAY—TIFFIN.

ANOTHER breakfast scene. We like that meal; it has not the regularity, the business-like air of a dinner; people think more of conversation, less of eating. At dinner one course follows another with the regularity of clockwork. At breakfast there is nothing of the kind; you flirt with an egg, you dally with the ham on your plate; the piquant flavour of your Bohea is mixed up, if in India, with the relish of a smart, amusing leader in the *Hurkaru*, or the sensible and far-seeing one in the *Friend*. At breakfast you feel you can be as short or as long a time over it as you like; you are independent, free,—your own master, and in the full enjoyment of the renewed life which a good night's sleep has given you; besides, you have the day before you. Away, then, with any further comparison between that light, free, intellectual repast, breakfast, and the heavy, constrained, animal meal, styled dinner. A man asks us to dinner,—we feel he wishes to feed us; to breakfast, we are conscious of a desire on his part for the amusement of our society, for our conversation, for whatever there may be in us worth drawing out; and while we would accept the first invitation with our hand on our stomach, did custom authorize such demonstrative action, we smile with pleasure at the second request, accept it with gratitude, and feel that our would-be matinal host has paved the way to friendship's bower.

Perhaps, after this eulogy, the reader will expect to be introduced to a very grand breakfast, graced with all that can make such a meal delightful,—perhaps even a wedding breakfast; who knows how high we may have raised expectation. Well, read on, expectant reader; and if you think we have treated you unfairly, don't ask us—*id est*, our book—to breakfast again; for, truly, it will be the sorest punishment that you can devise.

There were three at the morning meal we are about to describe: Ensign Hoby, the expounder of female characters; Ensign Earnest, the defeated steeple-chase jockey; and "Blazes," an immense bull terrier belonging to Earnest. The last could not talk, but he could do everything else that he was told to do; and as he sat at one side of the table, and caught with dexterity any pieces that were thrown to him, it was very evident that he, too, claimed to be one of the breakfast-party.

They sat in the large central whitewashed apartment of the bungalow, where Hoby and Earnest lived together. Everything in and about the room showed plainly that they were bachelors, and somewhat careless ones, too, as far as order and arrangement were concerned. The room itself was most simple; it had no windows, but large doorways at either end, leading out into the verandah, in one of which was placed a huge "kuskus tattee," similar to the one described in Mr. Plane's house. There were two other doorways, one on either side of the room; these led into the bed and bathing rooms of our young warriors, who had the centre room, in which they now sat, in common.

In one corner of this apartment stood a large wooden horse, covered with saddles, bridles, and horse-clothing; in another was a goolale,* with a basket of clay balls; in a third was a rack for guns and pistols, of which there was a goodly assortment. The walls were de-

* A peculiar kind of bow used in India to propel sun-dried clay balls. It is curious the accuracy with which those in practice can shoot with them.

corated with a few sporting pictures, and two nymphs of the ballet. A few riding-whips and a couple of hog-spears were hung on pegs.

Furniture there was not much to boast of. A couple of camp arm-chairs, half a dozen plain ones, the teak-wood breakfast-table, and that was all.

Earnest and Hoby sat at breakfast in pajamahs * and shirt-sleeves. To English ears, of course, this sounds very horrible; but the reader, possibly, knows not what India is in the month of May.

"Pass me one of those chupatties,† Earnest," said Hoby; "that early parade this morning has made me peckish. How do you feel after your ride yesterday?"

"Jolly enough. I wish I had won, though; it was a close thing, wasn't it?"

"Yes, all but a dead heat," Hoby replied; "where I stood in the stand, I thought it was one. I expect, however, Bessie has the legs of the Cape. Do you know that Fellows, who fell at the first jump, is only just sensible?—he was delirious all night. I saw the doctor just now as I came home."

"It was a nasty spill," observed Earnest: "I did not know myself, as I went over the first jump, that he had fallen, until I was almost on him; it was all Edgington and I could do to give him a wide berth. After the race I rode back, or was doing so, when I met the doctor with him in his buggy. I believe they bled him directly they got him home."

"The best thing too," said Hoby. "I don't think, by the bye, any one else was hurt besides he and Edgington; and with the exception of a lot of sticking-plaister on his forehead, which gave him a funny look at parade this morning, the latter is all right again."

* Light muslin or silk drawers, made very loose, and often used instead of trowsers during the day in hot weather, as also to sleep in at night.

† Unleavened cakes of coarse flour, much eaten by Europeans in India.

"Oh yes, he's none the worse for it. What fun it was when in the stand, after the race, he gave Miss Plane the lady's whip—he was as shy as any girl about it."

"Yes; and did you observe," said Hoby, "how haughtily she took it, and how she objected to give him her old one in exchange, which every one said she ought to do?"

"Of course I did," replied Earnest; "it took a lot to persuade her. She'd never have done it, after all, had not the general been there, and told her he thought it was the least she could do."

"And even then she did it with a bad grace. Depend on it," Hoby added, "the character I drew of her name will fit this haughty damsel."

"How handsome she looked!" Earnest continued. "Do you know, I think the colonel was a little smitten."

"Not a little—look here! my arm's black and blue from the effect of it."

"How do you mean?"

"Why, he was so excited about her beauty, he grasped my arm and pinched it, while he abused me for the character I had given her, till I thought he had gone clean mad. He laughed about it afterwards and tried to pass it off, but I'm sure he's spoony."

"What fun if he should really fall in love," said Earnest, "for they say he has never cared about any woman in his life; but, poor Edgington, how dismayed he would be if it were so, for I'll swear he's very far gone."

"Over head and ears," Hoby replied; "and that cold, haughty character of her's will attract him. Quite a little romance, too, his winning the race, and having to present the whip. Just the proper commencement for a love affair, is it not? Oh dear," he continued with a yawn, "I wish I were up to my neck in ice, for it's cruelly hot this morning, and yet the bheestie is watering the tattee well."

"There's but little wind," Earnest replied, "it's so early; but we can have the punkah. Here, bearer, call the punkah-wallah."

"Ah, that's better," added Hoby, as, after a minute or two, the air, agitated by the large fan, relieved them. "What could one do without punkahs and tattees in India? I've often thought how little people in England, much as they are told of it, appreciate the heat out here."

"It's impossible they *can* realize it, for there's nothing at home to compare it to, unless, indeed, they put themselves in the mouths of some of their smelting furnaces."

"Ah, by Jove," Hoby rejoined, "it's very wearying, this incessant heat. I often think life in India is mere existence. You've done, haven't you? Khitmudgar, take away the breakfast-things, and send my bearer with cheroots and fire. Now, Earnest, we'll have our matinal smoke; that cheroot, after breakfast, is I think one of the greatest pleasures in the day, and I've just time to take mine quietly before my company comes to be paid. When are your men coming?"

"In about half an hour," Earnest replied; "but I was officer of the day yesterday, and must write out my report first."

So saying, Earnest took writing materials, and began filling in the printed form for the relieved officer of the day, while Hoby drew one of the arm-chairs forward, put his feet on the table, and puffed away.

"I didn't visit the guards in the evening," Earnest continued as he wrote; "the colonel let me off on account of the steeple-chase. How much less duty we have to do altogether than the officers in the European regiments!—at the same time, I would rather command Englishmen."

"So would I," answered Hoby; "but so would *not* a great many, for they imagine Jack Sepoy perfection, and scarcely inferior to an English soldier. I think they are wrong, and that the day may come when we shall find he has been too much petted. In many points, the Madras and Bombay armies are better constituted than ours. Our respect for high-caste men, or rather our exclusion of all others, is, I am sure, a mistake; but that's an opinion which a man would get into very bad odour for, did he broach it."

"Were you to admit low-caste men into regiments, the Brahmins and Rajputs would not serve," rejoined Earnest, "and thus we should lose the best men in India for soldiers."

"Excuse me; I doubt your high-caste men being the best material for soldiers; but even allowing it to be so, I would have low as well as high caste regiments," said Hoby; "at present, all our army is of one stamp. I cannot exactly see danger in it, but I do see greater safety in my plan."

"You surely do not think the native army could ever be unfaithful," Earnest asked; "and if not, what could your low-caste regiments avail?"

"I cannot tell; but I think, that for an army levied in India, where so many creeds, sects, and castes abound, I would not confine the recruitment, as we do, to only Mussulmans and Hindus of certain grades; on the contrary, I would enlist opposing elements. Union, they say, is strength, but disunion in the native army would, I think, be our greatest safeguard."

Earnest's bearer interrupted them at this point, to say his company had arrived, and were waiting outside.

"Oh, they are rather too early," Earnest remarked—"but never mind; tell the subadar and jemadar to come in; and bring another table," he added to the bearer. "We shall get on better if we have separate tables, Hoby."

The bearer left to execute his orders, and the native officers appeared. They were in full uniform, and, as they entered, they saluted their officers in a somewhat stiff military style.

"Take a chair, subadar," said Earnest; "there's another for you, jemadar. It was rather hot coming here, was it not?"

"Very hot, sahib; but that does not signify, we are always glad to come into your presence."

"Especially on pay-day," answered Earnest, laughing; but call the pay-havildar and let's begin: I won't keep you out longer than I can help, such weather."

"Narain Sing, come into the sahib's presence," called out the jemadar, partly opening the door.

"Is it true, sahib, you won the race yesterday?" asked the subadar, who knew perfectly well Earnest had not done so, but thought the query would please.

"No; Edgington Sahib won it," answered Earnest. Why did you not come to see it?"

"My duties did not allow me to leave the lines. I must not eat the Company's salt for nothing."

The pay-havildar here appeared, with two sepoys, each carrying a large bag of rupees, which, having saluted Earnest, they placed on the ground, and then retired. Narain Sing produced his pay-lists, and squatted down on the floor near the rupees; Earnest reached his pay-book from a shelf, and the work of paying the company commenced.

Let us shortly describe the natives there present. The subadar was a spare man of about fifty, with quick, restless, green eyes, and greyish-brown whiskers and moustaches, which, by the bye, were very long and thick; so long, that the owner joined them together, and twisted them back in a long curl behind his ear. This gave him rather a ferocious appearance, but it was not borne out by the expression of his face, which was mild enough, and the whole manner of the man was indicative of a being in authority who was always fearful that his good-nature would get the better of him. His skin was of a yellowish brown, his teeth were very imperfect, and discoloured with the beetle-nut which he was even then chewing; his hair looked scanty enough, as far as you could judge from the little that peeped out from under his chako, which he wore in the room as he sat, for it is a mark of disrespect in India to uncover the head; he had, apparently, too much hair in his flowing whiskers and moustache to spare any for the top of his cranium. He was dressed in white trowsers, and a red coatee with green facings. In the way of ornament, he boasted small gold-fringed shoulder-straps (they could scarcely be called epaulets), and the principal decoration of a native officer, two rows of large solid gold beads, about the size of plums, around his neck. His chako, which was heavy and cumbrous, was even better calculated than those *we* use in tropical climates to concentrate the rays of the sun, and knock down our poor countrymen with, for the material was the same, and, moreover, it had no peak to shade the forehead and eyes.

Our subadar sat very upright in his chair, his sword between his knees, and his white-gloved hands resting thereon, bestowing great attention as sepoy after sepoy came in and received the month's pay.

The jemadar, who sat by his side, only differed from his superior in being much darker and much stouter, with black instead of greyish-brown whiskers and moustaches, and having only one instead of two rows of the golden beads around his neck.

The pay-havildar, seated on the ground, was in undress—that is, in light and cool native clothes. This indulgence was allowed him, for, having to see to each man's account, and pay out all the money, he could do so better and more accurately without the incumbrance of a heavy uniform to impede him. The principle is not a new one, for it is well known that in our English army when anything has really to be done, such portions of the uniform as can be dispensed with are invariably thrown aside, both by officers and men; but that does not signify: a man, of course, fights better when throttled with a high stock, and dressed in a way that allows him not the proper use of his limbs; at least, whether he does or not, so think the authorities, and one must bow to their superior wisdom.

The havildars and naicks (corresponding to our sergeants and corporals) were paid first, then came the sepoys, whose monthly pay was seven rupees: these all came in one at a time, received the amount from the pay-havildar, saluted Ensign Earnest with military precision, and departed.

But, the men being now all paid, the pay-havildar proceeds to count out what is due to the subadar and jemadar. There is a little discussion between them regarding certain deductions made therefrom, but being of a private nature, Earnest does not listen to it; and when it is settled, the subadar, with another salute, announces that all is finished.

"Then take them away," Earnest replies; "to-morrow we have target practice. Let the company be at the butts at five o'clock in the morning."

Both the native officers rise, salute, and retire; but the pay-havildar stops to give Earnest his month's pay, which was drawn from the treasury at the same time as that of the men. Outside can now be heard the voice of the subadar, who, having made the men fall in, calls out in English (for words of command in the native army are always given in our mother tongue), "Attention!" "Threes left shoulders forward!" "Quick march!" "Forward!" and the regular tramp of the men, as they march off to their lines, concludes the payment of the 3rd company, 99th regiment Native Infantry, for the preceding month.

"Now, havildar," says Earnest, "give me my 'tullub,'* and deduct that fifty I owe you, and also my mess bill—sixty rupees, is it not? Give me back the order I gave you for the fifty. I dare say I shall have to give you another before next pay-day. Now how is it? Let me see; so I get, including the company's

* The general word used in India for pay.

allowance, after all deductions, one hundred and thirty rupees, twelve annas, and three pice. Here, bearer, take my pay from the havildar, and mind you don't pay away an anna* without my leave."

"I say, Hoby," he added, addressing his friend, who at another table, surrounded by native officers, rupees, and sepoys, was going through the performance he had just completed, "I have not much to carry on with this month, only one hundred and thirty, after paying fifty I got from the havildar, and my mess bill. I wish I had won that race yesterday; the forty gold mohurs would have been a great addition to my finances."

"Never mind, you nearly won it, and must console yourself with that," answered Hoby laughingly; "you'll have better luck next time."

When Hoby's company was paid, the two were once more alone together. They drew up to the centre table again, and both put their feet on it.

"What shall you do with yourself till tiffin-time?" asked Hoby.

"Oh, this is my moonshee† day," answered Earnest; "he will be here soon, and then I shall have two steady hours at Hindostanee."

"When do you suppose you shall pass?" continued Hoby.

"In three months more, if I'm lucky. I passed the colloquial easy enough; I hope I shall get as well through the big go."

"Well, *I* hope to get a staff appointment without a P.C.‡ to my name—many do," said Hoby; "and languages were never my forte."

"Yes; but you have better interest than I have," answered Earnest, "and that goes a long way."

"Twelve o'clock, I declare," exclaimed Hoby, look-

* A copper coin, the sixteenth part of a rupee.
† A teacher of native languages.
‡ Passed college.

ing at his watch. "I'm to be with Edgington at half-past. We are going to the general's together."

"What's that for?"

"Oh! after the race yesterday, the old general asked Edgington, whom you know he's very fond of, why he never came to see him, and Edgington said he'd come to-day. 'Do,' said the general, 'come to tiffin, and bring Hoby with you.' I was standing by, and of course accepted."

"I expect Edgington was glad enough to do so," said Earnest; "Miss Plane, you know, is there."

"I know it," answered Hoby; "and it will be great fun seeing Edgington make love, for I'll swear he wants to do so."

"If ever he succeeds, Hoby, he's sure to tell her the character you gave her name, and she'll hate you for ever afterwards."

"She will do nothing of the sort, unless the cap fits; and then I shan't care about her hatred."

"But tell me," said Earnest, "what put that funny idea into your head about characters from names? Have you the same theory with regard to men?"

"Not in so great a degree. Your first query I cannot answer, for I know not precisely myself; it is intuitive, I suppose."

"I certainly agreed with you in many of the sketches you drew," added Earnest; "and yet it is odd I did so, for I never knew any girls with some of the names you painted."

"Not odd at all," continued Hoby; "it would have been very odd if you had not. My instincts in the matter are common to all, only I have perhaps studied the subject more than others."

"I never knew anybody else who had studied it at all," answered Earnest, laughing; "so it may certainly be called the Hoby science, for you are the first who have pursued it."

"Well, so be it; we all have our own crotchets, and

this is one of mine; but as I derive from it the greatest pleasure that can be derived from any science, I shall certainly not relinquish it."

"What pleasure is that, pray?" asked Earnest.

"The pleasure that the students of all sciences derive from the verity of their conclusions; in truth, I have seldom found myself wrong."

"Well," added Earnest, "we shall see if you are right this time. But here comes my moonshee, so adieu to everything but dry Hindostanee, and the absurd tales in the "Bagh-o-Bahar,"* for the next two hours."

An hour later, Hoby was driving with Edgington in his buggy down to the general's house at Deegha, a suburb of Dinapore.

Edgington was in great spirits; his success the day before, the manner in which that success had also been fortunate for Miss Plane, his possession of her old riding-whip, his anticipated meeting with her at the general's—all contributed to make him very joyous; and as they rattled along, through the bazaar that divides Deegha from Dinapore, he chatted away in great glee.

"It is not so," he replied, in answer to some remark that Hoby had made, regarding the transitory duration of all pleasures in life, "not so at all; those who find gratification *only* in selfish pleasures promulgate the theory; for true it is, that *their* pleasures pall; but those who seek for pleasure in the happiness of others never get satiated; nay, the more they indulge themselves, the more does their appetite for such enjoyments increase."

"But do you not think," added Hoby—who, because he saw the mood that Edgington was in, purposely assumed another, to draw him out,—"do you not think, that even the philanthropists you allude to tire

* A Hindostanee book, in which students are examined.

of their pleasures, when the good they do is met with ingratitude and unkindness; and when the happiness they look for is often frustrated, through the perversity of the beings they seek to benefit?"

"To some extent, yes," answered Edgington; "but they cast about for worthier objects, and forget their disappointments in the anticipated pleasure of future success."

"Ay, but then that is pleasure in anticipation, not in reality!" exclaimed Hoby; "and is it not true that the former almost invariably exceeds the latter? 'Man never is, but always to be, blest.' What knowledge of human nature is displayed in those few words! We all acknowledge the fact, more or less, and yet how we all struggle on, regardless of experience, for that happiness which we can never attain."

"*Perfect* happiness, I grant you," said Edgington; "but happiness, to a greater or less degree, we *do* arrive at continually. It is not in the nature of man to be perfectly contented with his lot, to want for nothing more, to wish nothing altered. I opine it is well that it is so, for the reverse would do away continually with all incentive to exertion; and the perfectly happy man would become, in very elysium—a pitiable object."

"And yet he would be happy," suggested Hoby.

"I doubt it; anticipation is an essential ingredient of happiness."

"At all events," remarked Hoby, "it is a state of which we can only form conjectures, for none have ever attained to it. But how absurd, after all, are our discussions as to happiness; we speak as if it was a state with its limits and boundaries defined—in short, as if *all* understood what was meant by the word; whereas, to each it has a different signification. Even in the abstract, happiness and misery are only comparative terms. You may ask a man, with reason, if he is happy, for the query with the adjective merely refers to the state of his feelings; but should you ask him if he has *attained* happiness, you must, to make your question clear, define to him what you *mean* by the word, or allow him to give you his signification thereof, and then answer with reference thereto. I'm afraid I've not made my meaning clear, and so will illustrate it on yourself. Now, tell me, are you——"

"It's quite unnecessary," interrupted Edgington; "I understand you perfectly."

"You'll understand me better," continued Hoby, "when you've answered my query. Now, tell me, are *you* happy?"

"Well, if I must answer, I'll answer truly," said Edgington. "Yes, happy as the day."

"So far so good. But again, is happiness yours? and to make your answer clear, explain to me first what you understand by the word happiness," said Hoby, while he looked at Edgington with a roguish smile.

"I'll do nothing of the sort," answered Edgington, laughing, and slightly blushing. "Why am I to be subjected to this inquisitorial process? But to come down to more tangible facts; I'm happy just now in anticipation of the good tiffin we are sure to find at the general's, and that's much more to the purpose, at this moment, than all the rigmarole we've been talking, for here we are at his compound gates."

"Edgington, Edgington," said Hoby, as they drove up to the house, "you are easily made happy—that is to say, *in anticipation*; but stake not too much on the cast. The tiffin you allude to *may* disagree with you; and remember, ere it's too late, that it's not alone what we put into our stomachs that we find hard to digest."

Edgington looked seriously at his companion for a moment, as if to ask what he meant; but Hoby was studiously engaged wiping the dust off his boots, and at that instant the buggy mare stopped of her own accord at the hall-door.

They were shown into a large and comfortable drawing-room, fitted up in a luxurious style. It contained no one but the old general himself, seated at a table writing, under the ever-waving punkah.

"How do you do, Edgington? Glad to see you, Hoby, he said rising. You're in the nick of time; we shall have tiffin in ten minutes. Come, take off your swords, put them in that corner, and excuse me for a little, while I finish this letter."

The swords, worn in honour of the general, were quickly placed on one side, and Hoby took up a book on the table, while Edgington strolled round the room, looking at some pictures hanging against the wall.

Hoby's book or pamphlet, for it was little more, opened at the fly-leaf, and he unconsciously read what was written thereon :—"Beatrice Plane, from her friend and admirer, Antonia Curtain;" he looked at the title —it was an American work, "Woman *versus* Man;" in his surprise he let the book fall, but muttered, as he picked it up, "I know not why it should astonish me, but still it *is* strange." A gleam of satisfaction passed over his face as he read once more in the title what he conceived to be the verification of the sketch he had applied to the name of Beatrice; but it fled in another moment, and gave way to a look of pity, as the figure of Edgington, still restless, and walking about the room, crossed his eyesight.

"Come here, Edgington," he said; "is not this a pretty sketch of Dinapore from the river?" pointing to a pencil-drawing on the table; "and see," he added in a lower tone, as Edgington stood by him, "here's a funny book," and he opened it at the title-page; "what a curious subject for the general to study, is it not?"

"Yes; what a strange title; what *is* it about? It is by an American woman," said Edgington.

"Of course it is," replied Hoby; "one of the strong-minded American women, too. I should like to read it; I've a great mind to ask the general to lend it me."

"No, don't; he might not like it; besides, see here," exclaimed Edgington, who had turned over the fly-leaf by accident; it's not his book, it belongs——" he stopped short, and looked at Hoby with some confusion. Strange fellow, that Hoby; he was intently occupied in endeavouring to make one of those pen-wipers in the shape of a woman with wide petticoats stand on her head.

"Come, I'll bet you a chick,* Edgington, I make this damsel stand on her head longer than you do; here's my stop-watch, will you try?"

"Oh yes," said Edgington, laying down the book very hastily; "you try first."

They were thus scientifically engaged when the general approached them.

"Well, anything to pass the time," said the old gentleman laughing; "what is it? a bet? I doubt you're being as expert at that as you are at steeple-chasing, Edgington."

"I owe you a chick, Hoby," said Edgington, rising and blushing as he did so. "Ah, there's the whip, I see, General, which Miss Plane won yesterday."

"Yes; she was using it this morning, and liked it very much. She's up-stairs; I'll send and tell her tiffin is ready," said the general. "Here, chuprassie."†

"Sahib!" answered the chuprassie, pushing aside the slight bamboo screen so quickly, that he appeared to have heard his master even before he spoke.

"Let the ayah tell the Missee‡ Baba tiffin is ready."

"That cut over your eyebrow is not much, after all, Edgington," continued the general.

* Four rupees. † A messenger.

‡ The word used by servants for young unmarried ladies.

"Oh no, sir; I found it had nearly healed when I dressed to come here; so I exchanged a lot of diachylon our doctor had put over it for this little bit of black plaster, which hides it perfectly."

"Fellows is not so lucky," observed the general. "I hear he'll not be out of bed for a week. But let us go now into the other room, Miss Plane will join us there."

So saying, he led the way into the dining-room, where a substantial tiffin was spread.

Miss Plane entered before they sat down; she bowed distantly to the general's guests, and said to him, "I had half a mind not to come down, sir; the heat is so excessive, that eating anything is quite out of the question."

"Oh, sit down, and try," he replied; "you must not starve yourself in India."

She did so with a languid air. She looked as pretty, or rather handsome—for the latter in her case is the better word—without her bonnet or riding-hat as she did with them. This, by the bye, always says much for a woman's beauty; for, alas! how few look equally well in both cases. Hers, however, was a style which nothing could much heighten; while the absence of all adornment enabled one more fully to appreciate the exquisite contour of her features and classical-looking head, to which the plain Madonna style in which she wore her lustrous and massive hair much contributed.

"Now, take some of that jelly," said the general; "I don't propose anything more substantial, as you say you have no appetite. Hoby, send Miss Plane some jelly."

"I'll take a glass of that wine, also, you have by you, Captain Edgington," said Miss Plane. "I see you still bear about you some marks of your fall yesterday."

"It is but little, however," Edgington replied. "I

hope your ride to the race and back did not fatigue you? It was very good of you, and all the other ladies, to come on such a hot and dusty evening."

"Yes, I think we deserve to be praised for the effort," she replied; "but in my case, I did it from the feeling that the sooner I accustom myself to heat the better."

"Well, I'm sure you were amused," said the general, who was busy with some cold beef and pickles, "to say nothing of the whip which you brought away for your pains."

"I thought you would win it, Miss Plane," interposed Hoby, "when you drew Major Bruce's mare, Bessie, in the lottery, particularly as Captain Edgington rode her."

"They all tell me you are such a wonderful rider, Captain Edgington," remarked Miss Plane; "how is it, then, you got such a fall, or 'purl,' for that seems the favourite word in Dinapore, yesterday?

"My horse fell, and—and—I—I mean—what could I do?" Edgington answered confusedly; "but as for my being such a capital rider, the fact is, there are several in Dinapore as good, if not better, than myself."

"You do not think so!" she coolly remarked."

"And why not, pray?"

"Because others do not; and I cannot suppose you an exception to the mass of mankind, and blind to your own merits."

"I scarcely know whether to accept that as a compliment or reproof," Edgington remarked, somewhat taken aback by her *sang froid*.

"As the latter, decidedly," she replied; "I never proffer the former."

Edgington, a little abashed, addressed himself with increased attention to his salad; and Hoby, who was evidently much amused, took up the cudgels for his friend.

"You do not admire modesty in the male sex, then,

Miss Plane; you think, in assuming it, we entrench on your rights?"

"By no means," she replied; "why should modesty be the attribute of women alone? But if by modesty you mean pretended ignorance, I admire it in no one."

"Pretended ignorance is a somewhat hard expression to apply to the case, is it not? For instance, *I* may know I am the handsomest man in Dinapore," he continued, smiling as he saw his face in the opposite mirror, and felt then, as he had always known, it was a very plain one, "still, if any one told me I was so, you would not surely have me bow in acquiescence, and intimate that I knew it well?"

"The case is an extreme one, and scarcely likely to occur," she replied, with a slight smile; "but we are exhausting the subject. Tell me, Captain Edgington," she continued, turning to him, "did you think you should win that race, yesterday, when you went over the last jump with Mr. Earnest?"

"Yes! I thought I—that is to say—I knew one of us—I mean that the race would be won by the fastest."

Having given vent to this rather unintelligible answer, Edgington blushed a little, and relapsed into his salad. Miss Plane regarded him steadfastly for half a moment, then fell into a train of thought, with her eyes on the table. A pause occurred,—one of those pauses which show that, at all events, some of the party are not at ease. Miss Plane broke it by commencing a conversation with the general, on the advantage of pickling walnuts at a sufficiently mature age.

How strange it is, that the first steps of love always make a man a goose. Here was Edgington, for instance, a man in no way wanting in conversational powers, with very fair talent, and peculiarly gifted in the art of small talk, as shy at the general's table to-day as a timid girl. He could scarcely open his mouth; when he *did*, it was to give vent to some remark which he repented of the next moment. He was continually intending to say something, and as continually thinking it might bear some other meaning; or that it was too general and vapid a remark, or was too particular and personal; or that it looked as if he wished to drag himself and his acts on the *tapis;* or that it was ill-natured, or pedantic, or vain, or foolish, or goodness knows what; for he found some objection to each and every sentence he thought of uttering.

How lucky it is for us poor men, that this state of things does not last; or what woman but would be wearied, bored to death, by her lover. It is, however, but of short duration; it is contemporaneous only with the first dazzling effect of the beauties or charms which enthral us, and nothing so soon dispels it as the conviction that our admiration is perceived by its fair object. If even we see it is perceived without favour on her part, nay more, with indifference, still if we determine to follow up the chase, the string of our tongue is loosened, and we can speak plain, and like ourselves. In a few words, it seems to be a state which all lovers pass through, more or less—the more they admire and love, the more stupid they are—and it also appears to be limited in period, and to cease with the time when the eyes have revealed the secret of that love, and it is become a tacitly acknowledged fact between the lover and his fair one that the latter is the admired object of the former. Woman has here a great advantage; to commence with, she does not generally fall in love as quickly as man, and the state we have described has long passed away in her lover ere she feels one particle of the flame which has been for some time consuming him. A woman in love is, therefore, rarely stupid like man, for she knows the ground she stands on, and in most cases her love at first amounts to little more than a mere *permission* for her admirer to love her; when later, however, a clear acknowledgment thereof passes her lips, it is poured into ears only too ready to receive it, and thus her position is very, very different from that uncertain state in which a man is when he feels the full force of the passion, is anxious to do all he can to produce a favourable impression, yet fears, like a very coward, that either word or glance shall reveal his secret; all which causes combined, give birth to the feelings we have attempted to describe above, and under which poor Edgington at this time most decidedly laboured.

But, how quick also is woman to see when a man admires her; nay, how well she can tell whether it be mere admiration, or love, that animates him; moreover, how sure is the discovery to give her an interest in him, even though she may feel that he never can be more to her than he is at that moment. Beatrice Plane rose from that luncheon table with the knowledge that Edgington was in love with her; and the discovery made her think a little. She cared nothing for him, she did not suppose she ever should; but it was a gratification to her proud nature, to feel assured of the impression she had made, and the more so, as, both from all the general had said of him and what she had seen herself, and notwithstanding the confused state he was in that day (which she cleverly attributed to the right cause), she knew that he was a man any woman might be proud to class among her admirers.

"Well, let him love on," thought Beatrice as she left the table, while a cold smile passed over her face; "I will give him no encouragement, and it will amuse me."

"I have been stupid enough," thought Edgington, as he held open the door for her to pass out; and "I dare say she thinks so. She'll look on me as a good steeple-chase jockey, and nothing more."

"She's all my fancy painted her," Hoby hummed to himself, keeping time on the mahogany with his knuckles.

Bubble, bubble, bubble, went the general's hookah, which he had just begun to smoke. It appeared a monotonous and melancholy sound to Edgington as he sat down; but he was out of temper with himself, and gladly sought relief in the cheroot, which, at a sign from the general, was offered him. A little more, and all three were enveloped in clouds from "sublime tobacco," which, whether on the heated plains of Hindostan or the snow-clad regions of the Poles, is equally prized, and will not lightly be displaced.

## CHAPTER VII.

BEATRICE'S LETTER—AN EVENING IN THE HOT WINDS—ADVANTAGES OF INDIA.

THE same afternoon Beatrice wrote a letter to her mother, in the following terms:—

"DEEGHA, DINAPORE,
"*Thursday.*

"MY DEAR MAMMA,—

"How tantalizing it is, that, after a separation of eighteen months, we are now within reasonable distance of each other, and still cannot meet. Somehow or another, though, I do not feel as if I was so completely separated from you as when oceans rolled between us; we cannot converse, 'tis true, but you can respond to my letters, and I to yours, ere the interest of the subject broached has died away, which was so often the case formerly.

"I know not why I write to you now—for I await your answer to my last—except that it be I want some one to commune with, and know no other being, as there is none in the world, except you, with whom I can do so.

"Do you remember telling me in England that I should be much admired when I came out to India? Well, you spoke true; I find I am quite the rage here, and, if it has no other advantage, it amuses me. One of the general's lady friends told me this morning that I am creating a regular sensation in this little world. I have had some proofs of it myself, as follows.

"I went yesterday to a steeple-chase, and as I entered the race-stand with the old general, the hum of voices ceased, and I felt I created no little impression. Only guess my surprise, however, when 'Ye gods, how lovely!' greeted my ears. The exclamation, I feel sure, was not intended to be heard by me, and I found it proceeded from an officer about forty-five years of age, who, I afterwards discovered, was the commandant of one of the native regiments here. I looked at him in my way, the way which you used to say I did so well, and I wonder he did not fall backward off the railing on which he was seated, for he was dreadfully confused. Later in the day, after I had been introduced to him, I let him know, in an indirect way, that I had heard him. Perhaps in this I was wrong; what do you think? But I could not resist the opportunity, when he asked me, with reference to a telescope he was adjusting, if I was far-sighted, to tell him I both saw and heard well! But I have one decided conquest to relate, in a Captain Edgington, who won the steeple-chase yesterday, and who, by an arrangement—too long to detail here—presented me with the riding-whip, the prize in a ladies' lottery, which I won, and to whom, in spite of all my objections, I was obliged to give my old one. He came to luncheon to-day with another officer of his regiment, the general having asked them both yesterday; and it was too absurd to see the sad state he was in,—I mean, how very much he was in love. Yesterday was not the first time I have met him; but it appeared, from his manner on the day he first saw me, as if the beauty which you have bestowed on your daughter quite took his heart by storm. At luncheon to-day, however, any doubts I had on the subject were dispelled; and I feel it is quite necessary to let him see I am not easily won, or goodness knows but my next letter to you might detail a proposal!

"You will be anxious to know what sort of creature he is. Most girls have a great objection—they call it delicacy—to discuss an admirer, even to their mothers, but you know I have no such feeling with you; we are,

I trust, too much alike in our natures, have too high an appreciátion of ourselves, and too common a contempt for the assumed superiority of man, to render any secrets between us necessary, or even advisable, on such points.

"He is gentleman-like, not handsome, but with, nevertheless, a very pleasing countenance; tall, brave (he showed the latter in the steeple-chase yesterday), and, from all I hear and the little I saw of him *before* he fell so much in love (now he can scarcely open his lips), he is clever enough. 'Do you like him, then?' I think I hear you say; and the only answer I can give is, that I do not *dislike* what I have seen of him. But you know me too well, I trust, dearest mother, to suppose I should ever fall in love until I saw clearly it was quite advisable for me to do so. Even then, I am sure, I should never attain that supposed elysium of feeling which poets and romance writers describe; for, irrespective of that peculiar madness not being in my nature, I would endeavour to commence *before* marriage the task which we both think so necessary *after* it, namely, the control of my lord and master; and I know that any but the smallest amount of love which will content a man would put me in a very bad position to attempt it.

"Tell me if you do not agree with all I have said; and depend on my keeping this aspiring captain at a distance, even though, as I acknowledge to you, he is not disagreeable, and though he is rich (I forgot this—it is an important point—it seems he has a private fortune), and would give all he has for one smile from me.

"Give my love to my father—of course he will not see my letter—and let me know in your next the exact day you expect to be here. I rode down to Patna the other morning—it is but four miles from here—and saw the house we are to live in; it is the largest and best there.

"The heat is insufferable. I did not picture to myself anything like this. I cannot exist for a moment without the punkah, and it bores me to death when I write, it blows the paper about so.

"Your affectionate Daughter,

"BEATRICE."

"P.S. Say something civil to the general in your next, which I can read to him. He allows me to do just as I will in his house, and I'm sure likes having me here. He is not bright though, poor man, and when we are alone it is an infliction. As to Captain Edgington's private fortune, I know not how much it is; but the story goes that a distant relation, rich as Crœsus, left him his orphan child and two large sums of money, one for its education and the other for my would-be lover."

When this letter was concluded, and Beatrice had taken the afternoon siesta, which is more or less common in India, a reinvigorating bath and toilet made her feel equal to the usual evening drive with the general. To her surprise, she found that the guests at luncheon were to be their companions in the carriage; for the general having a very good billiard-table in his house, and being very fond of the game, had managed to detain them, and pass a pleasant afternoon enough with its help.

The sun had but ten minutes more of his daily course to run as the carriage drove round to the door; but how different is an evening in India during the hot months and a summer evening in a temperate climate. Let us, reader, detain you an instant while we endeavour with our feeble pen to paint the former, and then judge for yourself if you can trace any resemblance.

Though the sun was not yet below the horizon, no one could see it, or had seen it for the last two hours, and this purely on account of the very large quantity of dust and sand with which the air was charged. The hot wind which had been blowing all day, though it had somewhat decreased in force since noon, had not yet by any means ceased, for it still breathed a continued hot current, varied every now and then by a strong and sudden gust, which sent up clouds upon clouds of fine dust into the air, previously, however, so tainted therewith, that the addition, though great at the moment it rose, did not seem, when once fairly in the atmosphere, to add to the obscurity or palpable thickness that prevailed.

Though the sun could not be seen, there was a kind of red and fiery glow in the dusty air, which accorded well with the dry and parched-up appearance everything animate and inanimate presented. Green, properly so called, was an unknown colour in the vegetable world; men and animals, loaded with dust, looked hot and weary; and when you met them, and saw the state they were in, you very naturally, if not abroad from necessity, asked yourself what pleasure or advantage you were likely to attain thereby!

As we write, we have before us one of those evenings, and we feel, alas! how utterly incompetent we are to bring the same before the reader; to describe the piercing nature of that hot wind, which penetrates all your clothing, carrying with it the impalpable fiery powder with which the air is charged; to paint the utter dreary desolation all nature assumes, as if, tired out in its contests with these choleric blasts, it had resigned itself to its fate, and ceased even to try to look green and gay; to realize for our readers in its extent the prostration of spirit engendered by such a scene, and how those subject thereto feel at such moments that India is a dear country at any price.

On such an evening did the general and his party, according to custom, start for their evening drive. They passed through the Dinapore Bazaar, the barrack-square, and then joined such of the other residents as had ventured forth on the road, or course, in front of the native infantry lines. The conversation in the carriage was not animated, the high temperature told on all; and it was not till they were met by Colonel Carstairs on horseback that much was said by any one.

"Good evening, general—good evening, Miss Plane," he said as he rode up and walked his horse by the side of the carriage; "this is pleasant weather, is it not?—the wind's as hot now as it was at two o'clock, and the sun is just setting. This is something like the hot winds up country, Miss Plane," he continued, turning to her—"at Delhi and Meerut, for example, where it blows hot all night, and we never take down the tattees at all."

"I can conceive nothing worse than this," Beatrice replied; "and I truly don't understand why anybody comes out on such an evening."

"To get exercise and an appetite," the general remarked. "Did you never face the hot winds, you would, in many up-country stations, have to stay in the house for nearly three months on end, as there it never ceases, day or night, for that time."

"Ah, indeed," responded Beatrice, who, after a short pause, turned to our hero, and said, "Do you remember, Captain Edgington, the first morning I met you on this road, and——"

"Of course, I remember it perfectly," interposed our hero very quickly.

"I did not mean that—you interrupted me," she remarked, colouring; "I was going to ask if you remembered, that morning, telling me India had many advantages? Now that I hear, see, and feel so much against the country, I would beg you to detail some of them, for it would be a relief."

"I will willingly do so," he replied cheerfully, and apparently at his ease, now that he had a given subject to discuss. "India is the best country in the world for a poor man, for a talented man, for an energetic man, and for a lazy man. For a poor man, because he is exempt from many of the miseries that poverty entails in England. Here, we all mix on nearly equal terms, and the poor man is not looked down upon by those richer than himself; for in India, individuals are not measured by the length of their purses, as at home, but rather by whatever there may be good or bad, agreeable or the reverse, in their composition. India is a good country for a talented man, for, the market not being so stocked with that article out here as in England, it is very sure, sooner or later, to command its price. In like manner is an energetic man sure to succeed, for India offers a large field to enterprise; and being a comparatively nèw country as regards most arts, manufactures, inventions, and sciences, the man with energy, fairly directed, cannot fail to find many paths to success. I think I said India was a good country for a lazy man: how many are there out here, earning, at all events, a decent livelihood and doing little, who would starve at home doing twice as much. If they earn little, they want little to live on, and so are many of these comparatively happy, who, had they remained in the mother country, would have been miserable objects, sinking deeper and deeper into that poverty which they lacked sufficient industry to surmount. Those who belong to none of the four classes I have described, I would counsel to avoid the sunny East; for truly such an evening as this," he added in conclusion, with a smile, "does not allow me to name climate as one of the Indian advantages."

"There's truth in much you have said, Edgington," remarked Colonel Carstairs; "but you have by no means exhausted the subject and the advantages of India. *I* know many others," he added, turning to Miss Plane, "which, if you'll allow me, some day I'll detail to you."

"By all means. I shall be glad to know them," she replied; "but at present I am by no means satisfied with Captain Edgington's details. I am neither a poor man, an energetic man, nor a lazy man—in short, not a man at all. What advantages, then, has India for me, or for any woman?"

"That question I cannot answer as readily as the last," Edgington said; "for it requires a deeper insight than I possess into the wishes, hopes——"

"Let me answer it for you," interrupted Hoby, shortly, "for I'm sure I can do it better. *May* I do so, Miss Plane?"

"Of course. I seek for the information; I care not who tenders it."

"Then I would, with all deference, remark that, as talented and energetic men find in India a field for their science and enterprise, *because* the market is not overstocked with these two commodities, in like manner beauty, and the numberless charms that woman possesses, are more prized, and receive on the same account more admiration and homage out here than at home. This I conceive to be the greatest advantage ladies have in India; or if I am wrong, and it is not esteemed as such by the fair sex—at least by the unmarried portion—then did my sisters and cousins in England sadly deceive me, and I, in consequence, err greatly in my estimation of England's daughters."

"You most certainly *do* err, if you think that this questionable advantage would weigh in the scale with many," she replied with a frown; "and as even you yourself, with strange generosity, except married women from its influence, can you name me the advantages India holds out to them?"

"The advantages their husbands derive are their own," suggested Hoby with a constrained smile.

"Yes, but may they ask for none for themselves apart from their husbands?" she inquired.

"They may ask; but I know of none they can obtain," he replied with a laugh; "for as the husband, if good for anything, will naturally rejoice at any happiness the wife enjoys, so cannot the advantage be, as you propose, exclusive."

"A very pretty argument in favour of conjugal unity," she remarked; "but after all your learned details, Mr. Hoby, I'm still as ignorant as ever respecting the advantages of India for ladies."

"*I* will enlighten you on that point, Miss Plane," interposed the colonel; "but it must be under more favourable circumstances than the present; in a cool room, for example, with the thermometer at something reasonable, and not on a dusty road, with the hot wind blowing in your face."

"I shall leave you the task then, sir," said Hoby; "for with your predilections for India, I am sure you will draw a glowing picture; and I truly have but little more I could add to what Miss Plane, to my grief, tells me has in to way enlightened her."

"I see the course is nearly empty," the general remarked, as he aroused himself from what had looked very much like sleep. "Drive home," he added to the coachman—"I will put you down," he continued to Edgington and Hoby, "at the corner of the square, which is close to your mess."

"How very suddenly the night comes on in India," remarked Beatrice, as they drove homewards. "I do not think the sun has set more than ten minutes; and see, it is nearly dark."

"Yes; we have little or no twilight," Edgington said; "and it is a sad want in a country where, for ten months out of the twelve, you cannot be out with comfort more than half an hour before and after sunset and sunrise."

"Another Indian advantage," Miss Plane remarked, smiling, as she looked at our hero.

Edgington smiled in reply, as he answered, "*I* am not such a great advocate for India, as many are, Miss Plane; Colonel Carstairs, for example, who has just left us, will not allow that England is in any way preferable to India; and will certainly, if you broach the subject, try hard to convince you that *because* India has no twilight, *therefore* twilights are very objectionable. That is not, probably, the argument he will use; but his reasoning will amount to it."

"Yes," remarked the general, "Colonel Carstairs is infatuated about India. I think most men become so who never go home. With some it is a case of 'sour grapes'—they *can't* go to England, and so they perhaps wisely determine to think India perfection: others get such fixed Indian habits and customs, they care not to change them; and finding they can only indulge them out here, they try to persuade themselves, and the rest of the world, that they are after all in the best place."

"But you have been home, sir," said Beatrice, "more than once: are you, then, an advocate or an opponent of India and its customs?"

"Neither," he replied; "we have both advantages and disadvantages out here. I know not whether to class getting rid of you two at this corner as the former or the latter," he continued, turning to Hoby and Edgington, as the carriage stopped: "the former, perhaps, for I'm tired, and I dare say you are so too. You are just in time for your mess—there's the bugle. Good appetites I will not wish you, for eating heavy dinners in the hot winds is both unwholesome and irrational. Well, good night to you both: he'll sleep best who eats least; remember that. Drive on, coachman."

## CHAPTER VIII.

THE RAINS—CHARITY—BEATRICE AND HER MOTHER—EDGINGTON'S BUNGALOW—LOVE AND ITS POWERS.

The hot winds have passed; it is the height of the rainy season, namely, the month of July. Since our last chapter, a great change has come o'er the face of the country: then all was dry, parched up, and withered; now everything is green, moist, and spongy. All nature is wet, not only wet, but soaking wet: the long green rank grass would drench you up to your waist did you walk in it; the roads are one mass of puddles, and where "cucha," *id est*, not macadamized, they are impassable for wheeled carriages. The Ganges was then a decent-sized river; you could see across it, ay, and plainly too, for a rifle would have carried its bullet to the opposite bank. See it now! Don't tell us that's a river, or at least allow it's the mouth of a river; for look, it's all water lower down; *that*, surely, is the sea. What, no!—a long way from the sea!—nonsense! Five hundred miles by the river's course! Is it truly so? It seems astonishing; yet we must believe you, and only affirm we've seen nothing like it in Europe.

Ah, well it's a noble river,—and so that's the mighty, the sacred Ganges! the stream into which thousands upon thousands of Hindu bodies are thrown yearly, to insure them a safe passage to heaven! See! see! how it rushes eastward, its turbulent and discoloured waters breaking into thousands of white-crested waves as it struggles in its course with the strong opposing wind. Truly it is very beautiful, it is sublime, in its might, its grandeur, its majesty! No wonder the ignorant and fanatic Hindus, casting about for things to worship, have fixed on this noble river the "Gunga Jee"* as an object. We pity their faith, though we share in their admiration. Oh! would that, as it roars along in its wild and impetuous course to the ocean, it would proclaim, in words as loud as the noise of its waves, the existence, the omnipotence, of that Almighty Hand which set its waters in motion, and teach the Hindu worshipping on its banks where alone his prayers should be directed!

So thought *not* Beatrice Plane, as from a window of her father's house at Patna she watched the river in its course. Hers was not the religion to form such a wish, for it was a text faith, and a text faith alone. Following strictly, as Beatrice did, a creed of form, ceremony, and confession, she naturally held that the only essential points were a rigid performance of those duties; and thus charity found no place in her devotions, which, indeed, being of the ultra high-church order, could scarcely be expected to give it birth; if, even more, that exclusive religion did not make her deem it a scandal to her sect to bestow a charitable thought on any who were not on her side.

Beatrice had never considered the religious state of the Hindus; she scarcely, perhaps, knew the difference between the Hindu and Mussulman creed; but she *did* know that neither were Christians, let alone high-church; and therefore, had she thought at all on the subject, she would have felt sure (oh! what a comfortable and cheering conviction) that they would be damned, as surely as—as—*she*, Beatrice Plane, being most decidedly a religious girl, chanting her prayers whenever she had an opportunity, and following out strictly the forms of her sect, was among the happy and chosen few who had no cause for fear.

Truly it is a very comfortable religion, this of Beatrice Plane's; a sort of religion to hug oneself with, to

* The name used by the Hindus for the Ganges, which also signifies their respect for it.

think of with satisfaction by the fireside on a cold winter's night, when the wind and sleet are driving outside—a religion, alas! not unknown in England, and of course, if you believe its advocates, the essence of all that's right and proper.

But in this instance at least we do Beatrice wrong; for, poor girl! as she gazed out of the window she merely thought the Ganges was a very grand object, and no idea of her own or the religion of others crossed her mind. We know not, then, how we were led into comments on that portion of her character; however, it is written, so let it pass. The reader knows Beatrice better now than he did before, and that's something gained.

"Oh, *do* come here, mamma," called out Beatrice to Mrs. Plane, who was in the next room; "there's an enormous country boat, sailing up the river, has just broken her mast. Come quick, come quick; it's such a strange sight—mast, sails, and all are dragging in the water, and the waves are breaking right over the boat. What a number of natives there are on board, and what a dreadful noise they are making; I can hear them quite plain now the window's open. Look, look! there are three men clinging to the mast and sails. I wonder if they'll be drowned. They are trying to pull them on board with ropes. No; can you make out what they are doing?"

"I think they are afraid the boat will be swamped," Mrs. Plane replied, "and that they are going to cut away the wreck. Upon my word, the boat is in great danger, for see, she's drifting down the current quickly, and they can do nothing, hampered as she is with those enormous sails and cordage."

"Yes, you are right; I see them using their axes. They don't seem to think much of the men clinging to the mast, who, anyhow, must be pretty well exhausted, for they've been half the time under water."

"Is it not dreadful!" remarked her mother, as the

last few strokes separated the floating hamper, which, with the three men clinging to it, drifted away down stream much quicker than the boat, for the latter still presented a large surface to the wind.

"I think they'll all be drowned," remarked Beatrice. "I can't see them at all now—yes, there they are; but I only see two. The boat's trying to row in to the shore. How the wind blows! Ah! there's another boat sailing up, and it will pass very near the men. I suppose they'll be saved now. Let's sit down—I'm tired of standing."

They took seats at the window. The boat which approached was a budgerow,* a more manageable kind of craft than the one which had lost her mast. It carried but one large square mainsail (there was too much wind for the topsail), and as it was running right before the wind, it rode easy enough on the troubled waters. It was evident, from the course it held, that it would pass but a few boat's lengths from the wreck of mast and sails. To all appearance, the men (there were only two left—Beatrice was right, one had been washed away) would be saved; at least, so would anybody have thought who looked on, and did not know the utter indifference of the natives, and their supineness in such matters. Mrs. Plane *did* know it, and she shook her head as she said,—

"Were there a box with one hundred rupees in it attached to those floating masts, I am sure the budgerow would stop and try to save it; but its only two "dandies,"† poor men, who can pay nothing for their deliverance, and unless there's perchance a European on board, who'll *make* them stop, they'll pass on."

"No; they are all natives," exclaimed Beatrice; "two baboos,‡ apparently, have just come out of the cabin. They all see the wreck now, for they are point-

* A boat used by the wealthier classes for journeys on the river.

† Boatmen. ‡ Natives of the better class.

ing to it. I hear the men in the water calling; surely the budgerow people will try to save them. They are very near now—they are close. Well, that *is* dreadful! they've passed, and are coolly watching the wreck as it floats astern."

"You'll get accustomed to such sights in India, my dear," remarked Mrs. Plane. "The budgerow people probably thought the floating masts might injure their boat, if they went too close, and they care little for each other's lives."

"See! the boat that had the accident is near the shore. The floating masts and sails are so far away now, I can scarcely distinguish the men on them. Another five minutes, and the wreck will be hid by the point below. Why don't the men try and swim to land? I thought all the natives swam well."

"So they generally do," answered her mother; "but the waves break so, I suppose those two are afraid to try. Well, there's nothing more to see now, for they are nearly out of sight; they are like ducks in the water, and won't drown easily."

"Yes; let's get under the punkah again," said Beatrice, suiting the action to the word, and taking up the worsted work she was engaged on. "Now, tell me, mamma," she said, after a few minutes' pause, during which Mrs. Plane was occupied with household accounts,—"tell me, mamma, what you think now of my two admirers; do you hold them both as cheap as you did when you arrived a month ago?"

"I know them better now," Mrs. Plane replied; "and think of both, that while you might do better, you certainly might also do worse."

"Which is your favourite?" asked Beatrice: "that is, Which would you rather I married of the two?"

"If I were obliged to make a sudden choice, I should prefer the colonel," answered Mrs. Plane.

"Why? will you tell me?" asked Beatrice. "Captain Edgington has certainly more in him; the colonel is insufferably stupid, and it would bore me to death to be tied to such a man."

"Yes," said Mrs. Plane; "but then the colonel could offer you a better position than Captain Edgington. Your pension as his widow would be larger in case of his death; and then you would, I think, be happier if you married him than the captain. I see you look surprised: I'll tell you why I say so. You are very like me, dear Beatrice, on some points, and would, I am sure, never be content in married life to submit to your husband in all his whims and fancies. You would, in short, as I do, like to rule your own household—to rule your husband too, of course for his good; and from one or two things I have seen in Captain Edgington, I almost doubt your accomplishing it with him. The colonel, on the other hand, I feel sure you could twist and turn as you would; and though I allow he *is* somewhat shallow, what then? you cannot have everything, and in choosing a partner who is a mild, easy-going man, you must necessarily be content to take him with the defects appertaining to those qualities."

"All that I allow," Beatrice replied; "and as I am in love with neither, I can weigh the advantages of the one fairly against the other; but I do not quite agree with you in what you think of their temperaments. Men of Colonel Carstairs's stamp are very often fond of showing their authority in little things, and are then *most* obstinate and difficult to manage. Captain Edgington, on the contrary, would, if I judge him rightly, always yield if you could convince him the plan you proposed were better than his own; and very much rather would I undertake the latter task, and hope to succeed, too, than fret and fume at the dogged obstinacy of a simpleton, whom no conviction would change or alter."

"Well, my dear, it is a question on which your future happiness so entirely depends, that I should be very sorry to attempt to bias your judgment,—more especially as you seem to me quite capable of exercising that judgment coolly, and without any of the absurd enthusiasm, or love as it is called, which is productive of so many of the ill-assorted matches one meets with. By the bye, have you ever found out how much Captain Edgington has—I mean how much beyond his pay?"

"No," replied Beatrice; "but he once mentioned to me, incidentally, the fact of his rich connection dying and leaving him his orphan girl and his fortune. But you may depend, dear mother, on my being careful; and as there is no occasion why I should marry at all just yet, I shall have plenty of time for reflection. I do not see why a very much better match than either of the lovers under discussion may not turn up; and though Captain Edgington may have a considerable private fortune, a civilian well up in the list (I'm sure there are many in India anxious to marry) would be more advantageous in every way."

"Then of the two, the colonel and Edgington, you decidedly incline to the latter?" inquired her mother.

"Yes; for though I do not suppose I should ever love Captain Edgington,—as he loves me, for instance, —I am sure I should *hate* the colonel before I had been married to him a week; and it's unwise, I think, in any case, to marry a man with that conviction."

"Oh, certainly," replied Mrs. Plane; "but, as you say, wait and see what will yet turn up. Tell me, does Edgington know he has a rival in his commanding officer?"

"I think he does," replied Beatrice; "you know he has never mentioned the subject of love to me, but he has nevertheless made love in a thousand ways; and latterly, when the colonel's attentions became more marked—in fact, nearly as much so as his own—he has fallen at times into deeply-desponding fits, as if he thought Colonel Carstairs, from his rank and position, *was sure* to win the day."

"*For goodness* sake don't let him do that," remarked

Mrs. Plane eagerly; "let them *both* live in hope; and so you can, when necessary, make your choice at your leisure."

Having delivered which sage and charitable piece of advice to her daughter, and accompanied it with a kiss, Mrs. Plane descended to family prayers followed by Beatrice.

We will leave them to their devotions, for we will not attempt to pry into the secrets of their hearts at such a time; but rather, accompanied by the reader, we will pay a visit to the pretty bungalow at Dinapore, where Captain Edgington lives alone, as it seems to us we have somewhat neglected our hero of late; and we wish much to know what his feelings and hopes are since we last saw him, two months ago.

Already we are there; the seven miles that separate Dinapore from Patna has not taken us long to traverse.

That is Edgington's bungalow, the one with the clumps of bamboos on either side of the compound-gate—it is a nice-looking abode, is it not? The flower-beds skirting the lawn are all in good order, and bespeak the care of the owner. The house is large and roomy for a bachelor to occupy all alone, while the numerous out-houses, with the natives lounging about, show that he possesses a goodly retinue of servants. That long, low building is the stables, where no less than seven horses stand; we may, perhaps, go in and look at them some other time, at present we are all anxiety to see our poor love-sick hero.

No tattees now obstruct the doors, which are mostly wide open, the morning being cloudy and comparatively cool after last night's rain, so we can walk straight in. There is Edgington: he is, we think, a shade paler than when we last saw him, and he wears a thoughtful brow, as he sits with a cheroot in his mouth, writing a letter. We need not disturb him as we look over his shoulder and read the epistle he is just finishing, for though it is hastily written, and his handwriting is none of the best, we can still make it out.

DINAPORE, *Monday*.

"I got your letter, dear William, two days ago, in answer to mine, telling you of my love affair; and thank you much for all the kind things you say in it. I find it difficult, however, to follow the advice you give me—not to embark my happiness in the pursuit until I am firstly convinced the object is worthy, and until I also see some signs of her reciprocating my affection. I *know* your advice is wise, when I think soberly over it; but I do not act upon it, simply because I am already too much in love to do so. With regard to her liking me, I must say I have not as yet seen many proofs of it,—sometimes I even think the reverse; but then I doubt if I make sufficient allowance for the reserved nature which she evidently possesses. Do you know, it is strange, but there is something in this very reserve, this coldness,—for it almost amounts to that,—which captivates me in spite of myself. I have told you before that she is very beautiful (the description I gave you of her by no means does her justice), and I fear this beauty makes me somewhat blind, or rather that I wilfully shut my eyes to the defects of her character.

"You will want to know what these defects are; and though, having said that I wilfully shut my eyes to them, I might with reason plead incapacity to inform you, I will be as candid with you, my dear brother, as I have always been, and endeavour to enlighten you.

"With her reserve, she is proud and haughty, and truly this is *all* I have seen that is against her; but this very *hauteur* makes her all the more captivating when she descends therefrom, as she sometimes does. And I keep on continually picturing to myself how delightful it will be when love, having once really entered her heart, shall thaw away this barrier, and when perhaps, from her very temperament, she will *then* love more ardently than the mass of women do whose affections are more easily awakened.

"*I sometimes* think this last-mentioned effect applies

also in my case, dear William; and that as I have never been in love before, this my first love, arriving at a mature age, has more strength and fervour in it than the oft-repeated loves of men who have experienced the passion a dozen times, perhaps, before they attain thirty.

Anyhow, I know that I love this girl with a force which sometimes appears to me unreasonable. She sees it all, I am sure, but she takes it much too coolly for me to flatter myself that I have as yet succeeded in touching her heart.

"Oh! another difficulty is in the way. I have a rival, who is no less than my commanding officer! You know what he is like, for I have often described him, and so I need not do so again—though I think Miss Plane sees that he is not particularly bright, and though I'm sure he has not as yet in any way won her regard, still a colonel is so much better a match than your poor brother, that I cannot help wishing he were anywhere but where he is. It is strange, Colonel Carstairs falling suddenly in love in this way, for he always railed against women and marriage,—declaring the first pleasant creatures only if kept at a distance, and that a man was a fool who committed the second. That he has now altered his opinion and would marry Miss Plane to-morrow if she'd have him, I'll swear: so it is a race between us; and I must say, to do him justice, that he does not take any unfair advantage, which he might, being my commandant, by keeping me out of the way.

"Such is the position of affairs. I know not what advice you can give me in the matter, or how you can help me; but write to me, old fellow,—you are the only person to whom I have said a word in the matter and sympathy in such cases is pleasant.

"I suppose you have lots to do now that you are adjutant of your regiment. I was thinking, only this morning, how much more fortunate I am in my promotion than yourself; for though you are not *unlucky*, I certainly am the reverse—a captain like myself, with only twelve years' service, being decidedly an exception in our army. I suppose, however, in a year or two at the outside you will also get your troop.

"This letter I am sure you will pronounce stupid—I feel it so, but my pen *will* discuss but one subject; and then, remember, men in love never write lively scrawls. I heard from our mother last overland; she writes in good spirits, and looks forward with much pleasure to my coming home soon. Alas, I cannot *now* tell her if I shall do so or not. The letter is full of Marion, who is now seventeen, and, our mother declares, the belle of the county. She would make you a nice wife, William. Why not go home and take a peep at her?

"Oh, one thing regarding my lady-love, I had forgotten to mention, and I am sure it is one which will raise her in your estimation. She is decidedly religious in so far as all the outward forms thereof can be regarded as proofs. Her reserve on other matters extends, however, also to this, and I can therefore give you no further information on the subject. But I will not say another word about her, or the next letter you receive from me you will not have the courage to open; for if I have not bored you dreadfully with this, then are you even more goodnatured than I take you to be.

"I wish I had been with you at your pig-sticking* party, near Kamptee: it is, I am sure, the finest fun in the world; and, without vanity, I think I may say, dear William, that if we were side by side in the saddle and decently mounted, he must be a good and a bold rider who would prevent one of us getting the spear.

"God bless you, old fellow. I have smoked two cheroots while writing this letter—the last is just out; and as to the soothing effect of tobacco, and tobacco alone, you owe, in my present state of mind, anything

* The popular name for boar-hunting.

lively, or even sensible, in this scrawl, I will at once say, good-bye.

"Ever your affectionate brother,

"ARTHUR EDGINGTON."

He directed the envelope to "William Edgington, Esq., —th Regt. Madras Native Cavalry, Kamptee," gave it to his bearer, and then strolled out into the verandah.

"How stupid I am," he said to himself, as he saw his servant leave the compound with the letter; "I quite forgot to tell William of the strange character which that curious fellow, Hoby, gave to the name of Beatrice; and yet *why* should I tell him?" He paced the verandah several times in deep thought. "It's very strange," he exclaimed, stopping suddenly, "how entirely her apparent character accords with a part of his prediction." Again he strode backwards and forwards. "But what a fool I am to think of it at all," he continued, as he struck the verandah pillar with a stick he held in his hand; "because Hoby fortunately divined, or rather made a guess at, some points, does that prove that he is to be right throughout? If I thought so — I — I — would try to conquer—— But who can look at that beauteous face," he suddenly exclaimed, breaking off into another mood, while his face brightened up, "and believe the owner to be all that he described—to be something terrible in the shape of a woman, for really the picture he painted amounted to that. *I cannot, and I will not.*" He sat down on a chair which chanced to be there, and covered his eyes with his hands for an instant; when he removed them, all colour had fled from his face. Oh, Beatrice, Beatrice," he continued in a low voice, which trembled with agitation, "how very *very* dear you are to me! What—oh, what is the secret of this spell which you have cast around my heart, under the influence of which I am a child in your hands? My waking thoughts,

Beatrice, are yours; my dreams have you, and you alone, for an object; I scarcely know myself since I have known you, so entirely am I changed. You are my world, my all, my hope, my life. Oh, take pity on my love, and return it with but a tithe of the affection I bear you; or else, Beatrice, tell me at once there is no hope, and add not further fuel to the fire which already consumes me!"

He relapsed into silence, and once more bent down his head in deep thought. He was calmer when he again spoke: "Strange, more than strange, is this power of love; for see how completely it enthrals those on whom it has fastened. How utterly unable are we to analyze it, to reason as to its nature, to understand it in the remotest degree! What volumes upon volumes have been written on the subject, and have they in any one respect added to our knowledge? How many of these books did I read, and yet what knew *I* of love until I met Beatrice Plane? No wonder that kingdoms have been won and lost for love; no wonder that the greatest good has been achieved, the greatest crimes perpetrated, in its pursuit—that the wise man, through its influence, has become foolish, the fool knavish, the brave timid, and the coward brave. This, all this and more, has been depicted, detailed, among all nations, all creeds, all classes, under the sun, and yet can it *only* be realized by those who, like myself, are suffering from the almost unearthly power it possesses!"

He ceased to speak, but every now and then his lips moved as if he still communed with himself. We would not willingly disturb him; let him think on; for if strong feelings, worked up to a painful tension, demand solitude as a right, it would be both ungracious and unsafe to arouse Edgington.

## CHAPTER IX.

THE BALL—THE PRETTY EURASIAN—PHILANTHROPY—THE POLKA—A PROPOSAL.

SIX weeks after the events recorded in the last chapter, the mess-room of the 99th regiment N.I. was one evening brilliantly lighted up. A ball was to be given by the officers of that regiment to the ladies of Dinapore and Patna, and all that could be, had been done to render the ball-room and its approaches lively and light. The flags of the regiment adorned the walls of the former at one end, while muskets and bayonets, arranged like stars against the wall, gave a still further martial and gay appearance to the ball-room.

The band of the regiment—a very good one, by the bye—was stationed in the verandah; and though no one had yet arrived beyond some of the regimental officers, it had already commenced operations, and was playing an overture in excellent style.

"The room looks well enough," said the colonel, who was walking up and down it with Hoby; "and, thank goodness, it's not a very hot night. How many ladies did we calculate would be here?"

"Thirty-two, sir," replied Hoby,—"that is, if Mrs. Plane and her daughter come, which Earnest, however, who sent the invitations, said was still uncertain."

"Oh, I was there to-day," remarked the colonel carelessly, "and they then had quite made up their minds to come; for Miss Plane, who has not been very well the last two or three days, is all right again."

"Then we shall have the full number," said Hoby. "It's time they began to arrive, for it's ten minutes past nine."

"There's a palankeen just come up," remarked the

colonel, as he heard the hŭn-hŭn-hŭn-hŭn, or grunting of the bearers; "who can that be?"

"Earnest has gone out to see," replied Hoby. "I hear Merton's voice, so I suppose it's his wife in the palkee."

The reader may perhaps remember, that Merton was the junior ensign in the regiment, and had married a girl with dark blood in her veins very shortly after he joined.

She came in, leaning on Earnest's arm. The colonel and the other officers present at once advanced to welcome her, which they did very kindly; and it somewhat reassured her, poor girl,—for this was the first ball, or anything in the shape of one, she had ever been at.

The colonel gallantly led her to a sofa, and sat down by her side as he remarked, "It's quite right, Mrs. Merton, that one of the ladies of the regiment should be the first in the ball-room."

"I'm glad you think so," she said; "but I had rather not have been the very first. In fact, I wanted my husband to wait a little, but he was in a hurry to come. See, John," she remarked to Merton, who was passing by, examining the decorations on the wall, "there's not another lady here."

"An additional reason why you should not regret having taken pity on our previously forlorn condition," remarked Edgington, who had just come in; "and see, you will not be long alone, for here comes Mrs. Bruce."

The colonel rose to shake hands with Mrs. Bruce, while Edgington sat down by Mrs. Merton, and endeavoured, by chatting away with her in a lively strain, to do away with the feeling of shyness which she evidently laboured under.

Mrs. Merton is worthy of a description, if only as a contrast to the fair daughters of Europe. She was not *a half-caste*: but was probably the daughter of a half-caste woman by an English father; thus she was only a quarter-caste,—or, in other words, was three parts English, and only one native. Many of these Eurasian girls in India are very pretty, and Mrs. Merton was perhaps as pretty a one as could be found. She was very small and slight, but her figure was in exquisite proportion, while her arms, hands, and feet were a study for a sculptor; her skin had a deep olive tinge in it, but it accorded well with its smooth and downy appearance, as also with her large jet-black eyes and blue-black hair, which, as is almost always the case with Eurasian girls, was immensely long and thick. She was just the age when girls or women with dark blood in their veins are the prettiest; she was barely sixteen, and pretty as she then looked, it was sad to think that, as is always the case, no trace of that beauty would remain when she attained thirty; for, in tropical climates, woman arrives earlier at maturity and fades quicker than in temperate regions. In character, Mrs. Merton was kind, gentle, very shy, without much sense in her pretty little head, and had an inordinate love of everything European, and a distaste for everything native, which is perhaps the general character of her class.

She was dressed in pure white, which of course made her skin look even darker than it was (it's strange that Eurasian girls *will* always dress in white), and boasted no ornament of any kind except a large artificial white rose on one side of her head. She looked altogether very pretty as she sat talking to Edgington, and so thought two officers who had just come out from England to join the European regiment at Dinapore, who were standing in a doorway opposite to where she sat, and remarked to one another how she would be admired in a London ball-room.

"Something so out of the common, isn't she?" lisped out the younger, a mere lad in his teens, and a consummate dandy and ape.

"Y—a—s. One requires change sometimes. Cussed

pretty, by Gad," answered his companion, taking a telescopic view through his eye-glass. "She looks nervous, though; I'll ask her to dance the first polka with me, and soon put her at her ease," he added, as he stroked what he fondly believed was a moustache.

Mrs. Bruce, having walked with the colonel round the room, to inspect the decorations, advanced to the sofa where Mrs. Merton sat; and Edgington resigning his seat, she, shaking the pretty Eurasian cordially by the hand, sat down by her side.

"This is as it should be," observed Mrs. Bruce, "we, the two first arrivals, are ladies of the regiment. I suppose you are very fond of balls?"

"This is the first I ever was at," replied Mrs. Merton, while her pretty olive cheeks assumed a richer glow.

"Indeed! Then I prophesy you'll enjoy it very much. Do you know that lady who has just come in?"

"No; who is she?"

"Mrs. Peters, from Patna; that's her husband, talking to the colonel. You ought to know her, she's a very nice person."

"I should like to know her, for I truly know very few ladies; but then I don't think John wishes me to go much into society."

"Well, if I get an opportunity, I'll introduce you to Mrs. Peters, later," replied Mrs. Bruce. "Good evening, Mr. Percy," she added, with a smile, to the officer of that name in the regiment, who approached her; "I know you are coming to ask me to dance, but its no use, unless its a sober, quiet quadrille, for I dance nothing else."

"No, indeed, Mrs. Bruce," said Percy, in his drawling tone, "I was bent on another errand. I was going to ask *you*, Mrs. Merton, if I might introduce that officer standing by the door there, the shorter of the two, with a glass in his eye. He came out into the verandah, where I was cooling myself previous to com*mencing* the work,—I mean the dances of the evening,

—to ask me if I could procure him the honour, and there he now stands, awaiting your decision."

"I don't know him, that is, I never saw him before. Oh dear, where *is* John? But, perhaps, I ought to say yes—*do* tell me, Mrs. Bruce?"

"I think you might venture, then," replied Mrs. Bruce, smiling, "even though your husband is not here."

"Very good. Mr. Percy, tell him yes—that is, that I—that you—yes, that you may bring him, and introduce him," stammered out Mrs. Merton, while she blushed immensely and smoothed her dress.

Percy crossed over to the aspirant for the introduction, who, leaning against the open door, had been coolly watching the foregoing scene through his eyeglass.

"You can come," drawled out Percy, lazily; "come along quick, though, for it's frightfully hot here, and I want to get out in the verandah again."

The introduction completed, the owner of the eyeglass, with a strong "young England" lisp, said,—

"Will you allow me the pleasure of dancing the first polka with you, Mrs. Merton?"

"Oh dear, I shouldn't mind a quadrille, but a polka—I—I—am afraid my husband doesn't like. Would you ask *him?*" answered Mrs. Merton with great embarrassment and hesitation, except the last four words, which she jerked out with much *naïveté*.

"Haw! I beg your pardon, I didn't quite understand you," answered the dandy with the eyeglass, which he kept in his eye all this time by a contraction of the muscles of one cheek.

"Oh, there's John,—*do* call him—I'll go myself," she continued, as she rose from the sofa.

"No; I'll fetch him," said Percy, who looked on, an amused spectator of the scene.

"Oh, thank you—thank you."

In another minute Percy had returned with Merton.

"John dear, this gentleman has asked me to dance the polka with him; *may* I do so?"

"If you wish it, my love," replied Merton, looking fondly at his pretty little wife.

"But I *don't* wish it — that is, if you don't like it. Was I wrong not to refuse at once?" she asked, looking anxiously at her husband, while he of the eyeglass twitched up the collars of his shirt with impatience.

"Dear Arabella, I wish you to amuse yourself—dance it by all means. You've kept this gentleman standing a long time," he added, bowing distantly to the eyeglass; "but I'm engaged for this quadrille which is now forming, so I must leave you."

"Mrs. Merton, are you engaged for this quadrille? No! Will you dance it with me, then?" said Edgington, coming up at that moment.

"Yes, of course," she answered, rising.

"Then the first polka is mine?" lisped the "young England" warrior.

She bowed an affirmative, as she went off with childish glee, leaning on Edgington's arm, to take her place in the quadrille.

The room has filled fast during the last few minutes, and the opening dance boasts no less than two quadrilles, with eight couples in each.

Crash goes the band, outside, with the opening bars! It's almost too loud, close as it is; but the music is excellent, and in another minute the quadrille has fairly begun.

Edgington, as he dances, is somewhat bullied by the punkah; for tall as he is, the fringe brushes his head every time he passes under it, and disarranges his hair not a little.

"I wish we had taken one of the top places," he said to his partner, as they finished the second figure. "That horrid punkah sends my hair all over my eyes every time I pass under it."

"Oh, bend your head. How very tall you are, Captain Edgington," remarked the pretty Eurasian, *looking* up at him.

"Yes, often too tall for comfort, as in the present instance," he replied. "But see, there's Earnest opposite; *his* head already looks like a mop from the same cause."

"Now then, Captain Edgington, we must dance, and not talk so much. See, we are all wrong in this figure," exclaimed his partner, as she laid hold of his hand and guided him into his place.

Edgington looked at her with pleasure; she enjoyed the dance so thoroughly—it did his heart good to watch her. "Ah!" thought he, as he regarded her pretty face, beaming with happiness and excitement, "Merton's not to be pitied after all, with such a wife."

"Oh, how delightful this is!" said Arabella, with a joyous face, as she returned to his side. "Dear me, I had quite forgotten about John: I *do* hope he's dancing."

"Yes, he's in the other set. Tell me, Mrs. Merton, has he got you that side-saddle yet, which I know he intended to get?"

"No," she replied. "I don't wish him to get it, though I love riding, for he can't afford it. He's already in debt two thousand rupees to the Agra Bank; * and then, a side-saddle is of no use without a horse."

"Let me lend you my small Arab," said Edgington kindly. "I have more horses than I can even exercise myself."

"How good of you! Will you really? I'll tell John directly after the dance. I *do* so long to ride; and, you must know, I can ride pretty well," she continued, looking up at him with a self-satisfied air, "for I had plenty of practice when I was younger."

"Now, good people, attend to the dance, or sit down," said Earnest good-humouredly, as he crossed over in the last figure but one. "It's difficult to get through a quadrille without *vis-à-vises.*"

"I'm so sorry: now *do* let's attend, Captain Edging-

* A bank at Agra which lends money to officers.

ton," said Arabella Merton. "It's all your fault, I declare," she added laughingly; "you talk so much, you drive the dance clean out of my head."

"Then you have a double pleasure, Mrs. Merton," said the general, who had just arrived with the Plane family; had entered unperceived by Edgington, and was then standing behind him, with Beatrice leaning on his arm.

Edgington had no time to speak, for he was obliged to advance in the figure, but he cast one glance at Miss Plane, and he thought she looked disdainfully, but with curious eyes, at his partner.

We may as well remind the reader, that six weeks have intervened since we last saw Beatrice Plane, and left Edgington in his verandah thinking about her and moaning over the intensity of his love. During those six weeks Edgington has not been idle, but has pressed his suit at every opportunity, and by every means in his power. That *he* is in love has long been a tacitly-acknowledged fact between Beatrice and himself, though he has never, as yet, trusted his tongue to say so. But as he can no longer doubt that she is aware of his object, and as she permits his attentions, he has great hopes for the future, and even flatters himself that she returns his affection to some little extent.

One thing puzzles him, however. The colonel has, during the said six weeks, been as unremitting in making love as himself; and though, when Carstairs is not by, Edgington is satisfied with the progress he makes, all his satisfaction and hopes are, perhaps, the very next day thrown to the winds, should the colonel and he be together in her society.

To a looker-on it would have been amusing enough to watch the game as it had lately been played by both. Each, of course, knew that he had a rival in the other; but, to the credit of both, be it said, that it in no way impaired their friendly and kindly relations to each *other*. That it was so, said much for the innate honesty and justice of Carstairs's disposition, however those good qualities might be impaired by the weakness of his character and the absence of intellect in his cranium; for in his capacity of commanding officer he might easily have thrown impediments in Edgington's way, with a view to leave the field clearer for himself. He, however, in no way did so; and his rival could not help feeling grateful to him, though dreading, at the same time, the effect such generous conduct, already hinted at by Beatrice, might have on her affections.

Thus each left the other free to press his suit, and, by mutual though unexpressed consent, they portioned off particular parts of the day, or particular days, to one another, feeling, as both did, that neither could do much when they were with Beatrice together. It was more than funny the way this was done; perhaps a short conversation the two had held that very morning, as they rode home from parade, will illustrate it.

Colonel Carstairs.—"You are president of that Court of Requests* to-day, Edgington; it will keep you engaged till twelve o'clock. I'm going out this morning, but shall be back to tiffin at the mess by one."

Captain Edgington.—"Oh, very good, sir; I shall probably go out after the court is over, but shall be back to dinner to make the first preparations for the ball to-night."

Colonel Carstairs.—"It will be a good ball, I've no doubt; I shall be there early to receive everybody."

Captain Edgington.—"I shall take a cup of tea at home before I come; it always makes me livelier for the evening."

Thus no contretemps could occur that day; it was quite understood, just as well as if it had been spoken, that the colonel had the Patna field to himself till half-past twelve, and then resigned it to Edgington, who was not to be interfered with during the afternoon; as also that

* A court for the adjustment of officers' debts.

the first dance at the ball was the colonel's, and that Edgington should not be in the way till that was over.

In spite of such and similar arrangements, it had frequently happened that the colonel and Edgington found themselves together with their lady-love; and it was at such times that all the rosy hopes which Edgington had formed the last time he was there received a considerable check. It was not that she appeared to favour the colonel in preference to himself, but it was that he could *then*, with the nicest scrutiny, discover no bias or inclination whatever on her part, and was fain to retire on such occasions with the conviction that if he *had* made any progress towards her regard, his commanding officer had apparently done the same.

He was always, therefore, dejected and downcast after such triform interviews; and as they acted on Carstairs in the same way, they both mutually avoided them, in as far as they could do so, by adopting the expedient we have detailed above.

It may be thought strange that each of these lovers should thus wilfully shut his eyes to the fact that another stood as high in his mistress's regard as himself; but it must be remembered, that neither had as yet declared his love, and as each hoped and thought he made more way when alone, it is really not to be wondered at that they avoided, as far as lay in their power, meeting in the presence of their lady-love.

The reader, who heard Mrs. Plane's sagacious advice to her daughter on the subject of her two lovers, can easily conceive, that if Beatrice followed the same, the consequences would be what we have detailed; and that both the colonel and Edgington would, on the whole, feel satisfied with the treatment they experienced from Miss Plane, though that satisfaction certainly received a check when they met in her presence.

Beatrice, though she treated them equally well, in order to let them both, as her mother said, "live in hope," had, in reality, a strong preference for Edgington. *That* she had when she discussed them with her mother six weeks before, and this interval had increased the feeling. We must not be supposed to mean that she loved Edgington: far, indeed, was she from that point—deep love, indeed, was not in her nature; but she had quite made up her mind, that if she married either it should be the captain, and she merely kept the colonel on the tenter-hooks of expectation and hope, as it pleased her to apply the plural number to her lovers, while, with all a woman's tact and cunning, she saw that she incurred no risk of losing Edgington's attentions therefrom. Had our poor hero understood better the character of his lady-fair, he might, doubtless, have caused a great diversion in his favour by applying judiciously a little of that very powerful touchstone for such natures, neglect.

Such was the state of affairs at the time the ball we are describing took place, and we hasten to return to it after this long digression, which, however, was necessary to keep the reader *au courant*.

The dance over, Edgington led the pretty Eurasian back to her seat, declined her invitation to sit down, on the plea that he must go out into the verandah to cool himself; and having attained a point outside whence he could command that part of the ball-room where Beatrice sat without being seen himself, he gazed, as lovers only gaze, at the object of his affections.

She had never, he thought, looked handsomer, as, dressed in pure white, with a string of costly pearls twined in her dark brown hair, she looked like the queen of that assembly, dispensing with the ornaments with which her attendants were adorned, knowing while she did so, that her beauty only shone forth the more lustrously therefrom.

"And can it be," said Edgington half aloud, as he leaned against one of the verandah pillars, almost overawed by the beauty on which he gazed, and feeling in every pore what Byron so emphatically describes as "the might, the majesty of loveliness,"—"can it be that that superb creature will one day, perhaps, be my wife? Oh what a thrilling thought, what joy, what happiness untold will then be mine; methinks I could pass my life in looking upon her and her beauty. But what reason have I to hope that it will be so?" He was silent as the events of the last three months passed rapidly before him. "Never mind; hope I have, yes hope, which shall make me brave everything, do anything, to attain what is now dearer to me than life. Such prizes are not lightly won, though all the more precious when gained; then let not my efforts relax, but hope on, hope on, my heart,—and do ye, my tongue and brain, work sagaciously, boldly, and in concert, to accomplish this great end!"

"Is that you, Edgington?" said Hoby, advancing from another part of the verandah, where, horrid creature! he had been smoking a cheroot; "are any theatricals on the *tapis*, that you are reciting and gesticulating in such a way? I lost the subject, however, for I was too far off, and did not like to approach until I had finished my cheroot, for the smoke might go into the ball-room. Couldn't you do it again?"

"Oh, nonsense," replied Edgington, considerably startled and displeased, though he knew it was useless to try and be angry with Hoby; "you lost nothing, I assure you; for whatever I may have said, I said to myself. I came out here to escape the heat of the ball-room, but I'm going in again now; won't you come? only not too close to me, or the ladies will give me credit for the scent of that manilla, which is somewhat strong in your neighbourhood."

So saying, Edgington strolled back into the ball-room, thinking, as he did so, it was lucky he had not spoken out loud, or Hoby might have heard his rhapsody.

Hoby stayed out in the verandah to air himself. *What he thought*, we don't know; but as he undid the breast of his jacket to shake it, and passed his hand through his hair to drive away any remaining smoke, he said aloud, "*That's* a case of up a tree." Whether he referred to the fumes of the tobacco, which he flattered himself he had got rid of, and which he might figuratively suppose had ascended into the neighbouring foliage, or what he alluded to we, cannot say; for the expression, to say the least of it, was vague, and he added nothing in elucidation.

A waltz had just begun as Edgington entered the ball-room, and he quickly, among the whirling couples, discovered the colonel and Miss Plane. As she waltzed beautifully—and so did Carstairs—the dance seemed to afford her great pleasure; and when, as they stopped for breath, her cheeks glowing with the exercise and excitement, she leaned on the colonel's arm, and looked up in his face as they talked and laughed together, it pleased not Edgington to see that she did so, or that she seemed so happy and contented with his rival.

"Good evening, Captain Edgington." He turned; Mr. Plane, in the act of taking a pinch of snuff, stood by his side. "How is it you are not dancing?"

"I've been out in the verandah to cool myself, and missed the beginning of this waltz."

"Ah, it's nice exercise," said Mr. Plane; "but I remember it always made me giddy. I did not know there were so many ladies in Dinapore as there are here. Have you had an ice this evening?"

"No; why?" answered Edgington.

"Only *I* have, and they are very well made; take my advice, and if you go into the supper-room, try the sparkling Moselle; I never remember tasting better."

"I'll not forget," said Edgington; "though I think I shall wait till supper-time."

"I'm afraid Mrs. Plane will take *me* away before supper. Our daughter, as you know, has not been very well lately, and Mrs. Plane will not let her risk anything from late hours."

"She's looking well enough to-night," remarked Edgington as the colonel and Beatrice stopped once more in the waltz; and a pang of jealousy shot through his bosom.

"Yes, I'm sure it's a mistake, leaving before supper. I shall go and try to persuade Mrs. Plane. Do you know there's nothing better than a ball to give me an appetite, and few things I enjoy more than the hookah after a late supper. Don't you think so?"

"What?—that it's wrong to leave before supper, or that you enjoy the hookah? I certainly agree with you in the former," answered Edgington listlessly.

"Hang that fellow! I wish he'd look where he steps when he waltzes. Horrid thick boots he must have had, too," exclaimed Mr. Plane as he hopped away on one leg; "never thought of apologizing either, I declare. My worst corn, too;—oh, what a shooting pain!"

He continued muttering as he limped away, and Edgington felt almost grateful to the careless dancer who had inadvertently rid him of the bore a conversation with Mr. Plane always entailed.

"Strange that he should be *her* father," Edgington thought; "how different they are. I scarcely wonder at her evident contempt for him, he certainly is insufferably stupid."

The waltz over, and Beatrice once more by her mother's side, our hero presented himself.

"I'm sure you enjoyed that dance, Miss Plane. I did not know you waltzed so well."

"Yes, I enjoyed it, for it's rare to find a partner who waltzes as well as Colonel Carstairs."

Edgington bit his lip as he continued: "Are you engaged for many dances this evening? None!—Will you then dance the next polka with me?"

"Certainly—but this is a quadrille now forming."

"Will you dance that also?" he asked.

She rose in reply, and put her arm in Edgington's.

"Do you mind taking one of the top places," he inquired, "for at the sides the punkah brushes my head whenever I pass under it."

"And disarranges your hair, Captain Edgington. Certainly, you shall be spared that calamity," replied Beatrice, smiling. "Tell me, did your pretty partner in the quadrille you were dancing when I came in, remark the fact, for I see it *is* sadly tossed."

"She's the wife of one of my brother officers, and this is her first ball. No; she did not remark it, but I mentioned it to her."

"She's very pretty," said Beatrice.

"Yes, she is so, and a very good little thing," said Edgington patronizingly.

"She would be flattered, no doubt, if she heard your opinion, and the way you express it," remarked Beatrice.

They had attained their places, and a pause ensued. Edgington was thinking if it would be wise to hazard a proposal that evening. His thoughts were interrupted by Beatrice.

"Come, talk, Captain Edgington; I detest a silent partner."

"Willingly; what shall be the subject? The one we were interrupted in to-day?"

"I forget it," she replied. "Oh, yes, philanthropy, was it not? A very dry subject for a ball, I think; but never mind, it's better than none. I thought your views chimerical—think you to change my opinion in the pauses of a quadrille?"

"The more merit, if I succeed under such disadvantages," replied Edgington. "You would not assent to my proposition that the exercise of philanthropy was the truest source of pleasure; and urged, on the contrary, that philanthropists, while running after the imaginary benefits they wish to confer on others, forget or neglect their own duties."

"I did so," she said, "and I am certain it is so, for

we have all enough to do in directing our own courses in life."

"Would you, then, advocate our living for ourselves alone, and that all our pleasures should be selfish ones?" asked Edgington.

"That we cannot do," she replied, "for we are all more or less dependent on one another. But how think you the world would go on, were all its inhabitants philanthropists? Would there not be an end to all great achievements, to all progress,—for what causes these? Is it not the many who aim at success, who seek to gain the top of the ladder and pay little heed, during their efforts, to their less fortunate comrades; who even use the unsuccessful as stepping-stones, if thereby they can mount the quicker. In your philanthropical world there would be nothing of this kind; emulation would not exist; the incentive to exertion in all would be wanting; and the only hope for the inhabitants of your imaginary planet would be their discovery, that individual exertion, with self as an object, tends really more to the public good than all their previous visionary attempts to improve and benefit one another. But now we must dance: think of what I've said, and answer it, if you can, when the figure's over."

Once more side by side, Edgington remarked, "You've made out an extreme case against me, because you have, unintentionally I believe, mis-stated my position. That in attempting to do good to others we should neglect either our own good or our own advancement, I never for a moment affirmed; I merely wished to support the statement, that the exercise of philanthropy was a true source of happiness. Now, I conceive no stronger argument can be used in support of a position than the results of experience, and these, surely, are on my side. Does not the experience of ages tell us it is true? Have we not all, with but few exceptions, felt it ourselves; and do we not see it elucidated every *day in our* acquaintances? Take the first really cheerful and happy man you meet—one whose happiness is not transitory and uncertain, but one who preserves to himself through life, even during its misfortunes, an under-current of pleasure—I will not affirm that this man is a philanthropist, but I will use the stronger negative argument, and ask you if you ever knew such a one selfish or wholly bent on the furtherance of his own schemes? I am sure you will allow that you did not; and if you admit so much, you surely will no longer controvert my position, which, in the mild form I put it, will not, I think, admit of denial, however it may be liable, in the exaggerated manner in which you stated it, to the objections and satire which you so cleverly brought forward. But see, I must stop, for we must dance again."

The figure over, Beatrice said, "Let's change the subject to something more lively. Do you know this is my first ball in India, Captain Edgington?"

"I suppose you've seen many in England?"

"Not a great many. At Cheltenham, however, where I was one winter, I saw a few."

"There's no great difference between English and Indian balls, is there?"

"Very little; were it not for that continually-waving punkah and the native servants in the supper-room, I should not know we were out of England."

"How do you like India now, after four months' experience?"

"Not much, though better than I thought I should. I think, whatever the advantages of India may be,—we have had one or two discussions on that point, remember,—that the climate is nearly the sole disadvantage; but then it's not a slight one, or easily got over."

"It is not, indeed."

"I remember your telling me, the first time I met you, when you showed me how to drink out of a ghurrah, that I should like India better than I then thought I should; and so far you were right."

"I shall never forget that morning," said Edgington with emphasis, looking at Beatrice to see how she received the statement. She cast down her eyes for a moment—it was but a moment, for she looked at him again immediately as she said,—

"No more shall I; for I think truly it was the hottest morning I've felt since I came to India."

"Surely she understood me," thought Edgington; "shall I say more?"

"*I* shall not forget it, Miss Plane, for it was our first meeting," he again remarked, in a low tone.

She made no answer, but looked down again. "Yes, our first meeting," he continued, "and it gave rise to——"

"Make Captain Edgington attend to the quadrille, Miss Plane," interrupted Hoby, as he advanced forward in the figure; "see, we are waiting for you both."

"Curse the dance!" muttered Edgington; "I'll say nothing more with the chance of interruption: there's the polka afterwards; then, at least, one can do as one will."

"Do you see all those natives looking in at the verandah doors?" said Edgington, as in the ladies' chain he held his partner's hand; "they think it a curious scene, and wonder that Englishmen and ladies find pleasure in an exercise for which they keep paid boys and dancing-girls."

"Yes. Do you think, then, that they despise us for it?" asked Beatrice.

"More or less, doubtless, they do so," Edgington answered; "but to English manners and customs they have now got so accustomed, that it, or anything else which is opposed to their habits, makes less impression on them than it doubtless did two generations back."

While the side couples were dancing the same figure, Beatrice said,—

"I have, ever since my arrival in India, been trying *to ascertain* what are the general feelings of the natives towards us; but I must acknowledge I have in no way succeeded, for I have met with so many conflicting facts."

"And so you always would," replied Edgington. "I could never comprehend why so many people, and even some by no means ignorant of India, always speak of the natives as a collective body, and quote an opinion as the opinion of the mass. In no country, I think, is there such a difference of feeling as in India on most subjects, and on none more so than the light in which we are regarded. In one point, however, I conceive they are nearly unanimous, namely, in their estimation of our power as a nation;—were *that* not so, our tenure of India would be very short-lived: but as regards the affection or hatred with which they regard us, it is as various, or nearly so, as are the creeds, sects, and castes."

"Caste among the natives is a curious thing," remarked Beatrice; "their jealousy on that point seems to me to be their ruling passion."

"It is so," said Edgington; "a native will forgive anything sooner than an injury, real or contemplated, thereto."

"Once more it's our turn to dance," said Beatrice, "and I think the last figure."

The quadrille ended, Edgington walked up and down the room with his partner; several times did a declaration of his love hang on his lips, but he was afraid to give it utterance; he was doubtful of the result, and fearful that his doing so might put an end to the fond hopes he had indulged in for the last few months. As they walked, Colonel Carstairs joined them, and said,—

"The next dance is a polka; may I dance it with you, Miss Plane?"

"I am engaged," she replied—"engaged to Captain Edgington."

The colonel replied, evidently piqued, "Why, he had the last dance, and—and——"

"And surely I may give him this one too, if I will," interrupted Beatrice with a haughty air.

"Of course, of course," Carstairs replied hurriedly; "but may I engage you for another dance, later?"

"I know not how long we shall stop, or if I shall dance much more," she said coldly.

"Then I can ask you again by-and-by," observed Carstairs, with assumed indifference. "Don't forget, Edgington," he continued, turning to our hero, "that you take the bottom of the table at supper; Bruce will have, that, as a bachelor, you'll do the honours better than himself."

"I'll do my best, sir," Edgington replied, as the colonel left them.

They continued their promenade in silence. Edgington felt hope beating high within him. Oh, how little will elevate or depress a lover!

The polka commenced, and our hero, for the first time in his life, held the girl he dearly loved around the waist. Much has been said for and against the polka,—the latter, we fear, will carry the day, for already is it banished from many coteries in London. It has had, however, if a short, a very brilliant run; no new dance ever was more popular, none will be more regretted. Peace to its ashes, if its death-dirge has really sounded! It may be, in future balls, that, when the dancers sicken of the tedious monotony of quadrilles, varied only with the giddy-causing waltz or the boisterous, romping country-dance, the fair daughters of Terpsichore will heave a sigh to the memory of the enchanting but much-traduced polka!

Sweet was the air to which the polka we now describe was danced; and long, long did that dance, that air, continue present to Edgington. He was more than happy as he guided his lovely partner through the crowd of dancers with which they were surrounded, and ceased only when, fairly out of breath, the kidded hand pressed his shoulder, and the voice of her he loved begged him to stop.

"You dance well, better even than Colonel Carstairs," said Beatrice, as she leaned on his arm; "but it's nearly over, I think; and, anyhow, I cannot finish it, the room is so very warm."

"If you fear not the night air, step outside into the verandah," replied Edgington; "I'm sure you'll find it a relief."

She nodded acquiescence. In another moment they were there, and all alone, for it was empty, with the exception of the band, which was at the further end, and too far off to overhear them.

"What a beautiful night," said Beatrice, as she looked up at the starry sky, across which a few thin and white vapoury clouds were driving. "See the full moon over the barracks yonder,—what a flood of light it pours down!"

"Beautiful indeed!" said Edgington, gazing on the lovely face of his partner, bathed in the halo of those soft and mellowed rays.

The tone of his voice caused Beatrice to look up, when she met that steadfast and loving gaze. She frowned for a moment; but she smiled the next, as she said,—

"Had we not better go in again? See, the dance is over."

"No; wait one moment—but one moment," said Edgington with much emotion. "What I am about to say, Miss Plane, will not surprise you, for it is impossible that you have not long ago read, what my lips have feared to utter. I do it *now* in fear and trembling. I love you, Beatrice,—deeply, sincerely, with all my heart and soul. Oh! may I dare hope that my affection is returned, in however slight a degree? Tell me it is so," he continued, as he took her hand, "and earth boasts not a happier man than Arthur Edgington this night." He paused for a reply, but none came; the hand, however, which he held between both his, was not withdrawn, and he continued,—" Beatrice, *dear* Beatrice—may I call you so? that permission, if accorded, is all I ask, all I crave. Tell me, Beatrice, will you grant it?"

"I will," she replied firmly, after a moment's pause. "You took me somewhat by surprise; but—but—there is my hand; you have it already, let it be my answer."

## CHAPTER X.

A FORTNIGHT BEFORE MARRIAGE—OPPOSING ELEMENTS—THE HEAD OF THE FAMILY.

In the lofty drawing-room of Mr. Plane's house at Patna, commanding an extensive view of the Ganges, a month after the ball detailed in the last chapter, sat Arthur Edgington and Beatrice Plane. It wanted but a fortnight of their wedding, which was to take place in the Patna church, while a comfortable and commodious budgerow had been already engaged by Edgington, in which to take the honeymoon excursion on the river.

Neither look as cheerful as they did when we last saw them. Why is this? The reader shall judge for himself.

"Of course I love you," Beatrice replied to Edgington's query on the subject, which wearied her more and more each time it was asked. "Of course I love you, Arthur: I have told you so a hundred times already; why, then, eternally repeat the question?"

"Because you do not act as if you did," replied Edgington with a sigh. "A month has now elapsed since our engagement,—how much pain has your coldness cost me during that time."

"What on earth would you have me do?" asked Beatrice, with a despairing face. "Is it my fault if our natures are dissimilar, and if I cannot be as demonstrative as you could wish?"

"If not your fault, your misfortune decidedly," answered Edgington, unjust and unkind in contemplating the despairing prospect he had before him. "Good God! Beatrice, what a future is before us, if in married life you show no further outward signs of affection than you have during the time of our engagement. Tell me, will this be so?"

"What a question to ask!" Beatrice exclaimed. "Of course, as your wife, I am bound to honour and love you; nor is there a possibility of my failing in the duties I shall then owe you. In trouble I will comfort you; in sickness I will nurse you, and do, in fact, all that my sense of duty prompts, and that a wife takes on herself at the altar."

"I suppose your answer must satisfy me, Beatrice," replied Edgington, with a sigh; "but surely something *besides* a sense of duty will animate you in all such wife-like acts?"

"Though other feelings will of course exist, I might, if I trusted to them, fail or relax in my efforts; but what my religion teaches me I ought to do, I most certainly shall do," she replied, with a calm and dispassioned countenance.

"Ah, Beatrice! did I not hope that marriage would alter you somewhat on such points, I should truly be very miserable. I not only hope it, however, but I am sure it will do so. Some fault, probably, in those who had charge of your education, has taught you to cover your warmest feelings with this snowy mantle, and allow them to appear but in a very subdued form. Tell me, dearest—for we will now discuss the matter quietly—were you always, do you think, as cold in manner as you are now?"

"I believe I was," replied his intended; "and of one thing you may be sure, your constantly remarking it only increases the fault, if fault it be. Let me alone. I have told you I love you; let that love bear its fruit in peace, taking its own time to do so."

"I believe you are right," Edgington replied, with a deep sigh, taking her hand as he did so. The beautiful hand—for Beatrice's hand was very perfect—lay in his own without life or motion. What would Edgington *have given* that the slightest return of pressure had been accorded him, that it had even been drawn away; anything, anything better than this dreadful, dead-like, icy nature, in the girl whom he loved so madly. He looked at her face: it was like sculptured marble—almost as white, quite as inanimate. He trembled with agitation, excitement, and despair, drew her towards him, and kissed her passionately, in the hope of calling forth some life, some show of feeling, in the statue at his side.

"Oh, when, *when* will he go away, and leave me; 'tis now five o'clock, and he does not often stop so late." Such were Beatrice's thoughts, as she submitted, with the resignation of a martyr, to the infliction.

Another moment, and Edgington paced up and down the long room, with rapid strides, while Beatrice sat watching him, calm as he was excited, and only wondering when this visit, longer and more tedious than usual, would come to an end."

He stopped suddenly before her, and said with firmness, "Do you think it possible, Beatrice, that we shall be happy together after we are married?"

"Why not?" she replied; "You love me, and I'm sure I love you; what, then, but happiness should lie before us?"

"Do you *really* love me, Beatrice, dear Beatrice?" he exclaimed, in a transport of delight, falling on his knees at her feet; "Oh, why did I for one moment doubt it," he continued, as he pressed her lips with a passionate kiss.

"Now get up at once, or I'll never tell you so much again," she continued, directly she had succeeded in releasing herself from his embrace. "You see, I *dare* not show you any affection, and must be even colder with you than my cold nature—for cold again I warn you it is—dictates."

Edgington blushed as he arose from his knees—blushed at the impetuosity of feeling which made him assume the posture. He quickly recovered himself, however, and continued his promenade to and fro in the long room.

Presently Beatrice unconsciously yawned, as she sat on the sofa. Edgington heard her, and stopped again.

"Do you wish me gone, Beatrice?" he asked.

"No, not gone," she replied; "but I should like the conversation changed. You have never told me much about Marion Paris, whom you were left guardian to. She's fifteen years old, is she not?"

"Sixteen," replied Edgington.

"Is she, really. She's pretty, I hope?"

"The belle of the county, my mother tells me."

"I'm glad of it; I detest ugly, gawky girls," Beatrice remarked. "See, it's a cool evening, and the sun will soon set; suppose we go into the garden, till the carriage comes round for the evening's drive."

"As you will," Edgington answered, listlessly opening the low window.

"If you'll allow me, I'll smoke a cigar," he continued, when, a minute or two later, they trod the carefully-kept gravelled path, which extended from the verandah nearly to the river-side.

"I accord the permission," she replied, smilingly, "with the old conditions—that you keep at a reasonable distance, and to the leeward side."

"The effect a cigar produces is certainly very calming," observed Edgington, a few minutes later, as he emitted a thin volume of gray smoke from his lips, with much gusto and relish."

"I hope you'll often smoke, then," remarked Beatrice, from the other side of the gravel-walk, "for I'm sure it must be good for you; but you quite understand, that you are not to smoke any more in the house after our marriage than you do here now. I even dislike my father's hookah in a room, but cigars would be dreadful."

"I have promised it long ago," he answered, "and of course I shall keep my word; but I dare say, as time wears on, like many other ladies in India, you'll get accustomed to it."

"Well, wait till that time arrives, if it ever comes," she answered. "And now tell me—you said the other day that you had hoped, before you knew Miss Plane was to be Mrs. Edgington, to get leave this cold weather, and join a large boar-hunting party in Bengal. I have thought of it since, and can see no reason why you should not go, and I too, for I long to see some of the Indian field sports."

"If you really think you would like it," replied Edgington, with renewed interest for the being on the other side of the gravel-walk, "I have no doubt it could be managed. But remember, if we do go, and it bores you, the fault is yours, not mine."

"Oh, certainly; but why should it bore me?"

"Because, unless you take an interest in the sport itself, there is not much in such an expedition to amuse you."

"But I do, or rather shall take an interest in it. All such scenes, where danger forms part of the sport, always had a charm for me. Besides, I suppose *I* can ride sometimes, while you are hunting the boars, and that will be a great pleasure. Oh yes; another gratification, and not a light one, will be mine—I shall see my newly-married husband excelling the many, for, riding well as you do, you will of course be A 1 in the field."

"Dear Beatrice! we will go by all means," answered Edgington, with a gratified and happy smile, crossing over the gravel-walk as he spoke, quite forgetful of the interdicted cigar; "it will, as you say, be a great pleasure, and I shall enjoy, beyond measure, seeing you ——"

"Forgetting yourself again, I declare!" exclaimed Beatrice, stopping in her walk. "Do you want to drive me into the house? Now, pray, return to your side of the path."

"Devil take the cheroot!" added Edgington, with some warmth, flinging it away as he spoke. "I beg your pardon for the expression," he added a minute later; "but I have paid penalty for it in the loss of a good Manilla."

"You were wrong to throw it away," she quietly observed; "you will only have to light another, to calm yourself with. Remember, you told me a cigar always soothed your feelings when excited."

"You tantalize me dreadfully, Beatrice," said Edgington.

"That is a long word, and so long since I heard it, or used it myself, I almost forget its exact signification. If I remember right, however, we were taught at school it meant to torment with false hopes; pray, how have I done so?"

"You first attract and then repel, Beatrice. You remind me of those magnet playthings children use with little boats in a basin of water: the loadstone attracts the tiny bark, but no sooner is it near, than, presto! the negative side of the rod is presented, and it is driven away. Even so in my case," he added, with a careless laugh, "the latter effect is produced, for I return to my own side of the walk, and, as you rightly prophesied just now, light another cheroot."

"I doubt but that also will be thrown away quickly," she remarked; "for here comes the servant to tell us the carriage waits. On the principle that the attractive and repellant side of the magnet are presented alternately, I ask you to come with us for the drive. You can ride back to Dinapore just as well when we return, —for I suppose you've nothing to do there,—or even after dinner, if you'll wait so long."

"You are very good," he replied, with a smile; "and in spite of the chance of future repulsion, I obey the magnet this time, and will come. The game we have *been discussing* is a pretty one," he added, after a short pause; "but even children tire of its sameness, if repeated too often—remember that."

"Sahib, the carriage waits," said the turbaned slave, with a respectful salaam, falling behind directly after he had spoken.

"The game should be varied, then," remarked Beatrice, with a side glance at her lover.

"And how, pray?" asked Edgington.

"By repelling *first*, and attracting *afterwards*. It then becomes quite a new amusement," she added, laughingly. "But I must run in, and put on my bonnet. I'll tell my mother you'll stop and dine, and you cannot, in all gallantry, then desert us."

So saying, Beatrice went into the house, leaving Edgington on the grass-plot, watching her figure until it entered the bow-window. "Strange girl, strange girl," he repeated slowly to himself; "and stranger still, this strange girl, in another fortnight, is to be my wife. Be it for good, or be it for evil, God only knows; my heart sometimes misgives me when I think of the future. But how beautiful she is! and how deeply that beauty has enthralled me! Her very coldness, too, e'en while it repels, attracts me. Am I wise, though, to marry with such feelings uppermost? But away with all such thoughts; in any case, 'tis too late to ponder them now." He whistled an air, as he strolled round the house, trying to drive all gloomy ideas out of his head, and so far succeeded that he met his future wife and her parents at the carriage with a cheerful countenance.

"The cold weather is coming on apace," observed Mr. Plane, after they had been out a few minutes; "the air is sensibly cooler now after sunset."

"Yes," said Edgington; "I wish, however, we had as long a cold weather here as they have in the North-west Provinces; there, certainly at that time, the climate is perfection for three months; here, in Behar, perhaps for two; in Calcutta, for one. Long or short, however,

I can conceive nothing more enjoyable than the Indian cold weather, while it lasts. Whether it is that we enjoy it more because we suffer so much from heat, I know not; but I can remember nothing in Europe before I came out to equal, in its perfection and exhilirating effects, a bright Indian day in the height of the cold weather. You have yet to feel all this, Beatrice."

"Yes, and I shall enjoy it, too. Oh, mamma, I have not told you that about January, if Captain Edgington can get leave, we are going to join a grand boar-hunting party in Bengal. I long to see the sport, for I've heard so much of it."

"And it will please you much, if you are your mother's daughter," answered Mrs. Plane. "I shall never forget the only really good thing of the kind I was ever at. No, not the one I saw with you, James," she continued, seeing that her husband was about to speak; "*that* was a wretched affair; there was only one man who could ride at all in the party, and truth compels me, James, to add that it was *not* you. No, no, I mean the party below Calcutta, where all the best riders in the tent club were present."

"I could ride very fairly at one time," replied Mr. Plane, somewhat nettled at his wife's remarks; "but I had a fall which shook me sadly when I was young," he continued, addressing himself to Edgington, "and I never had as much nerve across——"

"Which do you intend shall be Beatrice's riding-horse?" asked Mrs. Plane of Edgington, coolly interrupting her husband.

"Oh, my little black Arab," our hero answered; "he's in every way the best lady's horse I have."

"Bring him down here some day this week," said Beatrice; "and as the evenings are so much cooler now, we can take a ride together."

"To hear is to obey," replied Edgington with a bow.

Mrs. Plane looked at her daughter, and found her

daughter was looking at her. The expression, really without meaning, had reminded both of a conversation they had held that day as to the possibility of Edgington being an obedient husband. It did not alter, however, the opinions they had then severally expressed, the mother thinking it was no easy task to accomplish, while Beatrice was confident of eventual, though deferred success.

"How curious a carriage would look in India without syces running by its side," remarked Beatrice a few minutes later; "as strange, or nearly so, as one in England with them."

"Is it not wonderful the excellent condition this constant running keeps the syces in," said Edgington; "we have been driving fast ever since we came out, and look, neither of them are in the slightest degree distressed, or even out of breath."

"I remember, about five-and-twenty years ago," said Mr. Plane, "when I was assistant to the magistrate at Chittagong, which station, as you probably know, is at the north-east corner of the Bay of Bengal, and where the houses are all built on hills——"

"Oh, papa," interrupted Beatrice, "I'm sure Captain Edgington cannot care about——"

"Not *that* story, James, I beg," exclaimed Mrs. Plane; "there is not the slightest point in it, and I've heard it so very, *very* often."

Edgington smiled, and Beatrice saw him do so.

"I shall, at all events, allow Captain Edgington to form his own opinion on that point," said Mr. Plane to his wife; "but it shall be another time, and when you are not by, in order to spare you the story you've heard so often."

"Thank you," answered Mrs. Plane quite coolly.

Nothing worth relating occurred during the remainder of the drive, or during the evening Edgington spent with his intended; but when he rode back to Dinapore that night, he was conscious that the attractive side of the magnet had been invariably extended towards him since the garden scene.

We have endeavoured in this chapter to show the terms on which Beatrice and our hero stood to each other a short time previous to their marriage, and we can see no object in dwelling longer on this period in our history. The reader will, therefore, suppose the intervening fortnight to have elapsed, and the marriage concluded with all the *éclat* befitting such occasions; for when next he is introduced to the fair Beatrice, she will have changed her name, but whether for the good or ill of the contracting parties, the future course of our tale will inform him.

## CHAPTER XI.

A COLD-WEATHER ENCAMPMENT—GOING TO COVER—BOAR-HUNTING IN BENGAL.

About seven o'clock on a bright morning in January, 1856, on the low land, or churs,* bordering and intersecting the mighty Ganges near Berhampore, might have been seen a sight which, though familiar enough to the majority of Anglo-Indians, would have puzzled English eyes.

Six tolerable-sized tents, with a few small ones for servants and cooking, formed an encampment on a spot devoid of trees, and around was the scene enacting which we now wish to describe.

On one side of the encampment, no less than five-and-twenty elephants, ranged in two lines, and picketed to the ground with ropes, or chains attached to one leg, regaled themselves off the fodder which was abundantly strewed before them, keeping up, at the same time, an incessant flapping with their large ears, and a continual waving to and fro of their lithesome trunks, to drive away the flies and insects buzzing around. The mahouts, or drivers, in groups of four or five, in their rear, clustered around small fires made in the ground, as they baked on metal dishes their morning meal of chupattees,† and then smeared them with ghee.‡

Near the largest tent of the encampment a considerable amount of cooking was going forward, and a crowd of attendant khitmudgars, or table-servants, waited

* Islands and low land with rank grass and other vegetation, but devoid of trees.

† Cakes of coarse and unleavened flour.

‡ Melted butter, often kept and used long after it is rancid.

around to carry the dishes when ready into the canvas abode, which was used as a breakfast and dinner tent.

A great number of picketed horses in all parts of the encampment were, with few exceptions, devouring their morning feed of gram, which is the common food in India for cattle. And as eating was the order of the hour, the syces and grass-cutters* were also taking their matinal meals, as they squatted on the ground near their steeds.

In short, it is very evident the encampment, both human and bestial, are taking their breakfasts; let us go into the long tent, where, from the clatter of plates, knives, and forks, it is certain the said performance is also going on, and perhaps we shall find a spare seat.

We recognize two faces as we enter. One lady, who, from her striking beauty, cannot easily be overlooked, we perceive at once to be her whom we have hitherto known as Beatrice Plane, but who is now Mrs. Edgington. Her husband sits lower down the table, and the rest, eight or ten in number, are strangers. No! that is Mr. Peters, the magistrate at Patna, who rode in the steeple-chase, and there's his wife also!

"This is your first expedition of the kind, Mrs. Holland, is it not?" asked a fat man from the end of the table, of a short and red-faced lady seated opposite, during one of the pauses he allowed himself from the good things before him.

"What, my first expedition pig-sticking! No, thank goodness, I've seen some dozens altogether; for Holland always takes me with him."

"Why give it that dreadful name?" asked Mrs. Edgington. "Boar-hunting—anything would be better."

"But it's *not* boar-hunting," answered Mrs. Holland, —"at least, what they call boar-hunting in some parts of Germany, where they've a lot of dogs, and all sorts of

* Generally speaking, every horse in India has two attendants, viz., a syce or groom, and a grass-cutter; the latter cuts grass daily for his food.

nonsense, to bully the pigs with. Here, in India, we do it in the proper style, and call it pig-sticking, which is the only right word for it."

"I shall judge of the appellation better when I've seen the sport," remarked Mrs. Edgington; "but the associations called up by it are not enticing."

"That's *because* you've never seen it; don't you think so, Holland?" asked his wife. "Doesn't the very name put you in a glow of excitement?"

"It does indeed, Nancy," replied her husband, a jovial indigo-planter. "They may talk as they will of all other fun, but nothing comes up to it."

"I declare it's a shame," said Mrs. Holland; "you'll never let me try my hand at a spear; I expect you think I should beat you, and so you always stick me at top of one of those lumbering elephants."

"Where you are certainly safer," replied her husband. "No, no, Nancy, petticoats have no business after pigs, excepting in a howdah* on a steady elephant."

"Howdah, indeed! And do you think I'll be cooped up in that way?" remarked his spouse. "No, thank you; if I must ride an elephant, it shall not be in a howdah, but where I can feel a little free, on a simple guddi."†

"Please yourself there," said Holland; "but a guddi is surely not so comfortable. Is it not time to get ready?" he continued, appealing to the oldest man at the table, a civilian (that is, a member of the civil service) at Berhampore, named Hope; "the morning's getting on."

"I think so," Mr. Hope replied. "Here, chuprassie, let the elephants and horses be got ready."

"Tell us, Mr. Hope—how did you manage to get such a splendid line of elephants from the rajah?" asked Edgington.

* An enclosed square or oblong-shaped receptacle for seats, generally used for tiger-shooting.

† The common pad or pack an elephant always carries on his back.

"By simply asking for them," replied the old civilian. "The rajah is liberal enough in that way."

As Edgington rose from the table to prepare for the hunt, he turned to his wife, and asked, "Who goes with you in the howdah, Beatrice?"

"Mrs. Peters, I believe. Is it not so?" she continued to that lady.

"Certainly!—being both ignorant of the sport, we shall be good companions," Mrs. Peters answered.

Edgington and Beatrice had now been married nearly three months, and, as the reader may remember, this was the boar-hunting expedition which they had spoken about at Patna.

Edgington, alas! as may well be supposed, was not happy with his wife, and he was only too glad to join in any excitement like the present to get rid of, or rather to forget for the time, the feeling of unrequited affection he laboured under.

The party began to leave the tent, to see about their horses, and to prepare themselves for the sport. Look! as we emerge once more outside, how different is the scene. There is no eating *now* going on; all is bustle and movement. Two of the biggest elephants are kneeling down, while the howdahs are being made fast on their backs; the others require no preparation, for their guddis or packs have not been removed, and they are ready to start at any moment. Saddles are being girthed up on many nice-looking beasts, and we are sure, from their excitement, they know the sport that awaits them;—like old hunters, in England, know what hounds and red coats mean.

And, talking of red coats, how are the Nimrods now under discussion habited? Do they rival their brethren at home in the fox-hunting field, or have they a distinct and characteristic uniform of their own? Truth compels us to say that neither is the case, and we admit it unwillingly, for we wish to interest our fair readers in the coming scene, and we know they would think it more picturesque, could we paint the riders as habited in some gay and uniform colours typical of their employment. The habiliments are, however, various—let us mention a few.

Mr. Hope, the old civilian whom we saw at the breakfast-table, has just come out of his tent; we will take him as the first example. What a funny hat he has on his head; it is in shape like a mushroom, and white, too, like that vegetable. It is called a "solar topee," or sun-hat, and it is made from the pith of a tree. Light as a feather, it is quite impervious to the sun's rays, and it is, without exception, the best covering for the head in tropical climates that can be devised. Had it been used for European troops in India during the last quarter of a century, we are afraid to guess how many valuable lives would have been saved, ingeniously sacrificed under the present system, through means of the Glengarry cap or patent-leather shako. Mr. Hope is further habited in a blue jacket, coming down considerably below the waist, but not so low as to get between him and his saddle; which comfortable garment consists of a light double-linen material, stuffed with cotton and sewn throughout, to insure the said cotton not moving. It is also a great protection from the sun—it is warm in cold, cool in hot weather, and very light and easy.

Thin white breeches and top-boots, with hunting-spurs—the boots with the tops such as our forefathers loved—completed Mr. Hope's attire, and a sensible one it was.

We need not detail others at length; they varied, inasmuch as some wore red instead of blue cotton padded jackets, and black jack-boots instead of tops. Again, the "solar topees" with some aspired to the shape of the jockey-cap, but the material was always the same.

The general character of dress, as the reader will perceive, was similar, the points studied being protection from the sun, lightness, ease, and a firm seat in the saddle. Oh, would that Government would dress our cavalry soldiers on the same sensible principles!

The Nimrods all carry spears in their hands, which is the only weapon allowed in "pig-sticking." The spears are very plain and simple affairs; they consist of male bamboo rods, from five and a half to six feet long, with a heavy piece of lead fastened at the top, and the spear-point at the bottom.

The said point, including the iron receptacle for the bamboo, is about one foot long, and round in shape to within four or five inches of the extremity, when it becomes flat. The weight of the leaden mass made fast around the top of the spear helps to give force to the thrust, for it causes the spear to descend heavier. The spear is never thrown, in fact never allowed to leave the hand unless it be torn away by force; but it is, nevertheless, necessary to have this weight, as when the hunter "jobs" down suddenly on a boar at the side of his horse, were the weight not there, he would probably fail in driving the spear home.

The spear in Bengal is always used and carried over-handed,* and from its length not exceeding six and a half feet, it is evident that a boar cannot be touched with it until he is close to or alongside the horse, more especially as the spear is grasped nearly two feet from its top. This close proximity, which must always be attained before the boar can be speared, constitutes one of the dangers of the sport, for the infuriated pig, on such occasions, does all in his power, and often succeeds in ripping up and wounding the horse at his side, if even he does not get the rider's foot into his mouth. But these and other dangers which "pig-stickers" and their steeds incur, will be better understood when, later, we are with the party in the field.

* In the Bombay and Madras Presidencies we believe the spear is carried under-handed, in the same way as a lance is used.

Custom having reconciled us, as it has all who have killed boars on the plains of Hindostan, to the expressions "pig-sticking" and "pig-stickers," the sounds *now* call up but pleasant recollections of perhaps the finest and most exciting sport under the sun, but we readily confess that the time was when we naturally shared Beatrice's objection to the appellations, and thought it showed a lack of taste in the first Anglo-Indian sportsmen to devise them.

The sun had been above the horizon about two hours as the party, mounted on horses and elephants, left the encampment. The weather was beautiful, with the bright sun and rarefied atmosphere peculiar to the height of the Indian cold season, and the happy faces on all sides showed how much pleasure in anticipation was shared by both the ladies and hunters present.

It is a picturesque sight, that long line, as it winds over the plain. Let us take up our position by the side of that dry nullah, or water-course, and watch it.

First come three of the hunters themselves, of which Captain Edgington is one. The flea-bitten Arab which he rides was bought in Calcutta last cold weather for no less than two thousand rupees (£200), and is, as you see, a perfect picture of symmetry. Perfect as it is in shape, however, it is no less so in temper and disposition, for it possesses *all* the good qualities for which these four-legged sons of the desert are famous. Docile as a child, gentle as a lamb, affectionate as a woman, no lion is bolder and more ready to face danger, no greyhound is fleeter, no wild zebra more excitable, more full of life and spirit, than this noble horse. As a "pig-sticker" (for, strange to say, the appellation is used for both horse and rider), he is invaluable; but on this point the reader shall judge for himself later. Mr. Hope, riding a large bay Arab, is by Edgington's side. It is, to say the least of it, a very handsome beast, but it seems restless, and the unusually long bar of the curb-bit tells a tale of an unpleasantly hard mouth, possibly of a runaway disposition. Mr. Peters, whom we remember at the Dinapore steeple-chase, is the third; he bestrides a small country-bred tatoo, or pony, while his own steed, led by a syce, follows them.

Habit is everything. See how little these horses care about the huge elephant following in their wake, so close that his ever-moving trunk, as he waves it to and fro, brushing his sides, fore-arms, and head, almost touches them. It is the largest and finest riding-elephant of the whole, and, as such, has been chosen for the howdah in which are seated Beatrice Edgington and Mrs. Peters. They will have a fine view of the sport, sitting as they do certainly fourteen feet from the ground, and perfectly secure, too, on the luxuriously-padded seat. What a little mite of a fellow the mahout, or driver, seated on the elephant's neck, looks; and yet he is by no means a small man. He is, by the by, as fond of the elephant as a father of his child, for he has been with it many years, and the mountain of flesh under him is obedient to the slightest word or the faintest movement on his part, as he sits on its rough and bristly neck, with his bare legs behind its huge ears, often guiding it with the smallest action of his feet, or even his toes.

Next in order comes Mr. Holland, mounted on a large and powerful Cape horse, for he is no light-weight, jobbing with his spear at imaginary pigs at his side, as he rides listlessly along, smoking what he declares is "the best manilla, by a long way, he's tasted for months."

A young indigo-planter, named Black, from a neighbouring factory, is with him, on a light racing-looking country-bred mare; and Mr. Holland, between the puffs of his cigar, is giving the first theoretical lesson in "pig-sticking" to his young friend, who has never yet tried the sport.

Then come some eight or ten led horses, each held by his syce or groom, for most of the riders have at least three nags in the field.

Behind them, in solitary grandeur, on the smallest elephant of the whole (and seated on the plain hay cushion or sack which all these beasts carry) appeared Mrs. Holland. Her ardour and enthusiasm were not to be quelled, and her cruel husband having, to use her own words, "refused to let her ride after the pigs, she'd see what she could do with a spear on a small elephant;" and so there she sat (using the guddi or pack for a side-saddle) like any Amazon of old, with the hog-spear upright at her side. Fruitful in expedient, she got over the difficulty which necessarily existed from her elevated seat and feminine dress, by enveloping her feet in a canvas sack, used for coarse flour, which, as she justly remarked, if not as elegant as a large shawl, was much more convenient, it was so easily slipped on and off.

"Who knows," she said at starting, as she ascended with some difficulty, spear in hand, to her position on the kneeling elephant,—"who knows but I may be in luck to-day, and that a boar may stand at bay near where I am. Yes, I can easily reach him," she added a minute later, essaying a thrust with her spear, on the off side, and going through a gymnastic movement as she did so, which, with her innate sense of modesty, we are sure she would not have attempted had she not relied on the friendly offices of the sack.

"You'll scarcely manage it, however, Mrs. Holland, unless the elephant is kneeling down," remarked one of the bystanders, convulsed with laughter as he spoke.

"Then kneel down he *shall*," answered the intrepid huntress. "Here, mahout! do you hear? unless the elephant does all I want, you shall feel this spear; and it's sharp enough to make you jump again," she continued, applying it playfully between the driver's shoulders, amidst the roars of laughter of both Europeans and natives assembled around, which followed her out of the camp, and along the whole line, up to the moment we present her to the reader.

"Why, goodness, Nancy," exclaimed her husband, who then saw her for the first time since breakfast, "what *can* you want with that spear?"

"Never mind, Holland—that's *my* business. Though I mayn't ride, I suppose I may carry what I will on the elephant?"

"And is it on the same principle you have that sack over your legs?" asked her husband, laughing, as he saw, for the first time, the extraordinary appendage.

"No, Holland, it's not; but I suppose you wouldn't like to see your wife perched up here, on this apology for a side-saddle, without a habit, or something in its place, and natives walking below by the side of the elephant. If you would, say so, and I'll fling away the sack?"

Mr. Holland did *not* say so, but he rode up close to her, and a smart conjugal conversation took place between them, which not for the world would we interrupt or overhear.

With the exception of one or two riders, who were somewhat late in leaving the encampment, and who are now pushing their way to the front, the rest of the line, pursuing its tortuous route across the plain, consists of the elephants, who shuffle along in admirable disorder, making no little dust as they do so. Each of these beasts bears his rider on his neck, and in one or two cases very black and scantily-clad villagers, who, only too glad at the prospect of seeing the boars, who destroy their crops, killed, have volunteered to show the likeliest spots where they may be found.

A little more than a mile from camp they all halted at the side of a grass jungle. The latter word is almost anglicized, and we need not explain its meaning; but the former has here a different signification to what is supposed. We have nothing in England to compare to the long rank grass in Hindostan; it is so thick that a man can scarcely push his way through it, and so high *that the* tallest elephants traversing it are often not visible. Where this grass exists, it is a very favourite haunt for hogs; but it is quite impossible to drive them out of it into the open plain, excepting with a line of elephants, who, keeping just close enough to each other to prevent the boars doubling back, generally succeed in forcing the majority of the swine, masculine and feminine, into the open country.

The grass jungle on the side of which the party halted, was oblong in shape, nearly a quarter of a mile long, and two hundred yards wide, which rendered it very convenient to beat thoroughly. The elephants were formed in line at one of the short ends; the large beast on which sat Mrs. Peters and Mrs. Edgington took up his position in the centre of the row, when, the horsemen having dispersed themselves on either side of the jungle, Mr. Hope—who had been unanimously elected as manager of the field—gave the elephant-drivers the word to advance.

Advance they did, and it was an imposing sight to see that apparently invincible and moving black mass of five-and-twenty elephants traverse the short space of open that intervened. In the centre, rendered conspicuous by his great size, and the towering howdah on his back, was the elephant on which the two ladies were seated, and near one of the ends rode Mrs. Holland, on her comparatively small beast, which, if one might judge from the apparent height of the grass in front, would, with its Amazonian rider, be completely covered when once it entered the jungle.

The grass proved even higher than anticipated, for every elephant on entering was hid, except the large one in the centre, the top of whose head could still just be seen. In short, of all that long black line, nothing remained visible excepting the one single head, with the mahout and howdah behind it, floating, as it were, on the tops of the rank vegetation. The elephants, drivers, Mrs. Holland, all, all were lost in that now moving sea of grass.

As they proceeded, however, the height of the jungle that surrounded them became somewhat less, and every now and then the head of an elephant, with its driver, would appear, or the trunk of another, as he lifted it on high. At last even poor Mrs. Holland, on her small elephant, was visible; but she knew it not, and preserved the posture she had assumed in the high grass, to prevent herself getting hurt. She lay along the cushion, with her face resting on it, and the sack still enveloping the lower part of her dress. When first seen in this position, at top of her little sturdy charger, our indefatigable huntress looked such a strange object, that a peal of laughter rang forth from either side of the jungle.

"Mrs. Holland, Mrs. Holland!" called out Mrs. Peters, from the howdah, "the grass is lower now; do sit up and see. Never mind their laughing," she continued, as our Amazon recovered her sitting posture, with some difficulty though, on account of the sack, and looked angrily at the spectators; "you did much the wisest thing you could do—it must have been very dreadful with the grass all round your face."

"Bad enough, any how, without being laughed at," responded the sufferer, in a great rage, loud enough to be heard in the howdah; "I declare they are laughing still; Holland shall take notice of——"

Alas! at that moment the grass became again high, and poor Mrs. Holland, helpless to stay her steed, ceased speaking, and became once more hid. Whether she resumed the recumbent attitude we cannot say; but a few minutes later she emerged from the side of the jungle, having evidently had quite enough of the attempt to pass through long grass on a small elephant.

"Glad to see you out again, Mrs. Holland," remarked one of the riders; "I was afraid, when I saw you going in, that you would not find it answer on that small beast. I hope neither your face or hands are cut with the grass."

"Oh no," replied Holland's better half, whose anger was never long-lived, and who had now quite recovered her temper; "no, thank goodness, I escaped pretty well, but I'm blest if I ever try long grass with a small hatti* again. I shall stop outside in future," she continued, arranging her sack as she spoke, "unless a pig stands at bay in the jungle, when, of course, in I go, 'cowt cui cowt,'" she concluded, with the remarkable talent she possessed for murdering all foreign tongues.

By this time, the line of elephants had advanced nearly half way through the jungle, but nothing had occurred to show that pigs lay there. The riders were getting impatient outside, and their faces lengthened as the possibility of this favourite spot being drawn blank presented itself to them.

"Why, hang it," said Edgington, "we surely shall find some pigs here; I never saw a better spot."

"A sure find generally," Mr. Hope replied; "but stop a bit, we are not through it yet. Howdah ahoy!" he continued, in a loud voice, with his hand to his mouth.

"Yes—what is it?" answered the silvery-toned voice of Beatrice, at the top of the grassy sea.

"Can you see nothing, or hear nothing?" asked Mr. Hope.

"No, nothing," replied Beatrice; "but the grass is so thick that——"

A noise like the sharp blast of a trumpet, always made by an elephant when he is startled, and produced by the use of his proboscis as a musical instrument, suddenly interrupted her, and awoke the attention of all present. Another moment, and the same elephant stopped, trumpeted again, and turned suddenly round, as the grass in front became violently agitated. Beatrice and Mrs. Peters stood up, and looking down out of the howdah, saw several moving black objects through the cover, which seemed in a state of great commotion,

* Hindostanee word for elephant.

running to and fro. One they observed to advance in their direction, and when close to their elephant, with a sudden and violent grunting it rushed past, doubling back the way they had come. Even their enormous beast did not like it, he swayed his huge body to and fro, and half turned round, shaking the howdah violently as he did so. It required a smart application of the sharp iron goad on the top of his head to keep him in his place. One pig had thus doubled back, but he was the only one; the rest—and there seemed to be five or six more—had rushed on with many savage grunts, and would of course be found again as the line advanced.

"Were there many?" called out Mr. Hope again, from the side of the cover.

"Yes, we think a great many," Mrs. Peters replied; "but one has gone back. I see the grass moving again a long way ahead," she continued to Beatrice; "and I'm sure we shall soon find some more. How the noise that elephant made startled us both, did it not?—such an unnatural noise, too. Ah! there it is again," she added, as one of the farthest elephants, having evidently come on some more pigs, went through the same performance.

"Hurrah! hurrah! they'll soon be out now," exclaimed Mr. Holland, flinging away choice Manilla number two, which he was smoking, and standing up in his stirrups to see as far as possible into the grassy jungle.

"Tally ho! tally ho!" called out Edgington from the other side of the cover, as a large pig dashed out near him, and sped across the plain. Scarcely, however, had he and Mr. Hope started in pursuit, when they simultaneously pulled up, looked at each other with disappointment in their faces, and returned to the jungle-side.

The reason was good,—it was only a sow that had broken cover, and nothing is fair game but a grisly boar. This is partly because the lady-pig cannot fight like her husband, and is therefore comparatively contemptible prey, and partly because it would be impolitic "to kill the goose that lays the golden eggs."

But two hundred yards now separated the line of beating elephants from the open plain, and the grass in this space being agitated every here and there, it was evident that more than one family of pigs were in front.

"The whole place is moving," said Mrs. Peters in the howdah, laying hold of Beatrice's hand as she spoke, with a half feeling of fear; "why, there must be at least twenty or thirty wild boars before us."

"An immense number certainly," answered Beatrice with composure, looking forward at the small remaining space. "What *will* they all do when they are driven to the very end?"

Three simultaneous "trumpets" from different elephants showed that more pigs had been met with. Of these, however (as is always the case when the line is near the end of the cover), many doubled back, charging the elephants as they did so, who all began to get very unsteady; for the hogs with their tusks often cut those animals' legs. Many boars, however, rushed on, and added their quota to the confusion and noise that reigned ahead.

Now is the most exciting moment of all to the pig-sticker, and, on the oft-recognized principle that pleasure in anticipation exceeds pleasure in reality, the most enjoyable. The boars are before him in the remaining narrow strip of grass; they *must* come out; and in front lies a plain from one to two miles long, with no cover for his enemy. There are evidently enough, and more than enough hogs, to find employment for all the riders; and, O enjoyable thought! when enough boars have broke to engage all the waiting spears, the elephants will stand still, and await the return of the hunters, ere they cause more of the grisly monsters to face the plain.

The horses, especially all the old pig-stickers, know

this moment as well as their riders, and show their excitement in different ways. Some will not stand still for a moment, but move restlessly from side to side, turning round, and lashing out perhaps at any object in their reach. Others, again, stand quite motionless, with their legs slightly extended, their ears pricked, and their heads towards the cover, positively trembling with pleasure, and watching as anxiously as their riders the scene before them.

The general excitement was shared, in no small degree, by Mrs. Holland; what to do with herself, or her spear, she did not know. She could now, from the side of the grass, occasionally see the pigs, and she constantly urged her mahout to make sudden, but, of course useless, dashes into the cover, in the hope that fortune would smile on her endeavours, and that she might give "one, only one boar a spear."

The distance between the beating elephants and the open country has still further decreased, and the small strip of jungle seems now literally alive with pigs. Another moment and some of them *must* break cover. Yes, there go two already,—right, right away into the open!

"Tally ho! straight ahead!" "Two of them!" "Regular tuskers, by Jupiter!" was roared out by several voices; and Mr. Hope, Edgington, Holland, and the young indigo-planter dashed after them. On, on they sped, each horse vying with the other who should first overtake the fleeing boars, and carry off the palm of "first spear." The pace was terrific. No heed was taken of inequalities in the ground, of the numerous earthen mounds surmounted with grass, of fissures or cracks in the black earth, large enough to take in a horse's leg up to the shoulder; in short, of any of the "spill" producing causes which they dashed past. There was no *time* to look twice at all these things,—there never is, under like circumstances, if the "pig-stickers" in pursuit deserve the name.

The start which the pigs had obtained, while the riders gathered up their reins, and before they got their horses into speed, did not exceed two hundred yards, and yet, after the four horses had thus run at racing speed for more than a quarter of a mile, the distance between the pursuers and pursued had in no way decreased.

"Nonsense!" will some of our readers exclaim; "what, good horses, such as these are described to have been, and going at racing speed, not catch a pig in a quarter of mile?" Ay, we answer, quite possible; for in half a mile, three quarters, ay,—even in a good mile, will first-rate horses be often puzzled to come up with the wild hog of Bengal.

Form not your opinion of him, reader, from the animals called pigs you see in England; this creature, we assure you, is of quite another genus; for, with the courage of the lion and the ferocity of the tiger, the wild boar of Hindostan unites the speed of a hare.

The race continued; the flying pigs ran side by side, straining every nerve to attain the still distant cover, while their four pursuers followed in eager haste; but, with all their exertions, still holding relatively to the animals they pursued the same distance that they had at starting.

The ground they had traversed hitherto had been pretty good; but its character now changed. It was no longer tolerably smooth and even, but cut up with many dry water-courses, which quite interdicted the same furious speed being kept up. Scarcely, indeed, had they begun to cross it, when Mr. Hope, on the hard-mouthed bay Arab previously alluded to, tumbled head over heels into one of these ravines, which was somewhat concealed by long grass growing on the banks; and both he and his horse disappeared at the bottom. It was quite impossible for the others to stop and help him, as it would have been, probably, a long affair, and, indeed, is never done in such cases.

The riders were thus reduced to three. The diminution of pace as they crossed the broken ground was all in favour of the boars—for these animals can run as fast, or very nearly so, on bad as good ground; and thus, when, after the lapse of two or three minutes, an even surface was again obtained, the pigs were, if anything, further ahead at that moment than they were when the race commenced.

Everything in this world, however, has an end, and so has a Bengal boar's powers of running. Quick as any horse for a quarter of a mile, and well able to run half a mile at full speed; if pressed at the same pace for more than three quarters, his wind is exhausted, and the savage hog, trusting no longer to flight, stands at bay and fights to the death. Though, therefore, the boars were farther ahead of their pursuers at the moment the raviny ground was passed than they had yet been, this state of things did not last long, and every stride the horses now took lessened the distance yet to be gained.

About this time the boars separated, as if with the intention of distracting their followers; and while one, and the larger of the two, held on the straight course, the other diverged considerably to the left, and looked as if he purposed to swim across a small arm of the Ganges which was in sight.

Edgington, on his flea-bitten Arab, was close behind Mr. Holland when this separation took place, who, turning his head, called out,—

"I'll take the left boar, Edgington; I can manage him alone, and we *must* bag them both. Do you two kill the other." So saying, he left them, and was soon far away in pursuit on their left.

Edgington glanced at his companion at his side, as they now momentarily neared the infuriated pig, which could be seen champing its huge white tushes, and looking back in the way boars *do* look when they mean mischief. Our hero was pleased with his survey; the young indigo-planter looked all determination, and was holding his mare well together, though he carried his spear in a way that showed he was as yet new to the sport.

Edgington did not even know his name; but he knew this was his first pig-sticking expedition, and how anxious he must, therefore, be to get the first spear. Wishing to give him that pleasure, and hoping to have other opportunities for the honour himself before the day was out, he said,—

"Do *you* ride up and give the first spear, and I'll follow behind. See, you can catch him now if you push on, for he's nearly run out."

The young indigo-planter, a boy of nineteen, did not reply, but with that courage and love of sport which is so general in the Anglo-Saxon race, he closed his heels on his horse's sides, and dashed forward to encounter single-handed the enormous boar before him, quite forgetful at the moment that he had not the slightest idea which was the best way to do it.

He was not long in catching the pig in its then blown condition, and when some fifty paces in its rear, he dashed forward, and sought to spear it in the back. But the boar, who had no idea of running any farther, stopped short in his career ere young Black reached him, and facing round, awaited his antagonist with eyes full of rage, and the white foam covering his tushes, as he ground them together. The impetus which the mare had on her, as she dashed forward at her rider's bidding, was so great, that even if Black had wished it, which he truly did not, he was powerless to stop her. He, therefore, passed at full speed close to the now stationary boar, and, inexpert in the use of the weapon he held, merely pricked him slightly in the shoulder as he did so.

Little or much though, it was still "first spear;" and as the blood trickled slowly from the non-important wound, and Edgington saw it, as he rode up to the scene of action, he called out,—

"Well done, indeed! first spear and first blood are yours. Now be careful what you do, for that boar means mischief, and will fight to the death, if ever blue boar did so. Look out, by God! for he's coming at you *now!*" he added, a moment later, as the pig, in a perfect paroxysm of rage, eyed the young planter and his horse, as they stood some seventy yards off, and putting his head slightly on one side, rushed at them with the speed of the wind.

It was but a moment, and Edgington, though he yelled out with all his might, "Ride at him—don't wait for him!" was too late. The young planter heard him not, or, if he did hear him, had no time to act; for the boar was upon him at the same instant, and only too true in his impetuous charge, caught the bewildered mare on the fore legs with the whole of his ponderous weight, rolling her to the ground as a round shot would have done. As she fell, and the boar flew past her, the avenging tusk ripped open her belly, forming a long and deep incision as clear and defined as a razor could have done it.

The poor lad on her back of course fell with her, but did so cleverly, for he fell free of her, and sprung on his feet again the next moment. Beside him lay his mare, his poor mare, so dearly loved, kicking as she lay on the ground, with a portion of her entrails protruding through the wound. The savage boar who had caused the mischief stood some sixty yards off, again champing his now bloody tusks, and preparing for another charge.

Edgington had, of course, seen, when too late to prevent it, the fatal onslaught, and he now saw the imminent danger the young planter was in. He was at his side almost as soon as the lad recovered his feet, and placing his Arab and himself between the unhorsed horseman and the boar, said quickly,—

"Get further away, and don't stand near me at all. The boar will charge again directly. Never mind your mare; you can't take her with you, and it's as much as your life is worth to stand here if he charges again, and I miss him."

Thus admonished, the young indigo-planter unwillingly left his poor mare's side, and retired in the direction Edgington pointed out, which was neither behind nor at right angles to where our hero and his horse stood, but in a direction between those two points.

In so particularly giving the direction where his companion was to retreat, Edgington judged rightly. Had young Black placed himself behind our hero, and had the boar charged, if not stopped in his career by Edgington's spear, he might have continued his onslaught in the same line against the young planter; whereas, on the other hand, had Edgington's companion placed himself at right angles to where his deliverer stood, the boar, being equally near to both objects, would have been quite as likely to charge down on the dismounted as the mounted hunter.

It was not long before the owner of the poor mare had placed such a distance between Edgington and himself, that the former judged him safe. Satisfied on this point, he turned all his attention to the hog in his front, who, motionless as a statue, watched our hero with his small and savage eyes, probably anticipating as easy a victory in this as the last case.

Edgington patted his Arab's neck, who seemed to return the caress, and gently pressed against the bit, as if impatient to get nearer the hog at bay. "You shall go directly," our hero muttered to his steed. "Bless him, I believe he'd stand on the boar, if asked to do so. Now for it, Mr. Pig," he added, laughingly; "one of us must conquer before we leave this place, and it's time to commence operations."

So saying, he allowed his horse to advance at a foot-pace towards the boar, which, as we stated before, stood some sixty yards off; but the Arab had not moved far, when the hog, without further warning, came thundering down at him.

Edgington's good horse, from long practice, knew what was to be done, and he had, of his own accord, altered the foot-pace to a gallop in less time than it takes us to write it. The boar and he met half-way; but our hero took care to pass to the near side, as the pig shot by on the right. At that instant, with fatal precision, Edgington dug the spear in between the shoulders of his enemy, but with such force, in consequence of the speed at which they met, that he was quite unable to draw it out again; and the weapon was wrenched out of his hand, and carried off by the hog, the shaft standing in a sloping direction over his head, while the iron point stuck fast in his shoulders.

Neither Edgington nor the boar ran far after the encounter; and when our hero had reined in his steed and turned round, the pig was already standing a hundred yards off, watching him, with the spear sticking in his back, which oscillated like a pendulum placed topsy-turvy, on account of the leaden weight at the end.

Had not another spear been get-at-able, and our hero alone, without another pig-sticker to help him, no course would have remained open but to endeavour to recover the spear, by making a dash at the boar, and wrenching it out of his back. But this proceeding—always dangerous, on account of the leaden weight on the top of the shaft, which, on the smallest movement of the pig, may strike him who attempts it a serious blow—was not necessary on this occasion; for the unhorsed young indigo-planter still held his own spear, and, seeing what had occurred, fearlessly advanced to offer it to Edgington.

Our hero did not, however, allow him to come far on his way, for he galloped up, and, taking it out of his hand, cautioned him to keep at a respectful distance. "There's lots of life in the animal yet," he remarked, "though I hope soon to finish him with this," feeling the point of the weapon as he spoke, to make sure it was sharp enough.

As he rode quietly back to the scene of action, the wild boar, who stood watching his every movement, was a sight which, could any painter transfer it cleverly to canvass, would make his fortune by the sale of his picture among the pig-sticking fraternity of Bengal alone. The enthusiasm for boar-hunting becomes almost a madness with those who have tasted the sport in its perfection. Nor can we wonder at it; for, search the world through, where will you find as worthy, as noble an enemy as the grisly hog of Hindostan? Always savage, even wantonly so, and therefore more dangerous to meet than a tiger in the jungle, as the latter will generally retire if allowed, and the boar will often charge in very wantonness, the wild boar of Bengal, when once wounded, is a very demon in ferocity and courage. Little cares he for his own life in such cases, if, in dying, he can revenge himself on his destroyer. Often may a wounded boar be seen close to a jungle-side, which, if he once entered it, would set pursuit at defiance, scorning to take advantage of the cover, which, perhaps, ten minutes before, when unwounded, he had sought hard to reach. In such cases, with his stern, perhaps, against one of the jungle bushes, or the rank grass, which would so quickly hide him from his tormentors, there will he stand with anger in his eyes, and his cheeks speckled with the foam which flies from his mouth as he champs his tushes, darting forward every now and then in a savage charge; and though generally baffled in his attempts, and perhaps more and more wounded at each and every effort, resigning his vengeance only with his life, giving and asking no quarter!

Edgington's enemy, on this occasion, had, however,

no jungle to retreat to, even had he wished to do so, which the expression of his eyes told plainly he did not. He was truly a splendid boar, a true "blue boar," as they are called; when of mature age they become blue-black; and his formidable curled tushes showing whiter than ivory on the dark ground of his face, were in themselves a sight to make a pig-sticker dare much for them. As he stood, his shoulders and fore-arms were covered with thick blood, which bubbled forth all round the spear-point fast between his shoulders, and ran down his neck and legs to the earth. The shaft of the spear, as we have before stated, inclined at an angle of forty-five over his head, and as he watched Edgington, he often looked up at the bamboo above him and the lead on the end, as if trying to make out *why* it was that whenever he moved from side to side, the bamboo also moved, and the leaden head moved most of all; at which times, also, the pain between his shoulders was much increased.

Fair reader, do you feel pity for the boar who suffers all this pain? Believe us, it is unnecessary. The boar does *not* feel for himself; he *feels* not the pain, for all his powers are devoted to revenge, and his whole being, with each and every faculty, is bound up therein.

Edgington was in no way doubtful as to the issue of the combat about to be renewed, but he would, at the same time, have felt thankful if his old spear were not fast in the pig's back. It was not that he felt more at home with his own spear than with a stranger's, but it was that the pig when he now charged carried an extra and formidable weapon, in the shape of four pound weight of lead at the head of the spear-shaft, which was [illegible] than Edgington's saddle, and which, striking [illegible] force of the hog's speed, was quite enou[illegible] horse if it hit him on the forehead, or [illegible] leg. The danger was, moreover, so[illegible] by the fact that the spear-top incl[illegible] or right-hand side of the pig; a[illegible] passes on that side, to enab[illegible] spear with the right hand, the chance of collision was, of course, thereby increased.

Our hero saw all this, and duly weighed it as he returned with the new spear; but all the thinking in the world could not alter the facts, and beyond his determination to try and lessen the danger by endeavouring to spear the boar as he stood, or, in other words, to ride so suddenly and so fast at him, that he would not have *time* to charge, he did not allow himself to anticipate danger, even for his dear Arab horse, for whose safety he truly concerned himself much more than for his own.

As he cantered back after these cogitations, he did not do so in a direct line with the pig, but rather as if he purposed passing him; but when his horse was about one hundred yards off, he suddenly turned him straight at the boar, and putting both spurs into the Arab's flanks, rushed up at almost railroad speed. Quick as he performed this manœuvre, the savage and wily pig was not behind him, for he, too, started at full career to meet his antagonist, the spear in his back swaying fearfully as he did so, and the leaden head threatening destruction to anything or anybody it struck. There was no time to think of the danger, for the next moment they met; and just before Edgington buried his spear in the boar's neck, the dreaded leaden top struck the Arab a violent blow on the shoulder.

Both stopped quicker after this second encounter than they had the first time—Edgington's horse, because the stroke had lamed him, and the poor pig had now nearly received his *quietus*.

Though lame, the Arab was but slightly so, and [illegible] his rider's wish to return and despatch [illegible] required neither courage nor skill to do [illegible] bleeding to death, and on Edging- [illegible] was quite unable to advance a [illegible] e died as he had fought, game to [illegible] efforts up to the last moment to [illegible] regardless of the repeated spear-thrusts he received, until nature could hold out no longer, and he sunk at the Arab's feet, a noble example of the courage, ferocity, and endurance of his race!

"I'm *so* sorry about your poor mare; how is she?" asked Edgington, as young Black came up to see their now lifeless antagonist.

"Very bad, I fear," he answered; "I much doubt if she'll ever run again. What an enormous beast!" he continued, putting his foot on the boar; "no wonder he sent my mare flying as he did. Tell me—about the mare—what can I do? She's a great deal too badly cut to walk back to camp."

"Let me see her," Edgington said, jumping off his horse and leaving him where he stood. "Never mind my Arab; he won't stir, or if he does, it will only be to follow me. Poor fellow," he added, looking back, "I fear he's somewhat lame from that nasty blow he got with the leaden head of your spear in the last charge."

On reaching the spot where the mare lay, Edgington, who had somewhat studied the veterinary art, saw at a glance that she could not live many hours, and that it was but lost labour to attempt removing her to the camp. He told his young companion so plainly, who was not a little distressed thereat, notwithstanding that he had himself guessed as much.

"Ah, Captain Edgington," said Black, with a doleful face, "she *was* such a good mare, and so fond of me, poor thing! I shall never forget her; she is the first horse I ever had that was *all my own*, and, I dare say, I loved her the more for it. Tell me," he resumed, after a moment's pause, as he gazed at the poor animal before him, breathing heavily, with its eyes glazed and staring, "was it my fault that the boar knocked her over and wounded her?"

"Oh no," our hero replied, unwilling to pain him; "such accidents must happen every now and then. See, here are our syces coming; the pig brought us here a pretty good pace, or they'd have arrived long ago. There are two villagers with them, we'll send one to get a hackery* to take the boar to camp; and as for your poor mare, my dear fellow, I fear you can do nothing but let her die where she lies."

The young indigo-planter did not speak, but he knelt down by the head of his dying steed, and, bending over, pressed his lips to her muzzle. When he arose, tears were in his eyes, which he quickly, however, brushed away, and turning to Edgington, said, "Yes, I'll go back with you now, but I'll leave my syce here with the mare till she dies, and he shall go and get her water from the next village. If the syce does not return to camp again by the evening, I'll ride out myself and see if there is still any chance for her. I speak of riding out again quite naturally," he added, after a moment's thought, "I'm so accustomed to riding *you*, my poor mare; but I quite forget I've not another animal to cross, either to come out here on or to avenge your death with."

"Don't let *that* distress you I beg," remarked Edgington, "my stable, with every horse in it, is at your disposal during the whole of the meet, and I doubt not you'll have many opportunities to avenge your favourite's death."

"You are very kind," said young Black, looking gratefully at our hero; "but suppose a similar accident befalls one of your horses?"

"I'll take my chance," Edgington replied, laughing, "and so will my nags,—they are all pig-stickers, and as such it's part of their duty."

Let not the joking tone of our hero induce the belief that the offer he made the young indigo-planter was a small one, or that it cost him nothing to make it. Edgington was passionately fond of his horses, and it was no little thing to risk them with a young and inexperienced "pig-sticker." But he pitied the poor

* Native cart.

lad for the loss of his mare, and with his truly kind heart, had the sacrifice been twice as great, it would not have prevented him doing all he could to cheer up his companion.

On their walk back to the jungle where they had left the elephants, for Edgington would not hear of riding while his companion walked, they discussed the events of the late encounter, and the young indigo-planter observed,—

"Though you say it was not my fault my mare was killed, I fear you only say so because you think the reverse would pain me. From the way in which I saw you act afterwards, I feel sure I did wrong in allowing the boar to charge me while I was standing still—tell me, is it not so?"

"It is," Edgington replied: "when I saw the pig charging I called out to you to ride and meet him, but you did not hear me,—and even if you had, it was almost too late. Avoid the mistake again: always *meet* a boar in his charge; and I feel sure that before even this day is over, you'll be so good a hand at the sport that you'll astonish yourself. You possess the two necessary qualities to make a pig-sticker—you ride well, and have lots of pluck; all the rest will come of itself. See, there is Holland coming up, I wonder if *he* killed his pig; his horse seems all right enough anyhow,—more fortunate in that respect than we have been. I say *we*, for look, my Arab still limps a little."

"Why, what's this?" said Holland, galloping up with choice manilla number three in his mouth; "one horse, and that a lame one, between two of you?"

"Yes," answered the young planter; "my mare was cruelly cut by the boar, and is dying, if she is not dead already."

"Devil she is!" exclaimed Holland, preceding the observation with a prolonged whistle. "Tell me, how was it?"

Young Black detailed all the fight, and when the

acount was finished, Holland put his hand kindly on the young planter's shoulder and said,—

"You did not attend to me properly this morning, younker, or you'd have had your mare under you at this moment. However, never mind; I dare say the factory* can find you another nag."

"Now tell us what *you* did," interposed Edgington. "Of course you killed your pig? I need not ask you though, for I see your spear is bloody."

"Yes, he's pork at this moment, sure enough!" Holland replied, "but he did not give me much fun. I soon caught him after I left you, for he was pretty well blown, I expect, when he separated from t'other piggy; but he turned out a "jinking"† customer, and hang me if I could prod him, do what I would. Whenever I came near, off he'd go at right angles, and this big Cape, as you may conceive, is not the best sort of animal for that fun. Well, this went on for some time, and I began to think my friend was a regular cur, and would not fight, when, all of a sudden, coming up to a large tree in the plain, he screwed his stern in to it, showed me a decent pair of tusks, and, as plainly as pig could speak, asked me to come on. I advanced, nothing loth, expecting him to charge as I came up; but devil a bit of it—he seemed determined not to leave the tree. Well, after a time I lost all patience, and rode at the beast to finish him; but this great lumbering horse tripped when within ten paces of him, and falling on his knees—no, they are not much cut,—all but sent me flying over his head. If my Cape horse was stupid in falling, he was *not* stupid in getting up again; for I suppose he fancied the boar would be at him, and was on his legs like a shot. He was none too soon though, for the first thing I saw was the pig by his side, who without more ado took my foot into his mouth, though luckily he included the stirrup-iron, which saved me, I

* Indigo factory. † Twisting or doubling.

expect, a devil of a grip. My first spear, as he stood under me, went right through him, about the middle, and he wanted no more than that one spear, for I had hardly drawn it out of him before he was dead."

"Well," said Edgington, "he was not such a game fellow as ours. We are coming near the place where Mr. Hope fell into the ravine. My syce saw him riding back to the elephants, and he did not seem hurt."

"He went in a tremendous purl, however, did he not?" remarked Holland. "How odd it is that so few people *do* get hurt in a pig-sticking party, in spite of the number of spills."

Another ten minutes more found them by the side of the grass jungle, with everything much as they had left it. The line of elephants had not moved since their departure, and now stood ready to drive out more hogs from the narrow strip of grass in front. Mr. Peters, and all the other horsemen, had been away after boars with varied success, and some had not yet returned; but, including the two pigs killed by Edgington, the young planter, and Holland, four were already known to have bitten the dust. The large elephant which carried Mrs. Peters and Mrs. Edgington had been brought out of the jungle, and those two ladies had got down from their elevated seat on Mr. Hope's return; who, in spite of his and his horse's severe fall into the ravine, had escaped without a scratch. Shawls and cushions had been spread on the ground, and were occupied by the ladies and riders, while on one very large red plaid, which Mrs. Holland had given a servant to bring for her, that lady now reclined in state, relating some of her former sporting experiences, to the no small amusement of her listeners.

As may be conceived, questions and answers regarding what they had done, mixed up with commiserative and consoling remarks to the young indigo-planter, for the loss of his mare, occupied the first few minutes.

The conduct of the beautiful Mrs. Edgington on this occasion somewhat surprised the party. Her husband had not been away long, certainly; but still there is always more or less danger in pig-sticking, and all in that circle on his return, expected to see his wife look pleased, greet him kindly, and evince interest in his success. The latter she did, but neither of the former; and many who sat there wondered at the coldness of her manner.

Edgington spoke kindly to her more than once, but evidently shrunk from contrasting his behaviour with hers, and so, with a sigh, which no one, however, perceived, he eventually seated himself on one of the shawls near Mrs. Holland, lit a cheroot, and was soon as boisterous in his laughter as any of her listeners.

That good lady was in her glory; for though she had *not* succeeded in spearing a boar, she *had* succeeded in persuading her listeners that she only lacked the opportunity to do so; and, thus mounted on a little pinnacle of fame, she had launched forth in animated descriptions of former exploits, all in the sporting line, which, if somewhat exaggerated, were not the less amusing, the more especially as, when she told some deed of surpassing wonder, and any one of her listeners insinuated a doubt as to his capability of believing it, unless somewhat modified in form, Mrs. Holland would strike the leaden head of her spear on the ground, as she held it upright at her side, and mildly state, looking hard at the disbeliever, "that she'd take her oath it was a fact!"

This, of course, clenched the business, for *that* tale at least; for who, with any decency, could doubt when such undeniable proof was proffered; and Mrs. Holland had it all her own way to begin a fresh history, a shade more marvellous than the last.

But ten minutes more, and all the party had returned, and the voice of Mr. Hope calling the riders to mount closed Mrs. Holland's *séance* for the time being.

In many cases fresh horses were mounted; for all felt sure of immediate sport: no one doubted that many pigs still lay before the elephants, though, during the time the riders were all away, and everything was still, more than five or six had broken cover and stolen away to distant jungles.

Edgington discarded the Arab he had previously ridden, which still limped a little, for a sound horse, and, agreeably to his promise, mounted the young indigo-planter on, next to the flea-bitten Arab, the best pig-sticker in his stable.

The ladies remounted their elephants, Mrs. Holland always spear in hand; and all being once more ready, at a word from Mr. Hope the line moved forward.

This time they had not long to wait: five pigs, of which two proved to be boars, broke simultaneously, and took away with them four riders.

"Do you keep with me," Edgington remarked to young Black, as they sat on horseback together at the side of the cover; "that is, if you like to do so."

No sooner were the words out of his mouth than a boar broke near them. "This fellow will do," he continued,—"come along;" and in another instant they were side by side coursing over the plain.

This pig took not the same direction that the last two had done, but bore away to the right, on which side Edgington had accidentally heard there was some low and thin grass jungle, which one *could* ride a boar through, though likely to lose him in it at any moment. The said jungle was evidently the hog's goal; and not being quite half a mile from the grass they had left, though both Edgington and the young indigo-planter tried hard to prevent it, the pig dashed into its friendly cover, when they were but twenty yards in his rear, untouched and unscathed.

"I think I can keep him in view through the grass; you stop outside, ride round, and view him again if he breaks," Edgington said quickly to his companion as he dashed into the grass after the boar. Young Black pulled up short, and watched Edgington as he proceeded.

Riding pigs in grass jungle is only practicable, as we have stated, when the grass is both thin and short; and it is always even then more or less dangerous to do so, on account of the strong chance you encounter of a fall. In such jungle the grass generally grows in patches, and thus bare spots are met with; but the ground is always bad for riding, both where the grass is, and where it is not; in the former case on account of the earthen mounds that spring up round the roots of the rank vegetation, and in the latter from the many holes the pigs and other animals make in the earth, and which cannot often be seen. Fissures, or cracks in the ground, caused by the heat of the hot-weather sun, are also sure to abound if the soil happens to be what in India they call "black earth."

A boar running in such grass is more likely "to jink," or turn short, than he is in a plain. We presume he sees more probability of escaping his pursuer thereby; and it is, of course, much more difficult to follow him. Edgington had hard work to keep his pig in view; and seeing, as he shortly did, that the hog was not likely to run through the cover, he called to his companion to join him; for in such a case, with a jinking pig, two spears are much more likely to succeed than one.

Young Black was soon by our hero's side, and for a minute or two they together chased the jinking boar through the grass; and though one occasionally lost him, the other kept him in sight; but neither could succeed in touching the wily beast with the spear.

"He'll stop presently," remarked Edgington to his companion, as they rode side by side; "that is, if we don't lose him first. I see he's nearly blown."

Our hero prophesied rightly; another moment, and he did stop, in a little open spot some thirty yards wide.

"It's my first spear this time,—that is, if I can get it," said Edgington with a laugh, as he dashed into the open space by the side of the young planter.

"Yes, whoever wins it shall have it," answered Black, also laughing, and grasping his spear firmly as he spoke.

"Alas!" as Mrs. Holland had justly remarked in one of her sporting anecdotes that very day, "nothing is certain in this life." Poor Edgington made sure the spear was his; but even while he exulted in the thought, his horse put his foot into a hole, that received the leg up to the knee, and rolled heavily to the ground, flinging our hero forward, as it were, into the pig's mouth.

Not twenty paces intervened between him and the grisly boar, when, somewhat stunned, though quite conscious of his position, he looked up. But danger there was none; for, though the hog had charged our hero the moment after he fell, young Black had received the charge on his spear with fatal precision; and thus, when Edgington expected to see a live boar about to rip him open, he saw his companion quietly seated on the perfect pig-sticker he had lent him, and the hog dead at the horse's side.

"Well done, indeed! two boars, and two first spears," exclaimed Edgington, taking his solar topee or pith hat off his head, and looking into it. "Ah, just as well I had this on, or I should not be talking now. See, the crown is split in two,—regularly in two," he continued putting his fist through it. "It saved my head, that's very certain; for as it is, I feel a little shaky. Look at my villain of a horse, too, how coolly he takes it," he continued, after a moment's pause, during which he shook his head and twisted his neck about, to make sure neither was broken. "See the beast munching away at the grass as if nothing had happened. Yes, by no means a bad boar you've bagged, *Black,* or are they bad tushes he carries; and I'm devilish glad, for both my sake and yours, that you killed him so cleverly. Remember, I prophesied you'd be a good pig-sticker. Well, I feel somewhat shaky still; but a cheroot will put me to rights, I hope." Saying which, our hero pulled out his cigar-case, and, seated on the ground where he had fallen, had what he called "a short though satisfactory smoke" before he arose.

One of the pad-elephants, which had been sent after them, appeared shortly, and on it was the boar hoisted; after which our two Nimrods retraced their steps to join the party at the old cover-side.

It was tiffin-time when they arrived, and they found a large table-cloth spread under the shade of a neighbouring tree, covered with good things. The whole party were soon reassembled; and then commenced one of those out-of-door cold-weather tiffins, which live long in the memory of all those who have enjoyed them. Each recited in turn his morning's experiences, while bitter ale, sherry, and champagne were passed round. The programme for the afternoon's sport was arranged; the boars already sent to the encampment counted; the "first spears" noted in Mr. Hope's pocket-book; and then, when the after-tiffin cheroots were ignited, and each hunter, stretching himself on the ground, literally revelled in the anticipated pleasure of yet two days more of such sport, it was exultingly declared, and assented to by all, that there's no fun in the world like "pig-sticking."

## CHAPTER XII.

### A CHEERLESS HOME—THE WISH REALIZED.

"I CANNOT agree with you, Beatrice; nor, pardon me, can I allow it. All the house expenses I will make you over most willingly, and shall be very glad if you will look after them; but to give you over my agents' and bankers' book is surely a little too much."

"There we are, as usual, at variance," Beatrice remarked; "you can have no expenses that I may not know of, where then does the objection lie? You are occupied with your regimental affairs, and have not as much time to look after such things as myself. In the same way with my father and mother, he attends to his civilian's duties, but she manages everything in that way. See how well it has answered with them, and how his pecuniary affairs have prospered. What I ask is surely not unreasonable."

"How often shall I repeat to you, Beatrice, that the relations of your father and mother cannot be accepted by me as a precedent in our case. I would not for the world say anything of either that their daughter may not hear; but I assure you I should be very sorry that you attempted to act towards me as she does towards him; and I am quite certain that under such treatment I should not be as submissive as Mr. Plane."

"I will not argue the point further with you, Arthur; perhaps some future day you will see your error. But with regard to my father and mother, I cannot allow that their example is not one we might both safely follow; and, in truth, it distresses me much when you speak of them in the disparaging way you have done *to-day*, and a hundred times before."

"Neither to-day, nor at any other time, have I meant to do so, Beatrice. If you did not, or rather had not, so continually quoted your parents, as examples for ourselves, I should never have said one word against them. But when you do so, you drive me into a corner, and I am then obliged to say what I think, which has never, however, amounted to more than that, in their conjugal relations, they need not be a pattern for us. However, let us now talk of something else, and try if we cannot pass the rest of this day without a discussion."

The above conversation took place in Edgington's bungalow, at Dinapore, whither Beatrice and he had returned after the boar-hunting expedition. It will do as well as any other for an example of what occurred almost daily between our hero and his bride. From the day of their marriage, Beatrice had tried hard to gain that ascendancy over her husband which she had always seen so successfully practised in the case of her parents; and it was no slight annoyance to this proud and imperious woman to acknowledge to her mother, whom she continually saw, that up to the present time she had not much advanced in her purpose. However, she by no means despaired of eventual, though but partial success; for Edgington (who was willing to sacrifice much to avoid such discussions) had often yielded to her, being anxious to prove that he sought not to exercise the dominion over her, which he could not but see was her object with him; and Beatrice argued on the strength of such concessions, that time, and the wearying method she pursued, would some day accomplish her end.

Aware, however, from experience, that when Edgington did not readily yield, and she could not bring forward any argument to convince him, the mere fact of her opposition was ineffectual to move him, she, like a wily tactician, did not, in such cases, prolong the argument, but was content to defer her hope of victory on the disputed point to a later and more favourable period. It was this system of action which made her drop the contest in the conversation recited above; but while she did so for the time, she was quite determined to renew the subject, when future concessions on her husband's part in other matters had drilled him more into the habit of deference to her wishes.

That happiness in the wedded life of our hero did not exist, with such feelings and objects actuating Beatrice, we need not assert; but, alas! this was not the severest trial he underwent. Many wives follow the course of Edgington's bride; but affection is generally mixed up therewith, and compensates, in some measure, to their husbands for the tyranny they undergo. In the present case this palliative was wanting; Beatrice had not loved Edgington when she married him, though she had liked him as well as her nature permitted; and this liking never had, and never would, ripen into love. It was not in her being to love; she truly had never experienced the feeling, and she could not, therefore, appreciate the misery that the want of it caused our hero. With him it was different; for, possessed of a very affectionate and loving disposition, but one that had never until now been awakened to feel that strongest form of devotion, *love,* when the flame was once kindled, it burnt with extra lustre on account of this delay, and thus made his feelings for Beatrice, when he married her, of that kind that can least brook neglect from the loved object. That she did not love him as he loved her, he well knew when he married; but how many thousands besides our hero, both men and women, have rushed on matrimony with the same knowledge! Edgington, like many, did so, with the hope that stronger feelings would be formed in his wife after marriage; but few have been disappointed to the extent that he was, inasmuch as many beings do not exist formed of the same cold materials as the heartless Beatrice.

Edgington had since his marriage done all he could

to awaken affection in his wife, and bitterly failed. It was not that she acted unkindly, for, with the exception of trying to domineer and rule him, she was guilty of no *active* unkindness; but it was her *passive* unkindness which cut him to the quick; her utter want of all feeling and demonstrative affection, which made him daily feel more and more how hopeless was the task he had undertaken. Ere the time of which we write,—and it was but four months after their wedding,—poor Edgington had nearly given up the attempt in despair. Once or twice during that interval it struck him, that if he tried a little of that potent touchstone, neglect, and was himself more chary and less lavish of his affection, it might possibly arouse his wife to try and win back what otherwise she might lose altogether. But our hero was wrong in his calculations; the coolness of manner which, doubtless, before marriage would have stirred Beatrice's nature, inasmuch as it then portended a loss of the state she had yet to gain, had no such effect now. When Edgington tried the experiment, he certainly found his wife more agreeable, inasmuch as she did not momentarily dread a display of affection on his part, and was therefore more unrestrained in her conduct; but he could not perceive that she was in any way more tender in her manner towards him; in short, she seemed to be quite satisfied with the changed state of affairs, and to wish for no further alteration.

"Oh," thought Edgington, as day after day, and week after week, he pondered these subjects,—"oh, how unutterably wearying is this continued attempt on my part to awaken affection, when I begin to fear even the germ does not exist. It cannot go on thus for ever: the cord of love may be much strained, but it will snap at last. Do I *now* love Beatrice as well as I did? I fear to answer the query even to myself, so strongly do I feel that if my love is not yet impaired, the day must arrive, and that shortly, when it must be so,—nay, more, vanish altogether, from continual contact with her icy nature. And how sad that I see no course by which I can avert this coming state of things —no road to escape it—I, who have always thought of happy married life as the most blessed state on earth, who now, with the wife that I have, could forget, overlook all her faults, did she but show me affection. Where are the dreams I indulged in when I first knew her, that the cold manner apparent to all would vanish when brought in contact with a husband's love, and that the love in her case would burn the more brightly, being a new feeling planted in the virgin and hitherto barren soil of her affections. Alas! the new feeling has not found birth,—the soil is still a virgin and hopelessly barren one,—and I am doomed for life to sit down and watch it, making no efforts to improve its condition, knowing too well that all such will be fruitless."

That our hero thought all this at one time in the order in which it is stated, we do not affirm, but the ideas here embodied in words were continually present to him; and as day after day, and week after week, passed without any change for the better, the indifference, at first feigned, to call forth affection, became real and substantial; for he was progressing to the point of thinking that, though legally he had a wife, socially he had none, as not one feeling beat in common between him and the being who bore the appellation. In short, not to weary the reader with details which, from what has previously been told, he can picture to himself, two months had not elapsed from the date of the short conversation detailed at the commencement of this chapter, and consequently but six months after their wedding, when Edgington had virtually reached this state. He had, in fact, gone one step beyond it; the society of his wife bored him; for, with perhaps a natural revulsion of feeling consequent on the violence done to his oft-proffered affection, he now saw no charms in the authoress of his woes. Her stately manner was nothing but a proud demeanour; her ready wit but an engine of unkindness; her religion but a mask for uncharitableness; her reserve a want of candour. His ear could distinguish no melody in her voice; and though the last effect produced, it too came, and tore up rudely whatever little spark of affection still remained in his heart. No beauty of person or feature now attracted his eyesight; nay, when he gazed, he would wonder, and ask himself where the beauty lay which had formerly so enthralled him, and which, he knew, still existed in the opinion of others.

Edgington!—Edgington!—Beatrice is the same; it is *you* that have changed. You are now the more reserved, your manner is the colder; and though we believe you might yet be won back, might once more see with your former eyes and hear with your former ears, we know it is not Beatrice who will cause this second change; for though she sometimes grieves to see how thoroughly you are estranged, she is too happy in the liberty of thought and action she now has—too thankful to escape the dreaded ordeal of your demonstrative affection, to wish things to be as they once were.

The hot weather of the year 1856 had commenced when Edgington's love had cooled down in this manner, or, to speak more correctly, had vanished altogether. The course of wedded life between our hero and his beautiful partner flowed perhaps smoother under this altered state of things than it had done before. He, as we have stated, was now thoroughly indifferent, and she, only too glad to be relieved from the tedium and weariness his former love entailed, did not try to revive it.

Coupled with this relief, however, was the unwelcome conviction that her influence with her husband had diminished, and the cessation of what she *now* saw were useless attempts to gain the upper hand allowed more peace around our hero's board than it had yet known.

Though the daily course of their lives flowed smoother

now than it did when he was always striving to gain her love, and she the dominant power, nothing could well be more miserable than the existence they both led under this comparatively smooth surface. Edgington felt keenly the conviction that he was united to a woman with whom he never could know happiness, and that not for him was domestic joy or the thousand associations called up by that one word, home!—while Beatrice's proud spirit was sorely wounded when she became conscious how insignificant a person she had become in her own circle, as also how utterly she had failed in realizing the dream of her youth—a home, and a husband acknowledging her mistress.

It was when Edgington first felt the cheerlessness that reigned under his roof, that, casting about, as all will under such circumstances, for some ameliorating phase, his thoughts reverted to the former object of his solicitude, Marion Paris, who, as the reader knows, was with his mother in England; and as he had, since his marriage, given up the idea of furlough, he felt a longing desire for the society of the young girl whom he had loved as a child, and who, he thought, would now cast a ray of sunshine on his desolate path. The idea, once entertained, grew daily in strength; but our hero could not disguise from himself that, considering the age of his young *protégée*, and the fact that she was but a very distant connection of his own, he certainly must receive his wife's willing consent ere he ventured to ask her to become an inmate of his house; and that, should Beatrice, when asked, show any disinclination whatever to the plan, he would be in no way justified in pressing it on her.

Edgington was a man who, having once made up his mind what course his conscience would approve, followed out that path at all risks, and in spite of any disappointments or misfortunes the doing so might entail on himself. Having, therefore, determined that *Beatrice* had the full right, if she wished it, to object to

Marion being asked to join them in India, and that if she did object, though ever so slightly, he must not try to remove her objection, it was with no little anxiety that he broached the subject one morning as they sat in the verandah of their bungalow, taking tea after their early ride.

"Beatrice, you have often heard me speak of Marion Paris, the girl left under my charge some years ago, and who is now with my mother in England?"

"Of course I have," Beatrice replied; "you told me once she was a great beauty, did you not?"

"Yes," said Edgington, pouring out a cup of tea; "my mother says she's very lovely. There's much about her in the letter I received by the overland yesterday; would you like to hear it?" he continued, producing the letter.

"Certainly, if you'll read it. Are you not neglecting your duties to your *protégée*, Arthur, in leaving her for so many years alone with your mother?—why don't you send for her out here?"

"That is the very thing, dear Beatrice, I wished to speak to you about," answered Edgington joyfully, unable to hide the pleasure the query gave him.

"Dear Beatrice" was not as usual a term *now* as it had been some months since, and the beautiful wife blushed when she heard it. She answered quickly, however,—

"Then I have forestalled you. You had already proposed to yourself doing so, and were going to tell me of your intention."

"By no means," Edgington answered. "I had certainly thought of it, and thought I should like it, for many reasons; but I never for a moment entertained the idea of doing so, unless you gave your full and willing consent."

"And why should I *not* do so?" said his wife, drawing herself up, as she spoke, in her own old manner, reminding Edgington of the period when he loved so deeply. "Your affection for your *protégée* is not likely to arouse the jealousy of your wife."

"I hope not," he answered, with a sigh, as he remembered how little that wife cared for his love, as, also, how indifferent he had latterly been to the fact; "but I still thought it right to ask your permission."

"Which I give readily," said Beatrice. "It will be a pleasure to me as well as to yourself to have her. I sadly want a companion to relieve the monotony of this Indian life, and a young girl like Marion is just what I fancy."

"Then it is settled," Edgington said; "and I'll write home by the next mail, so that she can arrive here before the cold weather. Now hear what my mother says about her," he continued, as he opened the letter and read,—

"Marion knew not exactly whether to be pleased or not with your marriage. She has a very lively recollection of you in India, and having, since her father's death, always regarded you as filling his place, she is, like so many young girls, scarcely willing that another, and one she has never seen, should now claim so much of your affection. When I first told her, she said most naïvely, after a moment's thought, 'Tell me, what will Arthur's wife be to me?' 'How do you mean?' I asked, for I did not understand her. 'What relation will she be? You have always told me that Arthur is no regular relation, only my guardian; what then will his wife be?' 'Your guardian's wife,' I replied, laughing; 'is not that enough?' She thought again for a few minutes, and then said, 'I suppose I *ought* to love her very much?' 'By all means,' I replied; 'and when you see her, I have no doubt you will.' 'Oh, then, I'm not obliged to do so before?' 'Scarcely; it is difficult to love a being one has never seen.' This seemed to satisfy her; but an hour later she came up to me, and said in the most simple and natural way, as if the conversation had only just concluded, 'Yes, dear aunt, I feel I *shall* love Arthur's wife very dearly when I know her,—that is, if she will let me do so; and if you like, I'll write and tell her.' Was it not all very nice? and can you wonder at my loving the dear girl as I do?

"I have so often described her to you, that I will not risk repetition; but each mail, when I write, it appears to me as if I had not said enough about the fascinations of her manner and person in my last. She is just at that age when every month makes a change; and go where she will, she excites universal admiration. Not her least charm is her utter unconsciousness of her rare beauty. I call it rare, because her Greek descent on her mother's side has given her such a lovely and perfect Grecian profile, that the style is somewhat rare, even in this country, where beauty is sown broadcast through the land. She had looked forward so much to seeing you when you came home on furlough, that she was not a little disappointed, like myself, when she heard it was not to be; and she now sometimes wonders if you will ever send for her out to India. *I* have wondered too, so many girls now go out and marry well in India, that if you thought it good to send for dear Marion, I would put no difficulties in the way; but unless you wished, on your own and your wife's account, for the pleasure and companionship her society would give you, I think she is quite as well with me in England."

"That is all," said Edgington, as he closed the letter; "do you like the slight sketch of Marion that it gives?"

"Exceedingly; how well your mother writes—yes, Marion will doubtless be a great acquisition in our house. She will amuse me with her original and *naïve* ideas; and as she is, I am sure, the very opposite to myself in character, we shall, I doubt not, become fast friends."

"*C'est une affaire décidée,*" said Edgington, as he

balanced himself on the two hind legs of his chair, and placed his feet against the verandah pillar, in the true Indian style. "It's almost cruel to take her from my mother; but she never expected to keep her beyond her present age. `Now, let me see: this is the middle of April; my letter can reach home by the end of May. Two months to prepare for the journey makes it July. Say she leaves England beginning of August, she'll be in Calcutta by the middle of September, and up here next October, just in time for the cold weather. It couldn't be nicer. The only difficulty is, her coming out overland alone; but my mother will find some one to take charge of her, she's sure to manage it. I'll just tell her what we want, leave it all in her hands, and I'll bet the flea-bitten Arab in the stable against anything his equal, if it can be found, that Marion is in Calcutta next September."

## CHAPTER XIII.

### CALCUTTA—A WARM WELCOME—MARION PARIS AT HER TOILET.

Nearly six months have elapsed since the conversation recorded in the last chapter; and Calcutta, at sunset, one warm Sunday evening towards the end of September, 1856, is the time and place. The course, or esplanade by the river-side, is thronged with carriages and horses, while a few palankeens may also be seen in the crowd, giving the idea which palankeens always do to new-comers, of suffering on the part of the four two-legged unfortunate beings who bear the ponderous load.

The fast-flowing Hoogly, an arm of the mighty Ganges, running at the side of the road or course, is covered with ships of all nations, straining at their anchors as the ebb-tide rushes by them. In honour of the day they all carry their national flags; and perhaps in no port of the world can such a mixture of union-jacks, tricolors, lions and eagles rampant, stars and stripes, with other devices, be seen. Indeed, ships from all countries are there—from Norway, from Sweden, from Denmark, from England, France, Hamburg, and the different ports of Northern Germany; from Holland, Spain, Italy, Greece, and Turkey; from America, Australia, China, Penang, Burmah, and many places in the eastern seas,—there they all lie side by side, cheek by jowl, testifying by the difference of build, the cut of their rigging, the comparative cleanliness or otherwise of their exteriors, and the language spoken on their decks, whence they come; but all uniting in proof of the world-wide commerce, the prosperity, and the affluence of the metropolis of British India.

Calcutta has been called the City of Palaces, and, in truth, such parts of it as can be seen from the course warrant the appellation. The extensive "midan," or plain, to the left, is bounded at the further end by that part of the town known as Chowringhee, all the houses in which face the open, and in point of size and architecture are superior to many surrounding Hyde Park. At the Calcutta end of the plain, from its huge size looking like the parent of all the others, stands Government House, a noble pile of massive stone, without any of that elaborate decoration, or fretted carving, which so often destroys the effect of similar edifices. Facing it, at the further end of the open, is Fort William, a stronghold of no mean importance, which looks, however, from the immense space it covers, as if it would require a regular army to garrison it. Thus all Calcutta visible from this point is grand and imposing; and as it is always the first part seen by new arrivals, it has probably given birth to the name mentioned above, which many other portions of the city do not justify.

Let us leave Calcutta, however,—it has been described a thousand times before,—and turn to the population taking air and exercise on the course and esplanade at the river's side. Though the crowd before us belongs to the metropolis of India, which is also, of course, the abode of many wealthy natives, we can discern no gay Eastern equipages, no Oriental show or pomp in the moving throng; for Calcutta, unlike Delhi, Lucknow, and other cities in the interior, is very British in its habits, and to the English tastes have even the wealthy natives succumbed. The carriages, for example, which now pass in review are such as may be seen daily in Hyde Park, while the harness and saddles are English all over; so much so, indeed, is all this the case, that as we stand and see the long line of horsemen and equipages go by, we wonder much how very un-Indian it all looks.

The English portion of the crowd are both in carriages and on horseback. Observe the pale and emaciated forms of many reclining in their luxurious chariots, telling plainly that the burning clime of Hindostan is no congenial home for them; while the radiant complexions and blooming cheeks of a few fair girls on horseback announce a but recent arrival in the tropics. All are not, however, of these two classes; some who have been long in India look well and strong enough, though, even in their case, the olive-tinted complexion plainly bespeaks their protracted abode.

It was known in Calcutta by telegram, on the day of which we write, that the overland steamer would arrive that evening. She had been telegraphed from the different stations on the river as she passed up, and sunset was the time they awaited her above Garden Reach, the point where the overland vessels lie. As the way to Garden Reach is but a continuance of the road or course by the river-side, many of the crowd before us are now on their way to the steamer to see the new arrivals, to stare at them as Anglo-Indians always *do* stare at anybody fresh from home, and to pick up any stray scraps of news.

It is with a party standing on the deck of the vessel, some five minutes after she had been made fast to the quay, that we have now to do. They are three in number, and two of them we know—Mr. and Mrs. Peters, whom we left on the boar-hunting field in January last; but the third, a young English girl about seventeen years old, we have not seen before; still the reader will guess her, and rightly, to be Marion Paris, who, agreeably to the request of her guardian, Edgington, has just arrived from England.

"There's no occasion, Miss Paris, to take more with you than the carpet-bag you have in your cabin," said Mrs. Peters. "All your other luggage will come naturally to-morrow. You must introduce me, however, to the chaperon you had on your way from England, that I may thank her, in the name of Captain Edgington, for her kindness. I'm so glad we were here in Calcutta to receive you. You know we are to go up country together, and drop you at Dinapore. Mr. Peters and myself go further, on to Cawnpore, where he has been lately appointed. See, there is our carriage, and we can drive home whenever you are ready. Will you get the few things you want out of your cabin, and give them to my ayah,* who'll go down there with you, and we'll await you here."

"I shall not be a moment," answered Marion Paris, with a smile, as she tripped down the ladder, or staircase, to the lower deck.

"How very pretty, is she not, Edmund?" said Mrs. Peters, turning to her husband.

"Yes," he replied; "she's pretty and handsome both; and really I know not which is the better term for her, the two qualities are so blended."

"Captain Edgington told us in his last letter," observed Mrs. Peters, "that she was thought pretty at home, and I expected to see a pretty girl, like one sees every day in England; but she's much more than pretty—she's downright beautiful."

"Hush! here she comes up the stairs again," Mr. Peters remarked, as Marion ascended with a young lady but very little older than herself, and advanced to where they stood.

"Here is the lady, Mrs. Peters, who has kindly taken charge of me, and brought me safely all the way from Southampton. Mrs. Campbell—Mrs. Peters. She could not have done it alone, I'm sure, matronly as she looks," added Marion, with a merry smile, a moment later, when the introduction was completed, "for I was very refractory more than once; but luckily she has had Mr. Campbell to help her."

"I assure you, Mrs. Peters, I did not willingly undertake the charge," said Mrs. Campbell, laughing; "for

* Lady's maid or nurse, for they perform both offices.

truly I did not think my age warranted it. However, Mrs. Edgington, who brought Miss Paris on board at Southampton, begged me to do it; so I agreed at last, and threw all the responsibility on my husband."

"Whom we bored to death between us, I am sure," added Marion, putting her arm fondly round Mrs. Campbell's waist. "Here he comes, Mrs. Peters, to tell you how glad he is to get rid of me."

A few minutes later, Marion having taken her place in the carriage with Mr. and Mrs. Peters, drove off; but not before the young girl had extracted a faithful promise from her late chaperons that they would let her know the next day, at the very latest, where she might find them.

"And so this is Calcutta," said Marion, as they turned the angle of Fort William, and the city lay before her. "It is really very beautiful. Do you know, it seems like a dream my being out here," she added, pressing her hand to her eyes. "I've thought of it, and dreamt of it, too, so much."

"The dream is realized at last," observed Mr. Peters; "and I truly hope India will not disappoint your expectations."

"Oh, I'm sure it will not," replied Marion; "at least, I think not. It is all so new, so strange, it will take me two or three years before I've done wondering, and then I shall be—— Oh, tell me!" she exclaimed, breaking off suddenly, "what's that large black box those men are carrying on a long pole? See, the side is a little open; and how strange—there's a black man in it!"

"A palankeen — have you never heard of them?" asked Mr. Peters.

"Dear me, yes. It's what people travel in, out here, is it not. How I should like to try one—it must be such fun."

"That you can easily do, when you will," said Mrs. Peters, smiling; "but I doubt your liking it much, at least for a long journey. I travelled once, myself, seven days and seven nights dâk, that is in a palankeen, and was very sick of it, I assure you, before it was over."

"Well, my first shall be a shorter trip," said the beautiful girl. "How do we go to the place where my guardian, Captain Edgington, is?"

"By one of the river steamers," Mrs. Peters answered. "You'll enjoy that, I'm sure, for you'll see some fine scenery, and that noble river the Ganges."

"Do we go on the Ganges all the way?"

"No; this is the Hoogly, and we pass up it into the Ganges. At other times of the year the steamers go another way, through the Sunderbunds, as there is not water enough higher up this river."

"Shall we see many alligators? They say the Ganges is full of them."

"Dozens of them, I've no doubt. Did you see none coming up from the Sandheads?"

"I believe two or three were seen, but I did not see them. What fun it will all be—when shall we start?"

"In about a week, I think. Can you ride?"

"Yes—no—that is, not well; but I long to learn to ride better."

"We'll ride together while you are here," said Mrs. Peters. "I've a nice quiet Arab for you."

"How *very* nice. I have a habit. Tell me, have you ever seen Arthur's wife—I mean Mrs. Edgington?"

"Yes! We saw her at Dinapore, where they now are," Mrs. Peters answered.

"Is she a nice person? Shall I like her? I do so long to see her, and yet am almost afraid. I *want* to love her very much."

"Which she'll allow, no doubt," said Mr. Peters laughingly, and thinking it no great hardship to be loved by the charming speaker. "We neither of us knew much of her, and so cannot tell you much. She's generally thought very beautiful."

"Oh, that I knew. Is she glad I'm coming?"

"I'm sure she must be," answered Mr. Peters; "but I've not seen her since Captain Edgington wrote home for you."

"See there, Miss Paris," said Mrs. Peters, "that's our house across the plain—the one with the carriage standing at the door; at least it's where we are staying with some friends."

"Please don't call me Miss Paris. I long to be called Marion again; and surely, as you have charge of me, you may do so."

"Well, Marion it shall be," said Mrs. Peters, taking the young girl's hand in hers. "Now, I'm going to be inquisitive, and ask you your age?"

"Seventeen! Should you have guessed me to be as much?"

"I think so. You are tall, too, for your age: why you are nearly as tall as I am! But here we are at home. Now remember, though it's not my house, it belongs to a very dear friend of mine, who will be as delighted as we are to have you, and you must manage to feel quite at home as soon as you can."

"Oh that I'm sure I shall; you are so very, *very* kind," replied Marion, as she stepped out of the carriage and stood among the crowd of white-turbaned servants, who flocked around to render assistance, and to see the new Missee Baba* just arrived from England.

When the party had passed in, and before the carriage drove round to the stable, the syces and others left outside remarked, in no measured terms, on the beauty of the new arrival.

"Koob soorut!"† said an old white-haired and

* Young lady. † Very beautiful.

white-bearded servant—"fit for Mahomed's paradise The English girls are many of them angels, but I'v never seen such perfection as this before."

"What word is that?" said another. "She i certainly beautiful, but *our* Missee Baba is quite a good!"

"May-be, may-be," replied the old man; "but thi one seems not to belong to earth. Did you see the golde hair on her head—the rays of the morning sun are nc brighter; and then her eyes — I'm an old man, but could not look at them long."

"Here, Mehemet Ali!" called out an ayah, as sh came outside, "the sahib* wants you; and Ramada go for me into Raneemoody Gully† and call my sister' daughter. The mem sahib‡ says she can be ayah t the new Missee Baba."

This disturbed the conclave and the discussion. Th carriage drove off, and the servants went about thei several duties in the house, with the noiseless steps fc which the natives are so famous.

If the reader will be as quiet in his movements a they are, he shall accompany us, when it is once fairl dark, into Marion's bedroom, where, with the help c the new ayah, she is preparing for dinner.

A greater contrast between two beings could not we be conceived, than that presented by the two girls. Nc that the young Hindu damsel was wanting in person charms: she was, as many of her class are, very pretty but it was altogether a diminutive beauty, a beaut that would not stand the march of time, a beaut which, young as she was—fifteen years old—was the in its zenith, and would fade from that hour. On th other hand, the English girl, tall for her age, was ju bursting into womanhood; and lovely as she was, needed no prophet to foretell that her beauty woul

* The master. † A street or lane.
‡ The lady—the mistress.

increase day by day, and gradually put on the developed and luxurious character, in the want of which, perhaps, lay its only present defect. The ivory whiteness of her skin, as over her bare neck and shoulders fell, in massive and lazy folds, the golden hair which the ayah tended, stood out in startling contrast to the dark but beautifully moulded arm which the Hindu girl placed upon it; while her face, as reflected in the glass, with its large swimming dark-blue eyes, smiling mouth, pearly teeth, and wondrously perfect Grecian profile, startled her young attendant by its excess of beauty and contrast to her own dark visage, as, in the discharge of her duties, she saw it suddenly reflected by the side of her own in the mirror.

The young ayah could both speak and understand a little English; and when Marion saw her start, as their eyes met in the glass, she said,—

"What's the matter, you are not frightened, are you?"

"No; I only jump because I never before see such beautiful face as Missee Baba got."

"Oh, that's all, is it?" laughed out Marion. "I expect, ayah, you are beginning your flattery early. Now, you need not be so long doing my hair; I should have done it in half the time myself."

"Missee Baba's hair very much and very long; not easy do quickly. Nearly finish, however."

Marion resisted all the ayah's entreaties to let her put some ornament on her head; and the simple toilet completed, sat down on the bed, under the waving punkah, chatting with the Hindu girl until the dinner-bell sounded.

We will not follow her down stairs, or dwell on her short stay in Calcutta; for other and more momentous scenes demand our attention. Suffice it to say, that the week passed quickly. Marion rode with her kind friend Mrs. Peters every morning, went with her to Government House, and one or two evening parties, half turned the heads of a dozen would-be lovers, was made more of than she had ever been before in her life, and left the City of Palaces, thinking that, "putting those dreadful mosquitoes and nasty prickly heat aside, Calcutta was great fun."

## CHAPTER XIV.

MARION PARIS—DINAPORE—CASTE—THE MARCH.

THREE months have flown. It is New-Year's Day, the first day of blood-stained 1857—that year eventful in scenes which have thrilled the hearts of thousands with horror; which have brought mourning and deep, deep sorrow to many an English hearth, awaking also the indignation of the civilized world. Tragedies so terrible that tongue cannot describe them; cruelties so fiendish that very devils must have perpetrated them; suffering, the recital of which makes the blood run cold;—these, all these, did the sun of India look down upon before the close of that year; for over and over, and over again, were they enacted on Hindostan's burning plains.

At this point in our tale we would wish to pause. Hitherto we have pursued our way over comparatively smooth waters; and we know not how we shall succeed now that we are about to enter the stormy seas in which the remainder of our history lies. Whatever little powers of delineation we possess may be utterly at fault, when we once tread on this, to us, hitherto untrodden ground; when we are called upon to portray the hopes, the feelings, the fears, of those who, though living, had death constantly before them,—not death alone, *that* were not so fearful to contemplate; but death rendered terrible by hideous torture, by protracted suffering, by dishonour. Oh! for the pen with power to describe all this—to depict it on these pages in its dreadful reality—without exaggeration, without colouring on our part, to describe the scenes as they really occurred; and let the reader, in perusing details of one act in that dreadful drama, appreciate in some degree the horrors of the whole.

We are, perhaps, somewhat anticipating events. It is only the first day of the new year, 1857. All India is at peace, and to all appearance likely to continue so. Time enough when the cloud bursts upon us; we have yet a quiet interval to pass through.

But we must "hie back" before we can proceed. A merry party were Mr. and Mrs. Peters, with Marion Paris, on their journey up country to Dinapore, which took some eight or ten days to accomplish. It was impossible not to be cheerful when in contact with the charming Marion: full of life and spirits, she appeared to be endowed with an extra stock for the express purpose of bestowing portions on her companions; and, fresh to everything herself, she gave freshness to every subject under discussion; and interested the listener in her *naïve* views, however erroneous they might be.

Marion was, in every sense, new to the world. The calm, retired life she had hitherto led, quite precluded any knowledge of the evil passions which often actuate mankind in the struggle for life, power, and riches; so that, knowing little or nothing of the worst side of human nature, and the limited experience she *had* attained being all in favour of her theory, she could not understand, nor would she believe, that wickedness was the prevailing attribute of her fellow-creatures, to be looked for and suspected under every fresh action or phase of existence.

Marion, on the contrary, believed that good preponderated over evil, as vastly as happiness exceeded misery on earth. Nor can we blame the grounds of her belief; for it found birth, not in her experience alone, but also in the deep well of charitable feeling she possessed; and what good, what excellence can exist in mortal without that Godlike attribute? Marion Paris, in truth, was charity itself; while deploring faults in others, she did not harshly judge,—her first impulse was to wonder if, under the same circumstances, she would herself have fallen; her second, to think of any palliating circumstances that existed. Enthusiastic on the score of religion, her worship was not one of form and ceremony, but a child-like devotion to the Giver of all good, which palpably influenced her actions and her intercourse with others. But (with Mrs. Edgington in England, from whom she had received her religious education) she could not see why religion should ever beget dissension, much less the spiritual pride which vaunts itself on its own excellence, and casts out as unworthy all who follow not the same path.

Her young heart, keenly alive to the sorrows of others, would sustain much unkindness itself before it rebelled, and then would forgive as quickly as it had been slow to take offence. In short, to sum up the more prominent points of Marion's character in a few exquisitely beautiful lines, she seemed to have attained and realized the state prayed for in the immortal words of Pope:—

> "Let not this weak unknowing hand
> Presume thy bolts to throw,
> And deal damnation round the land
> On each I judge thy foe.
>
> "If I am right, thy grace impart,
> Still in the right to stay;
> If I am wrong, O teach my heart
> To find that better way!
>
> "Teach me to feel another's woe,
> To hide the fault I see;
> That mercy I to others show,
> That mercy show to me."

And truly if the mercy of Heaven were meted out to this young girl according to her exercise of the attribute on earth, then need not Marion Paris fear to stand before her Maker.

We have been led into describing the character of this charming girl, whom we now declare to be our heroine. We had not intended this; the character would, we thought, require no description—it would declare itself as the tale proceeded. So we thought; and we should have acted consonantly, had not diffidence stepped in and made us doubt our powers to effect this, by far more difficult, mode of delineation. On the other hand, to state the character (always present as it is to our mind's eye) in so many words, was easy enough; and, anxious not to fail in doing justice to a being whose excellence requires an abler pen than ours to portray, we chose the easier, and probably more successful course.

Well, to "hie back" once more. A merry party, as we have said, were our heroine with Mr. and Mrs. Peters on their river journey up to Dinapore. Mr. Peters was in good spirits, as he had been appointed to a higher position at Cawnpore, whither he now wended his way, than he had yet held in Behar and Bengal. Mrs. Peters was happy in the elevation of her husband, happy in the acquisition of a friend in Marion, whom she already loved dearly, and, more than all, happy in thinking that four years' more work for "her dear Edmund," with the increased allowance which the post he was to fill at Cawnpore would give him, and they might both leave India for good, to pass the rest of their lives at home, in the society of their children—three in number—whom they had left in England, on return from furlough, five years ago.

Why Marion was happy we cannot say,—she was always happy, the dear girl,—and then, we had forgotten, she was soon to see her guardian Edgington—"her dear Arthur," whom she loved with the same feeling of attachment, mingled with respect, she entertained for him when they parted nine years before.

Thus all three were happy, and, as we have said, it was a happy journey until its termination, when Edgington warmly greeted his charming *protégée*. Her delight at the meeting was great,—she had dreamt of it nightly ever since she left Calcutta; and now, when she looked at Edington's somewhat careworn face, and, with her old fond manner, declared he was very little changed, and she should have known him again anywhere, our poor hero's eyes filled with tears, as he involuntarily contrasted her kind and affectionate ways with the icy influences he had been subject to since marriage.

"This is Beatrice, Marion," said Arthur, when he had a little recovered himself.

"Oh, Mrs. Edgington!" exclaimed Marion enthusiastically, though somewhat awed by the stately figure before her. "I *have* so often wished to see you, to know you well, to—to—to—love you, if you will let me. Do I annoy you by saying so?" she continued timidly, conscious of the chilling influence which Beatrice's manner exerted on every one with whom she came in contact.

"Annoy me, by no means; I shall be glad if you *do* love me," Beatrice answered. The words were kind, but no kindness of manner accompanied them—the chilling influence remained unaltered, and poor Marion, disappointed, though she knew not why, turned once more to Edgington.

But little worthy of relation occurred during the two months and a half which succeeded, and which brings us up to the date mentioned, namely, the 1st of January, 1857. Marion, of course, lived during this interval with Edgington and his wife, and, on the whole, passed a happy time. Her affection for her guardian, and his love for her, increased day by day, as continual intercourse revealed to each the many good and amiable qualities of the other. We make use of the words affection and love; but let not the reader suppose that this mutual regard partook on either side of more than what their positions justified. Whether it might have done so under other circumstances, it is idle to inquire;

with Marion, of course, the fact that "dear Arthur," as she still called him, was married, quite precluded the possibility of such a supposition, which indeed was evinced by the ordinary and unrestrained kindness and affection of her manner, from which she would naturally have shrunk, had she not felt that her fondness for her guardian was of a nature which she might freely indulge in. Edgington, on his part, loved Marion dearly, but it was with a continuation of the love he had borne her as a child; and though it is true that he often, in the secret chambers of his heart, drew comparisons between her and his wife, to the, of course, manifest disadvantage of the latter, he always reproached himself the next minute, and was doubly cautious how he allowed his imagination so much liberty in future.

Beatrice held on the even tenor of her way. She was not of a jealous disposition,—it was one of the few advantages of her character; and having become as attached to Marion as her nature permitted, the society of the young girl afforded her pleasure, while a keen interest was excited in the bosom of this passionless woman, in watching the development of a character so entirely the opposite of her own.

Marion had long since given up treating Beatrice with the warmth of manner which was so natural to her to exhibit towards those she loved. Her impulsive nature, which had been checked by Beatrice's coldness, had, almost unconsciously, taken upon itself another tone in her intercourse with her guardian's wife; and though the two lived together in the utmost harmony, no one would have thought, who saw them when alone, what a well of deep feeling, of warm and impulsive affection, existed in the breast of the young girl.

Marion could not also but perceive, though she had long combated the conclusion, that Edgington was not happy with his wife, while the effect that Beatrice's manner had exerted in her own case, did not allow her to remain long ignorant of the cause. Sincere and deep pity for her guardian accompanied the discovery, she fully appreciated his kindly and loving disposition, and realized in all its bitterness the sorrow he must have gone through ere he too had attained to the cold and careless manner which, as we have before explained, he now adopted towards his wife. Learning these things did not increase Marion's affection for Beatrice; but, as we have before said, she was supremely charitable, and thus while, from that time, her pity for Edgington made her interest in him all the stronger, she thought, on the other hand, there might possibly be much that she did not know of, many palliating circumstances for Beatrice,—anyhow, the very nature of her guardian's wife seemed cold, and therefore she ought to be pitied. "At all events," thought Marion, when she found that, in spite of these excuses, she still blamed Beatrice, "at all events, I must not constitute myself a judge in the matter."

Having argued thus, she went on trying to love Beatrice, because she was Edgington's wife, as much as Beatrice would let her, and succeeded so far in breaking the icy bonds around the immovable heart of this passionless woman, that, strange to say, her affection was in some measure returned; in short, Beatrice learnt to love Marion, with the exception of her own mother, better than she had ever loved any one else.

It must not be supposed that the beautiful Marion had been ten weeks in Dinapore, and had, during that time, won no admirers—quite the reverse was the case. She was the talk of the whole place; both at Patna and Dinapore was she allowed to be by far the prettiest girl —the belle of the station; and more than one ball had been given which report said owed its origin to the desire of the giver or givers to see her dance—to be able to look at her for a whole evening.

Edgington's house, in the palmiest of his bachelor days, had never been so besieged; the morning calls were innumerable, so much so that they wearied him, and he often took refuge in his own room, where, with a book, he managed to amuse himself, well aware that when Beatrice and Marion were with his visitors they had all they wanted; perhaps even in some cases one person too much; for among the callers were some who had paid Marion marked attention, and who would, doubtless, have been glad of a *tête-à-tête* interview.

Marion took all this very quietly. She had experienced a foretaste of it during the few days she stayed in Calcutta, and by the present time she had got accustomed to it, had learnt to look on it as a fact which, while it sometimes bored, much oftener amused her; for hitherto, among her admirers, both in red and black cloth, none had been found to touch her heart. Thus, in this atmosphere of admiration of which she was the centre, she buzzed about with glee, having never as yet singed her own wings.

Some of our readers will, perhaps, exclaim, "Then she was not perfection, after all." Quite right. No, Marion Paris was *not* perfection; had she been so, we should not be writing of her, for she could not have existed; and if it be urged, in answer, that we have only hitherto portrayed her good qualities, and said nothing on the other side, we would shortly reply, that the fact of her being woman, a dweller upon earth, at once admits the impossibility of her moral perfection; but it surely is not necessary, therefore, that we should pick her character to pieces—a character in which the salient points were good, the character of a young and joyous girl of seventeen—to find specific faults therein, in order to demonstrate to the reader that we are not describing perfection in Marion Paris.

Such fault, therefore, as any strictly moral person can find with our heroine for allowing, in this light and careless way, attentions from the many, which it would not have been easy to define, and more difficult to check (even had she wished to do so, which, it must be confessed, she did not, for it amused her)—such fault, if fault it be, we freely admit she is chargeable with.

Among Marion's admirers were two officers of Edgington's regiment—Colonel Carstairs and Ensign Hoby. What, Colonel Carstairs again! Why, he was in love with Beatrice. True, but that was a long time ago, a whole twelvemonth; however, we are not bound to find excuses for him, and need only state the fact. It was very strange that a man of the colonel's age, who had spent his life raving against women and marriage, who had always shunned a petticoat, who had till quite lately plumed himself on his freedom and escapes from the toils laid for him by the fair sex, should, all within one little twelvemonth, fall in love with two girls, one after the other—girls, too, neither of whom laid any toils for him at all, but into whose chains he had rushed a willing captive; nay, more, either of whom he would at the time willingly have married, thus abjuring his former faith and proclaiming to the officers of his regiment, both young and old, that the precepts on the subject of wedlock he had expounded for years were false and hollow. We repeat, it is strange that it was so; but the solution of the mystery must be given by the reader, if haply, being a fair onc, more conversant with the powers, and engines of power, employed by her sex, than we are.

Yes, Colonel Carstairs fell in love with Marion almost at first sight. Unknown to himself, Beatrice's desertion had caused a void in his heart, a void in a newly-formed cavicle, which he was only too ready to fill up again. Marion's beauty attracted him vastly; he was one of those men who, when he married, would certainly marry for beauty. Pondering the matter over, he flattered himself that, with the opportunities he should have for making love, and the excellent position and standing he held in the service, it was not too much to hope for success. "Devil take it," he said aloud in his solitary breakfast-room as he rose from that meal, after imbibing nearly equal quantities of tea and thoughts of Marion Paris during its continuance, "there's *one* great comfort —Edgington can't marry this girl."

Hoby, our old friend Hoby, we have sadly neglected of late; but we must bring him forward again. He was a funny fellow, Hoby, as the reader may remember, with a queer dry humour of his own, and an odd way of saying things, which was very characteristic of the man, as his famous essay on names proved. He was, and still is, senior ensign of the regiment.

Hoby was over head and ears in love with Marion; he was a far-seeing fellow, and discerned in her all the qualities desirable in a wife. He was not sanguine of success, rather the reverse; how could he, an ensign, hope to win where his colonel wooed. Still he loved on; he thought that he saw that in Marion which would never allow her to marry for position alone,—and though conscious that he was not a captivating man, in either appearance or address, he knew that woman is not always won by those qualities. Still, his hope was small; but he clung to it, for he loved deeply, and its indulgence had become a necessity.

The heart of Marion, as we have said, was still her own, but in Hoby's society she found pleasure. His keen sense of the humorous amused her; his manly and honest views interested her; his sagacity and penetration caused her to respect him; and above all, for the possible success of Hoby's suit, the absence of all vanity, the conviction he continually gave her that self was not his god, made her *like* him; though beyond that point she had not yet advanced.

Such was the position of affairs at the date this chapter opened. The relief of the Bengal army,—that is to say, the destination of those regiments to change their stations, as usual, during the cold weather, had been published the November preceding, and, amongst others, the 99th N.I. was ordered to Cawnpore, when relieved by another corps which was now daily expected. Preparations for the march being now completed, tents in order, and the necessary carriage obtained, they only waited the arrival of the relieving regiment to start.

On a bright morning in the early part of January they left the station. The parade-ground was covered with hackeries,* laden with the sepoys' baggage, as the regiment, with the officers at its head, commenced the march. When still in the neighbourhood of cantonments,—in fact, until they had passed Doudpore, one of the Dinapore suburbs, the officers marched at the heads of their companies, while the band and colours preceded the regiment, the former playing the appropriate tune of "The Girls we left behind us." But once fairly on the road, the regiment was halted, the officers fell out, mounted their horses, strict discipline as to the manner the men marched was relaxed, and the 99th native infantry proceeded leisurely on its first day's march towards Cawnpore.

"We shall be at our ground by ten o'clock," said Edgington to Colonel Carstairs, by whose side he rode, "though we were somewhat later than you ordered in leaving Dinapore. However, things never go quite right the first day of a march."

"No," answered the colonel; "it takes three or four days for men and animals to shake into their places. I am sure we shall find some of the carts that went on last night on the road; they were so cruelly heavily laden."

"Yes, some of the mess-hackeries particularly. I saw one or two starting late yesterday evening, and I am quite sure their burdens will have to be reduced by one half within the next day or two."

"Indeed; those were the carts with the breakfast-things; it will be a nuisance if they are not up in time. I think the mess-breakfast on a march is very delight-

* Native carts.

ful, for one always sits down with a good appetite. I hope you have a good hackery to send on at night; but if at any time all is not ready in your tent, bring the ladies, and come yourself to our mess-breakfast."

"I thank you," replied Edgington; "but my carts are lightly laden, and will, I am sure, be always up by the breakfast hour. I do wish we had camels here for carriage, as they have sometimes in the North-west."

"I wish so too. What a difference it makes; with camels you can keep everything in camp till within an hour of the time you start yourself, and yet find all on the new ground before you."

"Yes, rather different to these horrid creaking hackeries, which must start at nine or ten o'clock the night before, to be up in time. Look at that thing," continued Edgington, as they passed one of those wretched apologies for carts drawn by two large black buffaloes; "it doesn't move more than two miles an hour, and the wheels on their wooden axles make noise enough to be heard that distance. Bad as bullocks are for carriage, they are better than these lethargic buffaloes."

"In hot weather especially," remarked the colonel, "for buffaloes can't stand the sun; besides, they must have water every mile or two. They are stronger than bullocks; but that's their only advantage, for they don't even move as fast."

"There's nothing like elephants for carriage," said Edgington; "you have then always your tents and baggage with you, and can stop when and where you like; besides, you are quite independent of roads. I've been on one or two shooting expeditions in Bengal, when we moved in that way from place to place, and enjoyed it vastly."

"'Tis indeed very enjoyable; and an elephant carries such an immense load that you want no more than two. It's not very expensive either to a man who moves about much; for though a good shikaree* elephant costs a lump of money, the baggage-beasts are not dear. You paid a thousand rupees for your elephant, did you not, Edgington? He's worth all the money I think."

"I believe he is; but I shall know more when I've seen him stand a tiger's charge. The mahout† declares, however, that he never flinches."

"I suppose Mrs. Edgington and Miss Paris will ride him on the march?" asked the colonel.

"Sometimes, I imagine; but they both like horseback better. They will ride their horses on the march to-day, and catch us up, I dare say, before we have gone much farther."

"Ladies enliven a march vastly," observed the colonel, "if they will only ride with the regiment, as they ought to do, and not trundle along in those antiquated palankeens. Don't you think so, Bruce?" he added to his second in command, who joined them.

"Certainly; my wife, you see, is an example to all others: there she is on ahead," replied the major.

"So she is, I declare," remarked Edgington, laughing; "why she must have left before the regiment."

"She did so," said Bruce; "we have marched a great deal together, and it's not often she's behind."

"I don't see why she should ride on there all alone, however," said Edgington, as he put spurs to his horse and galloped forward.

* * * * * *

"Horrid work this rear-guard," muttered Hoby to himself, as, about three or four miles behind the regiment, he plodded on his way, all alone, at the head of some twenty or thirty sepoys. "It's one of the bores of marching, and I really think the duty might be given

* Hunting. † Elephant-driver.

to a native officer. Nice prospect I have before me to-day," he continued, as the bullocks in a hackery—which his men had been urging on by twisting their tails, or poking them with their bayonets—stopped short, and bending down their heads, let the cross-bar of the hackery resting on their necks slip over their horns; "I'm sure this cart alone can never get up to camp before three or four o'clock, and some will very likely be even later. If I get there in time for the mess-dinner, I shall think myself lucky. Come, you gharry-wan,* get on. Your bullocks don't move a coss † in two hours."

"Not my fault, sahib; cart much too heavily laden," replied the driver, who, perched on the pole between the two bullocks' flanks, urged them forward every instant, by squeezing the small of their backs between his fingers and palms.

"Then get down, you rascal; why the devil should you add your weight?"

"Bullocks go better when I sit there, sahib," answered the Hindu, obeying the order, however, and getting down as he spoke.

The rear-guard is a small party left behind, under charge of a European officer, to see all the baggage-carts arrive safely at the next encamping-ground. The duty is an unpleasant one; for hackeries or gharries do not travel quickly, and the guard is supposed not to leave any behind. If the duty is strictly carried out,—and it is so in some regiments,—the guard does not often arrive in camp until dark; but most commandants, during a peaceful march like the present, merely require the European officer on duty to see all the carts off the old encampment-ground, and leaving behind a few of his men, to follow the regiment with the others. Colonel Carstairs required no more generally; but this

* Cart-driver.

† The general measurement of distance in Hindostan, equal to about two English miles.

was the first march out of the station, and he had thought it better to order the whole guard, with its officer, to remain behind.

Hoby voted the rear-guard a nuisance when he spoke just now; but he would have given a large portion of the current month's pay to be rid of the duty and free to ride on, when, a few minutes later, Mrs. Edgington and Miss Paris on horseback overtook him. They both looked beautiful, with the colour the early morning exercise gave them; but Hoby had eyes for the latter alone.

"What are you doing here, Mr. Hoby?" asked Mrs. Edgington, as they pulled up; "the regiment must be three or four miles ahead."

"Enjoying the pleasant duty called rear-guard," he replied, gazing at Marion's beautiful face and figure, rendered more fascinating than usual by her riding-dress.

"Oh, duty is it?" said Beatrice, touching her horse with the whip; "then we must not interrupt you. Now Marion, a good canter."

"I'm tired, and would rather walk a little bit; besides, I want Mr. Hoby to explain what this duty is," said Miss Paris.

"The details will scarcely interest you," Hoby replied, with a gratified smile. "I have to see that all the carts arrive safely at the encamping-ground. I did not know you purposed riding on the march; I hope you will often do so; it is surely better than the unpleasant motion of an elephant."

"I think so too," said Marion; "and I enjoy a ride through a strange country above all things. Why is there a sepoy with every one or two carts on ahead? Last night, also, when a number went out of the station, I remarked the same thing."

"To take care of the things in the cart, and to prevent both cart and driver bolting. Generally speaking, when a regiment marches, the civil power furnishes carriage, by pressing a number of drivers, with their hackeries, into the service: they are not over and above well paid, would, as a rule, rather stop in their villages, and are therefore apt to decamp if they find an opportunity."

"What a shame," Marion exclaimed, "to press them at all!—it's quite against our English ideas of liberty."

"So are many other things in this country," Hoby remarked; "but no remedy has yet been found for them. You must also remember that the natives of Hindostan, as most Asiatics, almost *like* to feel the iron hand of power on their necks; at least one would think so by their conduct; for when they have it not, they get discontented and turbulent."

"They are strange creatures the natives," observed Marion; "it seems to me that I understand them less and less every day."

"So much did I find that the case during the first six months after my arrival in India," said Beatrice, "that I wisely concluded it would be well to remain satisfied with such knowledge as I possessed at the end of that time. I have, consequently, long since given up studying their whims and habits. As for what they call caste, it is quite incomprehensible."

"Do *you* know anything about it, Mr. Hoby; tell us what is caste?" asked Marion, after a short pause.

"I can easier tell you what it is *not*," Hoby replied; "for to detail what it *is* would take some hours, and even then much would be left untold. It is not sense; it is not progress in the direction of knowledge and civilization; it does not beget charity or benevolence to others; it does not either create or increase religious feeling, for such religious forms as it enjoins are most childlike, unmeaning, and debasing; it does not check vice in any shape; it does not inculcate virtue, in our acceptation of the term;—shortly, it does good to no one, while it has, doubtless, been one great cause why the Hindu mind has, during many past centuries, made but little advance towards the attainment of even a proper appreciation of morality."

"What a strange thing it is! If it has all these disadvantages, why is it followed—at least, what are the inducements it holds out to its votaries?" asked Marion.

"It is supposed by the Hindus to be of divine origin; they receive its mandates with their mother's milk, and we all know how difficult it is to unlearn what we were taught as babes. Besides, with all its absurdities, caste, with its accompaniments, is a Hindu's religion: he knows no other. According to the caste he holds in this world, will be his abode in the world to come; and believing this, as they do, we cannot wonder at their jealousy regarding it."

"Why do they think it is of divine origin?" asked Beatrice.

"Because their religious books state it to be so. The story goes that four races of men proceeded from the Creator at the creation; and, according to the parts of the Creator's body from which they sprung, are their honourable or dishonourable states in this life and the life to come. The Brahmins, the highest caste, are said to have come out of the mouth of Brahma, the creator; the lowest class, called Sudra, from his feet; the two intervening classes from his arms and legs; and, according to caste theory, all mankind owe their origin to one of these four classes, or to marriages between different castes, which is, however, strictly forbidden. The Hindus also believe that the descendants of these four classes are perfectly distinct and separate to this day, and that though each class has been divided, and subdivided, into perhaps hundreds of other castes or sects, each of the divisions now existing may still be traced back in all purity to one of the four original fountain-heads from which all mankind are descended."

"Tell us more about it," said Beatrice; "it is interesting."

"I don't know very much of the matter," said Hoby; "I believe it would take almost a life's study to master the subject; but the little information I have is at your service. As you may both opine, from what I have already said, *caste* cannot be purchased, cannot be attained by good deeds, cannot be bestowed by any earthly potentate, is not transferable—in short, can be possessed by hereditary descent alone. The Shastras, or religious writings of the Hindus, lay down certain rules and ordinances, agreeably to which each *caste* is to conduct itself. These are, however, generally speaking, confined to the most trivial and childlike forms and manner of doing different things. They relate, firstly, to the hereditary occupation (which is supposed to belong to each particular caste and to descend regularly from father to son); secondly, to the rites and ceremonies of marriage,—the bride being always, I may observe, of the same caste as the bridegroom; thirdly, to the union and communion of each caste, and the mysterious sympathy this exercises in that caste circle; and fourthly, to the selection, manner of cooking, and eating food. There are also other subjects on which directions are given, but the above are perhaps the principal points,—at least, they are all I remember. If any of these regulations are transgressed, the caste is broken: once broken, the casteless being is an outcast in every sense of the word. His own family will not recognize him, eat with him, or have any social intercourse with him whatever; never eligible to mix with those of other castes, and now thrown out by his own, he is truly alone in the world, with the conviction always present to his mind that his eternal state is compromised by his error. Strange to say, however (unless when the delinquent is very obnoxious to the heads of his caste circle), a few rupees expended on a 'burra kanna,' or feast, will reinstate him, whatever the fault may be he has committed. A greater absurdity, if possible, exists in the fact that if a man does a thing contrary to his caste, but is not seen to do it, or if seen, it is not reported, his caste does not suffer, nor is his happiness in a future state endangered. The penalties being, however, heavy which follow a known transgression of the rules of caste, it is only natural to suppose that the votary of its rites is responsible for his free actions alone; in other words, that by following out strictly the ordinances given him he is safe, and that he can only fall by wilful transgression. Not so at all; this would be much too simple and just to suit the anomalies, the absurdities of caste principles. The Hindu may lose his caste by an accident, by being forced to do what he resists to the death. For instance, if any one unseen puts a bit of beef into a Hindu's food, and he, poor fellow, eats his dinner not knowing it is there, his caste is gone; or if a Hindu is forcibly seized and *made* to do anything contrary to the rules of his caste,—that is, not forced to do it by threats or fear of punishment, but by actual brute force, so that he can in no way help himself,—still is his caste destroyed; as the fact that he acted against his will in this matter, or in ignorance, as in the first case I supposed, is in neither position accepted as an excuse."

"It does, truly, appear to be a wonderful institution," said Marion. "I remember once going accidentally near a native when he was cooking his food, and he threw it all away."

"Yes," said Hoby, "your presence polluted it, Miss Paris. The Hindus are no respecters of persons in all caste questions; but this same man, who threw away his dinner because your shadow fell on it, would probably be quite willing to perform the most menial office at your bidding. Such are the anomalies of caste."

"But surely," said Beatrice, "as marriages *have* sometimes taken place between beings not of the same caste, the four lines and their branches must have got more or less mixed."

"Most certainly they have, and most certainly is it opposed to caste rules that it should be so. But the truth is, this and so many other regulations have been formerly, aud are now daily transgressed, that purity of caste exists in the mind of the simple Hindu alone. Nevertheless, though the fact is so, though no caste is really pure, and no one can say from which of the four sources many of the present castes spring; theoretically it is supposed to be otherwise, and Hindus on this and many other subjects believe, what a very small exercise of their reasoning powers would show them to be false."

"You said each caste had a distinct hereditary occupation—was that so from the beginning?" asked Marion.

"Supposed to have been so by the credulous Hindus, who will believe anything. There were by tradition, as I said before, originally four lines or races of men proceeding from the Creator; namely, the Brahmins, the Kshatria, the Vaisya, and the Sudra. The first were at the head of all creation, and destined alone to fill the offices of priests and judges. They were also the advisers of kings, and destined to perform a few other very high functions. The second were all warriors. The third were the industrious class, to be employed on tillage, manufactures, and the like; while the fourth class were the menial race. As time went on, each of these four branches divided into several others, and these again intó more numerous divisions, which in their turn were again subdivided; so that at the present day the different castes of Hindus number some hundreds, and it is needless to observe that they have not strictly kept to the hereditary employment allotted by tradition to their forefathers. In fact, so much is the supposed original order of things upset, that Brahmins may now often be found performing menial offices for us Europeans, and even for the fourth class, or Sudras, who, in spite of the hereditary bondage of slavery, or rather servitude, assigned to them, have in many cases attained to honour, wealth, and distinction in our days, and in olden times I believe to even royalty itself."

"How do the Hindus get over these stubborn facts?" asked Beatrice.

"As they get over a hundred others which militate equally against all caste traditions—simply by ignoring them, when convenient to do so, or bringing forward some author who sanctions such deviations. The mass of Hindu writings on the subject of caste is very voluminous; some of the writings are pronounced sacred, and all are looked up to with reverence. Many, however, flatly contradict each other; and thus the Hindu, bent on finding an authority for any past or existing state of things, or any caste whim he may have conceived, has not generally to seek in vain."

"Then caste is not the same thing now that it was in olden times?" remarked Beatrice.

"Pardon me, I did not say so at all," resumed Hoby. "Some very old Hindu writings show, on the contrary, that even in those days there were almost as many departures from what are supposed to have been the original and divinely-accorded caste rules as there are now. I believe the almost numberless branches that have sprung from the four parent stocks have ever been, and are even in our day, yearly increasing; so that the whole affair is enveloped in greater confusion *now* than it was *then*: but in its baneful influence, which is really all with which we need concern ourselves, it is much the same to-day as it has ever been."

"Do the lower respect the higher castes? For instance, does a Sudra, or whatever you call it, respect a Brahmin *because* he is a Brahmin?" asked Marion.

"To a certain extent, yes; but very much less so than in olden times. The day was when to incur the curse of a Brahmin was a calamity dreaded by all, for it was supposed to affect both the temporal and eternal welfare of its recipient. Thus no one dared to speak or act against them in any way, and they were free to commit the greatest excesses and crimes. They had also in those times great prerogatives; they were only amenable to the laws in a very mitigated form, and their property was inviolable. All this is, of course, changed nowadays, and they do not therefore command the same respect as formerly; still they are looked up to even now; and this reverence is doubtless somewhat increased by the consideration which I cannot help thinking the Government unwisely pays to caste."

"In what way?" asked Beatrice.

"In many ways," Hoby replied; "none but high-caste men are enlisted as soldiers, and when enlisted, their caste prejudices are recognized, and even fostered. So it is in every branch of the service—the higher a man's caste, the better chance he has of employment under Government. The natives all see this, and it naturally keeps up their reverence for caste pretensions. The sepoys see it also, and it makes them arrogant and often useless; for, on the score of caste, they object to various things which much impairs their value as soldiers. Our recognition of caste is carried farther; for in the jails where criminals are confined, deference is there also paid to it. The prisoners are allowed to have their food prepared in the manner the rules of their caste point out (some time back, before the messing system was introduced, it was much worse), and if accidentally a European has come near it, or they conceive in any other way that it has become tainted, I know cases where their whims have been yielded to and other food supplied. Surely this is a mistake, and in prison discipline at least we should ignore caste altogether."

"I think so too," remarked Beatrice.

"My views in respect of caste are, perhaps, peculiar; at all events, they are opposed to the views of the mass of officers, civil and military, and therefore, mind you,

I give them with all due deference. In my estimation, we have all along made a great mistake in our treatment of caste: its rules and regulations are so undefined, so uncertain, vary so much in each and every caste division, that even were it wise to recognize it in our dealings with natives who voluntarily take on themselves government employ, it would be difficult to do so *only* to the extent really necessary; and therefore we should be, as indeed we are now, daily imposed upon. I doubt, however, *could* we define the necessary limits to which caste compels its votaries to adhere, the wisdom of recognizing it at all. I would, mind you, in no way advocate a crusade against it; this would do infinitely more harm than the course we have hitherto pursued, but I would in every *possible* case ignore its requirements, in *every case* treat low and high caste alike: the former should be as eligible for Government employ as the latter; and with regard to the army, where, perhaps, the greatest difficulty lies, inasmuch as high-caste men, would, at all events at the commencement of this new policy, object to enlist in regiments where low-caste men were entertained, I would have both high and low-caste regiments, treating them, however, in the same way, and showing no favour whatever to the former. Such a course would in a few years do much to lower the estimation caste is held in by the natives themselves, and might eventually—though that day is far distant—abolish it altogether. Another advantage we should derive, and no small one in my opinion, is, that whereas the Bengal army (an army of mercenaries without patriotism, serving their conquerors) is now all of one stamp, with the binding sympathies of high caste running through it,—and surely, therefore, a dangerous force for alien conquerors to maintain,—we should then have an army so constituted that if, from any unforeseen causes, a portion failed us, we might all the more, from that very reason, reckon upon the fidelity of the remainder."

"Upon my word, Mr. Hoby, we have to thank you for an amusing and instructive lecture on this wonderful thing called caste," said Beatrice; "it has taught me much I did not know before. From all you have said, you are, I presume, no admirer of the policy of the East-India Company."

"Pardon me," Hoby replied, "I should be sorry you left me with that impression. The only subject we have discussed is that of caste, and on that point I do not certainly approve of the policy pursued. Had others been brought forward, I should have had much to say in favour of the Honourable Company, who have certainly governed India during a hundred years in a manner that reflects credit on themselves and on our Sovereign."

"Well, Mr. Hoby," remarked Beatrice, "you must reserve your praises of the East-India Company for another time; our horses are now rested; you are so too, I suppose, Marion; so we will canter on and catch the regiment."

"Yes, I am quite ready," said Marion, as she gathered up her reins; "good-bye, and thank you, Mr. Hoby. I hope you will not be long delayed with those nasty carts; they creak enough to drive one mad," she added, as, putting her horse into a canter, she passed a ponderously-laden hackery, which, with its wooden axles, guiltless of oil, made noise enough to be heard half a mile off.

"There she goes," said Hoby half aloud, as he watched the two horsewomen cantering away, "and how different to the other at her side. What a contrast between the two characters! They are both beautiful, certainly; but even there the contrast is not lessened; attractive and repellant beauty differs nearly as much as beauty and its reverse. What a treasure she will be to the man who wins her—oh, that I could be the man!"

We must leave Hoby to finish his soliloquy alone,

and proceed with the two fair riders ahead. They were not long in catching up the regiment, which, no longer marching in sections of companies as when it left the station, now spread over a considerable extent of road, as the sepoys trudged on at their ease. Beatrice and Marion threaded their way through the crowd of soldiers, and a short distance ahead of the regiment came up to the colonel, Edgington, Bruce, and one or two others.

"Delighted to see you, ladies," said the gallant Colonel Carstairs; "always delighted to see you, but especially so in your present guise and positions. It is, I hope, an earnest that we shall often be blessed with your company on the march. I am glad that you both have the good taste to prefer your Arabs' backs to that of the elephant."

"You have caught us earlier than I thought you would," remarked Edgington; "I suppose, though, Marion, you were all anxiety to see what a march was like; or rather, that you both were, for it is equally new to you, Beatrice."

"Early as we are, we should have been up long, long ago," said Marion, "but we took pity on poor Mr. Hoby with the rear-guard, and somehow the conversation turning on the natives and caste, he told us an immense deal about it all."

"Did he?" said Major Bruce; "well, now retail it to us for our benefit; it will help to kill two or three miles of road."

"Bless me, I couldn't repeat one-half he said; besides, I have had enough of caste for a week at least. Oh, I see Mrs. Bruce on ahead; I shall canter on to her, Beatrice. It *is* such fun, this gipsy sort of proceeding, living in tents and marching; only gipsies don't ride generally, and that's the best part of it," she added smilingly to the colonel, as she touched her steed lightly with the whip before starting ahead.

"I'll come on with you, Miss Paris; I want to speak

to Mrs. Bruce," said the colonel, touching his somewhat lethargic charger (the old Cape who ran in the steeple-chase) with the spur.

"Come on, then; but quick. A race, who catches Mrs. Bruce first!" called out Marion, starting off at a gallop, her merry laugh ringing the while through the clear and bracing morning air.

Away they went; but the colonel had no intention of racing with his fair antagonist, so he followed at a sharp gallop, and arrived at the goal in time enough to be laughed at by the merry Marion for his defeat.

Twelve miles accomplished, and they arrived at the encamping-ground. The scene that met both Beatrice's and Marion's eyes was new, and pleased them with its novel and picturesque appearance. The spot chosen was a mango-tope, or grove of those beautiful trees, the thick foliage of which caused a deep and luxurious shade in striking contrast to the glaring day outside. In the fore part of the grove, facing the road, from which it lay some two hundred yards distant, were arranged in line the sepoys' tents, simple affairs enough, of which there was one long one for each company, while immediately behind them the tents of the native officers stood. Deeper in the grove, and studded about without any apparent regularity, were canvas abodes of all sizes and shapes, from the large double-poled mess-tent to the small hill-tent. In fact, whichever way the ladies looked, canvas houses, of different forms and various sizes, appeared; for officers in India, when not on active service, march luxuriously enough, generally with two or sometimes three of these temporary habitations. All these snow-white abodes, placed at different points in the deep shady vistas formed by the mango-trees, gave an idea of camp life which was far from displeasing; for it suggested repose during the noontide heat, and the possibility of being out of doors without a hot sun shining upon you. The encampment abounded also in animation and life; every here and there horses were picketed, carts just arrived were being unladen, cooking in many impromptu fireplaces was in progress, and numbers of servants were running about, getting all ready for the arrival of their masters.

Shortly before arrival, the halt was sounded; men and officers fell into their places, and the band struck up a lively air as the regiment marched up and formed line in front of the grove previous to being dismissed.

"It's a pretty sight altogether, and I've enjoyed this first day's march vastly," said Marion to Edgington, as he helped her to dismount at the door of the splendid tent he had provided as a day-habitation.

"I was sure you would like it; and now we are fairly started for Cawnpore," our hero replied. "I'm as hungry as a hunter; you must have an appetite, too, after your long ride, so come along, dear Marion, and enjoy your first marching breakfast."

## CHAPTER XV.

THE MORNING TEA-PARTY—SHADOWS OF COMING EVENTS—THE BENGAL ARMY.

In the verandah of Edgington's roomy bungalow at Cawnpore, at seven o'clock in the morning, a fortnight or three weeks after the march, were seated a party of ladies and officers enjoying the tea and chat so often indulged in after the morning exercise.

The party, with the exception of Mr. and Mrs. Peters, who brought Marion up to Dinapore, and who were now inmates of Edgington's house until their own was got ready, were all of the 99th native infantry.

Colonel Carstairs, who lost no opportunity of being near Marion; Hoby, who never willingly absented himself from her he loved; Bruce, who enjoyed the society of Edgington's circle,—were all present: for there had been a parade that morning, and our hero, as they passed his bungalow in returning, had asked them to come in.

Beatrice and Marion had just returned from the ride which they daily took, and sat in their riding-dresses, sipping their tea, and looking quite as beautiful as it was their wont to look.

We know few things more pleasant than these early tea-gatherings, so usual in India. People have certainly more ideas in their heads, or at all events express themselves in a fresher strain, during these cool hours than later, when the heat of the day makes talking almost an exertion. Edgington's tea was excellent; the manillas on the table and in the mouths of those who smoked so early were "first chop;" and though there was but one speaker at the moment we introduce the party to the reader, what he said engaged the attention of all.

"A curious circumstance was reported to me this morning," said Mr. Peters, "by a peon * of the kotwalli.† It seems that yesterday the police in the village, on the north-west side of Cawnpore, received from other villages still further on, small chupattees, baked hard, about three inches in diameter. Immediately on their receipt, the policeman of each village baked four or five others, and sent them to all the bustees ‡ in his neighbourhood. My informant told me that two or three of these cakes came to Cawnpore yesterday, were immediately multiplied by the police, and then sent off to all the places around. I heard all this by accident early this morning, and during my ride I met the kotwal § "Hoolas Sing," and asked him what it meant. He with me had heard of it only to-day, and is as much in the dark as I am. He thinks, however, it is very likely something in the shape of a circular connected with the pay of the police,—a kind of round-robin for an increase of wages,—and at all events of no consequence."

"Singular, certainly," said Edgington; "the same thing has occurred elsewhere—at Futtehghur, if I mistake not. There's an account of it in the last *Friend of India* I received. Here, bearer, bring the *Kubber ke khagux* ‖ which is on the table in my room. I wonder what it all means."

"Nothing, probably, or rather nothing that *we* can care about," said Mr. Peters. "It's a funny proceeding, though,—a regular Arabian Nights method of sending news about, is it not, Miss Paris?"

"Quite romantic," answered Marion. "Perhaps each cake had a note hidden inside?"

"A bright idea, but not at all probable," remarked

* Messenger. † Police-office. ‡ Villages or hamlets.
§ Police-officer. ‖ Newspaper, or, literally, paper of news.

Edgington; "for whatever it is, it's meant simply as a sign or token; but here comes the *Friend*. Ah here's the article; shall I read it out?"

"Do, by all means," said several, and Edgington read as follows:—

"One morning towards the end of last month the officials of Futtehgurh were in commotion. From thannah after thannah there arrived little chupattees about two inches in diameter. They were accompanied by all kinds of reports from puzzled thannahdars, and set the European world in a fever of speculation. It appeared that a few evenings previous, a chowkeydar from Cawnpore ordered a chowkeydar in Futtehgurh to make and bake twelve chupattees, such as the one he showed. Two he was to retain; two more were to be given to each of the five nearest chowkeydars. The order was obeyed, and all night long there was running and baking of chupattees. The five obeyed orders also, and distributed their message to twenty-five, and so the affair went on in geometrical ratio, the cakes sweeping over the district at a speed at which no Indian post yet travels. The wave has not stopped yet. It reached Allahabad in a few days, and to all appearances will include the whole of the North-west. Everywhere the police are the instruments of conveyance, and everywhere the police are unable to afford the least clue to the meaning of so strange an effort.

"What does it mean? In France such an occurrence would immediately be attributable to the agency of the hidden leaders of the Marianne. On the Continent, some revolutionary hero would probably be thrown into prison, till he accounted for what he knew nothing about. In India, however, though conspiracies are possible, secret societies are not; and speculation is again at fault. Are all the chowkeydars about to strike for wages? or is anybody trying a new scheme for a parcel-dawk? Is it treason, or a jest? Is there to be an "explosion of feeling?" or only of laughter? Is the chupattee a fiery cross, or only an indigestible edible? a cause of revolt, or only of the cholic? Is the act that of an influential malcontent, or only of a fool? All these suggestions have been offered, and we may add one more to the crowd. The despatch may have been the consequence of a vow made by some policeman, aided by the intense ignorance which distinguishes the force. These speculations, however, afford no light; the only clear fact appearing to be this—the police obey orders without knowing whence they are transmitted. They ought to be prohibited from transmitting signals not authorized by a European."

"What's the date of the paper? By that account, this sign has been through Cawnpore before—ten or twelve days ago at least. Perhaps you misunderstood the peon as to the time, eh Peters?" asked Bruce.

"Misunderstood him?—that's not likely; besides, as I tell you, I saw the kotwal afterwards," Peters replied. "No; what the meaning of it all is, or why it's happened twice in this way, I don't know. But, Edgington, let me see," he continued, stretching out his hand for the paper; "it says here in the *Friend* that the chupattees were sent from Cawnpore *to* Futtehghur. Now this time they are travelling the other way, down here *from* the Futtehghur side. The sign or symbol as it were coming back."

"*The Friend of India* asks what it means, and I think we may do so too," said Edgington. "It's impossible, however, Peters, it can mean anything of consequence, or be a sign understood by all through whose hands it passes; for were it so, the secret could never have been kept."

"I am not so sure of that," remarked Hoby; "it's astonishing how very close the natives can be when they like, and also astonishing how sympathetic caste union will make a secret quite safe even if many are its depositaries."

"Well, whatever it is, it's a mystery at present," Peters remarked, "and a mystery that's likely to continue, as far as I am concerned; for I would not walk very far to know it."

"There we differ," Hoby added. "I would walk from this time till this time to-morrow to learn it—ay, and eat or drink little by the way."

"What, then?" said Peters; "do you think it some mighty affair, some great state secret, handed about by chowkeydars* who can scarcely write their own names, and who would surely not be chosen for such a purpose. Besides, who in John Company's land is to hatch such a secret? Tell me that."

"Your query I cannot answer. I only say, and say again, I'd very willingly walk all to-day in the sun to find it out."

"Hoby, you've got some idea in your head about it," said Colonel Carstairs. "Out with it, man; it will relieve you to get rid of it. I'll swear you *have* some fancy, from the way you answered just now."

"You are right, sir; I have; but I know you'll all laugh, if I tell it," replied Hoby.

"An additional reason, surely, why you should do so, Mr. Hoby," remarked Marion archly; "I like laughing."

"Quite right, Miss Paris," continued the colonel; "besides, if Mr. Hoby is not now *made* to speak, he'll go away with a character for wisdom which, perhaps, after all, he's not entitled to."

"Now, Hoby, it's no use delaying; the company's against you, or, at least, your silence; so make a virtue of necessity," remarked Bruce.

"I think you are right, major," said Hoby; "and as my idea is perhaps worth little, you shall have it without further preface. You all heard the other day of the mutiny at Berhampore—the 19th native infantry, who got an idea into their heads that the new cartridges had pig and bullock fat in them. Is it not possible that this chupattee mystery may be connected with that mutiny?"

A roar of laughter was all the answer he received. It was so loud and long that some little time passed before he could speak again.

"I prophesied you would all laugh; and, see, I am a true prophet. You do not join in the merriment against me, ladies; that is, however, only because you

* Native police.

have not been long enough in India to appreciate the folly of my supposition, and——"

"But Hoby, Hoby," broke in Bruce; "where can be the connection between a mutiny in one of the lower stations in Bengal and this chupattee affair up here?"

"Does the Berhampore mutiny stand quite alone, Bruce? Answer me that," rejoined Hoby.

"Yes; there's been no other. There have been reports,—certainly,—at Barrackpore,—that——"

"Not at Barrackpore alone, Bruce," interrupted Hoby; "but from several stations in the army have reports been bruited about that the sepoys think *something is going to happen;* that they are dissatisfied with this new cartridge; and that, in fact, they are uneasy, unquiet. I have myself a chit* from an officer of the 19th, at Berhampore, written as far back as last January; and *then*, speaking of his regiment, he says, *it is shaky.* The event has shown how shaky it was; and can you—can any other man who knows anything of India, the natives, and caste sympathy—suppose that the 19th stand alone in this business; that the disaffection which caused them to break out is not shared elsewhere? I do not wish to be an alarmist," he continued, as he saw Marion listening intently to what he said, and as he thought, at the same moment, that his colonel might officially disapprove of such sentiments; "I do not wish to be an alarmist, and I dare say the Berhampore mutiny will be the first and last; but when you ask me, Bruce, what possible connection these chupattee messages can have with the Berhampore affair, I answer, that though the mutiny there stands alone, disaffection in the army has not been confined to that station."

"Hoby is right in some things," remarked the colonel; "not that *I* attach any importance to this

* A letter.

chupattee business, or that I think disaffection has spread in the army. The latter is the sort of tale to frighten old women with, and it's never likely to happen with Jack Sepoy, as long as he gets his pay regularly. Besides, if there were any discontent, we should have heard of it from all quarters; for it's impossible a regiment can be disaffected and the officers not know it. We should all laugh, and naturally, at any one who told us the 99th was discontented; and in the same way of the 1st, or any other regiment at Cawnpore. But one thing you said, Hoby, reminded me of a trifling circumstance which occurred last week. The subadar of the grenadier company, Mehu Lall—the fellow with the tremendous long white moustaches—was at my quarters on some duty or another, and after a long preamble—I could not guess what he was driving at—he asked me if it was true that the Government were going to convert all the sepoys to Christianity. It was such an absurd idea, that I nearly tumbled off my chair laughing. Only fancy old Mehu Lall made to subscribe to the thirty-nine articles! I laughed, as I tell you, till I cried again; and at last, I suppose, the old subadar saw the absurdity of the idea himself, and laughed with me. When we could laugh no more, he told me that it was, or rather had been, a current report here; but that, of course, none of the native officers of *our* regiment believed it."

"Did you notice it any further, sir," asked Bruce.

"Dear me, no; what good would *that* do?" remarked the colonel. "A foolish, idle, childish report—the less noticed the better. No, no; Jack Sepoy is easily aroused, but he's just as easily pacified (see the Berhampore case, for example); and whatever his faults are, he's loyal and stanch to the backbone."

"We saw a sepoy of our regiment to-day," remarked Beatrice presently, "who appeared to be quite a different kind of man to the others,—a different caste of face, and a large black beard."

"With such funny, sharp, twinkling eyes," added Marion; "and after a little bit two others with the same sort of faces joined him."

"Sikhs, probably," remarked the colonel. "We have about twenty-five in all. By the Government order we may enlist upwards of one hundred; but I'm not sorry we have no more. They sadly spoil the look of a line, with their long beards by the side of the smooth-faced Brahmin and Rajput. I cannot understand myself how the Government allow them to be enlisted; they are low-caste fellows,—or rather, they've got no caste at all, and many of them in a regiment would, I am sure, demoralize its tone. The spirit of our army is its high caste; destroy that, and you destroy the soldier's self-respect, which is the strongest staff we lean on. Now, good morning, ladies; I should like to sit and chat longer, but this morning I can't. Good-day, Peters; ferret out the chupattee business,—it's your duty to do so; but you'll find, if you do, an illustration of the mountain and mouse fable. Now, old Cape, come near the steps," he continued to his horse, as he was about to mount. "When I was as young as you, Mrs. Edgington, I could spring up without a stirrup. Can do it still, for the matter of that, Miss Paris, for though I *have* been two-and-twenty years in India, I'm still as active as——"

As what, they were not told; for the colonel, as he spoke, wished to illustrate what he asserted, and tried to gain his horse's back by a spring from the verandah steps. He was successful, for he lighted on the saddle; but the Cape, frightened at his master's unwonted activity, started off with a bound, and the sentence was left unfinished. Our gallant colonel had him in command, however, before he reached the compound-gate, when, bowing to the party in the verandah, he passed out on the road.

Beatrice then turned to Hoby, and said, "Do you remember the lecture on caste, Mr. Hoby, you gave

Miss Paris and myself on the march? Colonel Carstairs, I see, holds a very different opinion."

"Our colonel has, of course, much more experience than I have," Hoby replied.

"I cannot say that *I* quite agree with all the colonel said," remarked Bruce. "Regarding the Sikhs, for instance, I *know* they are good soldiers, and I very much doubt any natives of Hindostan fighting, without European leaders, as the Sikhs fought in both the Sutlej and Punjab campaigns. The Khalsa army was, without exception, the most formidable enemy we have encountered in India since our rule began. I have no doubt, therefore, it would be well to entertain a large number of these men in the Bengal regiments. The Sikh, it is true, has no caste,—the only superstition of the kind he holds is a veneration for cows, which is, as you all know, common to the Hindu,—but he is, perhaps, all the more useful on that account, and the sepoys do not look down on him as they would on a low-caste man; they rather, on the contrary, regard him as they do one of us—a being of a different race, out of the caste pale. The fact, therefore, of a large number of Sikhs in a regiment would never prevent high-caste Hindus joining its ranks."

"I would even go farther than you," added Hoby. "I am sure the Sikh is a better soldier than either the Hindu or Mahommedan of Hindostan. Better in every way; superior in physical strength, more ready to do rough work, he will handle the spade as willingly as the musket; he requires none of the absurd preparation to cook and eat his food which the Hindu does; he will go anywhere, fight anything, live and mess with Europeans, if required to do so; and, more than all, he does *not* hate us as the Mahommedans do (conceal it as they will); nor is he bound by caste sympathy like the Hindus, which bond of union amongst the latter is, I sometimes think, the most dangerous element in our army."

"But as this bond of union, as you call it, does not bind the Mahommedans and Hindus together," remarked Edgington, "I cannot see why it is dangerous. It might be so were our soldiers all Hindus; but mixed as they are, I see no objection to it."

"I am quite aware," Hoby replied, "that the opposing element of Hindu and Mussulman has always been regarded as our safeguard for the fidelity of the native army, and doubtless it is so in a very great measure; but is it not possible some question might arise which would enlist the sympathies of *both*, and where should we be then? If, on the other hand, instead of two, you had three, four, or even more classes devoid of sympathy with one another, would not our safety be so much increased by each and every additional opposing element? It is on this ground alone—putting the comparative excellence of high and low caste men out of the question—I would enlist as many Sikhs as I could get; and as high and low caste Hindostanees will not herd together, I would also have some regiments expressly for the latter in which not a Brahmin or Rajpoot should be admitted."

"Let us turn from theory to facts," said Edgington, after a short pause, during which no one had thought it necessary to answer Hoby; for they all knew his crotchets regarding caste, did not agree with him, and were sure they could not change his opinion. "Did you see in yesterday's *Hurkaru* that the sepoys at Barrackpore were also supposed to be in a state of excitement about this new cartridge, and that the late fires there are attributed to it?"

"Yes," replied Peters; "I saw also that the native officers had been doing all they could to stay the feeling, but the idea was, they were afraid of their men, and, at all events, had done no good."

"Is it to be wondered at?" asked Hoby. "The promoters of the disturbance were probably high-caste Brahmins, and a native officer of an inferior caste always pays deference to these priestly beings—another advantage this of your Brahmin sepoy!"

"You are quite incorrigible, Hoby," said the major, laughing, "with your caste ideas."

"Perhaps I am, major; but I detest the way we act in the whole matter. The way we truckle to caste, the deference we pay to it, the impositions we allow to be put on us as to its requirements. I look elsewhere out of the ranks, and I see the Mussulman do things opposed to the Koran, the Hindu act contrary to his caste rules, and yet——"

"Where do you see this?" interrupted the major; "only in little matters at all events."

"Which of us who have Mussulman and Hindu servants have *not* seen it? How long would any Mahommedan khitmudgar* stop in his master's service did he act strictly up to the edicts of the Koran? How long the Brahmin Sirdar bearer if he was as particular about his caste as a sepoy? Will your Mahommedan sepoy stand by while you eat ham, bring it to you on a plate, or wash the plate afterwards? No! but your khitmudgar or khansanah will do this. Will your high-caste Hindu sepoy wash your feet and wash the basin after it? No, but your Brahmin bearer will do so. I do not of course mean to imply that sepoys should perform such menial offices, I argue simply on the caste question, and bring forward these examples to show the truth of what I stated, that out of the ranks both Mussulmans and Hindus act in opposition to their prejudices. I will now go a step further, and ask why our house servants do these things? The answer is plain, because they would not otherwise get service; and if, again, I ask why our sepoys object to much that falls within a soldier's duties, the answer is equally plain, because they know well our weak policy with respect to caste. The whole argument seems to me to lie in a

* Table-servant.

nutshell, for as the rules which fence round caste with the Hindu, and the obligations of the true believer are both very elastic, and as they can be passed and transgressed when it suits the purpose of either Hindu or Mussulman, why then, forsooth, should we truckle to either in the ranks; nay more, why put ourselves in a position that we must argue the question at all, and out of the millions in Hindostan, numbering so many creeds, castes, and sects, confine our army to those alone who, we well know, will give most trouble in time of peace, and are not, in my opinion, the best men obtainable for war."

"Well but, Edgington, about the Barrackpore affair," asked Major Bruce, who wished to get away from the caste question. "The *Hurkaru* did not speak of it as anything serious."

"Not exactly serious, but it thought prompt measures should be taken," answered Edgington; "and I think so too. All old officers agree that the army is not, nowadays, what it was; the men are neither so satisfied nor so obedient as formerly, and I feel certain a few really severe measures would do Jack Sepoy good. I partly agree with you, Hoby, in thinking we have petted the sepoys too much, though I cannot think that in our consideration for his caste we have acted unwisely."

"My opinion is worth no more than another's," Hoby rejoined; "and I have spoken my share."

"So we all have, I think," added Bruce; "and I wonder we have not driven you good ladies away with the dry and 'shoppy' subjects we have been discussing. Do you know the meaning of that slang word, Mrs. Edgington?"

"No," answered Beatrice.

"It means anything connected with the shop," he said, laughing; "and as the army is *our* shop, and the sepoys our stock in trade, we have been talking 'shoppy'!"

"Oh, indeed!" exclaimed Marion; "but why should

you think the subjects have not interested us? I'm afraid you've a very small idea of women's mental powers, Major Bruce, and think nothing but light subjects can engage our attention."

"I stand reproved," the major answered, getting up from his chair; "and I'll not sit down again—that shall be my punishment."

Hoby rose also. "Come along, Hoby," continued the major, "we'll go together, and, *en route*, I'll see if I cannot make you think better of Jack Sepoy than you do. Adieu, ladies! Miss Paris, I will read up some very scientific subject to discuss with you next time we meet, after which, perhaps, you will forgive me for supposing you were bored to-day."

## CHAPTER XVI.

### THE BACHELOR'S BALL—A PROPOSAL—THE RAJAH OF BHITOOR.

The hot weather of 1857 has begun, and begun, too, at that very hot station, Cawnpore. The heat in India is bad everywhere, but it is worse at some places than others. A sandy soil, want of vegetation and trees, buildings with pucca roofs and white-washed fronts, off which the sun is reflected, each of these makes a station hotter than its neighbours. Cawnpore having most of these heat-producing causes, it has often been said, that but a sheet of brown paper lies between it and the infernal regions.

On a Monday evening, in the middle of April, 1857, the Assembly Rooms at Cawnpore were one blaze of light, for a ball was given that night by the bachelors at the station. Those new to India would have thought it much too warm to dance, and so truly it was; but the monotony of station life is great in Hindostan, and people readily enter upon anything which promises amusement, and temporary forgetfulness of the heat.

The ball was well attended. Cawnpore is a large place, and the difficulty in getting ladies enough together for a dance, which is not uncommon at out-stations, was not felt here. As the greater part of the civil service members, with their families, were present, there was a fair sprinkling of black coats, a thing always desired in India; for, contrary to the rule at home, black has certainly the preference of red amongst young ladies, or mammas looking out for husbands; and thus the sons of Mars, who elsewhere carry all before them, must be content in the sunny East to follow their brethren in plain clothes.

Of course the officers of the 99th native infantry were present, and with Edgington Beatrice and Marion had come. It was but the third ball the latter had seen in India, and she had looked forward to it with the pleasure natural to a young girl, increased, no doubt, in her case—or she would not be one of Eve's daughters—by the knowledge that her remarkable beauty caused a sensation in any assembly she entered. In truth, Miss Paris, on the night in question, was decidedly the belle of the ball-room; none of the men doubted it; and if not allowed by any mother who thought her own pretty daughter quite on a par with our demi-Grecian damsel, beauty is so much a matter of taste, that a unanimous opinion regarding it is never to be looked for.

Marion's beauty had never shone forth with greater lustre than it did on that night. The enervating climate of India, so destructive in the long run to good looks, is often at first favourable in its effects. It refines the complexion, it takes away, if it exists, the too redundant bloom of health, and gives a delicate and spiritual aspect to the face, which with beauty of a classic style, such as Marion's, is strictly in keeping. Miss Paris, in short, looked handsomer this evening than she did at Calcutta or Dinapore. She was of such tender age, that every week improved her appearance; and when Edgington met her as she came out of her room dressed for the ball, he started with wonder at her rare beauty. There was a charm in the face of his *protégée*, which was very peculiar; it was, if we may so express it, the charm of contrariety, or, in other words, the opposing character of her features, typical of both stately and lovable beauty. This it was which made it so winning. We have stated before, how perfect was her Grecian profile; it was almost too much so (forcing, as it did, on the mind of the beholder the idea of majestic and unapproachable beauty), had it not been so completely relieved by the expression of both eyes and mouth, which were lovable to a degree, and shone out in this character the more prominently from the ever-present contrast they had in the haughty Grecian profile. Her profuse golden hair, in keeping with both the qualities mentioned, she wore generally *à la Madonna*, and low behind, in a thick Grecian plait; but this night she had twisted a part into a massive coronet, which, while it usurped the place of any other ornament on her head, added to the height of the already tall girl, and gave a queenly attribute to its possessor, which Edgington had never seen her wear before.

"How do you like me so—I mean with my hair done in this way?" asked Marion of her guardian as she met him.

"I like it much. It makes you almost too handsome, though, Marion; you've broken hearts enough already, so it's scarcely fair you should bring fresh forces into the field."

"What nonsense, Arthur! Now go and call Beatrice, or we shall be late. No, there's *not* plenty of time; for though perhaps you are *blasé* as regards balls, remember I'm not."

Our readers must surely remember Mrs. Merton, the wife of Ensign Merton, of the 99th, the pretty Eurasian who was at the Dinapore ball? She is here in the Cawnpore ball-room, dancing the first quadrille with Hoby, as Edgington, his wife, and Miss Paris enter. Mrs. Merton has known a long time that poor Hoby is in love, as also that he has a rival in his commandant. Her hopes are, however, all on Hoby's side, for she likes him much; and believing, as she does, that girls generally accept the first offer (this belief, by the bye, is very general with her class, and she, poor little thing, had done it herself), she hopes he will speak soon, and not miss his chance by waiting too long.

"Oh, there's Mrs. Edgington and Miss Paris!" she exclaimed as they came in; "and I declare Miss Paris looks handsomer than ever. Oh, I see her hair's done differently. Isn't she beautiful? I can't keep my eyes off her. If I was a man, I should fall in love with her at once."

"But suppose she did not return your love," said Hoby with a slight sigh, which, however, did not escape his partner, "you would only then be heaping up sorrow for yourself."

"It shouldn't be so, however; I'd love her so that I'd *make* her love me. She looks so lovable that I'm sure she'd return love with interest."

"Women have their fancies as well as men," said Hoby, "and love does not always beget love."

"I'm sure it has not in one case," remarked Mrs. Merton, dropping her voice in a confidential way. "Miss Paris doesn't care a bit about the colonel; it's not likely that she should, either, for he's old enough to be her papa." The pretty Eurasian looked slily at Hoby as she said this, to see how he received it; but the dance cut short her observations, and his answer, if he intended any.

After the quadrille, Mrs. Merton sought her husband. "John, dear, I wish you could do something for poor Mr. Hoby; he's in a sad way, I'm sure—desperately in love with Miss Paris, and thinks, foolish fellow, he has no chance."

"And what can *I* do in the matter, Arabella?"

"A great deal. Encourage him. All men in love want encouragement. Tell him of your own case with me. I would have told him myself if I had not been ashamed. In fact, make him speak to Miss Paris; it's all that's necessary."

"I have my doubts there, though I think she likes him better than she does any one else," Merton replied; "and, anyhow, Arabella dear, we must not interfere in the matter; Hoby is no fool, and can manage for himself; so just check your womanly desire to help on the match, *and let* not your pity for Mr. Hoby spoil your pleasure to-night. There's no reason, because you've got into the scrape of marriage yourself," he added, squeezing her arm, as he led her to a seat, "that you should wish to drive every other young girl into it."

"What nonsense, John. You don't deserve to be talked to to-night, and so I'll leave you," she added, with a bright smile, as Edgington came up to claim her hand. "What, a polka, Captain Edgington! I can't say no; and you don't wish me to, do you, John?"

"By no means," replied Merton laughingly, "for I intend to dance it too. Ah, there's my partner waiting, and she won't wait much longer," he added, as he ran off and left his pretty little wife with Edgington.

"This is your polka, Colonel Carstairs," said Marion, rising, as that officer came up with many a smile to claim it. "If I remember right, you engaged me for this polka a fortnight ago, when the ball was first talked of."

"Yes, Miss Paris, and have danced it many a time since then in anticipation. Though I've not danced much the last few years, dancing with you is——"

"If we don't begin soon, it will be over, so let's leave the talking till later," interrupted Marion somewhat hastily, "and, in the mean time, I'll conceive all the pretty things you meant to say."

As they whirl round in the dance, let us enlighten the reader as to how Colonel Carstairs' suit progressed. He had never made love in so many words, but he tried to look love whenever he met Marion, and he continually paid her a long string of compliments; anticipating which just now, she interrupted him. She was at a loss to understand all this. In her opinion, the colonel was much too old for a lover; nor could she believe that a man of his age and position would fall in love with a young girl like herself. Still, at times his looks *looked* so much like love that she became alarmed, and had latterly invariably stopped him at the commencement of any complimentary string. In her manner to him she was, however, as unreserved as ever; he had never spoken love, and she was at times almost ashamed that the idea of its possibility had been allowed a place in her imagination. She also intuitively felt that the best way to keep things as they were was to act as if such relations between them were impossible, and she therefore treated him with the free and open manner natural for a girl to assume to the commandant of her guardian's regiment.

Colonel Carstairs, on his part, knew not exactly what to think. He had a great idea of the importance of his position in a worldly point of view, and felt sure the rank and *locus standi* his wife would have must tell in his favour. Still he sometimes thought, from sentiments Marion had uttered in his hearing, that she was not likely to be dazzled by such advantages, and then he felt somewhat desponding. Did she love him? He had asked himself the question that very day, and answered it in the same breath in the negative. Did she know he loved her? That question he could not answer so easily, and two hookahs smoked while he pondered it did not enable him to come to a conclusion. "One thing is very certain," said the colonel, as he finished the second hookah,—"if she doesn't know it now, she never will know it until I speak; so I see no use in delaying any longer. Yes—yes—I'll pop to-night at the ball. I can certainly get her alone; and Mrs. Edgington seems determined at their house never to leave us."

The resolve was made, and the colonel got himself up that evening with unusual care. When he came into the room, however, and saw Marion looking so supremely lovely, his heart failed him; he felt as so many have felt before him, and will feel to the end of time, that he was not worthy of such a priceless jewel; that if she were not so perfect, so intoxicatingly beautiful, he could then propose with better heart, with more hope of his suit being accepted. Having stopped where she could not see him, and watched her for a few minutes, he turned off into the supper-room, and drank two or three glasses of champagne, after which, strange to say, he felt once more hopeful, and determined, at all events, to know his fate that night.

After the polka came a quadrille. Marion did not dance it,—she was tired, and Colonel Carstairs sat by her side all alone.

"I shan't get a better opportunity," thought the colonel, "why the devil don't I begin?"

"Because the Indian climate makes one so nervous, Colonel Carstairs——"

"By Jupiter! how do you know what I was——"

"Miss Paris, they want another couple in the nearest quadrille, will you dance it?" said Mr. Peters, coming up at that moment.

"No, thank you, not this time, I'm so tired, Mr. Peters; I'll dance the next with you instead,—will that do?"

"By all means;" and Mr. Peters disappeared to find another partner for the vacant place.

"I was saying," continued Marion, "that because the Indian climate makes one so nervous, I am sure all the green tea which people drink is very bad, and I've persuaded Mrs. Edgington to have no more in our house. We have had none to-day, and I feel much better for it."

"Is that all," replied the colonel, with a disappointed air; "I was in hopes, from the way you began, that you had read my thoughts, Miss Paris, and intended to—to—encourage——"

"What *do* you mean?" asked Marion, quite bewildered.

"Never mind, it was a foolish fancy," continued the colonel, "but I wished to say something, and *dared* not say it. Will you listen if I say it now?"

"Of course I'll listen. What could you want to say that you dared not say? I don't understand you."

"This, Miss Paris, that I have never made love in my life" (he gulped the last words as he thought of Beatrice, and thought, perhaps, Marion knew of that episode) "and therefore——"

"Therefore you have saved yourself from a great deal of worry and annoyance, Colonel Carstairs, I can quite believe it," said Marion hastily, anxious to escape from what her woman's tact told her was to follow.

"You misunderstand me, Miss Paris,—not wilfully, I hope. I was about to say that, being unpractised in the art of love-making, I know not in what words to tell you, to—to—propose to you, later, to share my humble lot in life, and by so doing make me a happy man."

"It has come at last," thought Marion, with a sigh, "and I must answer."

She was silent for a few moments ere she replied,—

"I do not misunderstand you, Colonel Carstairs; it would be prudery to pretend it, and I truly grieve to pain you by saying it cannot be. I am very young, unused to the ways of the world. If I thought anything in my conduct had led you to hope for a favourable answer, I should feel even more miserable than I do at this moment. You have been very kind to me, and I like you very much, but my liking can never become love."

"With time it might," urged the poor colonel, clinging, like the drowning man, to the last chance of winning what he really knew not how much he prized until Marion's answer showed him how poor his chance was,—"with time it might, Miss Paris, and I will be very patient."

"No, Colonel Carstairs; time, though it may increase the liking, will never give it the character of love. But I cannot talk about it," continued poor Marion hastily, with a half-hysterical sob, which, however, she instantly suppressed; "the subject is as painful to me as to you.

Forgive me, I beg, for any pain I may have caused you. See, we shall be noticed. Say I have your forgiveness; don't deny me that," she urged, with her eyes full of tears; "you truly know not how miserable I feel already at causing you sorrow."

"Yes, my full forgiveness," replied the colonel, after a pause, more affected than he had ever been before by woman's words. "But, good God, I have nothing to forgive—if any fault there be, it is mine—mine, Marion (let me call you by that name once, but this once, for the first and last time), in supposing that a man of my age, with my blunted sensibilities, who has lived alone till he is fit for no other existence, could win the heart and hand of a being all youth, beauty, and freshness, like yourself. My forgiveness, indeed!—none but an angel would have asked for it. Ah! Miss Paris, happy, thrice happy the man who wins you!"

"Will you take me into the supper-room? I feel very faint; a glass of wine-and-water will do me good," said Marion, rising, her face ghastly pale.

Carstairs gave her his arm, and they passed to the supper-room. The snow-white arm which rested on his trembled violently, and he feared at one time she would fall by the way. The wine-and-water revived her, however, and she said,—

"It was the heat more than anything else, and I must get a little cool air. Will you take me outside for a minute or two?"

When there, the colonel said, "May I make you one final request, Miss Paris, and then drop——"

"Oh, not again," she said beseechingly, looking up at him with a half-feeling of fear, in the comparative solitude of the verandah.

"You mistake me—my request is not hard to grant. Will you allow what has occurred this evening between us to remain unknown to all others?"

Marion pondered a moment ere she answered, "Yes,

I will make the promise; but it must be coupled with a promise on your part not again to renew the subject."

"I promise," he replied, with a deep sigh.

"And *I* promise," said Marion. "Now let us go in," she continued, anxious to bring the scene to an end; "the cool air has done me good. Leave me when I am seated; I would be a little alone. Nay, I will say good-bye here; I see Mrs. Peters, and can join her. Good-bye, Colonel Carstairs; believe me I shall always think of you as a very dear friend." She shook his hand kindly. Another moment, and Carstairs was alone.

The poor colonel felt miserable. Who would not feel miserable under such circumstances? He felt doubly miserable, because Marion, even in refusing him, had made him love her the more. Oh, of all the shapes which sorrow assumes in this sorrowful world, there are not many more acute than that the poor colonel laboured under. Up to this time, hope had cheered him; but now all was blank despair. To return to the gaieties of the ball-room was impossible; he sent word by a servant to one of the ball stewards that he felt unwell, and was obliged to go home, and another half-hour saw him upon his plain charpoy bed, tossing about under the waving punkah, half dreaming, half thinking of Marion Paris, and the painful promise he had made her.

Events in the world wag on, in spite of the misery felt by any number of its inmates; and the ball at Cawnpore was not a whit less gay for the sudden and heavy cloud which had overshadowed two beings that had entered those doors blithesome and happy.

We say two, for Marion felt for poor Colonel Carstairs more than she cared to own to herself. She pitied him with all her heart; what he had said touching the lonely life he led, haunted her all that evening, and for poor Marion the ball had no more pleasure. It was, of course, the first proposal that had ever been made her.

"I trust this first is the last," she said to herself, when, a little later, she sat by Mrs. Peters on the sofa, hoping that no one would disturb her train of thought; "for truly it has made me very miserable."

Marion was not, however, long allowed to dwell on the subject. "She *must* dance." "That set was incomplete without her." "She had promised to dance the waltz." What could she do? Dance she did, and in the exercise and excitement found relief. But when, as time went on, she saw not the colonel in the gay and whirling throng, and she pictured him in his solitary bungalow, a prey to grief, she could have cried from very heaviness of heart; for she had, alas! for the first time in her life, caused heavy sorrow to another.

Marion, sweet Marion! you have yet to learn that in this world the compensating scale holds good in your own character as in everything else. If from your susceptibility you feel pleasure more keenly than the mass, you will taste the cup of bitterness in a like ratio. Let not the knowledge, however, when attained, change your nature. Were all the world like your sweet self, how small the sum of human ills that mankind need bear!

The general commanding at Cawnpore was in the ballroom,—General Wheeler, a brave old soldier, who, in spite of many years spent under a tropical sun, retained all the energy and determination of his youth. The gaieties of the ball pleased him; he knew well how necessary such relaxations and amusements were to vary the monotony and *ennui* of station life, as also how constitutions, debilitated by the enervating influence of climate, take out a fresh lease of endurance, activity, and life from such scenes.

Mr. Blank, an old Bengal civilian, with snow-white hair, who held the highest civil post at Cawnpore, and was known far and wide for his hospitality and social disposition, sat on a sofa with Mrs. Bruce. Ices had just been handed round; and as they enjoyed this greatest of all luxuries in India, the conversation ran thus,—

"A capital ball, certainly, Mrs. Bruce; I hope you have performed your share of the dancing."

"I've danced twice already, and I really think there are dancers enough without me."

"Yes, there's no lack of ladies; and truly Cawnpore boasts many a pretty face," remarked Mr. Blank. "Mrs. Edgington, who sits opposite, I think very handsome. I knew her father formerly, and her mother too; the expression of her face reminds me of her mother."

"I knew Mrs. Plane slightly at Patna, myself, and I think there is a likeness. What a sad affair that was, Mr. Blank, with the 34th native infantry at Barrackpore, the end of last month. Of course you heard it. A sepoy attacked the adjutant, and none of the guard interfered. I'm glad the Governor-General so soon after disbanded the 19th, who had mutinied at Berhampore; for such a severe punishment will have its effect. Tell me, what do you think of all this discontent in the army; I see there are reports of it from many stations?"

"I hope we have seen the last of it," Mr. Blank replied, "and I hope that when it's all past, certain reforms, much wanted in the native regiments, will be carried out. But we are here to dance, not to discuss military matters, Mrs. Bruce; will you allow me the honour of your hand for the quadrille now forming?"

"With much pleasure," replied Mrs. Bruce, as she rose from her seat. "I observe, somehow, that neither military men nor civilians will discuss these matters with us ladies. Why is this?"

"Because in ladies' society more agreeable subjects naturally present themselves," gallantly remarked Mr. Blank. "Shall we take this place? Mr. Hoby, will you and Miss Paris be our *vis-à-vis*. I'm glad, Miss Paris, you do not allow the gentlemen to be idle, but keep them to their work, or pleasure, I ought to say; for pleasure it must be to dance with you. If you have a spare quadrille later, I hope you'll grant it to me."

While the dance was in progress, a noise outside proclaimed the arrival of some person of consequence; and a few moments later, a native, attired in the eastern style and with regal magnificence, entered the ball-room. His height, perhaps somewhat above the general height of man, was increased by the head-dress he wore, which was a conical-shaped cap, surmounted by a magnificent white feather. He was of a sinewy, if not a stalwart build, his eyes were coal-black, a moustache shaded his lips, which were peculiarly thick and African in their character, and a large bushy black beard descended to the jewelled hilts of the dagger and pistols in his kummurbund.* He advanced with perfect possession to where the general sat, and accosted him.

"Who is that?" said Marion to Hoby, with whom she was dancing.

"The Rajah of Bhitoor, Nana Sahib. He is very fond of English society, and comes, they tell me, to many of the balls here."

"What is he—an Indian chieftain?" asked Marion.

"So far a chieftain, that he has a fort and palace a few miles from Cawnpore. A fine man, is he not?"

"One can scarcely see him for jewels," replied Marion, laughing, "so I can't say; but I don't like the expression of his face at all. Such great ugly thick lips, and such a savage face altogether."

"His big beard makes him look savage," remarked Hoby; "it is nothing else."

Half an hour later, the Rajah of Bhitoor, Mr. Blank, the old civilian, and Major Bruce stood together in one of the entrances, discussing the mutinous spirit which

* A shawl worn round the waist.

had manifested itself of late in the army. Nana Sahib could speak English, but Mr. Blank and Major Bruce were good Oriental linguists, and the conversation was conducted in Oordoo,* the common language of the country.

"Many people now connect the chupattee circular and the mutinous spirit together," remarked Mr. Blank. "What does your Excellency think?"

"If I knew the meaning of the chupattee sign, I could better answer the question," the Nana replied.

"Have none of the intelligent natives near you suggested any explanation?" asked Mr. Blank.

"The suggestions have been nearly as numerous as the chupattees," replied Nana Sahib; "but I have never thought it worth my while to try and unravel the mystery."

"You think, then, it is nothing of consequence?" said Mr. Blank.

"I don't think so, I know it," the Nana replied. "What! an important secret in the hands of thousands of chowkeydars! The English are much wanting in wisdom if they give it any value. It may be a freak of some wealthy native, who can afford to pay for it, to cause wonder in the council-chamber at Calcutta. It may be an experiment of some company, to organize a telegraph which shall beat even your lightning one; it may be a thousand things I have heard suggested, but I *know*, it is nothing which can engage the attention of sensible men."

"Your excellency has heard," remarked Major Bruce, "that the 19th native infantry were disbanded at Barrackpore this month. Will that severe step, in the native opinion, stop the mutinous feeling?"

"It has stopped it already, I consider," the Nana replied. "Is it a light thing for a thousand men to be turned loose on the world, to lose their all? His

* Hindostanee.

Excellency the Governor General did well to take so decided a step, and turn those rascals adrift who had been unfaithful to their salt."

"What an absurd idea has been reported," said Major Bruce, "amongst the native soldiers, that the Government meant to Christianize the army. Whence do you think it sprung? The Company have always been so careful on the subject of religion, that I should have thought it the last report which would have gained credence."

"Who can say where it originated," the Nana replied. "The Sirkar * have, I think, done very wrong to notice it. Such foolish tales, fit only to amuse and astonish children, should be allowed to die out in the obscurity from which they sprung. But what does it all signify, —the tomasha † is at an end; the Government have shown their power, and need not trouble themselves further in the matter. This discontent in the army has not reached the regiments here, has it?"

"Oh, no," replied Major Bruce; "they are all faithful to their salt. My regiment heard the report, but laughed at it."

"They are sensible men," replied the Nana with a peculiar smile and a curl of his thick upper lip; "and I'm glad you have found it out. Who is that young and handsome lady opposite to us."

"Which?" asked Mr. Blank. "There are two, and both very handsome."

"The young lady," replied the rajah, "with the golden hair twisted over her head."

"Miss Paris. She lives with Mrs. Edgington, near whom she is sitting."

"She is very beautiful," said the Nana, "and so, indeed, is the other lady. Are they staying at Cawnpore for some time?"

* The governing power.

† Spectacle, noisy scene. No English word has its exact meaning.

"Yes," replied Major Bruce. "Mrs. Edgington is the wife of Captain Edgington of my regiment."

"Your regiment is——"

"The 99th."

The Nana said nothing, but he gazed at Marion with his fiery eyes, while his lips moved as if he muttered to himself. Miss Paris, accidentally looking up, caught his passionate gaze fixed on her, and started as she did so. She did not blush: she turned pale, and moved uneasily in her chair. She was frightened; but why, she could not say. Certain it is, however, that we all occasionally see people we take a great and sudden dislike to, with as little ground or cause as Marion had for her aversion, or the sudden fear that assailed her.

Supper, which was shortly after announced, distracted her attention; and with the peculiar facility which youth has for discarding unpleasant subjects, she had, ere it was finished, almost forgotten the love episode with Colonel Carstairs, and the fiery gaze of the rajah of Bhitoor.

She was not destined, however, poor girl, to finish the evening in peace. Nana Sahib, who admired her more than any woman he had ever seen, asked Mr. Blank to introduce him. The old civilian did so, but repented it the next moment, when he saw how perfectly scared Marion looked, and how utterly unable she was to give answers to the few sentences in English which the rajah addressed to her. Luckily Edgington came to her relief; and the Nana, seeing how impossible it was to engage the young girl in conversation, turned to Mrs. Edgington, whom he had been introduced to at the same time, and taking a seat near, managed, while talking to her and her husband, to feast his eyes on Miss Paris's beauty.

Oh! could Edgington have read the thoughts then coursing the brain below that waving ostrich-plume; could the knowledge possessed at that moment by the jewelled rajah at his side have been shared by only one true English heart in that assembly, the Nana's throat would assuredly have been clutched by the officer he addressed, and a horrible scene in the direst calamity experienced by Britain in the nineteenth century would have been avoided.

## CHAPTER XVII.

BEATRICE'S DEPARTURE—MUTTERINGS OF THE STORM—CAUSES OF THE MUTINY—NANA SAHIB.

A FEW days after the ball, the post one morning brought a letter for Beatrice from Patna. It was written by her father, but dictated by her mother, the latter being too unwell to hold a pen. It was not a long letter, and ran as follows:—

"PATNA, April 17, 1857.

"Your father writes this letter, dear Beatrice, at my request: I am in bed, and far too unwell to do more than dictate; I cannot even do that long, for the doctor recommends perfect quiet. The night before last you nearly lost your mother; from eleven till one the doctor thought there was but little hope, for the fever had flown to my head, and I was in a very dangerous state.

"I am better now, but still not out of danger. I insisted on the doctor telling me the truth this morning; he, foolish man, thought it would frighten me. [It did not a bit, Beatrice. I write this for myself—James Plane.] I should be easier if you could come to me, and I write to tell you to do so. Captain Edgington can make no difficulties, and you must come quickly. By Palkee Gharrie Dâk you may, I calculate, be here on Saturday, if you leave the morning after you get this letter. When I am better, you can easily return to Cawnpore the same way. I depend on your coming, and I shall therefore expect you by Saturday at the latest.

"I can add nothing to the above, which your mother

dictated. She is very ill, and wishes you to come quickly; so we expect you.

"Your affectionate Father,

"JAMES PLANE."

Beatrice was fond of her mother; whatever little space her heart gave to affection was nearly filled up with her mother's image, and the above letter frightened her sadly. Edgington made no objection to what she had, however, decided on doing before she consulted him; and she left Cawnpore that same evening. It was the first time she had been parted from her husband; but the very cool relations they now stood in to one another prevented anything like real grief being felt on either side; not quite so, however, as regarded Marion, for Beatrice had unconsciously learnt to love this young girl, whose character, while thoroughly the opposite of her own, had never jarred against the pride which Mrs. Edgington cherished, while it had in its affectionate and trusting disposition leant upon her as much as the cold and passive nature of Beatrice allowed. She felt parting with Marion, therefore, much more than she did with her husband, and promised her to return as soon as Mrs. Plane's health permitted it. Marion, on her side, grieved also at the absence. It required very little to call forth affection in her warm heart; and at the moment of parting with her guardian's wife she recalled but the few acts of kindness received—nay, even blamed her own conduct, which had, she thought, prevented their being more numerous.

Well, Beatrice was gone, and Edgington left alone with Marion—not quite alone, though, for the reader will not forget that Mr. and Mrs. Peters were our hero's temporary guests until the house they had taken in the civil quarter was ready for them. It was well that it was so, for Edgington was not insensible to the scandal which might have attached itself to his beautiful *protégée*, had she and he, during his wife's absence, been the solitary inmates of his bungalow.

A few days after his wife's departure, Edgington received a letter from her, with the intelligence that Mrs. Plane progressed favourably, and that if all continued well, she hoped herself to return to Cawnpore in another month. "Even if my mother is quite well before that time," wrote Beatrice, "I will stay so long, for it is not impossible she may be sent to Europe, and, in that case, I shall not see her again for years." Edgington, of course, made no objections to this arrangement; and Mr. and Mrs. Peters having kindly, on Marion's account, consented to remain his guests until Beatrice's return, the remaining portion of the month of April passed in such sociable happiness as the heat of the weather permitted.

About this time it began to be doubted by the more sensible portion of the officers at Cawnpore whether the native regiments at that station were, on the whole, quite loyal and trustworthy. As we have previously explained, two mutinies, though unaccompanied by violence, had already occurred in lower Bengal during the months of February and March. Reports of disaffection at many stations in the Bengal Presidency had also found their way to Cawnpore. Occasionally the reports in the bazaar had gone a step further, for it was bruited that the regiments at Cawnpore also shared the disaffection; but whenever it was attempted to trace these flying rumours to their source, it was found that they had none—or, at the most, none of sufficient importance to justify them. Now, however, affairs somewhat changed: the bazaar reports became more clear and specific; the budmashes, that is to say the idle and vagabond class, in and around Cawnpore, took upon themselves a bold and impudent tone when they addressed Europeans; a wild rumour that the Company's raj, or government, would soon be at an end, was whispered by native to native; and, more significant than all, a reserve, a secrecy, a dislike to be interrogated as to their causes of annoyance, seemed to pervade all the native soldiers from subadar to sepoy.

A little before the disaffection assumed this tangible shape, the new muskets, which were to supersede the old and almost useless "Brown Bess," were directed to be issued, and, of course, with them the cartridges, which were supposed, with more or less truth, to be the cause of the outbreaks which had already occurred. These cartridges, we would state for the information of the very few who do not know it already, were supposed by the natives to contain (or, what is much nearer the truth, a report was industriously introduced into the ranks, by certain leading natives of Hindostan, that the cartridges did contain) both pig and bullock fat, in the prepared paper used in their manufacture. Now, the Mahommedan regards the pig as unclean, the Hindu is forbidden by his caste rules to touch bullocks' flesh; thus both in biting the obnoxious cartridge would do violence to their religion. This was the plea given, at that early period of mutinous 1857, for the disaffection in the native army,—and, doubtless, it was, to a very great extent, a true one; but there can now be but little doubt that the credulity and the prejudices of the sepoys were used as tools by designing hands, and that the mutiny of 1857 would have occurred, or at all events not been long delayed, if the cartridge question had never existed.

As, however, we are not writing a treatise on the Indian mutiny, or even its history, but only the tale of one act in the drama, we need not enter at length into the above questions, though we must briefly do so to the extent to render clear the motives of the actions we have to detail.

From what we have already said, it will be seen that we believe the sepoy army to have been merely the tool used in the Indian rebellion,—in short, that the outbreak was *not*, as supposed at first, merely a military revolt, but in reality a huge political movement, having for its object no less than the overthrow of the English empire in Hindostan. That this was known by the sepoys themselves, we do not believe; they were worked upon to act as they did through their religious prejudices, aroused in a cunning manner by the actors in the political conspiracy. These movers or instigators of the rebellion were for the most part Mahommedans, and they were assisted in a very remarkable manner by accidental circumstances, which timed in most fortuitously for their undertaking, and made their task so much the easier.

In a few words—We conceive the rebellion to have been a premeditated scheme long before the cartridge question appeared on the *tapis*. The movers therein, perceiving the deficiencies,—which some have erroneously supposed the causes of the rebellion,—in the army,—such as the paucity of officers with regiments, the lack of sympathy between officers and men, the petted condition of the sepoys, &c.—supposed it possible, through these and other means, to create a rebellion in the ranks. At that very moment, by an extraordinary chance, it so occurred the Indian Government resolved on a step (the introduction of the new cartridges) which gave a much easier mode of working on sepoy sympathies than had before existed.

We believe the head movers in the conspiracy availed themselves of the fact in a cunning manner, *first* spreading an undefined report that the Government meant to christianize the whole army; and *when* time had been given for this report to excite the fears of the sepoys, and they were well prepared to receive and believe as true any plausible means which could be shown for its accomplishment, *then, and not till then,* was the suggestion made, which spread like wildfire through the land, that the new cartridges contained both pig and bullock fat, and that their introduction would necessarily convert the whole army to Christianity—or, in other words, which was much the same thing, would, with both Hindu and Mussulman, destroy their religion.

But we will return to our tale. At the time that the disaffection at Cawnpore assumed somewhat of a substantial shape, a havildar of Edgington's company, a man who had received much kindness from our hero, and was truly attached to him, came one morning, and after making some official report said,—

"Sahib, will you swear not to give my name as narrator of what I will tell you, and then I will speak."

Edgington promised.

"Sahib, there is great discontent in the regiments about this new cartridge. Neither Hindus nor Mussulmans will use them, for they will lose their caste. We were told long ago that the Sirkar meant to make us all Christians, and now we are ordered to bite cartridges with pig and bullock fat. Sahib, harm may come of it—you can do nothing to prevent it. You thought of going to Europe last year; will you not go now, and take the Missee Baba with you?"

Edgington questioned the havildar closely in what way evil could arise; but the man seemed almost frightened that he had said so much, and would say no more. He repeated his request, however, that Edgington should go away.

"That I cannot do," our hero replied: "even had I before thought of it, what you have said would prevent my doing so."

The havildar would say nothing further; he even tried to modify what he had already said; reminded Edgington of the promise, passed to other subjects, and went away.

"I have done my duty," he remarked to himself as he returned to the lines. "I have paid the debt of gratitude I owe—I can do no more!"

His conduct was not strange. It tallied with the Hindu character: he had done what he could to induce his officer to escape the impending danger—he had not been successful; and his scruples forbad him to betray his companions.

What did Edgington do? He pondered upon what he had heard, but it was no more than he had heard before in the hundred and one reports which ran through the station daily. He thought of sending Marion away; but where to send her—where would she be safer than she was with him? The spirit of disaffection was not confined to Cawnpore, and he could not send her out of India. What steps, then, could he take as a military man to warn the authorities? Report the fact to his commanding officer; that was the obvious course. But what had he to report? It was but little, still that little should be told. He ordered his horse, and rode to his commandant's quarters.

He told his tale in a few words, keeping back, according to his promise, the name of his informant.

"Why, Edgington, it's no more than any old woman out of the bazaar will tell you. I'm sorry you've had a hot ride for nothing. That *our* regiment's stanch I'll take my oath; other officers must look after their own men. I would report it to the general, but upon my word it's not worth it. Suppose the men won't use the cartridge, what then? They will be punished; and, anyhow, what danger have *we* to apprehend. No, no, my dear fellow; go home quietly. I believe an order is now coming out, if it's not out already, that the cartridges are not to be bitten at all when loading; and then all will settle down. Thanks for coming, however: it was your duty, and you did well. Now, good-by, for I've a lot of work I must get through."

Reader, remember! this was before a single Englishman or woman had been sacrificed to the religion of the sepoy; and the idea that such atrocities could be committed was not *then* believed by any one. It was, however, even in that day, infatuation on the colonel's part, a willing shutting of his eyes to the cloud so soon to burst; but it was not a singular instance—there were thousands of others. Even *after* the mutiny had commenced, with all its attendant horrors—*long after* the expressions "stanch" and "loyal" excited but disgust and distrust in the many—still were numbers found who would not believe in the faithlessness of those below them, and who, to the last moment, nourished, fostered, and disarmed not the snake which stung them.

All who have read the incidents of the Indian mutiny must have been struck with this characteristic point amongst both civil and military officials at that time. How very general it was; how few the exceptions. The solution may, we think, be found, firstly, in the confiding nature a life amongst abject dependants engenders; and secondly, in the proficiency most Asiatics attain in the art of deception.

The end of April at Cawnpore passed in the manner we have detailed. Many felt that all was not right, and no one more so than the brave old general, whose position, with but two companies of European soldiers at his command, was far from enviable. He could not do much, however, nor did he dare, at that period, to do anything indicative of apprehension; but he sent over to Oude for a regiment of irregular cavalry, and having urgently applied for further European aid, awaited, with others, the course of events.

The month of May commenced—that month which at home calls up associations of green fields, trees budding into leaf, and hawthorn-covered hedges; but which, in India, speaks of fervent heat, fiery winds, and clouds of heated dust. It is just two years since our tale commenced, and it is the same thing now which it was then. The hot winds blow from morning till night; kuskus tattees are drenched with water for sixteen hours out of the twenty-four, by dusty and indefatigable coolies; but the state of India, alas! is far from the same. The superficial observer may not see it; but how deceitful the apparent calm! For has not the eve of the mighty convulsion arrived, and those who see furthest guess little what is to come.

The rajah Nana Sahib arrived at Cawnpore from his fort at Bhitoor, and he arrived with a goodly retinue. But he had often done so before; he was fond of English society, and his arrival caused neither wonder nor speculation. He visited the general, and, report said, tendered him any assistance in his power, in case of a disturbance. When this was bruited about, no one doubted that the rajah was sincere in the offers he had made, for he had always been friendly to the English, he had been so much in their society, had so often asked parties to his palace at Bhitoor, that all thought he would be only too glad to show the British Government how sincere were his offers of friendship.

After his visit to the general, he, among other calls, came to Edgington's house. He had come, he said to Edgington, who received him, to see Mrs. Edgington and Miss Paris, and ascertain personally that they had not suffered from the fatigues of the ball he had met them at a fortnight ago. Our hero told him of his wife's absence, and sent for Marion, who was in her room. The servant who called her, merely said a visitor had arrived, and the astonishment of Miss Paris was great when she saw who that visitor was. There was no retreating, however; and though much confused, nay, almost alarmed, for there was something in the Nana's face that sent the blood back cold to her heart, she was obliged to sit down and endure his presence as she best could.

The sudden antipathy which the young girl had conceived to the rajah was very remarkable. Edgington had reasoned with her about it the day after the ball, for he had seen it only too plainly, and was unwilling that, should the rajah again address her, she should repeat it. On that occasion she could give her guardian *no* reason for her dislike and fear of the chieftain, excepting that she avowed, with a blush, he had looked at her as she had never been looked at before; and as she left the room directly after saying so much, evidently to avoid any further discussion, Edgington had not renewed the subject. Upon the rajah calling at his house, he could not, in common civility, deny Miss Paris; besides which, Edgington was not unwilling that Marion should have an opportunity of getting over what he considered a childish dislike.

Nana Sahib, who had perceived at the ball how disastrous was the effect which his amorous gaze had produced upon Marion, did his best during this visit to undo the mischief he had then done, and by talking principally to Edgington, and looking but seldom at Marion, he achieved his purpose so far, that, after his departure, she acknowledged to her guardian she thought herself mistaken in thinking he had looked at her rudely on the ball night.

"But I dislike the man excessively, dear Arthur, in spite of that," she continued; "and I do not suppose it is at all necessary I should like him, for he is *not* an old friend of yours."

"By no means," Edgington replied; "and as long as you are not rude to him, dislike him as much as you will. What do you say; shall we go and see his old palace at Bhitoor? I fear the weather is too hot."

"Oh, *much* too hot," joined in Marion, only too glad to have an excuse put into her mouth against a trip she dreaded. "I was glad you did not promise him to come. Perhaps, next cold weather, when Beatrice is here, and one or two officers will join us, we might make up a nice picnic to the place. But the idea, during these hot winds, of being cooped up eight or nine hours in a gloomy old castle, with the gentleman who has just left us as a companion, is surely not an enticing prospect."

"You are right, Marion; and we won't go," said Edgington, as he lit a cheroot. "Now, I'm going have my first smoke to-day, and will you, like a dear girl, sit down to the piano and sing me my favourite song?"

"Which is it?" asked Marion, with a bright smile, as she seated herself at the instrument. "You say you like all my songs."

"The one you sing well. Now, you can't make a mistake, for there is *but one* in which you excel, vain Miss Paris," answered Edgington, as he stretched himself on the sofa with a laugh.

Marion sung: whether it was the right song, we don't know, but it was a very sweet one; and the coolie at the tattee outside listened with all his might, and quite forgot why he was there as he did so. The tattee became dry, the room became warm, but Marion sung on, while Edgington and the coolie listened.

## CHAPTER XVIII.

NEWS FROM DELHI—PREPARATIONS—MARION'S DREAM—THE END OF MAY.

Tuesday morning, the 12th of May, 1857, found the bazaar of Cawnpore in a state of great excitement. News had arrived during the night of the mutiny at Meerut, of the march of the mutineers upon Delhi, of the native troops in that city joining them, and of the massacre of the Europeans at the latter place.

News of all kinds in a strange way is always, in India, first received by natives, so that when the above startling intelligence was being passed from mouth to mouth in the native quarters of Cawnpore, the officers in cantonments were going through their morning duties, or taking their morning exercise, quite unconscious of anything extraordinary having taken place.

Such news, however, runs apace, and a couple of hours later it was the one subject of conversation and wonder in the native infantry lines and the European officers' mouths.

There was this morning a "tea gathering" in the verandah of Colonel Carstairs's bungalow, and several of his regimental officers were present, when a native mahajun, or banker, from the town, who had in his hands some of the colonel's business, came and detailed the disastrous intelligence.

Horror sat upon every face, as the broad outlines of the Meerut and Delhi massacres were related; but some did not believe, and among the number was the colonel himself, who had such a rooted conviction of the loyalty of Jack Sepoy and the gentle nature of the Hindu, that it required much more than a mere bazaar rumour to convince him that anything so utterly improbable had occurred.

"I'll tell you what," he exclaimed, as he coolly lit his morning cheroot, "I'll bet a gold mohur it's not true; and I'll prove it very soon. The Delhi paper's due to-day—I'll send and get it. Here, orderly, go and get my letters and newspapers from the dâk office. Yes, let him ask for yours, too, Bruce. Now, we'll just smoke quietly till he returns, and then, baboo, you shall take back the denial with you to the bazaar."

"God grant it, sahib," said the mahajun as he sat down at a respectful distance; "for, if true, sad days are coming on."

The banker spoke with sincerity. He was of that class who, throughout all the after troubles, prayed for success to our cause. All the monied and commercial class did so, for they well knew that no security of property would exist under either a Mahommedan or Hindu government. By any disturbance, by any change in the existing state of things, they had nothing to gain—much to lose.

The orderly returned. There were no up-country papers, and only one letter—for Major Bruce.

"Strange, certainly," said the colonel; "but the paper does not always arrive regularly. The report must be false, however; for the telegraph would have brought the news before this, if true. When do they say it occurred, baboo?"

"Sunday and Monday, sahib."

"The telegraph may have brought it, sir," said Hoby, "and the general may have thought it well to keep the secret. What was the meaning, by the bye, of what I saw yesterday? Some classies,* by the assistant adjutant general's order, were taking powder and ammunition up to the old thirty-second barracks; and later in the day——"

* Men employed to pitch tents, move ammunition, and the like.

"Great God! it's true enough!" broke in the major, who had been reading his letter; "from my brother at Furruckabad," he continued, striking the epistle on his knee, "and they know all about it there."

At that moment General Wheeler's aide-de-camp rode into the compound, came up to the verandah, and said,—

"Colonel, the general wishes your attendance at his quarters. No hurry; finish your tea first. Well, Bruce, what news of the Sky Races—are they to come off?"

"I really don't know," Bruce replied, rising, walking up to the questioner's side, and patting his horse. "Your Arab seems in good condition for them." The major continued, but in a low voice, "Of course, you've heard it all; this letter from Furruckabad confirms it. Take it with you if you will, and show it to the general."

"Yes; horrid, is it not?" the aide-de-camp replied, taking the letter; "but don't speak of it before that native."

"Oh, he knows it; they know it in the bazaar; every one in Cawnpore will know it in another hour."

"Good morning," said the aide-de-camp as he rode off at a quiet trot. "It can be kept dark no longer," he muttered to himself; "and the general may as well do whatever he means to do openly."

The tea party broke up quickly, and each wended his way home, or called on some other friend to discuss the matter. They parted with different feelings; the greater part, though horrified at the wholesale massacre that had been perpetrated, did not anticipate that the mutiny would spread further. There were probably, they thought, some circumstances. both at Meerut and Delhi, to explain it—some circumstances which aggravated the sepoys, that they did not know of; and the idea that their own regiment, the 99th, could follow the example set them, did not for a moment enter their heads. "Did not their native officers assure them daily the regiment was loyal to the back-bone; and did they not see it whenever they went into the lines, whenever they spoke to any of the men?" "They did not believe *any* of the Cawnpore regiments were disaffected; but their own regiment, the 99th—bah!" "I only wish I were as certain of getting a lack of rupees," said a lieutenant much in debt, to a brother officer, during their walk home, "as that our sepoys will stick to us through thick and thin."

A few there were, Edgington and Hoby among the number, who did not look so hopefully at the future. "Ce n'est que le premier pas qui coûte," said the latter to our hero; "*that* is passed, and God only knows where this will stop. I believe our regiment is stanch, but of the other regiments here I know little; and who can say what example, backed up by caste sympathy, may do either with them or our own men?"

"True," Edgington replied; "I should feel much more confidence in their loyalty if we had a thousand European bayonets at Cawnpore. But I *do* trust this Delhi affair is exaggerated: women and children killed, the former worse than killed,—I can scarcely believe the sepoys would be such brutes."

"Well, we shall know more, possibly, to-day," said Hoby, as he turned into his quarters. "God grant it be so; and God grant, above all, that both here and throughout India those in authority will awaken to the danger!"

They did know more, and that self-same day. Further and further details reached Cawnpore by letters, both English and native; and before evening they knew, if not all the circumstances of the Meerut and Delhi revolt, quite enough of the terrible scenes enacted.

Edgington did not allow the accounts, in all their terrible reality, to reach Marion. Much that, in the course of a few days, he both heard and read was quite unfit for a young girl to know; and though he told her there had been a mutiny at Delhi, he did not detail to her any of its horrors.

Our readers will perhaps be anxious to learn how the account of this rebellion up country was received by the native force at Cawnpore. "In the most satisfactory way," as Colonel Carstairs himself expressed it, four or five days after the intelligence arrived. That officer had himself carried to the general the assurance from the subadars* and jemadars* of the 99th, of the unchangeable loyalty of their men; and he (the colonel) had reason to believe the same thing had occurred with all the native infantry regiments at the station. Equally satisfactory was the case of the one native cavalry corps at Cawnpore (the Oude Irregular Cavalry, before mentioned, had been sent away, serious doubts being entertained of their loyalty), the troopers of which unanimously expressed their disgust at the conduct of the mutineers, and begged their claim to be registered, that if a cavalry regiment should be sent to fight at Delhi, theirs might be chosen.

Some few there were, however, who, in spite of all this, doubted; and when, a very few days after the news of the Meerut and Delhi mutinies arrived, intelligence reached Cawnpore that the troops at Ferozepore had also risen, while those at Meean Meer (Lahore) had been disarmed, these few felt that any day might turn Cawnpore into a scene of bloodshed such as had been enacted at Delhi, and that not an hour should be lost in preparing in the best possible manner for such a contingency.

Luckily the general commanding was fully alive to the critical position in which things stood. Though, during many years spent in Hindostan, he had never seen the sepoy exhibit himself in the light which those latter-day events had called forth, he did not, like Colonel Carstairs, deem it impossible that others of

* Native commissioned officers.

the same caste and race would follow the example set them by their brethren. And when day after day passed by, and the citadel of Delhi, the palace of the Mogul princes, remained in the hands of the mutineers, and the new sovereign they had elected still sat on his blood-stained throne, he was not unconscious what a temptation this apparent weakness on our side gave to the rebel movement.

The European force at Cawnpore at this time, numbering but one hundred and fifty bayonets, with a very few guns,—for which, even, there were not sufficient gunners,—was quite insufficient to enable the commander to show such an imposing front as would warrant an attempt to disarm the troops. He was therefore, though unwillingly, obliged to resort to other tactics, and while acting as if he placed the fullest confidence in the sepoys, make such preparations as he could to meet any outbreak.

Here, however, arose another difficulty. Any defensive operations would argue a doubt as to the loyalty of the native soldiers, and to conduct any such without their knowledge was simply impossible. It was therefore resolved to disseminate a belief that the fortifications and other measures adopted were necessary owing to the unsettled state of the North-Western Provinces, and were, in fact, to repel any outward foe, not to guard against home treachery.

Nana Sahib, the rajah of Bhitoor, had, as we have previously stated, offered any assistance in his power; and as no one doubted the sincerity of his offer, the general commanding applied to him for aid, which he promptly furnished, sending two hundred infantry, one hundred cavalry, and two guns, to be disposed of as the general thought best.

There were two spots in Cawnpore which appeared eligible for the intrenchments those in authority determined to construct: one was the magazine; the other, two buildings known as the European hospital-barracks. The latter point was chosen, and an intrenchment some five feet in height was hastily thrown up, inclosing the said two buildings.

Fifteen lacs of rupees (£150,000) being in the treasury, both General Wheeler and the civilian in charge were aware that it held out a great temptation to the troops to mutiny, and it was therefore determined to place it all within the intrenchment. But the treasury was guarded by a body of sepoys; and on its being intimated to them that the unsettled state of the country rendered necessary its removal to a safer spot, the native officer of the guard, calling his men together, replied with all apparent submission, but in a manner that showed he intended if possible to carry out his point, that no fear need be entertained for its safety from any body of rebels or budmashes in and around Cawnpore, as both he and his men would defend it with the last drop of their blood.

It was evident that any attempt to carry the point by force would only hasten the catastrophe which the greater part of the European officers now expected; and as delay was always in favour of the English, inasmuch as reinforcements might later arrive, it was determined to receive the loyal professions of the guard in good part, and, making a virtue of necessity, leave the treasure where it was.

With the object of showing the sepoys the confidence reposed in them, and on the plea that the commanders might be with their men in case of any disturbance from without, the regimental officers of each native corps were directed to sleep in the lines; and it spoke not a little for the bravery and devotion of England's sons, that this order, involving great nightly risks,—nay, certain death, if mutiny should break out,—was obeyed, not only without a murmur, but with alacrity and cheerfulness by all.

Edgington, as we have stated, had endeavoured to keep Marion as unconscious as he could of the horrors which had attended the up-country mutinies; and now, with regard to the state of Cawnpore, he in her presence treated the subject lightly. Miss Paris had, however, from others learned enough to teach her that sepoy revolts were not without danger at least to life and limb; nor was she ignorant, at this very period, that a mutiny at Cawnpore might be daily looked for.

When, therefore, the order apppeared that Edgington, with others, was to sleep in the lines of the regiment, it distressed her not a little. She fully appreciated the danger attendant thereon; and though not left alone in the bungalow, for Mr. Peters and his wife were with her, she during that time passed many a sleepless night, conceiving every sound she heard the outbreak of violence, and fancying all manner of evils for her guardian, Mr. Hoby and others, who, far away in the dark night, lay surrounded by ruthless savages, who under like circumstances in other stations had not hesitated to slay and kill.

One night about this time, as poor Marion lay tossing about in the restless sleep which was now her nightly portion, she dreamed a terrible dream. Unconnected and unnatural as most dreams are, this was no exception to the rule. Her mind, however, as continually happens with us all, took no note of its improbabilities and discrepancies, but when the horror of the scene she conjured up had attained its climax, she awoke with a piercing scream.

Her dream, as far as she could recall and arrange the confusion in which it was enshrouded, was as follows:—

The troops at Cawnpore had mutinied; and her guardian, Mr. and Mrs. Peters, and herself were shut up in Edgington's bungalow, besieged by a large body of mutineers. For two whole days and nights did the siege last; for the building was strong, and they were assisted in its defence by all the native servants in both her guardian's and Mr. Peters's service. At the end of the second day but little or no advantage had been gained by the besieging party, and the firing, which was kept up with little intermission against the walls, had ceased for a short time. Her friends and herself had assembled in a small room on the ground floor, and were taking some hastily-prepared tea after the fatigues and anxieties of the day, when they heard, as it were below them, a sound of digging, or rather excavating underground. Edgington, by whose side she sat, turned pale when he heard it, and declared to them his fears that the besiegers were driving a mine, which they would probably fire on the morrow. All night did the hammering sound continue. Sleep, of course, was out of the question, and they awaited daylight under the belief that it would usher in their last day on earth. Marion, in her dream, was calm in contemplation of the death that awaited her, for death had never inspired this young girl with the excessive dread it does many. The morning dawned, and on their surveying the rebel force from one of the barricaded windows, they were conscious that their numbers had been much augmented during the night. At last Edgington, who continued to look out after the others had retired in despair, called out they were saved, for that among the crowd he saw Nana Sahib, the rajah of Bhitoor, who had paid them a visit but a few days before; and that he doubted not the accession of strength was owing to the rajah's troops, who would certainly persuade the rebel sepoys to raise the siege. Shortly after, a messenger with a flag of truce appeared, and, on being admitted into the bungalow, said he had been sent by the rajah to offer them deliverance; but that one condition must be accepted therewith, which was, that the Missee Baba (Marion) should be given over to his master, as the rajah loved her, and wished to marry her. Edgington and Mr. Peters refused to capitulate on such terms, and poor Marion, who felt she would willingly lay down her life for them, could not make up her mind to the dreadful sacrifice offered, and did not, therefore, combat their resolution. As the messenger retired, he told the servants the offer he had brought, and added that, on the refusal being received, the mine which was prepared under the house would be fired, and that all those not killed by the explosion would be at the mercy of the besiegers. The servants, who had hitherto fought bravely in defence of their masters, then came in a body, and insisted on the terms being accepted, adding that *they* had accepted them already, and were about to open the doors to the besiegers. Edgington and Mr. Peters remonstrated; but even as they did so, a guard of the Nana's entered the house, followed by the rajah himself, who advanced to claim his bride. He took her hand, in spite of Edgington's attempts to prevent him, and passing his arm round her waist, was about to remove her, when poor Marion awoke with a shriek as we have stated.

So long and terrible were the cries she uttered, that Mrs. Peters, who slept in the adjoining room, was at her bedside as she opened her eyes, red with weeping. Marion's first impulse was to throw herself on the bosom of her friend, as she fervently thanked her God it *was* but a dream, and clung to Mrs. Peters with the feeling of fear such dreams produce in even those waking moments.

"Oh, such a terrible dream, Mrs. Peters! Tell me nothing has happened!"

"Nothing, dear Marion—nothing. Compose yourself, my dear girl," added Mrs. Peters; "I am here—no one can harm you."

"But it was so real, so life-like," continued Marion, as she trembled violently; "and yet I cannot think what made me dream it."

"What was it, tell me?" said Mrs. Peters, knowing that its recital would calm her young friend. "Now, begin at the beginning; I'm not at all sleepy, and can sit with you as long as you like."

Marion did so. As she proceeded, the absurdities she had not before been conscious of struck her; and she had so far recovered her composure when she concluded, that she said,—

"A foolish dream, was it not, Mrs. Peters; and a vain one too?"

"Not likely to be verified at all events," her friend replied. "Remember, the rajah is a firm friend to the English; besides, no Hindu may marry a Christian. But it was a strange dream, and I do not wonder it frightened you. Now, do you think you can go to sleep quietly, dear Marion¿ Remember, I am in the next room, and will come any moment you call. You will break hearts enough yet in sober reality," she merrily added, kissing the beautiful girl as she sat up in bed, "without inventing extra conquests in your dreams. Now, God bless you, and dream no more; or at least, only dream pleasant dreams."

We have, at the cost of possibly wearying the reader, detailed Miss Paris's dream at length. It will in after-scenes account for the terrible aversion and fear with which she regarded the Nana; but we must not anticipate, and we will now return to the arrangements going on in Cawnpore—the defensive arrangements in case of an outbreak.

The intrenchments we have alluded to progressed daily, and a large quantity of powder was brought in and buried. The guns,—they were but few,—were placed in position; and as one of the two buildings enclosed by the defensive earthwork had a thatched roof, tiles were placed over the thatch, to lessen the chances of fire.

More could not be done, and the days now passed with dreadful anxiety to many. Some,—their number had much decreased lately,—still affected to treat all these defensive measures as unnecessary. They were quite sure the sepoys would be faithful, and had never in their lives slept with a greater feeling of security than they now did nightly in the quarter-guards of their regiments. The mass, however, during the last few days, thought otherwise, and were ready at a moment's warning to send their wives and families into the intrenchment.

The reader must not suppose that the inhabitants of Cawnpore were confined to the civil and military officers in the service of the East-India Company. The town itself, apart from the cantonments and the civil quarter, was large, and filled with a numerous population. The greater part of these were of course natives, Hindus and Mahommedans; but there were also many Europeans engaged in trade or mercantile pursuits, besides a fair sprinkling of Jews, Parsees, and Armenians, all of whom had as much to dread as the Europeans themselves from a sepoy revolt. Latterly, that is to say, from the 20th of May, as the danger became more imminent, great numbers of these had, with the sanction of the authorities, passed the nights in one of the European barracks; and such of the civilians and officers as lived in out-of-the-way spots also sent their wives and children to the same place every evening.

Edgington, however, kept Marion at his bungalow, as it was not far from the intrenchments, and he did not wish to expose her to the inconveniences others suffered, until he was obliged to do so.

In such times may be seen, in all its force, the love of property inherent in many. Now, and a little later, when it was still more a case of life *versus* goods, numbers of the shopkeepers would not leave their stalls at night,—they preferred the risk of death, surrounded by their household gods, to the safety of the rendezvous, at the cost of abandoning for a few hours their merchandise.

An exodus from Cawnpore also began at this time, but it was principally confined to the rich natives, whose property was easily removed, and who, foreseeing the dangers that threatened, sought elsewhere safer resting-places.

It will be remembered that the treasure was still in charge of a sepoy guard, they having virtually refused to allow of its removal to the intrenchments. But the loyalty of the sepoys becoming daily more and more doubtful; and reinforced as the authorities now were by the troops sent from Bhitoor, they determined to take the charge, by force if necessary, out of the hands of these men, and transfer it to a guard composed of the Nana's troops. Strange as it appeared at the time, however, those who had hitherto been its custodians made no objection to this arrangement, and the change was peaceably effected.

Thus ended the pleasant month of May. As if to make the misery of the Cawnpore inmates all the worse, the latter portion of the month was frightfully hot; and we need not observe that, with the existing state of things, not an hour's peace or repose from the heat was allowed to the European sufferers. Twenty times every day was a report spread that the troops would mutiny that night, or that the plan of the rising was settled, or that emissaries from some up-country station had arrived with details of further mutinies, the usual massacre of the Europeans, and extravagant promises from the king of Delhi to all soldiers who showed their hatred of the Feringhees by zaf kur-ing (butchering) them. Every day did the lower order of natives around Cawnpore assume a more insolent tone when they addressed the English; every day did the Government paper fall in value, at first twenty, then thirty, forty, and even fifty per cent. below par; every night did a part of the Europeans pass a hot and miserable night at the great rendezvous in the European barracks;—and thus dawned Monday, the first day of June, in the memorable year one thousand eight hundred and fifty-seven.

## CHAPTER XIX.

THE RAJAH OF BHITOOR—REINFORCEMENTS GAINED AND LOST—THE STORM GATHERS—IT BREAKS.

NANA SAHIB! Are they not almost household words in English mouths? Are they not the personification of all we can conceive terrible and to be hated in human nature? Does not the name call up the idea of a perfect devil in man's shape,—a being full of treachery, cruelty, cowardice, and every despicable vice—void of compassion, void of any heavenly-born attribute, gloating over the hellish torments he inflicts; in whose ears the manly shriek of anguish, the supplicating voice of woman, the cry of childhood, finds no response,—a being execrated by the whole civilized world, and calling up a blush in every honest man's cheek, that such an incarnate fiend should wear his own shape?

Yes, Nana Sahib, this is the inheritance you have gained for yourself; be it our lot to increase, if it be possible, each and every one of these feelings, and to hand you down to posterity as—as—what you are, for we truly know nothing on earth with which you may be compared.

Before, in further pages, we paint the acts of this monster, let us say a few words on his antecedents. The lives of great criminals are generally supposed to possess an interest; and the Nana may assuredly claim a front-rank place in that crowd.

He was the adopted son of Bajee Rao, the ex-Peishwa of the Mahrattas, who, on his death, left the Nana nearly the whole of his vast property, amounting to *forty* million rupees. On the Peishwa's death, Nana

Sahib petitioned the Government to be acknowledged his heir and successor, and that the jaghire* of Bhitoor should descend to him. This was not granted, and we presume the first seeds of his animosity to the English were sown at that time. Though not so rich as he would have been, had he inherited the large pension allowed by the East-India Company to the ex-Peishwa, the four millions sterling which he received made him one of the wealthiest men in the country.

He lived in his fort at Bhitoor, and associated much with the English, attending many parties at Cawnpore, and often inviting the officers, both civil and military, from that station to hunting-parties and *fêtes* at his palace. He was tolerably well educated, spoke English besides one or two Eastern languages, and had read some of the famous English authors. He was agreeable in conversation; recognized, apparently, the advantages of western civilization; and was, as almost all natives of rank are, a gentleman in his manners.

That Nana Sahib had the right, as well as every other chieftain in India, to take up arms against the English, and try to drive the foreign conquerors from his country, we cannot doubt. All nations have the right to throw off a foreign yoke, no matter how attained; and we know of nothing to except Hindostan from the rule. Had the late war in India been simply a war of independence, who conscientiously in Europe could have decried it? But it was not so. Patriotism has no existence in Hindostan; the mass care little who governs them. We have, however, in former pages, stated at length what we conceive were the causes that led to this war, and who were the movers therein, and it is not, therefore, necessary to repeat all this. With respect to Nana Sahib, however, and other chieftains who have taken up arms against us, it is *not*, we conceive, the simple fact of their having done so which

* Estate.

should make us decry them; but because the act was generally accompanied with black treachery—because it was always attended with revolting cruelties, therefore are we justified, in *all* their cases, in dealing out a heavy punishment, now that the day of our ascendancy has dawned; while to the vilest of them all, the cruel monster of Bhitoor, we trust, when caught, the hangman's rope will be his speedy doom.

"Good news—good news!" exclaimed Edgington, as, on the morning of the 2nd of June, he broke into the breakfast-room, where sat Mr. and Mrs. Peters, with Marion, the latter making tea; "good news, indeed! Two companies of Europeans—the Queen's 84th—have marched in this morning from Allahabad. But that's not all; half a battery of Oude Horse Artillery has also come: so now, dear Marion, you may, I think, sleep quietly at night, for you will be well guarded."

"It *is* good news," said Mr. Peters; "when and where did you learn it?"

"I saw the two companies and the guns myself; the former, I suppose, were expected, but the latter, it seems, we owe quite to chance, for they were on their way to Futtyghur, but the officer in charge came here, as a portion of the troops with him had mutinied."

"Well, it's an ill wind that blows nobody good," Mrs. Peters remarked. "Do you really think, Captain Edgington, that we may now expect peace and quiet?"

"I hope so," our hero replied; "and even if the worst came to the worst, and any of the regiments mutinied, with the European force and guns we now have, and those intrenchments to retire into, we could most easily defend the place until succour arrived."

"The intrenchments seem to me, though, to be paltry affairs," remarked Mr. Peters. "As a civilian, of course, I know little or nothing of such things; but the parapets are not higher than my chin, and a good jumper, horse or man, could spring over them."

"They might, certainly," said Edgington; "but

with guns belching forth grape from those mounds, and the musketry we can now place behind them, I much doubt any men or horses attempting the freak. Anyhow, the intrenchments are the best that could be constructed at such short warning, and I'm only too glad we have them. No; I'm in earnest when I say we are very, very fortunate to have received these reinforcements; for though I do not prognosticate evil, I have for the last three days been ready to take you into the intrenchments, Marion, at a moment's warning."

"How do you mean *ready?*" said Mrs. Peters. "You have not even had Marion's clothes packed."

"If we do go into the intrenchments," Edgington replied, "we shall go with very little. Marion's ayah has a small box prepared with a few necessaries. I have a carpet-bag; two light charpoy bedsteads stand ready in the verandah; my small hill-tent is packed; my gun and rifle are in their case, my pistols in my sword-belt; my hog-spear is with the mahout, who will bring it with him: the elephant will carry these few things, and not another article shall I attempt to move out of the bungalow."

"I think you are right," remarked Peters; "and I will to-day get ourselves up in as light marching order. There's no harm in being prepared. Unfortunately, I have no tent, and I expect that is the greatest necessary."

"Fortunately for me," said Edgington, laughing; "for you can take one of mine. If we go into the intrenchments, I never expect to see anything again that I leave behind; so, it may be, you will be the means of saving me a tent."

"I'll take it, then," replied Peters. "I wish I knew where to buy a pair of revolvers; I've nothing but old single-barrel pistols."

"Revolvers are not easily found at this moment," Edgington remarked. "Hoby, of our regiment, showed me a pair yesterday, he'd bought of a native for four hundred rupees,* which, when all was quiet, would certainly not have sold for a quarter the sum."

"Come, this is all very martial conversation," said Mrs. Peters, smiling; "but I don't see why you should have it all to yourselves, so I shall join in. Pistols were the subject, I think, and you regretted you had not a pair of revolvers, Edmund; but it never struck you that your wife might want something of the sort. See here," she continued, putting her hand into her pocket, and taking out a little pistol, six inches long, capped and loaded;—"see here; I was obliged to take care of myself, Edmund, and bought a tiny pair the other day in the bazaar. Marion has the other —in her room, not in her pocket," she continued, as Edgington started; "and we can both load and fire them to perfection. Yes; while you two have been away in the mornings, we've had a little practice on our own account; and I really don't now know which is the best shot. Which do you think, Marion?"

"I believe we are nearly even. I broke one ghurrah† more than you this morning, but then you beat me yesterday," replied Miss Paris, with an inclination to laugh at her manly exploits.

"Well, upon my word, the best thing I ever heard!" said Edgington, as he made all the teacups on the table ring from the force with which he struck the table. "It only requires circumstances, to draw out Englishwomen. Is it not so, Peters,—and are you not proud of your wife? I'm proud of you, dear Marion. Who'd ever have dreamt of *your* practising pistol-shooting?—Ha, ha, ha! capital, I declare."

"It is not what I would do from choice, dear Arthur, but I quite agreed with Mrs. Peters it could do us no harm to know both how to load and fire."

"And how long have you both been practising?" asked Peters.

* £40. † An Eastern pot for holding water.

"Just a week," Marion answered.

"A week!" Edgington exclaimed. "Why, I thought you *then* had no idea of danger."

"I had, though," replied Marion, "and so had Mrs. Peters; but we saw both Mr. Peters and yourself wished us to know nothing, for fear it should alarm us. We allowed you to think you had succeeded, but we determined, all the same, not to be wanting at the eleventh hour."

"God bless you, Marion,—you are indeed a treasure." After a little pause, Edgington, who had been looking at Marion with tears in his eyes, added, with assumed cheerfulness, "Now that we have done breakfast, let's stand in the verandah and have a little pistol-shooting all together. Get your pistol, dear Marion, and as you *will* be so warlike, let me give the finishing touch to your knowledge."

Reader, this is no solitary instance. Many and many English ladies learnt the same thing during eventful 1857. Many, with the cry of the dying and the wounded in their ears, loaded as fast as their husbands could fire. If ever female heroism stood out in the peculiarly bright colours which belong to it, it was on Hindostan's burning plains that year.

On the same evening two fires broke out in the cantonments, and two officers' dwellings were completely destroyed. These were not the first cases that had occurred: there had been two or three within the last week; and as Edgington, from his verandah, with Marion by his side, watched the flames shoot high in the air, he recollected but too well that the mutinies at Meerut, Delhi, and Ferozepore had been ushered in in the same way.

"Would to God, dear Marion, that you had never left England, or that I could send you away now," said Edgington, as he gazed, by the illumination one of the burning bungalows threw into his verandah, on the beauteous face of his *protégée,* whose hair shone like burnished gold in that red light, "for Cawnpore is not the place for you."

"That is the unkindest speech, Arthur, you ever made me. Know you not there is selfishness in that wish? It distresses you to see me in such scenes, and *therefore* you would have me gone. But you think not of the misery I should feel when I knew you were here alone. Would it not, then, be kinder to forget the pain my danger causes you, and let me remain where my inclination prompts, and where I am happiest?"

Edgington took Marion's hand in his, but answered not. A few minutes later he looked at his watch, by the light the burning bungalows still gave out.

"It is time for me, dearest, to go to the quarter-guard—I was a little late last night. Don't fancy I'm miserable there; we are a merry party in every way. We smoke and chat all the early part of the night, and my bed is as comfortable as it would be under this roof. Now, God bless you! Remember what I told you this morning; we are quite safe with the extra English soldiers we now have."

The night passed quietly, the fires burned out, and the inhabitants of Cawnpore awoke sound in life and limb to another day.

"Bad news!" said Hoby, coming into Edgington's room about eleven o'clock next morning. "I met one of the staff just now who told me a company of the 84th and one of the 32nd are to march at once towards Lucknow. It seems Sir Henry Lawrence has written to the general for all the Europeans he can spare. In my opinion, he can spare none; but, anyhow, they are to go."

"I'll tell you what, Hoby," said Edgington, as he rose from his writing-table, and put his hand on his friend's shoulder, "if it be so, God help us all! for two days will not pass over our heads before our sepoys mutiny. I *see* it in their very looks—could *you* see no change last night in their manner?"

"I saw what I——"

"Hush," whispered Edgington; "here comes Miss Paris."

"I have come to tell you some bad news, Arthur," said Marion, as she entered. "The gulundazes* of the Oude artillery have nearly all deserted. My ayah heard it just now, and came to me at once, *She* says the report is, the sepoys will rise to-night. These are sad times for us all, are they not, Mr. Hoby?"

"We must hope for the best, Miss Paris," said poor Hoby, who, confident as he was that not many hours would pass tranquilly, looked with anguish past words to describe on the fair girl before him, whom he loved with his whole heart.

The voice of Edgington's bearer, at that moment, was heard outside, as he said, "The Sahib is in his writing-room. I'll take him the books."

"No," answered another man's voice, "I'll take them myself;" and the next moment the chick† which separated Edgington's writing-room from the outer one was lifted up, and a sepoy in uniform, with the order-books under his arm, appeared. He saluted as he delivered them to our hero.

Edgington read them, made some laughing remark to Marion, and handed them to Hoby.

Hoby read, and returned them to the sepoy, who departed with another salute.

"Nothing bad in them?" asked Marion anxiously, during the silence which followed the sepoy's departure.

"Not exactly bad," replied Edgington evasively; "but leave us, dear Marion, I have some business I must talk over with Mr. Hoby. What *can* I say to comfort you, my poor dear girl?" he continued, as Marion rose from her chair with a look of great distress.

"Tell me all, Arthur; don't treat me as you do, in that respect. Have I ever shown, by my words or my manner," continued the young girl, with a proud move-

* Native artillery-men. † Curtain of thin bamboo strips.

ment of her head, "that I cannot bear to hear of danger,—that it unnerves me? Why then keep me in ignorance? It is not fair to me, Arthur, dear Arthur—is it, Mr. Hoby?—I ask you to plead for me. Tell me all, Arthur; I know already too much not to know more. Believe me, I shall meet any danger the better for knowing it beforehand; but now, seeing you keep things back, I fancy matters worse than perhaps they are. So you will tell me, won't you?"

Hoby spoke. "There is little to tell; but that little were I in Captain Edgington's place, I would tell you, Miss Paris. I feel convinced you are equal to hear anything, and that you should know all."

"Yes, Marion, you shall know what little you do not know already," said Edgington, "Two companies of the Europeans are ordered to Lucknow, where, it seems, they are much wanted; and neither myself nor any of the officers of our regiment are to sleep in the lines any more."

"The last news more than compensates for the first," said Marion affectionately; "though I suppose it bodes ill likewise. Tell me more,—why is the last order given?"

"*That* we don't know," Hoby replied; "but as the order applies to all the regiments here, save one, and that one I know is thought the most loyal, we must presume it is no longer thought safe for us to do so."

"At all events, dear Arthur, you will leave me no more of an evening. You will sleep here. And you, Mr. Hoby, you too will not again pass the night in danger. Oh, what a comfort all that is, and how very, *very* happy it has made me. I will go and tell Mrs. Peters;—she is getting a few things ready, in case we must go into the intrenchments. Arthur, the sepoy who was in here just now with the order-books looked at you *so* earnestly as you read them. Did *you* observe him, Mr. Hoby? I'm sure that man means mischief. What am I to do about my ayah; poor thing, she says she's sure to be killed if the sepoys mutiny and she's found in my service. She wants to ask you if it would not be better to go into the intrenchments at once."

"Oh, tell her the report the sepoys will mutiny to-night is no better than the same and like reports we've had for a whole week," Edgington answered. "Tell her, also, ten minutes at any time will take us into the intrenchments; and now run away, dear Marion, and leave me with Mr. Hoby."

But events crowd on, and we must not delay too much by the way.

The two companies for Lucknow left that same afternoon. Edgington saw them go, and felt he would give all he had to detain them. He was painfully conscious of the altered demeanour in the men of his regiment; he heard the same thing from other officers, and he now hourly expected the outbreak.

Another day passed, and on the following evening he sat in the verandah about ten o'clock with Mr. and Mrs. Peters and Marion. Hoby and Percy had both come there after the mess-dinner, and the conversation, of course, was on the one subject—the anticipated mutiny.

"I don't think even Colonel Carstairs now believes in the loyalty of our sepoys," Hoby remarked; "and I think he has been the last to give way. You, Percy, were one of their champions, and it took not a little in your case to make you think our men might follow the example set them elsewhere."

"I do not *now* feel at all sure," Percy answered, "that our men will mutiny, though it is, I fear, very probable. Either, in my opinion, *all* the troops here will continue faithful, or *all* will revolt. It will be no case of partial rising, for the sympathy which binds the sepoys together will come strongly into play, when one regiment has risen, and force the rest into the same path."

"I quite agree with you," remarked Peters; "the

only question is, whether it is still possible to keep them all straight. Great disaffection, doubtless, exists at this moment, and has latterly increased in growth. This is, I am sure, partly attributable to emissaries from other stations, and partly to the numberless reports which serve to inflame the sepoys' minds, and to the religious character given to the rising. More than all, perhaps, to the success achieved, and still maintained at Delhi, by the rebels. Many of the men, both here and elsewhere, would rather not revolt; but they begin to fear they are attaching themselves to the losing side; they fear the gibes, if not the hostility, of their comrades, and they, too, will probably, though against their own wishes, follow in the stream."

"It does not now, surely, at this eleventh hour, signify much *why* the men revolt," sagely remarked Mrs. Peters; "would it not be better, therefore, to employ whatever time we have in deciding how we shall each and severally act when the mutiny breaks out? otherwise the news will confuse us all, and we shall not know what to do first."

"As for Marion and myself, our plans are all settled," said Edgington. "The few things intended to go into the intrenchment are all packed and ready. If I am then called away, Marion will go on the elephant. You will surely go on the elephant too, Mrs. Peters."

"No," Peters remarked; "my buggy-horse stands ready harnessed, and we shall drive there. It's no use, I fear, attempting to send my other horses in."

"None at all," said Hoby; "I much doubt if every officer will be allowed even one horse. How could they be fed?"

"I shall take my favourite Arab, all the same," Edgington remarked, "and trust to keep him. It will be hard to part with all the others; but so it must be. Why, nearly a thousand persons will be in that intrenchment, including all the townspeople, and in this frightful heat too. Ah, Marion, if we do go in, you must make up your mind to great sufferings, if only from the crowd, the heat, and want of space."

"Between two and three hundred women and children alone slept at the barrack rendezvous last night," said Hoby, "and the heat was frightful."

"We shall all suffer, doubtless," remarked Marion, mildly; "but we must assist one another, and trust to the Almighty for deliverance. We *must* support one another, Mrs. Peters, must we not?" added Marion, as she nestled closer up to that lady's side; "for it will, doubtless, be very terrible, and nothing——"

"What is that light to the left over those trees?" broke in Percy. "See, it increases, and now flames dart up. Great God! it's the riding-master's bungalow on fire! Is this never to stop? Surely these fires must warn us."

"And they do so," replied Hoby: "at least they do me. Come along, Percy, we ought to go to the fire; perhaps we can be of use. What a noise there is in the direction of the cavalry lines. Good God! what does all that shouting mean? There go some officers to the fire," he added, as two or three horsemen passed at full gallop in that direction.

"Hark! there are many horses," Edgington exclaimed a minute later. "Surely it's more than the fire," he whispered to Peters at his side. "How quick the bungalow burns. I see the road now quite plainly by its light. Here comes Earnest, of our regiment; he'll tell us what it is. Holloa, Earnest," called out Edgington, "What is it?—going to the fire?"

"Fire!—no. What, great God! have you not heard? The cavalry's up! Hear how they shout. To the intrenchments, quick. Merton's away on duty, and I'm going to fetch his wife. We shall meet there, I hope; if not, adieu."

The clatter of hoofs told how quick Earnest sped on

his charitable mission. Edgington turned round, and saw Marion, with a pallid face, leaning against the verandah pillar; but in the momentarily-increasing noise he heard her voice, which firmly said, "I am ready, Arthur."

## CHAPTER XX.

THE MUTINY—THE INTRENCHMENTS—THE COUNCIL.

It was eleven at night, on Thursday, the 4th of June, when the events related at the close of the last chapter occurred. Seven hours have passed since then, and it is now six on Friday morning. The reader will kindly fancy himself inside the intrenchments, and may gaze around as we narrate what took place during that interval.

Half an hour after Edgington had hailed Earnest, and received the startling announcement, he and Marion stood within the defensive earthworks. No sooner, however, had our hero placed his ward in safety, than he passed out alone on his way to his commanding officer's bungalow, thinking it very likely he might be required on duty. Midnight sounded as he left the intrenchments; but the whole station was alive and moving. He soon met some officers, from whom he learnt the present position of affairs, which, in his hurry to place Marion in safety, he had not before had an opportunity to do. The regiment of cavalry had mutinied, had taken their arms and ammunition with them, as many spare horses as they could lay their hands on, and had gone off in the night, no one knew where.

"Then they committed no violence before they went?" asked Edgington of the officer who gave him this information.

"I believe not," replied his informer; "their main object appears to have been to get away with all their horses."

"And the infantry regiments, what are they doing?"

"Still in their lines; but how long they will stop, who can say? I've just come from the bazaar; the confusion there is tremendous. A large crowd, with numberless women and children, is on its way to the intrenchments. Were they very full when you left?"

"Not very," Edgington replied, "but filling fast. I must go and find my commanding officer,—you have not seen him by chance?"

"What, Colonel Carstairs?—Yes, I have; he is gone to the general's. I heard one of the staff say, about half an hour ago, that any orders given would be issued in the intrenchments, so I suppose that's the right place to go to."

Edgington turned back, and forcing his way through the dense crowd which blocked up the entrance, found Marion standing where he had left her, by the side of his elephant, while the mahout, with his assistant, was pitching the small hill-tent he had brought.

It did not take long to do this, and Edgington, having placed Marion's simple bed inside, persuaded her to go in and try to sleep.

He himself sat down in the open air on his charpoy, and awaited the arrival of Colonel Carstairs and the other officers of his regiment. At last, tired of watching, he stretched himself on the simple bed, and, in spite of the dreadful noise and confusion which raged around, fell asleep. It was six o'clock when he awoke, and he could not at first recollect where he was; but the crowd around, lying on the ground and in the verandahs of the barracks, with the earthen parapets in front, on which the guns were mounted, soon brought the reality before him.

Some of the officers of his regiment had arrived during the night, and among them was Colonel Carstairs. Our hero soon found him, and learned that, very early that morning, one of the infantry regiments had also left the lines, was supposed to have joined the cavalry, and to have proceeded with them to the *civil* quarter, two miles off, where all the treasure was lodged. The general, it seemed, had given orders for all the Christians in the town and station to go into the intrenchments, and was momentarily expected himself. Some officers, the colonel said, had, during the night, and early that morning, been to their regimental lines, to see if any hope remained of keeping the men to their allegiance; he, the colonel, had himself been to the 99th, but not a man would listen to him; many had warned him not to approach, while two sepoys had fired at him, as in despair he rode off.

"I never thought it would come to this," said the poor colonel with a heavy sigh. "I loved my regiment, and I thought they loved me."

"Have all the infantry regiments mutinied, then, sir?" asked Edgington.

"Very nearly so, I fear. All the officers who went told the same tale when they returned. One poor fellow was killed. I forget his name,—that young fellow doing duty with one of the regiments, who dined at our mess the other day. He could not understand what they said to him, and rode amongst them; they pulled him off his horse, and bayoneted him on the ground. Hoby was riding by and saw it,—dreadful, is it not?"

Mr. Blank, the old civilian, who was at the ball, came up at this instant.

"Have you heard the worst part of the business, colonel?"

"No; what is it?"

"Peters, who left the civil lines a little after I did, says the report there is that the Nana has joined the rebels, with all his troops."

"What! the rajah? That's surely impossible. He promised the general every assistance; and, as you know, gave troops to guard the treasure."

"Yes; for his own use, I suppose; for they had broken into the Treasury before *I* left this morning—that is, they and the cavalry together, who mutinied last night. What provisions have we here, do you know? Enough, I hope; for we shall be near a thousand souls in the intrenchments; and God only knows how long we may have to stop here."

"A month's provisions, I believe," said Edgington; "at least, I was told so."

"Where can all this enormous multitude be stowed?" said Mr. Blank. "The barracks can never hold them all; and then this cruel heat! These few outhouses will be the best places; for at least there will be some privacy there."

"Have you, then, no tent?" asked Edgington.

"Yes," answered Mr. Blank; "I never thought of it myself; but, thank goodness, my old bearer sent one yesterday. Only three of my servants have come with me—only three faithful out of thirty; for yesterday they all promised to come. My rifle, my papers, the clothes on my back, and that old English horse there, were all I saved; for I had not ten minutes before the cavalry were round the house. No, I saved another thing—that," he added, pointing to a large mushroom-shaped solar topee, or sun-hat, with which his bearer passed at that moment; "and I would not sell it at this moment for a thousand rupees. Fancy a June sun, and the comfort of such a covering! Whose elephant is that?"

"Mine," said Edgington.

"You don't suppose you'll be able to keep it here?" Mr. Blank asked.

"No, I know I can't. But I think it may be turned to some use. The mahout is, I believe, trustworthy; the elephant can travel an enormous distance in four-and-twenty hours; why should not notice of our position be sent down country to Allahabad, or Futtehpore at least?"

"A good idea. But I dare say the general has found other means to send the news. However, an extra string to our bow would do no harm," remarked Mr. Blank. "Hallo! Bruce; glad to see you. A doubtful sentiment, perhaps, when one looks around; but truly

I *am* glad. When did you come in? Of course, Mrs. Bruce is safe with you?"

"Behold her there!" Major Bruce replied, with an attempt at a smile, as he pointed to his wife, fastening herself the kurnauths* of the tiny tent they had brought. "Working hard and early. Lucky if the most delicate among us has not harder work before we leave this place."

"Have you brought much with you?" asked Mr. Blank.

"Much! That's all," he added, holding up a light carpet-bag he held in his hand. "The tent I sent in yesterday, before the mutiny. We were not so lucky as some others, and were glad to escape with our lives."

"Ah! how was that?"

"Strange to say, we heard nothing last night of the cavalry mutinying. We had gone to bed somewhat early, and were asleep when it occurred. My bungalow, as you know, stands by itself, and there was no noise to awaken us. I think, however, three of my servants knew it; for they had vanished this morning, probably with any loot† they could lay their hands on. I awoke at my usual hour, and was half-dressed, when my khansamah came rushing in, and told me the cavalry had mutinied last night, and that the Gillis Pultun‡ had risen this morning."

"Nearly the whole infantry regiment," said my khansamah, "are now on their way to the Treasury, and will pass by here in five minutes. I know that they will saf kur§ you and the Mem Sahib, if they find you here; so, for God's sake, run for your lives to the intrenchments. *I* will stop and bring everything you want afterwards." Even as he spoke, we heard the sepoys shouting on the road. I remembered Meerut and Delhi. Luckily,

* Sides or walls of a tent. † Plunder.
‡ 1st regiment. § Kill.

Mrs. Bruce was dressed. I snatched up my double-barrelled gun, stuck these pistols in my belt, passed out with her into the garden, then through the hedge into the compound of a native house, which stands near mine, gained the lower road, and came here as fast as we could."

"And your khansamah?"

"I have not seen him since; it is not more than half an hour since we arrived. Oh, here he is!" he exclaimed, as an old man, with a long white beard, supposed to be dressed in white, but so covered with black soot that the original colour of his clothes could scarcely be seen, advanced towards them, and made a low salaam to his master. "Well, Atma Sing," asked Bruce with much anxiety, "all right in the bungalow? what have you brought with you?"

"Khoda Lord Kurree" (God make you a lord), replied the Mussulman, with another salaam, "all is lost!"

"What, all in the bungalow? Nothing saved? All I have in the world! How was it?"

"The sepoys, sahib, as I expected, entered the bungalow and asked for you. I said you had gone to the intrenchments in the night. They abused me for being the servant to a Feringhee, who, they said, would in future be their servants,—at least, the ladies, for they would kill all the males. I was obliged, to save myself from violence, to speak as they did, and pretend to be with them. In five minutes they had taken everything valuable out of the house, for there were two hundred men looting it at the same moment; but they seemed in a great hurry to get on to the Treasury, and left all the heavy things. A subadar took your mare, sahib,—I mean the gray mare you call Bessie,—and wanted to ride her, but she kicked him off, knocked down two sepoys, who tried to stop her, and ran out of the compound. Before they left the bungalow they put fire in the thatch, and went away when it began to burn. All the other servants had run away when the sepoys first came in, and of course I could do nothing alone to put out the fire. I remembered the box with your papers in your writing-room (several sepoys had opened it, but left it when they saw there was nothing but paper inside), and ran in to get it. Part of the burning thatch fell on me, and I was much hurt; but I saved the box, sahib,"—pointing to it on a coolie's head—"and it is all I could save."

"So all I have is gone!" said poor Bruce with a sigh. "My mare, my dogs,—all in my house I delighted in. All gone in one fell swoop! It's somewhat hard to bear."

"Come, Bruce, your case is no worse than mine; I've lost everything too," said Mr. Blank, willing to console him.

"It *is* worse though," Bruce replied. "When this affair is over, if, please God, it be over quickly, you can get everything you want again, Blank; I cannot. How, do you ask? I am a poor man, I have a large family at home, and with the monthly instalments I pay to the Agra Bank my pay barely keeps me above water; how then can I rebuy everything? I have tasted poverty, Blank, been ground down with debt for years; you, I believe, have known nothing of the kind; how, then, are our losess equal?" Bruce concluded with a bitterness very foreign to his normal temper; but, during a long life in India, poverty had haunted him,—had prevented his visiting England and seeing his children. Was it then strange that the news he possessed nought but the clothes on his back was a severe blow?

To make after-events clear, we will now describe the intrenchments more closely than we have yet done. They consisted of a simple wall of earth, about five feet high, thrown up around two barracks and their out-houses. The space inside was a good deal larger than the buildings occupied, and was, at the time of which

we write, and for some days later, studded with ten
In a part of this open space, much exposed to the fire
an enemy from without, was a well, the only one in tl
fortification, and on which the garrison were depende
for water. On one side of the intrenchments was
church, and on the opposite side unfinished barracks f
the European infantry. The two large buildings withi
the intrenchments had verandahs, supported on mason
pillars, and the buildings themselves were plain ar
airy inside, for the purpose intended,—hospital barrack
One of them had a thatched roof, which, as befo
stated, had previous to this been covered with tiles,
decrease the chances of fire. Around the intrencl
ments, at different distances, were bungalows, wi
their outbuildings, other edifices, and compound walls

By noon all the Christian inhabitants of Cawnpo
were in the intrenchments, with the exception of a fe
shopkeepers in the town, who would not desert the
goods, as they believed the sepoys would simply mal
off with the treasure they had secured, and molest n
one. We say Christian in preference to European, f
a great many certainly did not come under the latt
head:—we allude to the Eurasians, or Indo-Briton
of whom there were an immense number, with the
families.

The numbers in the intrenchment might be roundl
estimated as follows :—

| | |
|---|---|
| Male Europeans, consisting of members of the civil service, officers, soldiers of the 84th, 32nd, and 1st Madras fusiliers, with a very few artillery-men ............... | 2( |
| Remaining Christian population of Cawnpore, consisting of merchants, tradesmen, clerks, pensioners, bandsmen, drummers, &c. &c. &c., of which some were European, but the greater part Anglo-Indian or Eurasian ........ | 2( |
| Ladies, women, and children, being the wives and families of all the classes above given ...................... | 3( |
| Native servants, who nearly all deserted during the first three or four days ................................ | 2( |
| Total ................. | 9 |

Thus, out of seven hundred souls in the intrenchments, exclusive of the native servants, but four hundred were men, and of these only about two hundred and fifty British-born; while not much more than a moiety of the whole number, or about two hundred and fifty in all, were fighting men by profession. When these numbers became known that day, many a bold-hearted Briton looked round upon the insignificant earthworks, on the seven guns mounted thereon (almost all of small calibre), and fervently prayed that the sepoys would content themselves with the treasure they had obtained, and not try conclusions with their late masters over the frail fortifications which would then be the only hope of the garrison.

It was very much doubted by *all*, on the day of which we write, whether any siege would take place. The sepoys had little to gain by it; had already secured a large amount of treasure; could now pillage the station at will; and it was therefore hoped they would decamp *en route* to that hotbed of rebellion, Delhi.

As the afternoon advanced, this hope increased; for while the garrison received intelligence which left them little doubt as to the rajah of Bhitoor having declared against them, they also learnt that at the head of all the rebels, and with the treasure packed on elephants, he had retreated north-westward.

This news was received with great joy throughout the garrison, and as, with the exception of a few marauding parties composed of sepoys and budmashes, and an occasional fire which broke out, the station appeared quiet, several officers mounted their horses, sallied forth, and visited their late dwellings, in some cases carrying away a few things they wanted, and in others bringing further information which left no doubt of the certain departure of the main body of the rebels. The bungalows visited were found, however, to have been more or less looted, while any horses left in the stables had been taken away.

Though all now hoped no siege would take place, pre parations were nevertheless wisely made that same after noon, in case their expectations proved fallacious. Th artillery was the first thing to be considered; and a the very few gunners they had were insufficient to ma it, volunteers for this service were called for from th infantry soldiers. Several officers, who understoo more or less of gunnery, also volunteered for the work and an artillery corps was quickly organized, differen men told off to the several guns, and this branch o service rendered as complete as circumstances allowed

The guns, as stated, were but seven in number—on 24-pounder and two 9-pounders, belonging to th Oude battery, which had fortunately arrived; as als four 6-pounders previously in possession of the garri sons. These had been placed in judicious positions and ammunition for each was now laid ready.

The buildings, and portions of them, were the allotted to different classes. In the barrack with th thatched roof all the women and children of the 32n were placed, as also the greater part of the wives an families of the townspeople. The other barrack wa given over to the soldiers and non-combatants, th latter, by the bye, professing their willingness to figh if occasion required it.

Nearly all the officers and members of the civil servic had tents for themselves and families; and to such a had not, the different out-houses mentioned were given

The hospital arrangements and medical departmen were also cared for—a portion of the thatch-roofe barrack being apportioned to the sick and wounde (already were there a few of both), while the medicine and surgical instruments were stowed away in a corne of that building.

Provisions for one month had been brought into th fortification; but these were generally of the most simpl kind. The staple food intended for the use of the garri son was attah (coarse brown flour), with which chupattee might be made, together with dall, a kind of pea. A few sheep and goats, to be killed later, were provided; but the rations did not go far beyond this; for such luxuries as tea, coffee, beer, and the like, which some had after the public stores began to run short, they only possessed from their own foresight in sending them into the intrenchments in time. Of rum for the use of the soldiers there was, however, a large quantity.

We have forgotten to mention, that early that morning the jail in the civil lines had been thrown open by the 2nd cavalry sowars, and that the whole of the prisoners had either joined the rebels or formed looting parties on their own account.

It is sunset—sunset of that first day in the intrenchments, and the crowd have come out from under the shelter which an Indian June's sun renders so necessary. It is evening, 'tis true; but an Indian evening during the hot winds speaks not of coolness or refreshment. The strong gusts of air which blow in fitful blasts carry with them, even at that hour, such heat as the denizens of temperate climates wot not of; and many in that curious crowd feel their suffocating influence the more painfully to-night for want of the cold-bath, which, in such weather, they usually take three or even four times a day, but which, for the last four-and-twenty hours, they have necessarily had to forego.

A party are sitting at the door of Edgington's tent, or rather on the open space between his and Mr. Peters's canvas abode. By an arrangement made that afternoon, the larger of the two tents was given for the use of Mrs. Peters, Marion, and Mrs. Merton (the pretty Eurasian), while Edgington, Peters, and Merton occupied the other. The latter officer, who was on duty when the mutiny broke out, and had foolishly made no fore-provision, had no tent of his own; so Edgington kindly gave him and his little wife shelter. We said the party were sitting, but "lying" would be the more proper word, for they boasted but two chairs between them all; and though two or three were sitting on Edgington's charpoy, which he had brought out, the greater number were lying down on the hot and dusty ground.

"This is not playing at soldiers," drawled out Percy, as he raised himself on one elbow, and rubbed off the lines of thick dust from under his eyes;—"this is the first day, but it's quite enough for me. Oh, what would I give for a refreshing mussuck."*

"If we have not worse to come," remarked Hoby, "we ought to feel very grateful. We've had nothing as yet but a day under canvas in the hot winds,—not pleasant at any time, but no great hardship in itself."

"But it is hardship," said Percy, "not to change your clothes all day in such weather, and that too with no excitement to keep you going. I'd rather, myself, if there were no ladies and children in the case, be shut up here for a week with guns booming all round, than lead the cooped-up life we have to-day."

"Well, there *are* ladies and children in the case," remarked Hoby, "and so we'll hope for the cooped-up life, even if it does bore you. Is it not extraordinary," he said, turning to Mrs. Peters, with a desire to draw the fair Marion into the conversation, "that Nana Sahib, after all his professions of friendship, should have joined the mutineers? I suppose the fifteen lacs in the Treasury were too potent a temptation."

"Or he's a traitor at heart," said Miss Paris with energy. She blushed the next minute, when she remembered her opinion had not been asked for, and that her dream had probably called it forth.

"I incline to your opinion, Miss Paris," said the colonel gravely, who, in a very few hours, had passed from excess of confidence in all natives, to the opposite extreme. "He is, I am sure, a cold-blooded traitor,

* A large skin receptacle for water, used by the water-carriers.

and has had not a little to do with the insurrection here."

"Well, I only hope he's satisfied with his booty, and gone off at the head of the rebels," remarked Edgington. "In that case, we should be more than strong enough to bring any three or four hundred sepoys, who may have stopped behind, to reason. Oh! the pleasure of going at them! We'd make up a body of volunteer cavalry, and show them how English officers *can* charge! I'd ask for no weapon besides my hog-spear; and if I got near them, I'd do some execution with it."

"It would be a capital instrument to have when they were bolting," remarked Percy, with his usual drawl, "and I should much like to catch that slippery rajah on its point."

"I fear," said Peters, "we are running on a little too fast. If the Nana has gone off for good, and taken the troops with him, I do not consider we are out of the wood, though to-morrow may see us out of the intrenchments. I saw a native to-day—he is now in one of the barracks—who has just arrived from Allahabad. He doubted the sepoys there being long quiet, and Futtehpore, he says, is in a state of great excitement. Lucknow, you all know, is in a bad way, and I fear there is going to be a general mutiny throughout Bengal and the North-West. Bless you! you needn't make such faces at me, Earnest," he continued, to that officer, who wished to remind him the ladies were there, and that he might frighten them,—"I quite understand you; but Miss Paris has talked over the matter with my wife so much, that I doubt anything we can say adding much to her information."

"If there *is* going to be a general mutiny in the army," said Carstairs, "I know not where the Europeans are to come from to stop it. We have not over many in this presidency, and what we have are all wanted at Delhi."

"What a row there'll be in England when they hear of it all," said Percy; "they'll be sure to think we are going to lose India."

Darkness had come on as they conversed, and none saw the form of a native servant who approached, and who almost startled them as he spoke.

"The General Sahib Bahadoor's salaam to the Colonel Sahib, and wishes to speak to him in his tent. The Major Sahib, Major Bruce Sahib, is also to come."

"The Major Sahib is in that small tent," the colonel replied, rising; "Good evening, ladies! I hope by this time to-morrow you'll have roofs over your heads."

* * * * * *

Eight, nine, ten o'clock, and still the officers called to the general's tent sat there, and the reflection of the solitary light within might be seen through the door-curtain. All was still; the greater number in the intrenchments had fallen asleep, to dream of trials on the morrow. The tread of the English sentinel, by the tent of the commandant, was the only noise that broke the stillness in that particular part of the garrison. But the sentinel was not alone, and he knew it. A few paces from him an officer lay on the ground smoking, and evidently waiting for the council within to break up. Eleven o'clock! They rise at last; what can have kept them for three long hours? They come out of the tent, and wish each other good-night with ominous brevity. The officer on the ground lets them pass, and then rises and follows one, who proceeds towards his tent alone. Edgington—for it is he—overtakes, and at the same moment puts his hand on the shoulder of him he addresses,—

"Bruce, tell me—nothing new—nothing bad, is there?"

"Yes," answered the major, "bad as bad can be. Nana Sahib has written a letter, a short letter, declaring himself in his true colours, and begging us satirically to prepare ourselves; for with all the force under his command he attacks us to-morrow. No time for more; good-night—it may be the last to many of us."

"And is it to be so, and is poor Marion to be mixed up in all the horrors of a siege? Oh, would I had never sent for her from England!" exclaimed Edgington as he retraced his steps. "And that hound the Nana: strange, that one part of Marion's dream has turned out true. Well, well, I dare say we shall all suffer much before any of us leave this spot; but I would willingly suffer more than any—ay, as much as all put together—to gain but five minutes face to face with this rajah."

## CHAPTER XXI.

### THE SIEGE BEGINS—ITS FIRST REALITIES.

It is nine o'clock on Saturday, the 6th of June. The intrenchments have much the same aspect as yesterday, but the space around has quite altered in character. Then it was empty, now it teems with life; then it was quiet, now thousands of voices, mingling together, cause the deep vibrating sound, indicating the presence of a multitude.

And it was no small multitude which had thus early sat down around the intrenchments. It consisted of the 2nd cavalry, of the native infantry regiments, then all in open rebellion, and of the whole force which Nana Sahib could himself muster. It numbered four thousand men, and nearly all these were trained soldiers. But it was an ever-increasing army; for not only did all the budmashes and lawless characters in the country round at once enroll themselves under the new banners hoisted, but from Oude, and the North-west, multitudes of soldiers, more or less disciplined, arrived, and took service under the self-styled king of the Mahrattas.

It was true that the Nana had the previous afternoon left Cawnpore with all the treasure, and been followed by the mass of the rebels. Why he came back none in the intrenchments knew, none know to this day; but from early morning to the hour mentioned, companies of infantry, troops of cavalry and artillery, together with a never-ceasing line of elephants, camels, and baggage-carts, poured into the space around the intrenchments, and completely surrounded the frail fortification, although keeping at a respectful distance.

In the verandah of the thatched-roof barrack sat a party of ladies, gazing with blanched aspect at such parts of the scene outside as the parapets in front enabled them to see. Many of the number were young girls, not long from England, who had never seen a blow struck or heard the sound of strife; was it then strange that they sat with parted lips and straining eyes, feeling a cold shudder run through their delicate frames, as they watched the preparations for the coming combat? The secret of Nana Sahib's letter had oozed out that morning, and all knew that the stern strife would shortly begin.

"See, there is another gun going across," said a young lady of eighteen, only married the previous month, and who little expected to begin her wedded life with such scenes. "They stop!—I think they are going to fire. Had we not better run into the barrack? Oh, how very dreadful this is!"

"No, they are going on again," said another lady; "but there is a body of cavalry to the right that we have not seen before. It is not large enough for a cavalry regiment, or even a troop, and I think it must be some officer or chief with his attendants."

"Yes," replied the first speaker; "I think so too; but without a glass I can make out nothing."

"There is a glass, and a very good one, in Captain Edgington's tent," observed Marion, who formed one of the party. "I'll go and get it."

"Is it safe to venture?" suggested an old grey-haired lady, with a peculiarly lovable face. "Some of the sepoys are on the top of the unfinished barracks, and might fire as you go across the open."

"O dear, Mrs. Brown! they surely would not fire at me," replied Marion, stepping out boldly from under the verandah. "They are men, at all events, and will not, I trust, injure women on purpose."

She soon returned with the telescope in safety; she knew not, poor girl, the danger she had run, or how soon she would find out the sepoys were *not* men, in the sense she had used the word.

"They are nearer now," said the newly-married lady. "Will you give me the glass? I dare say I can make them out." She looked through it. "I have not got the right focus. No, that's not right either. Will *you* try?" she added, giving it back to Miss Paris.

Marion adjusted it quickly, and looked for some moments at the body of horse, which had halted in front. When she lowered the glass, her face was very pale.

"It *is* a chief," she said in a low voice to the circle of ladies round her; "and I fear our greatest enemy. It is Nana Sahib; I can see his face quite plainly, and I know it well, for he called at our house not long ago."

"Are you sure?" said Mrs. Peters, springing from her seat as she spoke. "A rifle-bullet would surely reach him. Edmund, Edmund," she called out to her husband, who, with a party of officers was standing within call; "the rajah is among those horsemen. I am sure you could hit him with your rifle; oh, do try—the perfidious monster!"

Peters was quickly at her side. "I should like to try. Which is he? But perhaps it would be better not; they have not attacked us yet. What do you say, Colonel Carstairs?"

"Certainly not," said the colonel; "at least, without the general's leave. Hostilities have not commenced, and we might only hasten them by the attempt. But I'll go and find some of the staff, and be back directly."

"It will be too late when he comes back," continued Mrs. Peters; "they are even now moving off. See, they are galloping away."

"By all means, by all means," called out the colonel, as a minute or two later he came running back with Edgington, who had also a rifle in his hand. "Get your rifle, Peters; here's Edgington to help. Now, see which of you can knock over the scoundrel."

"Too late," said Peters; "they are gone, and are now well out of shot. I wish I had fired without asking anybody."

"Boom!" The low-mouthed roar of a heavy gun was heard at that moment, and a 24-pound shot struck the parapet before them, burying itself deep in the earth, but harming no one.

"Get in, get in, ladies, all of you, quickly," said the colonel. "The siege has begun, and you will be much safer inside the barracks."

Another instant, and the assembly sounded "To arms—to arms!" Edgington called out, "Perhaps they'll try to storm. God bless you, Marion dear; I'll come back before long. Sit well under cover. What, Mrs. Brown, unnerved already? Nay; you must set a good example to the young ladies with you," he said, in an assuring tone, as he saw the old lady totter as she rose. He went forward to give her his hand; but she fell on her knees, and lifted up her hands in prayer. "Nay, nay," he added; "pray if you will, and let all join you; but not out here in the verandah."

"Oh, the horrors of such scenes! Great God! give me strength to stand them!" ejaculated the old lady, as she rose from her knees, and looked up to heaven with clasped hands.

Rattle, rattle, rattle, went the enemy's musketry from some of the buildings, and a ball struck the barrack wall, passing through the crowd of ladies on their way to the entrance.

Some of them shrieked, all turned pale, as they quickened their steps, and were soon under cover.

The siege had now begun in earnest. The reports of cannon followed one another in quick succession, while the musket-balls fell as thick as hail in the devoted intrenchment, and every man in the garrison was at his post; for an attempt to storm was expected.

The enemy appeared to have but two guns. Th were both on one side of the intrenchment, and tl greater part of the rebel army were also on that sid consequently the storming party was expected in th quarter, and the greater part of the garrison we gathered there. The other sides, however, were f from safe; for bodies of sepoys hovered all round, kee ing as much under cover of the surrounding buildin as possible, and so the parapets had to be well mann on all sides.

Edgington and Hoby found themselves together the quarter most threatened. They both had rifles their own rifles—and fired as fast as they could lo Our hero had one of the Prussian needle-rifles, whi load so quickly at the breech; and with this murdero weapon for long shots, he harassed the enemy co siderably.

"That last shot told, Hoby. I saw the man I aim at fall. Hang it, he's up again. I think you co reach him. Try."

"No; there's no want of marks, and he's certair wounded. Let him go, and give the wound its chan —it *may* kill him yet. Do you see the third bungal from here—the verandah is full of men; I'll send r shot amongst them."

"Well done! you hit some one. Hang it, how th bolt under cover. There is the one you struck, lyi there. But, Hoby, Hoby! see, see! I think they a going to storm there to the right! A thousand in tl body at least, and there's their leader ahead, wavi his sword for them to come on. I'll try to pot hi If I miss, never mind, I shall hit some others in t crowd." "Crack!"

"Bad shot," said Hoby; "but——hurrah! tha one of our guns, and look what a regular lane t grape has opened out in the crowd! Twenty of th down at least! They don't like it—they waver—tl are going back. No, there is their leader again! a they advance,—how they shout! Here goes one pill for the rascals."

"It found its man, I dare say," said Edgington, "but all on this side the intrenchments are firing at them. How quick I can load this rifle; there, it's ready again, and now——"

"Ting!" with a sharp ringing sound, was heard, and our hero's rifle nearly dropped from his hand. "Close shave, that; it struck my rifle-barrel, and must have passed six inches from my head. I'll not be balked of my shot, however, and here goes once more for the leader; he's not more than two hundred yards off, and I can, when cool, nearly hit the bull's eye at that distance." A moment's pause—crack went the rifle, and at the same instant the native officer on horseback clapped his hand to his thigh, while his wounded horse, maddened with pain, approached the intrenchments at full gallop, his rider vainly trying to stop him.

Blood from both horse and man ran down the courser's side. The conical ball from Edgington's rifle had passed through the rider's leg, and entered the body of his steed.

"Now, Hoby," called out Edgington, who had watched with pleasure the effect of his shot; "now then, shoot him; he's more than a common soldier, remember. Ah! it's done already," he exclaimed, as the report of a musket sounded close to them, and the native officer fell heavily from his horse. "Well done, indeed!" he added to the private soldier who had completed the task. "*He* can never ride again."

"Noa, by St. Patrick; he's got a sittler now, at all ivints," replied the Irishman, with a broad grin.

The fall of their leader seemed to damp the courage of the storming party. They halted, as if undecided whether to advance or to retire.

"That's a murderous discharge of grape," cried out Hoby, as two of the garrison guns sent their numerous iron missiles into the crowd and struck down many.

"Yes, and it's enough for them too, for there they g right about. They run fast, but my rifle-ball will catc them," he added as he fired, and observed with satisfac tion one of the hindermost fall to the ground at th same moment.

An exclamation of pain, heard on their right, mad both Edgington and Hoby turn; when they saw th Irishman, his musket on the ground, wringing his righ hand, from which the thumb was clean shot off.

"Ah, the dirty spalpeens, to use me so!—as if th other hand wouldn't have done jist as well. Divil musket can I handle now. Bad luck to iviry mother' son of them! Arrah by Jases, and it's painful th thumb is,—at least it would be if it was there," adde the Irishman, quaintly, as he looked at the jagge wound. "And sure it's to hospital I must now go," h continued, as he picked up the musket with his lef hand, and hurried off, calling down all the evil he coul think of on the heads of "the nasty black bastes."

The storming party was beaten off. It was a ver poor attempt they had made, and it was evident to a they were wanting in that cool courage, that person disregard of death, which alone can render such attack successful. It was with great joy all who could appre ciate it saw this fact; with it their position was *not* s desperate, and all the officers within speaking distanc congratulated one another thereon.

But the fight was not over, though the stormin party had been discomfited. Every protection afforde by the bungalows, the unfinished barracks, the churcl the compound-walls was taken advantage of, and showe of bullets struck the intrenchments, the tents, an buildings within. It was now between eleven and twelv o'clock, so that the firing had lasted nearly two hour During that time, however, but two persons had bee killed; one an English serjeant, the other a nativ servant—both shot as they left the protection of th earthen walls and crossed the open. The sun had beer however, more powerful than the enemy's fire: and n less than four individuals, including one officer, had already been carried into the hospital-barrack struck down from its effects. The weather was dreadful; it was of that kind that no white face in possession of his sober senses would, under other circumstances, have dreamed of exposing himself to its fury for the space of five minutes; and now for two hours had the garrison been subject to the glowing heat. All felt it,—some more than others; but all suffered so severely that they were conscious, even on this first day, and during those first few hours, that the climate would, if the siege continued, cause them more distress than the enemy.

"O Heaven! I can bear this no longer," said Earnest, as he lay under the parapet mound, while Percy stood by his side, firing whenever he saw a likely shot,—a native, his servant, loading for him. "Percy, I shall become insensible directly; the sun strikes through my uniform cap right into my brain. O for a wet cloth to wrap round my head."

"My man shall get you some water," Percy replied, as he coolly took down his double rifle from his shoulder, after sending a sepoy, seated on the roof of a bungalow, down the thatch much quicker than he got up; "but about a cloth I don't know what we are to do—such things are scarce enough here. However, never mind, you shall have the only towel I have in my tent." So saying, Percy sent his man to bring it and the water.

"Thank you—thank you," said Earnest, in a somewhat low voice, for he was in that state, that another half-hour of sun, without an improved defence for his head, would send him far beyond the reach of any sepoy's bullet,—"thank you, Percy. What did you fire at last time?"

"An infernal sepoy, who had stuck himself at top of the large bungalow in front, and was squatted on the thatch behind a chimney, firing at anything moving in or near our barracks."

"And, of course, you hit the chimney."

"No, I didn't. The brute had his legs exposed as I sat; so I took good aim, and fired on the chance. expect I struck him in the foot, for he bent forwa and stretched his hands down, giving me a fair shot his body. I was quite ready for him, and let fly with m second barrel. Where I hit him I don't know, but I came rolling off the roof in fine style."

The water and cloth arrived. The water was in shallow earthen pan, which Earnest placed by his side and having dipped the towel in it, he wound the w bandage round his head. The effect was soon apparent he lost the oppression on the brain, which was fa hurrying him to death's door, and could once mo stand up and look about him.

"Now you are better," drawled out Percy, ta ping him on the back; "you must take it coolly th weather, if you mean to see the end of the fun."

"And how can I take it coolly with this curse uniform cap? Is it not folly—worse than folly," sai Earnest, "to see the absurd things the Governme puts on the heads of both officers and privates? We' now been out two hours, and three or four men hav been carried to hospital senseless from the sun. On perhaps two, will die; and solar hats, at the cost of on rupee each, would probably have saved them all. Wit heat like this (see! my pistol-barrels are so hot I can' bear my hand on them), to give a man a cap little bette than a cobweb on his head! Ah! what would I no give for a good solar topee!"

"Have you nothing, then, but your undress cap?"

"Sorry to say, I have not. I had to fetch Mr Merton, and then came here in such a hurry I had n time to bring anything. Mark my words, Percy; thre or four hundred of those large mushroom solar topee here would be worth a hundred men's lives at th moment. The sun is a worse enemy than the sepoy and the Glengarry cap may lose us India."

The enemy's artillery had not been idle both durin

and after the attack. They had fired incessantly with their two guns. One was a 24-pounder, the other carried lighter metal. They directed their fire principally against the two barracks and outbuildings, determined, as it were, to destroy them, and take away all shelter from the garrison. The round-shot from the large gun struck with tremendous force against the barrack walls, often making great chasms in them, and alarming the poor ladies dreadfully who had congregated inside.

On their first entering, Mrs. Brown, the old lady, had proposed to her companions, that they should all join in prayer to the Almighty, beseeching Him to avert the dangers with which they were threatened. Her proposition was joyfully accepted, and the soldiers' wives who were present also testified their willingness to do so. The whole crowd of women and children then went down upon their knees, and while Mrs. Brown, in a loud, clear voice, gave utterance to an extempore prayer, it was evident, from the manner of her auditors, how heartily they joined in its spirit! It was a beautiful sight, amidst the roar of cannon and the rattle of musketry from without, to behold that old lady, with tears in her eyes, craving the help of God in their imminent danger; and to hear the muttered prayers of nearly three hundred women and children, in accents of heartfelt emotion, following her words, and beseeching the Almighty to spare them and their brave defenders.

The prayer had, as all prayers have when uttered in sincerity, a soothing effect on the assembly; and when, as they rose from their knees, friends kissed one another, while mothers embraced their children, the serene aspect on the crowd of faces present would have formed a picture strongly illustrative of the power of genuine devotion.

About this time (one o'clock) the fire slackened, and the rebels around seemed much diminished in number.

As the garrison ascertained later, innumerable small bodies spread themselves over the town and station, bent on robbery, destruction, and murder. Frightful scenes were enacted that afternoon in the town of Cawnpore. We have already mentioned that a few of the inhabitants had declined to avail themselves of the protection the intrenchments offered; these were mostly half-caste, that is to say, Eurasians, but some Jews, Parsees, and Armenians were also amongst them. Very nearly all were killed on that day,—men, women, and children; none were willingly spared, excepting a few unfortunate girls, who were pretty enough to be reserved for another fate, though in their case death, deferred for perhaps days and weeks, was often their ultimate portion.

The poor Eurasian fugitives managed to congregate in bodies, either in the streets, or in one another's houses, and thus surrounding their families, and protecting them from death and insult with their last breaths, they showed how much of the Anglo-Saxon spirit they had inherited from their partially English descent. It was not only the Eurasians, Jews, &c., who were made victims that day to the insatiable cruelty of the sepoys: all the Hindostanees of low caste who had been in English service, and who unfortunately showed it by their dress, were also butchered; while torture was in many cases resorted to, either to gratify the revenge of any particular sepoy or to afford amusement to the many.

"Business first, and pleasure afterwards," was the motto of some, and these scattered themselves over the station, pillaging every house. Man cannot, however, carry off a greater load of valuables than rubbish, or more gold than iron; and in every dwelling was much that the robbers could not remove. They loaded themselves well, but much which they longed for was necessarily left behind. What should be done? They could not remove it all, and others would follow in their footsteps, and enrich themselves with what they forsook. *That*, at all events, should not be, was the resolution they came to in each case, and the house was consequently fired.

It was this selfish, this dog-in-the-manger feeling, which lit up Cawnpore that afternoon with dozens of fires. Every bungalow, every dwelling-house, every Government building blazed, and, joined to the shrieks of the sufferers in the bazaar, to the yells and shouts of the sepoys, to the booming of guns, and the rattle of musketry, it made one great hell of the place, and the hearts of many in the intrenchments sank as they gazed.

Spies, with the hope of reward, brought into the besieged, from time to time, details of all these horrors, and of a great deal more. They told how the Nana had hoisted two standards — one for the Mussulmen and one for the Hindus — and how hundreds upon hundreds flocked thereto; they told how many trained soldiers from Oude had crossed the river and placed themselves under the rajah's orders; they told of an accession of artillery on the rebels' side; how titles and rank had been accorded to many of the mutineers by the Bhitoor chief; and, above all, how confident the Nana's army was of the speedy reduction of the intrenchments. They told—and the ears of the besieged confirmed the news—how songs were sung, outside, in which the God of the Mussulman and the gods of the Hindu were thanked because the Feringhee rule had come to an end.

The afternoon wore on, the evening advanced, the night came, and still the rattle of musketry, the booming of guns continued. Darkness there was none, one-tenth part of the fires burning all round would have sufficed to render all objects clear; but as it was, no illumination conceivable could rival in splendour the bright-red glare under which the intrenchment lay. The garrison, worn out by the sun, the excitement, and anxieties of the day, for the most part slept—slept to dream of further horrors—slept on the hard and still hot ground where they had last stood, but slept soundly till wakened to take their turn of night duty.

How different the aspect here, and amidst the rebel body outside! Silence, with a leaden hand, weighs down on the intrenchments; but music, singing, and dancing hold their revels around, as the cruel sepoys exult over the many murders perpetrated that day.

## CHAPTER XXII.

### THE THIRD DAY—THE WELL—THE BURIAL.

When the weary garrison arose, next morning, from their disturbed slumbers, they were conscious of further preparations on the part of the besiegers for their destruction. Four batteries, one on each side of the intrenchments were in course of construction, on which guns were to be mounted, and it was evident, to the least initiated in the art of war, that the danger would thereby be much increased.

Daylight had ushered in musketry fire from all sides, and as it was almost certain death to remain in the more exposed parts of the inclosed ground, most of the ladies, who had passed the night in their tents, now grouped together in corners of the verandahs, or sought still greater security in the inside of the buildings.

It is not easy for those unacquainted with an Indian climate to appreciate the suffering the beleaguered garrison underwent now, and at a later period of their troubles. The mere fact of not being able to bathe and wash themselves properly, was no little hardship; but when we remember that not one of the appliances used in India to cool the air in dwellings could here be resorted to; that coarse food improperly cooked was their portion; that many had not one change of linen, and no clothes but those on their backs; that in most cases they had wretched beds to lie on, and were, from want of chairs, obliged to sit on the baked ground, or the dirty floor of the barracks; that no privacy existed, that all had to herd together, to eat and sleep with the multitude; that delicate ladies had to perform the most menial offices for themselves and others; that the eye was constantly distressed by the sight of pain; that the olfactory nerves were offended by the most loathsome odours; that death was always present, and meeting them at every turn; that success was, even to the most hopeful, a mere chance, and a painful end as the climax of their disasters, the expectation of the many; that all this, and much more, which delicacy forbids us to mention, had to be borne under the oppressive and deadly climate of India, during the month of June, when the besieged had to stand for hours in the sun. Then, if all these circumstances be kept constantly in mind as our narrative proceeds, though the reader will appreciate in some degree the sufferings of the Cawnpore garrison, the most vivid conception must always fall far short of the reality.

The distress consequent on many of these causes might be read in the faces of a small party huddled together in a corner of the verandah, where they were comparatively safe from musket-balls, at about noon that day. Though the batteries we mentioned were not yet completed, the besiegers could not wait so long, and had, about an hour before, commenced a furious cannonading from the four guns they now had. Two of these were 24-pounders, and it was dreadful to see the terrific holes they made in the barrack walls, or how, when the round-shot struck a verandah pillar it completely demolished it. The party consisted not entirely of ladies; a few officers were with them, who having been on duty behind the mounds all the morning, had now, as an old sailor there present expressed it, "their watch in barracks!"

"So most of us have seen the last of our horses," said Colonel Carstairs, "for there are not many now left in the intrenchments. It pained me, even in all this trouble, parting with my Cape; but I was only allowed to keep one, and I chose a younger beast. It was very necessary to turn them loose; they were dreadfully in the way here, to say nothing of the want of forage."

"Yes, sir," drawled out Percy, who was supposed to be dressed in white, but who, from the dust, gunpowder, &c., had a dirty-brown exterior; "we've too much to do to look after horses; the only two servants I had have bolted, and I believe mine is not a singular case."

"I've only one left," said the colonel.

"And I've none," remarked Hoby.

"Mine all went off yesterday evening," remarked Mrs. Brown.

"We've still one old khansamah," said Mrs. Bruce; "nothing, I'm sure, will make him desert us."

"So I thought of my head man," Mr. Blank, the old civilian, remarked; "but he disappeared early this morning."

"My ayah is still with me," said Marion, "and I really think she will stop, for she is a dear, good, faithful creature; but all Captain Edgington's servants have gone."

"Ay, but he has a really true attendant in that havildar of his company," Mr. Blank continued, "who came in here the first evening, and who is not now likely to go over to the other side. How refreshing it is to see such a case of real faithfulness amongst the mass of treachery we've met with."

This was the havildar who had warned Edgington of his danger, and who, though he would not betray his comrades, had, on the mutiny breaking out, come into the intrenchments, and clung to his officer to the end.

"I don't think, altogether, there are a dozen servants left in the intrenchments," said Mrs. Merton. "John and I only had one at first, and he went away the first night—ha!—ha!"

She was not the only one who cried out, as a 24-pound round-shot struck the barrack wall, a few feet to the right, and covered them all with the dust and *débris* of the masonry.

"Well done, ladies, upon my word! you stood it splendidly," said Mr. Blank, as he wiped the dust off his grey head, and who knew how necessary it was to keep up their spirits among the fearful scenes which surrounded them. "I'm proud of you all as Englishwomen. Such a sudden visitor might have startled soldiers, much more ladies. No; don't move, any of you; we are in as safe a place as we can find. See, this end wall of the verandah protects us, and no shot can come nearer than that one."

It is extraordinary how dangers constantly present lose much of their importance, or rather, how habit accustoms us to them. These ladies had been but four-and-twenty hours under fire, and the report of a cannon did not now make them start, or stop short a sentence they were uttering. This last was, however, an uncommonly near visitant, and though they had all screamed with momentary fright, another five minutes found them talking again as if nothing had occurred.

"It was somewhat of a spent shot," said Hoby, "or it would have gone right through the wall, thick as it is."

"Yes," remarked Marion tremulously, for she had not quite recovered from her alarm, "the shot that struck the other barrack while we were at prayers, went right through."

"Can any of you read Hindostanee well enough to translate this paper?" said Major Bruce, coming up at that moment, under shelter of the verandah. "It was brought in this morning, and is a copy of something the Nana has had posted up all over Cawnpore. One of the staff gave it to me just now, to see if I could get it translated. I'll find one of the regimental interpreters later, but I think they are all on duty at this moment. Well," he continued, going up to his wife, "you are standing it bravely, I see, my dear, and all these other ladies too. We saw, when behind the intrenchments, where that last shot struck, but I think you are all in as safe a place as can be found."

"Perhaps *I* can make out the paper," said Mrs. Merton, as she held out her hand for it. "I've had a great deal of practice with such writing."

Bruce gave it to her, and she conned it carefully over, as Mr. Blank said,—

"I saw my carriage this morning, Bruce, with my two greys in it, driving quietly along, and two black rascals sitting inside. A pleasant sight, was it not?"

"They've got every carriage in the station, I think," said Colonel Carstairs, "for plenty have been seen to-day."

"It's really too ridiculous," drawled out Percy, "to see those black hounds, who probably have never been in anything better than one of the native kranchies, riding about at their ease in Calcutta carriages. If it was not too much trouble, I'd keep a journal, and note down all such things. I'm sure it would make my fortune when we get out of this hole."

"Yes, I can read it," continued Mrs. Merton, "though I dare say I shall make some mistakes. It *is* by the Nana, and a most impudent, lying paper."

We will give the translation without any faults the pretty Eurasian may make, or the frequent stoppages with which she read it. It ran thus. It is now an historical paper, and illustrates to perfection how the gentle Hindu can lie, when he has a purpose to attain :—

"A traveller, just arrived at Cawnpore from Calcutta, states that in the first instance a council was held to take into consideration the means to be adopted to do away with the religion of the Mahommedans and Hindoos, by the distribution of cartridges. The council came to this resolution, that, as this matter was one of religion, the services of seven or eight thousand European soldiers would be necessary, as fifty thousand Hindostanees would have to be destroyed, and then the whole of the people of Hindostan would become Christians. A petition with the substance of this resolution was sent to the Queen Victoria, and it was approved. A council was then held a second time, in which English merchants took a part; and it was decided that, in order that no evil should arise from mutiny, large reinforcements should be sent for. When the despatch was received and read in England, thousands of European soldiers were embarked on ships as speedily as possible and sent off to Hindostan. The news of their being despatched reached Calcutta. The English authorities there ordered the issue of the cartridges, for the real intention was to Christianize the army first, and this being effected, the conversion of the people would speedily follow. Pigs' and cows' fat was mixed up with the cartridges; this became known through one of the Bengalese who was employed in the cartridge-making establishment. Of those through whose means this was divulged, one was killed and the rest imprisoned. While in this country these counsels were being adopted, in England the vakeel of the Sultan of Roum sent news to the Sultan that thousands of European soldiers were being sent for the purpose of making Christians of all the people of Hindostan. Upon this the Sultan issued a firman to the King of Egypt to this effect:—'You must deceive the Queen Victoria, for this is not a time for friendship, for my vakeel writes that thousands of European soldiers have been despatched for the purpose of making Christians the army and people of Hindostan. In this manner, then, this must be checked. If I should be remiss, then how can I show my face to God? and one day this may come upon me also; for if the English make Christians of all in Hindostan, they will then fix their designs upon my country.' When the firman reached the King of Egypt, he prepared and arranged his troops before the arrival of the English army at Alexandria, for this is the route to India. The instant the English army arrived, the king of Egypt opened guns upon them from all sides, and destroyed and sank their ships, and not a single soldier escaped. The English in Calcutta, after the issue of the order for the cartridges, and when the mutiny had become great, were in expectation of the arrival of the army from London; but the great God, in His omnipotence, had beforehand put an end to this. When the news of the destruction of the army of London became known, then the Governor-General was plunged in grief and sorrow, and beat his head.

"Printed by order of the Peishwar Bahadour."

"A most creditable document," remarked Percy. "It shows a power of invention which says much for the genius of the author."

"Of all the lying, bare-faced papers——Well, well; when I think of that Peishwar Bahadour and all his promises, I do think he's the most rascally of all rascally natives, and that's saying not a little. The rope is spun, I hope, that will hang him, and oh that I might be there to see!" said the colonel, who, as we have before remarked, was now as inveterate against the natives as he had previous to the mutiny been the other way.

Ping! ping! went the musket-balls, as they struck the barrack walls; but except one of the tiny messengers came unpleasantly close, they did not interrupt the conversation. Boom! boom! sounded the deep-mouthed cannon at intervals; but the noise did not cut short the reproaches poured out by female lips on the head of the Bhitoor rajah.

A new and unlooked-for difficulty was encountered for the first time to-day, and a dreadful one it was, being no less than a want of water in that suffocating heat. Large earthen jars, filled for the use of the soldiers and women, had been stowed in the verandahs of the barracks, and up to this time had sufficed, but were now dry. In the frightful heat which prevailed, and the exposure all were more or less subject to, drinking was a necessity every few minutes; and thus, when no more water could be had from the earthen pots, excruciating thirst began to torment the garrison. There was, as we have stated, one well in the intrenchments; but it was, unfortunately, in a part much exposed to the enemy's fire, and consequently the danger of drawing water from it was great. A man had been killed that morning in doing so; but it was at his fourth or fifth trip to the well, and he had, fortunately for others, filled one of the big jars, and was filling the second when he met with his end. The water he had procured had lasted till one o'clock; but now more was necessary, and must be had at whatever cost.

It was from musket-balls that the danger was so imminent; and *because* the sepoys who fired could plainly see, from under the cover of buildings outside, any one who approached the well, it was suggested by one of the soldiers to send a woman and child alone to draw water, as it was thought likely they would not be fired on. A volunteer was called for amongst the women assembled, and was soon found in a young married girl, the wife of a soldier.

"And it's three cheers you'll have, Mrs. Bailey, when you come back agin safe," called out the Irish soldier of yesterday, who had lost his thumb, "besides the blessings of all the thirsty souls in the barracks."

"And who doubts her coming back safe, Pat?" said a fine specimen of an English sergeant. "It's *because* she'll be safe we are sending her. I'm sure, lads," he continued, appealing to the others around him, "we wouldn't any one of us put a woman into danger for our sakes?"

"I hope not, indeed," was shortly replied by many.

"There's another way to look at it, men," continued the first speaker. "If, as we all hope, those sepoys will let women draw water peaceably, many a good soldier's life will be spared, and the chances of all to get through this scrape will be much improved. Enough of us will be knocked over behind the intrenchments, without flinging away our lives unnecessarily at that well."

"Very true, very true," was responded on all sides.

"So then, Mrs. Bailey, you are to go," said the sergeant, "and take one of the children with you for greater safety. Not that we think they'd fire at you, if you went alone; but with a child you'll be more than safe. Now, then, for a volunteer amongst the children. Here, you young scamps, all of you, who'll go and draw water from the well with Mrs. Bailey?"

"I will," "I will," "I will," was called out by nearly the whole juvenile crowd.

"Volunteers enough," remarked the sergeant, "so I must choose one. Come, you black-eyed urchin," he continued, putting his hand on the curly head of a fine boy of nine years old, "you shall be the man."

"What! my Bobby?" called out one of the women, advancing quickly from a sick soldier's side, whom she had been attending. "No, thank you, sergeant; not if every drop of water in the well was a bright golden guinea, should he go on such an errand."

"Then we must have another," said the sergeant, good-naturedly. "Come, what mother will let her child go?"

He waited for an answer, but none came. Many mothers drew their children closer to them, and showed by the act the sergeant might wait a long time before they spoke.

"I'se got no fader, or moder—leastways moder's dead, and fader's a long way off, fighting the blackies," called out a bright blue-eyed boy in the crowd; "let me go, sergeant, please."

"Ah, Willy, you are the very boy I'd have chosen, and you shall go," said the sergeant, who saw plainly no mother there would send her son; and who hoped, through this woman and child, to get rid of what was likely to become their greatest difficulty. "Now, Mrs. Bailey, take this bucket in one hand, and Willy in the other, and walk there and back quite quietly, for, believe me, there's no danger."

"Danger or not, sergeant, I'll go," said Mrs. Bailey, as she took the bucket. "Now, come along, Willy dear; we'll soon bring them all some water, won't us?"

Away they went towards the well, watched with eager eyes by all. Mrs. Bailey walked quite quietly, and as if she really thought there was no danger; for she stopped about half-way to pull on her shoe, which was down at heel. She arrived at the well, filled the bucket, leisurely and composedly, and returned, little Willy trotting by her side. The crowd greeted her warmly, but not with cheers, they felt intuitively that these might be misunderstood by any sepoys w heard them, and who had seen the woman and chi go and return.

"I thought so," said the sergeant, as he joyfully to the bucket from the hand of the bold Englishwoma "the sepoys are *not* such brutes after all, and Wil and you may draw as much water as you will witho fear; whereas it's as much as mine, or any other mai life is worth, to go to that well in the daytime."

The thirsty crowd scarcely waited for the bucket be set down, but teacups, mugs, pannikins, every co ceivable vessel, was hastily dipped into it, and in le than two minutes it was all gone.

"I'll go this time," said another woman; "we mu all take it in turn; and if the sepoys always behave well as they did with Mrs. Bailey, it won't be very ha work. In this way they'll see all the beauty in t barracks," added the speaker, taking up the bucket, a grinning from ear to ear with her enormous mouth, f in truth this last volunteer was by no means pretty.

Willy did not think it necessary to ask if he was go again; he laid hold of his new conductress's han and trotted off with her.

"Here, Willy, you need not come back emp handed. Take this little pot, and bring it back full f me," called out a fat woman, who appeared to be mel ing away with the heat, as she ran after the boy.

The woman and boy proceeded leisurely to the we filled their vessels, and were about to return, when t report of a musket was heard from one of the neare buildings. None of the lookers-on cared much f this, as musket-firing went on all day; but what w their horror to see a ball strike the ground, close to t woman, who screamed as it did so.

"Come back!—come back quick! Run for yo lives!" screamed out the sergeant; and at the sa moment, ping! ping! two more bullets struck t masonry of the well.

The woman screamed, forgot the child she had with her, and ran wildly towards the barracks. Poor little Willy, very pale and frightened, quite as much at the screaming and the calls from the barracks as at the bullets, which he scarcely understood, did not know what to do. He looked round for a moment, with a scared expression, and then putting both hands to his face, burst out crying.

Quick as thought, and much quicker than we write it, did the sergeant dash towards the well; but ere he had advanced five paces another bullet struck the ground, at the child's feet. "Thank God, it has not hurt him!" ejaculated the soldier, as he strained every nerve to reach the child quickly. Another half minute, and "He has him! he has him!" was passed from mouth to mouth in the crowd. "Now, sergeant, run back quick!" was shrieked out by more than one voice. The brave non-commissioned officer wanted not to be told; Willy had his arms round his neck, and he ran for his and the child's life towards the barracks.

More than one musket was discharged at him, and some thought, when a few paces from the well, he made a kind of spring as he ran, and that the child cried out; but it was probably fancy, for the next moment they arrived safely.

"Take him, take him," said the sergeant in a tremulous voice, as he put his arm on the shoulder of the nearest in the crowd.

"Good God! they are both bloody!" exclaimed one. "Art hit, Willy dear?"

The sergeant sank on the ground, but, looking up, said, "Tell me the boy's not struck."

"He seems to have fainted," said a woman who had him in her arms; "and there's blood on him; it may, however——" "The blessed child!—his arm's broke! See here!" she exclaimed, as she lifted up the hand, when all saw the bone was smashed just below the shoulder.

"Oh, my God! and I brought it on him," saic poor sergeant with a groan. "I knew *I* was don but I thought the child had escaped."

"Now make way, make way, good people, and crowd round a wounded man. Stand on one side, let me see what can be done." These words spoken by a short man, a surgeon, who bustled that minute. An assistant was with him, who at carried little Willy, still senseless, into that porti the barrack allotted to the sick and wounded.

"Now, where are you hit, my man?" said the geon kindly.

The sergeant pointed to his neck, but did not s

"Ah, so I see," the surgeon continued, aft moment's examination, ominously shaking his hea the information of the bystanders. "Come, tw three of you lift him up. We must take you in continued, addressing the sergeant, whose lips slightly parted, and whose eyes wore a fixed ap ance.

Three soldiers at once raised him, two by shoulders, while one supported his legs. "C sergeant, don't hang your head in that way; will rest it on my hand?" asked one of the shou bearers. "Why, the Lord bless us! Please, don't think it's any use taking him in, for—for— dead already."

And so it was. The bullet had passed throug child's arm, and entered the neck of the poor serg whose greatest agony in dying was the thought, he had sent Willy into the danger.

* * * * * *

"What case was that?" said one hospital assista another, who, five minutes later, came out from portion of the building where the sick and wou lay; "it seemed like a child crying."

"And so it was. A poor child shot high up i

arm,—amputation just below the shoulder necessary. I'm not wanted; they've got enough without me. Let's come outside into the verandah, and smoke a pipe; I feel faint from the close air, and it will do me good."

A few minutes later they were joined by a third hospital assistant. "Operation over, and successfully I hope?" said the last speaker, knocking the ashes out of his pipe.

"Over, certainly," answered the new-comer. "It was a worse case than they expected, and the arm had to be taken out at the shoulder. The poor child died under the knife."

* * * * * *
* * * * * *

Night has again closed in—night of the third day in the intrenchments. The cannon still roars at intervals, the rolling of musketry still strikes the ear. What is that measured tread we hear advancing? Six or eight men at least—probably the new men for sentry duty. "Halt!" says the officer with them, in a low tone, as they reach the verandah of the barracks. What is it they take off the brick floor? Three bags,—and a little one.

"That's the poor child shot at the well," says one of the men, as he takes the smallest bundle on his shoulder.

"Quick march!" The party moves on outside the mounds.

"Halt!" at the side of a well, near the unfinished barracks. A few short prayers, there's no time for more—the three large and the one small bag are thrown in, and the burial party returns into the intrenchments.

## CHAPTER XXIII.

### HORRORS OF THE SIEGE—A GREAT DISASTER.

"OH, Arthur, Arthur, when is all this to end? Are we never to receive any help? Have the English in other stations forgotten us? You shake your head. Then, surely we shall be released. Tell me, will it not be so?"

"God grant it, dearest Marion!" replied Edgington. "We must hope for the best. Relief is sure to come, but *when?*—that is the question."

"You think it will come too late? No? Then what do you think?"

"I think, while it may do so, it is not at all likely. The account of the mutiny must long ere this have reached Allahabad, and there, we know, help exists. No, no, Marion dear, you will awake some morning, and hear the shouts of true-hearted English soldiers advancing to our rescue, while they send the crowd of black miscreants outside flying before them."

"Oh, Arthur, *do* you really think so? Are you as hopeful, Mr. Hoby?"

"Yes, Miss Paris," answered Hoby, saying more, however, than he felt. "I see not how it can be otherwise."

"All we must do is to hold out till they come," said Edgington, "and, with the despicable enemy before us, I am sure we can manage it."

"How do you mean despicable, Arthur? Surely they attack us in every conceivable way."

"They do, but they are despicable as an enemy all the same. They are wanting in courage. Were it not so, we should not now be here to talk of it."

"Quite right," added Hoby. "With their numbers, and the artillery they now have against us, were that quality not wanting, they could storm the intrenchments any day."

"You think, then, that during the storming attempts we were in danger?" asked Marion.

"No," said Hoby, "they want the pluck to make such attempts successful. They'll never storm the intrenchments."

"But is not our danger much increased by the red-hot shot and the shells which they now throw?" asked our heroine, who, accustomed, in spite of herself, to the horrors of the siege, which had now lasted a week, talked of such matters with a possession that astonished her auditors.

"Not much, now that all the tents are taken down," Edgington replied. "I thought, when the two were burnt yesterday, we should have the order. But where are you to sleep now, my poor dear girl?"

"Let us do as some have done already, Arthur—make a hole under the intrenchment mound, and cover it with boxes, bedding, or anything; or, better still, spread a part of the tent over it. I'd much rather pass the night in such a place than in the crowd of the barracks."

"I've thought of it already," replied our hero, "and think it will be the best thing. It's cooler than the barracks at night; besides, you'll be much safer there from both shot and shell. Poor Mrs. Peters! had she been alive, she would have shared it with you, but I cannot consent to your being all alone there, and will offer the shelter to Mrs. Merton. Mr. Hoby and myself, when not on duty at night, will sleep outside near you, so you will not be at all lonely."

"It must be done to-day," said Hoby, "and I'll help you, Edgington. We are both off duty at four, and we'll do it then."

"That will be very kind of you," replied Edgington.

"It will also be safer for you in the day, Marion; but I doubt your being able to stand the heat."

"No, in the day I must remain here in the verandah, or in a corner of the barracks. I'm burnt enough already," remarked the poor girl with a smile, putting her hand up to her face, which was much disfigured with the exposure she had undergone, "and must not quite destroy my complexion."

"Dear, dear Marion," said Edgington, looking at her with much emotion; "oh that I had twenty lives, and could give them all to see you safe out of this place!"

"And that I could lay down my one," added Hoby, "with the same end."

"As you have *not* twenty, Arthur, and as you, having only one, Mr. Hoby, cannot well spare it, I shall accept neither offer; though, without banter, believe me, I know you both speak sincerely, and thank you from my heart."

Hoby thought that if a round-shot struck him the next moment, he should die happier for those few words: and he brushed away the tears which sprang to his eyes—tears not of sorrow, but joy, even in the scenes around.

What his companions then thought of, we know not, but silence fell on the trio. Silence, in such circumstances, could but bring before them acutely the horrors of their position; and as it lasted, they became momentarily more and more depressed. So is it ever in scenes of trial, danger, and sorrow (amongst those who have any good in their composition), each, with an abnegation of self, speaks words of comfort or hope, and tries, by the cheerfulness of manner assumed, to infuse the same into those around. But the moment comes when the effort can be no longer maintained, when each awakes to the consciousness that others have done as he or she—that they are all trying to deceive one another, while all see through the deception. *Then* silence falls on the party; then each, brooding alone o'er their common griefs, sinks lower and lower into the abyss of despair, which their charitable and assumed cheerfulness had, unknown to themselves, in a measure kept off.

We will leave our trio in this sad mood. Alas! we can say nothing to comfort them, and we have much to tell of what has occurred since the last chapter closed.

The well difficulties, which ended our last account, we will first mention. The dream that the sepoys would not injure the women and children when they drew water being at an end, other means to obtain this necessary of life had to be found. There was but one, and that was to fetch it at night, when, of course, from the darkness, the sepoys could not so well direct their shots. After the first three days of the siege, however, the besiegers left off firing at sunset for one or two hours, and the interval was taken advantage of to fill the large jars, while each also provided for the next day's wants of himself and family. At this time an immense number collected round the well, and as both sexes and all ages were present, then could best be seen the ravages more clearly defined each day that the siege, with its attendant horrors, worked on the multitude.

Poor little Willy was not the only child killed at this dangerous place. A few affected to believe that the child had been killed by accident, or rather that its death had been occasioned by the sergeant running out to fetch it. They, therefore, when water was scarce, continued to send any child they could get, and two or three more were killed or wounded before the practice was put a stop to. For the credit of humanity and the English character, however, be it stated, that these instances were rare; that a moiety of the accidents occurred when the children went of their own accord to the well; and that in the one or two cases that remained, the senders probably partly believed what they stated.

The exposure, the badly-cooked food, the tainted atmosphere, &c., had brought two enemies into the intrenchments, more to be dreaded than the sepoys' bullets. Cholera and small-pox had both declared themselves the third day of the siege, and had at the time of which we write, viz. a week after its commencement, claimed numerous victims. The impossibility of keeping apart those affiicted with the latter disease had necessarily given the contagion increased force; while cholera—which is, we believe, an epidemic in the atmosphere, sustained by dirt, close crowding, and the like—found a favourable field for its ravages in the heated and pent-up garrison. Of those whom we know, Colonel Carstairs and Mrs. Peters had both died from that dreadful scourge cholera. They were regretted, of course; the death of every European was so, for all left relations or friends behind; and every male body thrown into that well outside the intrenchments diminished the defensive force. But the death of the colonel threw an extra gloom over the surviving officers of the 99th native infantry, for he was generally liked, and had always been a kind commandant.

Marion, we ought to mention, had never forgot the grief she had caused the colonel in rejecting his proposals, and woman-like she had felt a greater interest in him from that time, so that his death caused her much pain, enhanced by the knowledge that his later days had been sombred by her act. Mrs. Peters's death had been a stunning blow to her husband, while it had bereft Marion of her warmest female friend, the only one in the intrenchments whom she knew intimately, and on whose bosom she could pour out all her sorrows.

But another of those we know had gone to his account this last week. Poor Earnest! what he had said regarding a number of solar hats being worth as many European lives, was exemplified, at all events, in his own case. He died from the want of one. His uniform cap, all he had with him, was no protection against the blazing sun, and the fourth day of the siege he was struck down at his post by *coup-de-soleil,* and died three hours after. In him the garrison lost one of its bravest defenders, and the 99th an officer they all loved.

The besiegers' artillery had increased daily, and they had now mounted, in the four batteries alluded to and in other positions, the following: — Two 24, three 18, two 12, two 9, and one 6 pounders, besides three mortars. The tremendous fire which was now, with little intermission, kept up against the devoted garrison, may thence be conceived; and, as appeared in the late conversation, hot shot had been resorted to the day before, to burn the tents then standing, and also with the hope of firing the barracks.

The besieged had, during the past week, made two sallies, with more or less success; and in the latter, which was the more successful, they had spiked some guns in one of the batteries, with but trifling loss to themselves. These sallies had been made during the night; and when the rebel gunners, thus taken by surprise, saw themselves opposed to bayonets in the hands of desperate Englishmen, they did not wait to try conclusions. But such success availed not, beyond the partial relief the spiked guns gave them. It mattered little how many of the rebel army were destroyed; their name was Legion, and others supplied their places. In fact, the Nana's force daily increased: it was, as we stated, at the commencement of the siege four thousand in number; but the immense reinforcements of mutineers received from Oude and elsewhere, together with the influx of budmashes from the whole country round, had swelled it to eight thousand men. The Nana's army was therefore formidable, if from its numbers alone, for the reader will remember that but four hundred men, including the non-military portion, had to defend the intrenchments against this host.

We have already detailed one storming attempt, the

second day of the siege; but during the week two others had been tried, with the same result. There was an immense amount of shouting, a furious cannonading, a brisk musketry fire on all sides from the adjacent buildings and walls; but a few discharges of grape, when the enemy were at a convenient distance, had settled the matter. Jack Sepoy could not stand it,—he lacked the courage; and though each called out to his companion, "Chulo, bhai—chulo!" (Go on quick, brother—go on!) none used the more magic words "Come on!" and while each encouraged, all halted; until another discharge of grape, sent into the wavering body, settled the question, and "chulo" (go on quickly) was the order of movement, certainly, but in the wrong direction.

As possibly some of our fair readers may not know what is meant by grape-shot, we will, for their benefit, explain. Grape is so called from its resemblance to a bunch of grapes, and consists of many iron balls, about the size of large plums, heaped together on a circular base, in the form of a perfect grape-bunch. They are then bound securely with canvas and ligatures to one another and the base on which they rest. When fired from a cannon, the balls separate soon after leaving the mouth of the gun; and as they are numerous and spread, they cover a large space, dealing wounds and death around. Grape is, then, as may be supposed, much more destructive at anything like close quarters than round-shot; and it was this grape which, when it entered the mutineers' ranks during their storming attempts, made them halt, waver, and finally run.

Of all extraordinary features revealed by the great Indian rebellion, none is more remarkable than the deficiency of courage manifested throughout by the mutineer sepoys. We have all read—we read now daily—how thousands are beat by hundreds; how strongholds are carried at the point of the English bayonet, though the besieged number as many as the besiegers, and have all the advantages of fortifications and position on their side. Our assertion cannot, therefore, we think, be disputed.

We say it is extraordinary, because so opposed to the idea entertained before the mutiny of the physical courage of the Bengal sepoy. That opinion, though perhaps it overstepped the truth, was formed on good grounds—the experience of numerous battle-fields in India, when the native soldiers, headed by English officers, vied with their English comrades in deeds of valour, and certainly never acted in a way to justify the low estimation in which their prowess is held to-day.

The causes of this change in the nature of the sepoy are very simple, and are so well understood, that it is only for the information of those readers who know nothing of India we would mention them. They are, firstly, the want of English leaders, of officers whose courage they respect, and whom they look up to, as natives never will look up to one of themselves; and, secondly, the demoralizing effect the act of mutiny exercised on the sepoy, the consciousness he had not been faithful to his salt, and was then fighting against the dreaded Gora logue.*

If any argument were wanting to prove the truth of this, it would be found in the different way, all throughout this mutiny, the few sepoys faithful to us acted—we mean, how much more courageous they were than their rebel brethren. Besides Edgington's havildar, already mentioned, there were a very few native soldiers in the Cawnpore garrison, and their courage shone out, when compared to the poltroonery outside. But not at Cawnpore alone was this so; during the Lucknow siege was the same fact noted, and it has received confirmation in many parts of Hindostan during these mutinous times.

It would be a matter of very nice calculation to

* Europeans.

decide, had the mutinied sepoys possessed the courage which was theirs before the outbreak, and consequently fought *against* us as well as they did formerly *for* us, what portion of our Indian empire we should possess at this moment.

We must mention a few more of the troubles the noble Cawnpore garrison, headed by their fine old chief, underwent, before they arrived even at the end of this first week.

The barracks were daily getting more and more riddled with round-shot, and consequently daily less safe and more confined. The walls in some places had great chasms in them; these spots, of course, were avoided, for they offered no safety from the enemy's shot; and it necessarily further crowded the remaining space. Now that the tents had been all struck, and their inhabitants were compelled to resort to the barracks for shelter, room was scarcer than ever; while as for any privacy, it was quite out of the question.

It was a dreadful morning sight to see that heterogeneous multitude in the barracks, all of whom had slept in their clothes, awaked oft and again during the night by the crash of a round-shot or the shriek of pain—to see them rise up to encounter another day of danger, trouble, and distress; to see them endeavour, with such small means as lay in their power, to continue clean in their persons, and avoid the vermin which already swarmed on many; to see young and delicate English girls, nursed in the lap of luxury, combing out their hair seated on the floor of the barracks, with not water enough to wash their faces—no clean linen, no clean clothes in the frightful heat pervading. To see all this, and a great deal more (which the reader can well imagine, or we have written in vain), was truly dreadful; and now to picture all this, the reality having passed away, may enable "the maids of Merry England, who live at home at ease," to appreciate, in some measure, the horrible trials suffered at Cawnpore by their unfortunate countrywomen.

The hole was dug that evening by Edgington and Hoby, under the intrenchment mound; earthen walls were constructed as sides to the habitation, at right angles to the mound itself; the pole of our hero's tent and another were placed across from wall to wall, and the tent kurnauths were spread at top. When completed, the result was a chamber six feet square, and four feet high, which you entered by descending two steps, with earth for the floor, earth for the walls, and canvas for the roof; and this was the only abode poor Marion had.

It had its advantages, however, in those wretched times. It was much safer than the riddled barracks, for being under the intrenchment, the shot and shell flew over it; and, again, it was cleaner; but the greatest advantage, in our poor heroine's eyes, was the privacy it conferred.

Bad as it was, it was very much better than other hiding-places of the same kind, of which there were many under the intrenchments very much smaller and with a more insufficient covering.

Edgington saw Merton, and offered him the shelter for his wife. He (Merton) was only too glad to avail himself of it, and thus Marion and the pretty Eurasian passed that night under its cover.

The next day, Saturday, the 13th, passed as its predecessors; but the misery of the garrison increased hourly, from the numerous causes we have detailed. That evening, however, a great calamity befell them, resulting in a dreadful loss of life and increased misery to the survivors. The reader will remember that the barrack, in which all the women, children, sick, and wounded were placed, had a grass-thatch roof, over which a covering of tiles had been placed, by the foresight of the general, before the mutiny had declared itself. It was, however, insufficient to preserve the building from the effects of the red-hot shot which the besiegers now launched at the hapless garrison, and about an hour before sunset it took fire. The assembly immediately sounded, and all possible means to extinguish the flames were resorted to; but without success, for the wind was strong, and they gained apace. No sooner did the besiegers perceive the disaster than they collected their forces, and under the supposition that the garrison would be mainly employed at the burning building, they threatened an attack on every side. The danger was imminent, so much so that the burning barrack had to be deserted, while the greater part of the defenders stood at their posts by the intrenchments. A number were, however, told off, as they best could be in the dire confusion that prevailed, to remove the sick and wounded, for all hope of extinguishing the flames were at an end; and this little band worked as men only can work under such circumstances. The scene was truly a terrible one: the flames leapt along in their destructive course; women screamed for their missing children; the wounded, or those unable to rise from sickness, yelled for help; the firing was hotter than ever; those on the parapets were fully engaged in driving back the storming parties; and a more terrific scene, in all its details, cannot be conceived.

It came to an end. The combustible parts of the barrack were consumed, and the four walls, with the verandah pillars (the inside filled with a smouldering mass of ruins), was all that remained of the building so urgently required for shelter. The attack had been beaten back, and the weary garrison now collected to ascertain what loss they had sustained by the fire. The names of the sick and wounded were called over; but, alas! to many there was no response; and the dreadful reality was shortly apparent, that about thirty of these had perished in the flames.

Oh, the misery, the dark and dreadful misery, of that night! Wives had lost husbands, husbands wives, parents children, and moaned over their losses with heartrending grief; while a crowd of women and children, now without any cover to shelter them, wandered around, the pictures of despair.

From that time a great change came over the garrison. The miseries they suffered were all doubled by this sad event, and the flame of hope, which had hitherto sustained them, flickered sadly, if it did not expire in many a manly breast. They did their duty, it is true; they daily hurled back on their tormentors the destruction intended for themselves; but they fought as men without hope, actuated, however, by the still more powerful courage of despair.

Then shone forth, in all its beauty, the excellence of woman's nature. Formerly they had been the comforted, now they were the comforters; they tended, with unceasing solicitude, their brave champions; all consideration of station was forgotten, and the high-born dame nursed the private soldier. They whispered words of comfort into the ears of their defenders; they reanimated the hope which had nearly died out; they girded the warriors for the fight, and greeted with smiles their return. As day after day wore on, and no help came,—as misery, suffering, and privation increased, so did the fortitude of woman appear in its brightest colours, for they moved like angels administering consolation in those blood-stained intrenchments.

## CHAPTER XXIV.

### SUNDAY—THE ASSAULT—ANOTHER DEATH.

WE must again pass over some days, for the events in each were so like the preceding there would be little new to relate; and to tread over and over again the same ground of suffering could avail nothing.

It is, therefore, of Sunday, the 21st of June, we will now write, though we must first recount such incidents worthy of notice as had occurred up to that time.

When the barrack was burnt, all the medicines and the greater part of the surgical instruments were lost. The fire had been so rapid, and the confusion in trying to save the sick and wounded so great, that the flames had reached that part of the building where they were stowed before they were even thought of.

This misfortune increased twenty-fold the sufferings of those on the hospital list. But a very few surgical instruments had been rescued; all further operations were therefore performed with much difficulty; so much so, indeed, that none but the simplest were undertaken, and a bad gun-shot wound, after the conflagration of the barracks, was tantamount to death.

The greatest misery suffered, however, was owing to the climate, and the dreadful exposure the besieged underwent, especially since the main shelter was destroyed. Now, little or none was to be had, and the sun claimed five or six victims daily out of the garrison number. A great many made holes, such as we have described, under the intrenchment walls, but the noonday heat was too powerful for them to remain there, and an idea may be formed of the dreadful suffering the sun occasioned, when we state, that though these places were infinitely safer than either of the barracks from the shot of the enemy, all preferred a corner of the still whole building, or even the shady side of a wall in the burnt one, to exposure under the intrenchments. The difference, as to safety, in the two places was very great; few, if any, were killed as they sat under the intrenchment mounds,—many lost their lives from round-shot, shell, or musketry in the buildings. The latter, from the numerous chasms in their walls, from the want of a roof in one case, and from being the marks against which the sepoys aimed the greater part of their fire, were very, very dangerous—truly, little better than the open; but then they gave some protection from the sun, and the poor refugees in the garrison preferred these chances of death, coupled with shade, to sun and safety behind the mounds.

The dead, of which there were now many daily, were laid out in the roofless verandah of the burnt barrack. At night a fatigue party came round, and carried them outside the intrenchment, to the old well before mentioned, which was the common grave of all.

The day after the fire, as the authorities knew not how long the siege would last, or when help might arrive, it was resolved by the general in command to reduce the ration food of the garrison by one-third. Of the wisdom, nay, necessity of this step, none can doubt; but it increased not a little the sufferings of the besieged. They had not too much food before,—now they literally had not enough; and whereas formerly those in health would give up a portion to make some little delicacy, such as soup or the like, for a sick or wounded friend, each now voraciously devoured his share, for craving hunger forbad any being relinquished. Meat was also now a rare thing; for the last of the commissariat sheep and goats had been killed some few days before, and it was only when a stray animal from the besiegers' camp wandered near the intrenchments at night, and was seized upon by the English soldiers, that the garrison tasted flesh.

Two or three of the very few horses kept in the intrenchments had died, and though thrown outside the mounds, they could not be removed further. Their bodies were not the least annoyance the besiegers underwent; they stunk within six hours of their death, and pervaded the intrenched barracks with a sickening effluvium, which was perfectly intolerable.

But the plague of flies was even worse. The dirt, the heat, the putrid carcasses around, brought them in tens and hundreds of thousands into the intrenchments, and every moment of the day was each of the besieged reminded of their presence. When any one opened his mouth to speak, flies flew down his throat; when he ate his food, he masticated flies with it: they were so thick that the floor and walls of the barracks were black with them, and it may easily be conceived how this ever-present and ever-increasing plague weighed heavily on the trouble-tried garrison.

It is Sunday, the 21st of June, and a larger crowd than usual is observed, early in the morning, around the intrenchments. All the adjacent buildings—or rather such portions of them as remain after the general conflagration—are filled with matchlock-men, and it is evident to the besieged that an attack on an unusually large scale may be expected. News had been received from outside, the previous evening, that the besiegers had sworn to take the intrenchments on the following day, at all hazards; but not much reliance was placed in the report, so many times already had the garrison been deceived. This time, however, truth was in the tale. The Nana's army, weary of the siege, and determined to extinguish the accursed Feringhee race at Cawnpore, had sworn, as reported, to do or die. Let us see how they kept their words.

We will go to that part of the intrenchments where those we know and take most interest in are present.

There, on the side certainly not the least threatened, stand Hoby, Edgington, and Merton; Marion Paris and Mrs. Merton are below them, in the small excavation made, off which the canvas covering has been taken. When Edgington had told his *protégée* of the attack momentarily expected, she had insisted on remaining near him and Mr. Hoby during its continuance; and as she truly was very much safer there, under the mound, than she would be in the barracks, our hero made no objection to her wish. Mrs. Merton was present in the same way; she declared John would fight all the better if she were near him; and then, as both she and Marion said, they would be useful too, for they would load the rifles, and save time in that way.

Before the attack begins, which may be fatal to some of them, let us regard this small section of that heroic garrison, and see what effect the horrors and privations undergone have had upon them. Those who had known Miss Paris only in the palmy days of her beauty, would not have recognized her in the emaciated being at the foot of that mound. Not that her beauty had all vanished; some of its characteristics neither exposure nor suffering could destroy. The perfect outlines of her face were the same, and they constituted no small part of her attractions. Her eyes, though they sparkled not as formerly, still told of the loving and gentle spirit within, still in their depths revealed the warm and impulsive nature of their owner; her beauteous golden hair, though sadly neglected, was there, but hastily twisted at the back of her head in folds, which, from their weight and size, had partly escaped the thraldom of the comb, and hung in dishevelled masses down her back. But nothing else of the Marion Paris of other days remained. Her dress, one mass of gunpowder and dirt, sat loose on her attenuated form; her poor hands looked as if they belonged not to living woman; her face, speaking of sorrow and suffering, had nought of the joyous aspect of yore. In short, the poor girl we picture *was* Marion Paris, it is true; but Marion after seventeen days of suffering, which had laid many a strong form in the dust, while this frail being was spared for, alas! perhaps still greater misfortunes.

Why should we go through the same task with the other four. Who knows not the sad havoc that sorrow and privations rapidly make in all? Let that effect be multiplied many times, and the result will convey some idea of the sorrow-stricken aspect of the remaining figures.

"Come down here a minute, Arthur—I want to speak to you," said Marion; "I won't be an instant, and Mr. Hoby can say the moment the sepoys advance."

"Well, what is it, dear girl?" asked Edgington, when the next moment he stood by her side.

"Will you promise me one thing, and promise it faithfully?"

"I will hear what it is first; I will make no blind promises."

"Very good, I will tell you. It is not likely to happen, but still it *may* be. If—if the rebels beat us; if they should storm the intrenchments, will you promise me, that under no circumstances I shall fall into their hands?"

"Not as long as I have life to defend you, Marion."

"Oh, Arthur, *that* I know; but you must promise more."

"How can I do so?"

"You *can*. You must promise that if the rebels enter the intrenchments, you will yourself shoot me."

"I, Marion!"

"Yes, you, Arthur; and oh! if you love me, make me not ask another for the boon. Nay, I will *not* do so. See, if you refuse me, I have the means myself. This little pistol, placed here," she continued, as, with a steady hand, she applied it to her temples, "will effectually do my bidding. But if I feel I am dependent on myself, I shall not know when all hope is gone. I may be hasty, and you, Arthur, may live to repent you granted me not the first earnest request I ever made you. I see you will say yes; say it, and I am happy."

Edgington was silent. The dreadful working of the inner man was depicted on his face. He looked at Marion, whose hand was on his arm, and he saw the countenance of a resolute, determined girl, who well knew what she demanded.

"I will do what you ask, Marion; but remember, I will do it at the last moment. I have given you the promise, let *me* judge when the act is necessary. And now, God bless you; I hear the sepoys shouting, I must to my post."

"God bless you, Arthur; and, strange as it may seem, He *will* bless you for the promise you have made me."

The storming party was advancing, even as Edgington looked over the intrenchment mound, or rather, the advanced force of the same, for they were not numerous. They had devised a new plan to screen themselves from the grape and musketry of the garrison, for every two men had a large bale of cotton before them, which they rolled along the ground, and advanced under its cover. The buildings and walls in their rear swarmed with others of the enemy, waiting to see the success of this new expedient.

"That dodge won't pay," remarked Merton, "ingenious as it is. The seventy or eighty men behind those bales can do nothing by themselves; and moving at the slow pace they do, we can pick many off with our rifles when they come closer, in spite of the cover."

"Yes," replied Hoby, "I see none of our men are flinging away their shots at the cotton bales. Wait a bit, we shall get a chance directly."

"There are three men, if I mistake not, behind the

nearest bale," remarked Edgington, "and they cannot all hide themselves. There, the back of one fellow is well in sight; I'll try if I can make a good shot with the needle-rifle."

He fired. The sepoy alluded to sprang off the ground, and fell full length, clear of the bale.

"Well done, indeed!" remarked Hoby; "but don't try it again. The main body behind may come on at any moment, and you would then be sorry if your rifle were empty."

"No fear, for I have two, and there's lots of ammunition. See, the ladies load fast enough, and here I am ready again," he added, as he took the rifle from Marion's hand.

"Immense advantage, certainly, the quickness with which that needle-rifle can be loaded," said Merton. "I hope Miss Paris and you are very careful how you do it, though," he added, looking down at his wife.

"Oh, it's much easier to load than this thing," replied Mrs. Merton, as, with an iron loading-rod, she rammed the bullet home in our hero's second rifle. "Have you not fired yet, John?"

"No; but never fear, you'll have plenty to do directly," replied her husband.

"What are they doing now?" asked Marion.

"Still coming on slowly behind the bales," said Hoby. "See, Edgington!" he continued, "an officer with some men have made a sortie, under cover of the nearest unfinished barracks, and there goes a discharge of grape amongst the rascals near the third of those buildings. Capital!—a couple of dozen are down, and the rest bolt!"

"Never mind that side," Edgington remarked; "we shall have enough to do here directly. Those cursed fellows behind the bales can't be more than a hundred and fifty yards off now: I wish another would give me a chance."

"Chance enough now," called out Merton, "there come the main body."

He was right. Innumerable numbers of the mutineers sprang over the compound walls, or came out from under the cover of the buildings, shouting to one another, as they advanced to the attack.

The three rifles in the hands of Edgington and his companions sent their leaden messengers into the crowd; but a discharge of grape was fired at the same moment, which did much more execution.

"Arthur, tell me, how is it now?" called out Marion anxiously from below.

"Well for us, dear Marion; many were killed then."

"Still they advance," said Hoby. "Now, Miss Paris, my rifle—quick."

"One minute—there it is. Now, Arthur, give me the needle-rifle; here's the other one ready."

Bang! bang! two more discharges of grape into the rebel ranks plough lanes in the advancing columns, and many bodies strew the ground, while the piercing shrieks of the wounded are heard even amidst the rattle of musketry and the roar of the guns.

"That stops them, I think; for, see, their leader is down. No—another has taken his place. Never mind; the nearer they come, the more we'll cut them up," called out Hoby.

It was a critical moment. The storming-party—and their numbers were great—had advanced to within a hundred yards of the intrenchments. A little more and they would arrive, scale the low walls, and then, from their immense numbers, no hope for the garrison remained. Nothing more could be done, however, than was doing. Every man, at his post, fired as fast as he could load, or as others loaded for him. Every gun that could be brought to bear on the advancing party poured in round upon round of grape and canister; and still the rebels advanced.

For a few moments, all in the garrison conceived the

end of their trials had come, and the death which instantly awaited them, and those they loved, made many a bold heart quail. The feeling soon passed, however, even as their danger became still more imminent, and was replaced with a fiery desire of revenge—a longing to kill, a craving to close with the advancing miscreants, in a hand-to-hand combat.

Another few minutes must decide their fate. The sepoys, under the influence of bhung* and other stimulants, had certainly fought as they had never fought before during that siege. Have they the heart, now that the prize is almost within their grasp, to make a final dash and conquer?

"No," roared out Hoby, "not this time, my friend," as he shot dead one of the most daring of the assailants, rushing up in advance of the rest. It would seem to be an answer to our question; and the triumphant voice, the words, reanimated all around him.

The shout, for many mistook it for that, was taken up by others, and the cheers, for which the mutineers saw no cause, made the nearest of the advancing party halt. They halted only a moment, but it was fatal to their cause; they could not recover the impetuosity of their former advance; those in the rear hesitated when they saw the leaders pause, and during those moments of hesitation, rounds upon rounds of canister and grape mowed down their ranks, while nearly every bullet from the intrenchments, at that short distance, laid low its man. A few wavered, turned, and ran. Again shouted the garrison, again did the deadly canister urge a retreat. A little more, and a wild cry arose from the attacking force, and *sauve qui peut* was the order of the day, as, in a confused crowd, the besiegers ran for their lives.

Then did one long-continued hurrah from the reprieved garrison rend the air; while grape, canister, and bullets were sent after the flying multitude, who

* An intoxicating drug much used by the natives.

stopped not until they had attained their cover, but left 150 bodies lying on the open.

Congratulations on their success passed round amongst the besieged. Edgington shook Marion's hand with deep emotion, as he told her how at one minute he thought they had lost the day; and Hoby assured her and Mrs. Merton that he was sure a dozen extra sepoys owed their deaths to the quick manner in which the rifles had been loaded.

The besiegers, as if in revenge for their defeat, shortly commenced a furious cannon and musketry fire on the garrison; but all remained under cover of the intrenchments, and it did little damage. A few lives had, however, been lost during the attack, and the surgeons commenced their rounds, under the intrenchments, to pick out the wounded, and do for them what little lay in their power.

"The coast is pretty clear now," said Hoby as he looked over the intrenchment mound. "I think Jack Sepoy has had enough of that fun to last——"

A short sharp cry made the others, who were below, look up, as Hoby sank on his knees.

"Great God! are you hit, Hoby?" exclaimed Edgington, who was at his side the next moment.

"Yes," replied the former, as soon as he had recovered from the first shock of the stroke; "a musket-ball here," pointing to his right shoulder with the non-wounded arm.

"How dreadful! I'll call a surgeon. Oh, Mr. Hoby, dear Mr. Hoby, what *can* we do for you?" exclaimed Marion, as her eyes filled with tears.

"Nothing," replied Hoby faintly; "I fear it's a bad wound. No, I'll not be taken to the hospital," he continued, as Edgington and Merton were about to lift him; "but take me below. I can lie on the ground there. It's still early, and the sun 's not hot."

"Oh, you must not lie on the ground, Mr. Hoby," said Mrs. Merton, "but on one of our beds."

"On mine," said Marion; "it's more under the shade. That's right, Arthur; here's another pillow to raise his head."

"Will you call the surgeon, Merton?" said Edgington. "Can you feel the bullet anywhere, Hoby?"

"No, but I feel a dead pain between my shoulders, far from where the bullet entered."

The surgeon arrived at that moment. He was one of the most indefatigable of that body which, perhaps, had during the siege been more worked than any other. He spoke kindly to the wounded man, and proceeded to examine him, tracing carefully the course the bullet had taken. The examination did not last long, and Hoby spoke,—

"It's all up with me, doctor, is it not?"

"I fear so," said the surgeon kindly. "It's no use deceiving you; you cannot live many hours."

"I thought so," said Hoby calmly, though he spoke with an effort. "How long shall I probably live? two hours?"

"Not longer, I think, my poor fellow, for the bullet has taken a fatal course. Since the surgical instruments were lost, many have died from gun-shot wounds, because the simplest operations could not be performed; but it will not be your case,—this hurt is beyond the reach of art. Now, God bless you! I will return if I can, and as soon as possible; but I am much wanted elsewhere."

So saying, the surgeon, a kind-hearted man, left. It was, the reader will probably think, a hurried visit; but in such scenes as we are describing even those on the brink of the grave cannot take up much of the time so urgently required elsewhere.

"My poor, poor Hoby," said Edgington, who had watched with anxiety the surgical examination, and heard with sincere grief the result. "And are we so soon to part? It is so sudden I can scarcely believe it. However, you are, perhaps, escaping the still greater trials reserved for us, and it may well be your fate is an enviable one. Far better to die as now, surrounded by those who esteem you, than to be torn limb from limb, as some of us may yet be, by those wretches outside, if even the bodily tortures we may then undergo are not rendered still more acute by agony of mind regarding the fate of those dear to us."

"True, Edgington, and I must not repine. Had it been granted me to live, and help you to guard from evil that poor girl (who, even as she sits outside there, I can fancy a fit inhabitant for a brighter sphere), I should have been thankful. But it was not to be," added poor Hoby, shifting his posture with a groan of pain; "and God's will be done."

"Ah, Hoby!" remarked Edgington, forgetting even his friend's approaching death, when Marion's fate was brought before him. "How different my position—how different the position of every man in these intrenchments were we alone, with no women or children to guard. When I think of it all, and what it may yet come to, the reflection almost unseats my reason." The signal for change of sentries and officers on guard sounded at this moment, and Edgington continued, "I must leave you now, dear fellow, and so must Merton,' for we are both on duty: his wife and Marion will, however, do all you want. Can they get you anything now?"

"Yes, water," replied the wounded man. "Fire is in my throat."

The water was brought. "Let me hold it to your lips," said Marion tenderly, as she knelt by the side of her plain charpoy bed, on which the wounded man lay. "Don't drink more at this moment; you can have it again whenever you want it."

Poor Marion! She knew not until Hoby was thus mortally wounded how much she valued him, how unconsciously he had become almost dear to her. We say *almost,* for the simple-hearted girl had never thought enough on the subject to know how very near the pleasure she took in his society approached to love. She and Mrs. Merton had retired while the wound was examined, and Marion, on hearing the surgeon's fatal opinion, had evidently wept, for the traces of recent grief were yet visible on her face—nay, the tears were still coursing each other down her cheeks, as she held the bowl of water to the lips of the wounded man.

"Now, God bless you, Hoby," said Edgington, taking his hand with an affectionate grasp. "God bless you, old fellow; you have been a warm friend, and never shall I forget you. It may be we shall all meet soon again; perhaps you only precede us."

"Good-bye, dear Hoby," said Merton simply, and burst into tears as he said it.

A little more and the two officers stood at their post under the mounds, with manly sorrow on their faces, and the traces of tears still in their eyes.

Mrs. Merton was a woman, and had all a woman's instinct. She had long seen that Hoby loved Marion, and she guessed the dying man would like to be alone with the young girl. She framed some excuse, promised to return presently, and left them.

A silence succeeded her departure; Marion knelt by the bedside, and bathed with water the temples of the sufferer, on which the dews of death were even then collecting, but neither spoke.

Hoby's gentle nurse dared not speak, for she felt a choking sensation in her throat, and was conscious she should give way to audible grief if she did so.

At last Marion started, as the wounded man opened his eyes, saw they were alone, and placed his hand on the thin and wasted fingers of his nurse, as they lay on the coverlet. "Nay, start not, Miss Paris,—I meant not to alarm you; but I see we are alone, and I would say a few words, after which I shall, I think, die easier."

Marion replied not; the little hand under his own trembled violently, but was not removed.

"I will not ask you if I may speak, it might pain you to answer," continued Hoby, with a weak voice, "and what I have to say can in no way affect your future. But it will be a great consolation to me before I die to utter what my lips have burned to say a long, long time,—what perhaps would never have been said had I lived; for then it would have called for an answer, —now none is necessary. The water once more; my thirst and weakness both increase."

Marion, with a trembling hand, placed the cup to his lips. Her face was very pale,—pale in spite of the unnatural colour exposure had occasioned.

"Miss Paris, I have loved you. Marion, I love you now, and shall with my last breath. Oh that this poor life had been given more immediately in your defence! that my death could have helped you, could have saved you from one particle of suffering! I loved you very soon after we first met, Marion; when you saw it not, when I dared not show it you. I have loved you ever since. I never expected success, for I knew I possessed not the usual requirements for woman's love; but still I hoped, fondly hoped, and daily prayed, that I might find favour in your eyes. Did you ever guess my love? So much you may tell me."

"Oh, Mr. Hoby! you will break my heart," Marion replied, while sobs choked her utterance. "Yes—oh yes! I did perceive it; I knew it long ago. You are too generous to ask me more; but I will add more," continued the kneeling girl, whose very nature was all love and kindness. "I never disliked it. I never, 'tis true, returned your love; the love of woman awakes not so quickly as man's; but later I might have done so—I—I—think I should have done so." Miss Paris covered her blushing face with her hands, as she whispered, "Have I said enough?"

"Enough! Oh Heaven! how can I thank you,

Marion? Marion! The name sounds strange to me, when uttered in your presence; but my lips know none more familiar. Yes—Marion—Marion—will—love—me—later," he continued, slowly muttering the words, while the expression of his eyes, and the dreamy mode of utterance, showed his unconciousuess of her presence.

Once more was the water placed to his lips by the trembling girl, and he drank eagerly. He shivered all over, as he finished the draught, looked at Marion with reason in his gaze, and said,—

"I am very near death—nearer than even the doctor thought. Yes, I am about to die—to die when I have learnt what makes life a thousand times more precious. Ah, Marion! *I* may not live to love you, but there are others more worthy than myself; and these troubles over, you will meet with some one who will rightly value your angelic nature. And then, if departed spirits are ever allowed to look again upon earth, I shall yet see and rejoice in your happiness. The thought that it may be so, smooths my passage to the grave. No! say it not, I beg!" he continued, with great excitement, as he struggled into a sitting posture, in spite of the acute pain his wound gave him, and clutching Marion's wrist with his wasted and bony hand, stopped short her declaration that she never could forget him or love another; "say it not, if you would save me from the bitter reproaches I should then heap on myself for my selfishness in having, when within an hour of death, spoken to you on such a subject. Oh! spare me that pang, I implore you! You do so; do you not?"

"Thanks, dear Marion," he continued, a moment later, when, amongst her bursting sobs, he distinguished a faint "Yes;"—"Thanks, dear girl; now shall I die truly happy. Help me to lie down again. So,—thank you, thank you. The pain of my wound is very great," he said, as he laid his head once more on the pillow, and the muscles of his face worked frightfully with the agony he endured; "such pain cannot last long, and it warns me to prepare for death. I must banish all earthly thoughts, and alone, Marion, I must call upon my God. Leave me, dear, *dear* Marion; but remain within call. You must be with me at the last; for of your angelic face, the last thing I shall see on earth, I would fain carry the recollection beyond the grave."

Five minutes passed, as Marion, steeped in woe, sat a few paces removed from the dying man, where he could not see her. Mrs. Merton came up, her eyes also red with weeping, and asked if she should go in "to poor Mr. Hoby?"

"No don't," replied Marion; "he asked me to leave him, as he wished to pray. He will call me, when he has done; and if you don't mind, I would rather then go in alone," she concluded, while a deep blush suffused her tear-stained cheeks.

"I couldn't well stop, if you wished it," said Mrs. Merton, with innate delicacy. "John could only now spare me for one moment." She kissed her friend, wiped the tears from her eyes with sisterly fondness, and left her.

Ten minutes,—it seemed an age to the sorrow-stricken girl. She began to fear death had closed the prayers. She, too, prayed as she sat, prayed for the soul of him who, while he had never aroused deep love, had awoke the first symptoms of the passion in her young and gentle heart. A weak voice interrupted her—"Miss Paris." Another moment and she stood by the bedside of poor, poor Hoby.

"The end is near, Marion; I can scarcely see you. So let me die," he said, as she put her hand in his, and he pressed it to his clammy lips. "Speak to me; let me hear your voice once more. I see your face—dimly."

"My dear, dear friend. Oh, more, *more* than friend —my loved companion!"

A smile broke o'er the lips through which the soul was even then passing. "O God, bless Ma—ri—on!" was whispered.

One short struggle—a gasping sound—and Miss Paris held the hand of a dead man!

## CHAPTER XXV.

CHANGE OF TACTICS—THE NANA'S OFFERS—LAST DAY IN THE INTRENCHMENTS.

We have supped full of horrors, but our task is not yet done. The Cawnpore garrison have suffered much, very much, but there is yet more to come.

After the failure of the storming attempt recorded in the last chapter, the besiegers changed their tactics. Hitherto they had fired principally at the barracks, to demolish them and destroy life; now their great aim appeared to be to disable the garrison guns. They could not storm; they could not take the intrenchments, and put its defenders—the accursed Feringhee race—to the sword, as long as those guns stood; so round-shot of every weight, from 6 to 24 pounders, were sent hurtling through the air day and night directed at the guns and their carriages.

It was with bitter and apprehensive feelings that the besieged saw this change in the offensive movements. Not a day passed, after the great assault, that one of the guns—on which rested all their hopes—was not either injured or disabled. If, then, the succour expected did not shortly arrive, the time must soon come when, devoid of artillery, they would become an easy prey to the ruthless miscreants without.

How intently did the noble garrison now strain their eyes, looking for that succour which came not! How many fervent and tearful prayers were offered up nightly, by that despairing crowd, to the Great Ruler of all things! But though morning succeeded to night, and night to morning, the view from the intrenchment mounds was always the same;—no change, no signs of the help in which now lay their only hope—if even it can be called hope when, long deferred, it "maketh the heart sick."

A crowning calamity now fell upon the besieged—one which, when it occurred, was whispered from mouth to mouth, as if its import was too sad to be spoken aloud: their brave general, the noble Sir Hugh Wheeler—that old soldier, who in all their trials had known how best to relieve them; who had directed everything; who, by the moral influence of his presence, had kept despair from settling on his companions, was wounded, some said mortally. The news was received with consternation; but a few hours later the report was modified: the wound was not mortal, and the sore-pressed garrison escaped at least that sorrow.

But death was making greater havoc than ever in the intrenchments. The exposure, the suffering, the numberless causes inimical to life, were now telling, from their continuance, in a multiplying ratio. From fifteen to twenty bodies nightly found their last resting-place in the well outside, where lay so many who had preceded them. Two more of those known to the reader now lay with the dead, for Lieutenant Percy's head had been taken off by a round-shot, as he helped to serve one of the guns; and Mrs. Bruce had died, apparently of no specific disease, but from the general suffering she endured.

The siege had now lasted twenty days, and the garrison numbers were much reduced. The reader will remember that, apart from the native servants, who very soon took themselves off, seven hundred souls had entered the intrenchments, inclusive of women and children. Of these, about two hundred and fifty had fallen up to this time, showing an average mortality of twelve daily.

That the spirits of the garrison were now at a lower ebb than ever, will be easily conceived: the only wonder is that they kept up any hope, that despair did not fall on the whole body; for, truly, history's page presents no more dreadful situation than theirs.

Great admiration and sympathy have been accorded to the surviving members of the Lucknow garrison, after the brilliant and unparelleled feat of arms they went through; and none can doubt they deserved it,—nay, that their heroism has not up to this day been sufficiently rewarded. But let us not, in the midst of the glowing applause their deeds, and others of a like nature, call forth,—in the midst of our rejoicings o'er the quieting aspect of India, forget to pay a tribute of heartfelt admiration to the heroic Cawnpore garrison and their leader. Let us not forget to drop a tear in remembrance of the many heroic spirits of whom it was composed, who, during the comparatively short time they fought and bled, suffered much more than any other besieged body in India.

Were it only from the want of shelter which the defenders of the Cawnpore intrenchments were subject to, their position was infinitely worse than that of the Lucknow garrison, or, indeed, than any other body of the many sore-tried sufferers at that awful time. Who knows India, and dreads not an Indian sun? Who, having felt the fiery blasts of June on Hindostan's burning plains, can fail to appreciate the dire sufferings, from this cause alone, endured by the gallant body whose deeds we paint? Oh! Englishmen, side with us! Let not the nations say heroism such as theirs passed by unhonoured in the British isles! The Cawnpore garrison (alas! they have nearly, very nearly all gone to their last home), who fought without hope, who freely bled in their country's cause, under hardships which pen cannot depict, which tongue cannot tell, deserve a monument at England's hands, set up in England's mighty capital, worthy to hand down their deeds to posterity, and vie with Fame, who already, on a loud trumpet, has achieved immortality for their names!

"It must finish soon, my poor fellow-sufferer," said Marion, as she lay her weary head on the wasted shoulder of the pretty Eurasian. "This day week we shall not be here."

"Where then?" asked Mrs. Merton. "Do you think we shall be saved by that time?"

"Either saved or lost. We can never hold out till then; but four of our guns are serviceable at this moment."

"How horrible, is it not?" added her olive-complexioned friend, as she lifted Marion's head, and looked into those gentle eyes. "What will, then, be our fate?"

"'Tis too horrid to think of," replied Miss Paris; "and, after full consideration, I have made up my mind not to risk it."

"I understand; and I suppose that's why you always carry that little pistol about you. I've no pistol, but I have a husband," added the slight Eurasian somewhat proudly; "and he'll not let me fall alive into the wretches' hands. Did you hear all the horrors perpetrated at Delhi on the ladies?" she asked in an undervoice.

"Yes and no. I heard a great deal from my ayah, and saw much in one of the Calcutta papers; but poor Mrs. Peters would never talk much about it; she said it was not a fit subject for me as an unmarried girl."

"And Mrs. Peters was right," said Mrs. Merton, taking up quickly the matronly dignity, which she feared she had somewhat compromised by her question; "but I, as a married woman, can assure you, that death is not nearly as bad as our fate would be in sepoy hands."

"So I suppose," Marion replied, blushing, though Mrs. Merton, even, could not see her face, laid again, as it was, on its former resting-place. "But let's change the subject. How ill poor Captain Edgington is looking; do you know, he has a continual low fever on him now."

"Ill, certainly; but poor John does not look much better. It makes my heart ache to see them both. Poor Captain Edgington, he has much to distress him. When did he last hear from his wife; and does he know if she is still safe at Patna?"

"He supposes so; he heard from her just before we came into the intrenchments. But the revolt may have spread down country, and he must, of course, be very anxious."

"Yes. How dreadful it must be for those elsewhere, who have relations in this garrison. I can never be thankful enough that I have been with John through it all. Dear, dear John, it would have killed me to know he was here alone."

"They say the well is running dry, Andrew," said a private soldier, not far from where our two ladies sat, to his comrade; "if so, we are all booked for a long journey, as I guess the sapoys will spare none iv us."

"There's not as much water as there was," replied the other, "but it'll last some time yet. I believe, however, the provisions is running short, and that's nearly as bad."

"I suppose they've so much to do below," remarked the first speaker, "they can't help us—leastways until they've helped themselves. The niggers in here say all Bengal's in a blaze."

"Unless they *do* help us soon they'll be too late, for sartain. Bill, who works the nearest gun to me when I'm on sentry, says we haven't much more ammunition."

"He be blowed. We've ammunition enough for the guns we have left; but how long will those be serviceable?—that's the pint."

It was not a cheering conversation which Mrs. Merton and Marion had listened to, but there was nothing particularly new in it. The want of provisions and ammunition, and the possible want of water, they had heard speculations about before; the truth being, that while both the former were really short, the well was not in a flourishing condition.

Another day! The same routine; the same thing over and over again. No succour—no tidings of it! Misery on all sides! The average number of deaths, and the hasty burial in the evening.

On Wednesday, the 24th of June, it was bruited around that a letter had been received from the Nana, offering terms to the besieged.

"Have you heard the terms offered, Bruce?" said our hero, coming suddenly upon that officer.

"Yes. The Nana guarantees the lives of all in the garrison, and boats to take us to Allahabad, if we will surrender," replied the major.

"And are we going to accept?" asked Edgington, with anxiety.

"I don't know," Bruce replied. "The thing is even now under discussion; but I fear there is little choice, for in no case could we hold out many days."

"The terms are favourable enough—too favourable, I fear," remarked Edgington; "for after the experience we have had, the Nana should not be readily trusted."

"We are to give up the treasure, the guns, and ammunition. I don't see that the terms are so very favourable," said Bruce.

"Who brought the letter?" asked our hero.

"A half-caste girl, named Jacoby. She's got a sister here in the garrison. She says the Nana is tired of the siege, and wants the two lacs of treasure we have."

"When do you think it will be decided?" asked Edgington. "I'm very anxious. I truly don't know whether the offer ought to be taken or not. I fear treachery from that rascal of a rajah; and yet what *can* we do, with but three serviceable guns left."

"We shall know in another hour or two," said Bruce listlessly, as he wandered on. "Were it not for my poor children at home, I would, as far as I am personally concerned, rather die behind these mounds. But there are others to think of."

Poor Bruce! he had been a miserable man ever since his wife's death. The affection he had borne her was of no ordinary kind; and when she was laid low, having died of no specific disease, but only of the heavy sufferings and privations she had undergone, his feelings were thereby all the more lacerated.

The question whether the terms should or should not be accepted was not decided that day. Due time for consideration was taken, and an answer promised on the morrow.

Opinions varied that evening among both officers and men, as to whether the treaty should be concluded. Under the circumstances, no one doubted the advisability of entertaining it, if any security could be taken for the due performance of its terms on the part of the Nana and his followers. But all knew how treacherously the rajah had hitherto behaved, and many doubted the wisdom of trusting him at all. Others, again, urged that there was no reason to suppose help would shortly arrive; that with the disabled artillery, scarcity of provisions, &c., they could not hold out many days longer; and that it was better to trust to the chance of the Bhitoor chief being sincere in his offers than to encounter the almost certain annihilation which must necessarily otherwise shortly be theirs.

The question in the council-chamber was decided in the affirmative; and the next day, Thursday, an answer to that effect was sent, under a flag of truce, to the Nana.

The messenger returned with the information that the rajah, on receiving the acceptance, had at once ordered hostilities to be suspended, and that he would himself shortly arrive in person to ratify and confirm the agreement.

Hostilities on the side of the garrison were arrested,

and the besieged body waited with anxiety the arrival of the chief.

It was somewhat late in the afternoon when he arrived, escorted by a small body-guard; and he proceeded at once to the general, who, assisted by his staff, drew up the terms of the agreement, which was duly signed and ratified on both sides.

Its terms were shortly: That the garrison should give up all their guns and ammunition, and that the treasure in the intrenchments should be ceded. On the other side, it was promised that carriage for the sick and wounded should be provided to the river-side; that the troops should take their baggage with them, as also their arms; and that a sufficient number of boats should be supplied to take the whole of the besieged down the river to Allahabad.

As the rajah left the intrenchments, he happened to pass near the spot where Edgington and Marion sat. He regarded the latter attentively for an instant, but she shrank from his gaze; he then smiled, as if he deprecated her fear of him, bowed politely, which courtesy our hero returned, and passed on.

"The oftener I see that man, Arthur, the less I like him," said Marion, as soon as she had recovered from the fright the Nana's presence gave her.

"Never mind, dear Marion. The treaty is signed, and we shall leave Cawnpore immediately, when you will, I hope, never see him again."

"God grant it," replied Marion, "for the sight of him unnerves me in a way I cannot account for."

It was decided, when the treaty was concluded, that a committee of officers from the garrison should go to the river-side at noon next day and inspect the boats, to see that they were in a good and serviceable condition for the purpose intended. This was done; and the committee were well pleased to find, that not only was there a sufficient number, but that many budgerows (a superior kind of native boat) were amongst the number.

On the return of the officers preparations were made to hand over the guns, ammunition, and treasure, according to the terms of the treaty. The fortification was thrown open, and immense numbers of the rebels came in.

"Why, they are twenty to one at least," observed Edgington, as he and Merton sat in front of the small hole, where Marion and Mrs. Merton had retired on the sepoys entering. "What chance should we ever have had in a hand-to-hand fight?"

"Not much, certainly, for they could crush us now in five minutes. I really think, after all, they mean no treachery, and that we are well out of this dreadful business."

One of the native officers of their regiment passed the spot at that moment. He started when he saw them, instinctively saluted, and said, addressing Edgington,—

"Sorry to lose you, sahib; but it's the word of fate. India is no place for Englishmen now: the Company's raj * is finished."

"Dekne se maloom hoga" (When we see it, we shall know it), replied our hero shortly, in that common Hindostanee expression, which has a more extended sense than even our translation, meaning that one cannot know a thing for certain till it has happened; or, that seeing is believing.

The native passed on. He saw his former officer was not inclined to converse with him.

Mr. Peters came up a few minutes later, in a towering passion. "Only think, Edgington; I saw that blackguard, Holas Sing, the kotwal, just now—the man who formerly couldn't salaam and cringe too much, and who, if you remember, spoke to me about the chupattee circular one morning. I dare say you forget my mentioning it; but he then assured me it could mean nothing."

* Government.

"I remember your telling us," replied Edgington. "It was a long time ago, and we had a discussion about it. Poor old Hoby was there, and was, if I remember right, the only one who thought it a serious matter. Plain enough what it all meant now."

"Yes," continued Peters, "and we were all stupidly blind. But to return to Holas Sing—I was sitting down when he passed. Of course he recognized me; but he is much too great a man now to salaam. 'Peters Sahib here and alone?' he said jeeringly. 'Where are all the kutcherry people? Well, sahib, found out the chupattee secret?' he added, with a grin, as he passed on. I could have knocked him down, the black hound."

"I've no doubt he was up to the chupattee meaning long ago, even when they first came here," continued Edgington. "It's very wonderful how the secret was kept."

"It is, indeed," resumed Peters. "One of the town people in here told me, after Holas Sing had passed, that the Nana has made him kotwal under his new government. The rajah seems to have made a lot of appointments, and doesn't dream that the English can oust him."

"What the future of India *will* be, I have no doubt," continued Edgington; "it will be ours. But the rebellion, the natives say, has spread far and wide. All the army has mutinied; so it will be no light job to restore order; nor will it be done with the European force we have in the three presidencies. Ah, well, I am talking of it as if *we* were well out of this business. We *may* be; God grant it! but I am very anxious, and shall not sleep much to-night."

The evening came on. The mass of the Nana's men left the intrenchments, and withdrew to their own side. An order was issued, that the garrison would march down to the boats the first thing next morning, and that what little baggage there was should be packed and ready. It took not long to do this; a bundle, a carpet-bag, a small box, was the extent of what even the officers intended to take, for tents and all such heavy things no one thought of for a moment.

The night came, the second quiet night the garrison had known behind those earthern walls. But all slept not well; so accustomed had many become to the incessant sound of musketry and cannon, the very quietude disquieted them; while some of the most desponding, as they tossed on their hard beds or the baked ground, fancied the stillness that reigned the precursor of a still more fearful storm.

## CHAPTER XXVI.

### THE INTRENCHMENTS LEFT—THE BOATS.

Saturday, the 27th of June, 1858, commenced like other days in the hot winds. It was cooler a little before sunrise than it had been for the last four-and-twenty hours; but soon after the great luminary rose, the air became hot again, and began to puff warm blasts, forerunners of the coming heat.

The 27th of June! Will it be noted henceforth as the anniversary of a national misfortune—of black treachery — of hard-hearted cruelty — of a cowardly massacre without a parallel. Or will the horrors that occurred on that day be speedily forgotten and passed by in history's page unnoticed and unmourned?

"Marion, are you ready?" asked Edgington from the outside of the small retreat before mentioned: "it's near sunrise, and we shall all leave directly."

"Just ready. Mrs. Merton and I will take nothing but this one box between us, and we are now packing it," answered Miss Paris, as she drew aside the canvas opening, and stood forth a shadow of the Marion of former days, with a countenance on which deep woe was so indelibly impressed, it made Edgington's heart ache to look at it.

"I hope you both slept well," added our hero; "the night was quiet enough, after the uproar of the last three weeks."

"No, we neither of us slept much," replied Mrs. Merton; "we were too anxious. Where's John?"

"Gone on some duty or other; he'll be back directly," Edgington answered.

"Here are two chupattees I saved from my evening rations yesterday," said Mrs. Merton. "I saved one for John, will you eat the other, Captain Edgington?"

"By no means; I'm not hungry, but perhaps Marion will take it."

"No, I've asked her already. Well, as all refuse, I'll take it myself," continued Mrs. Merton, who was hungry enough, but who, like a good little soul as she was, thought of every one's wants before her own.

"I suppose we shall none of us get anything to eat before we go on board the boats," remarked Marion.

"I imagine not—unless extra rations are given out this morning. Hurrah! here comes Merton with a pile of chupattees, and a lot of dâl."

"Breakfast for us all," said Merton, as he arrived with his treasures; "goodness knows when we shall eat again, so let's devour these quickly, for we are to start soon."

"I suppose breakfast, then, has been served out to the whole garrison?" remarked Edgington.

"Yes," answered Merton. "I thought it would be, and so I went to get our share."

"See, John," said his wife, "Miss Paris and I have got the few things we mean to take into that one little box."

"I see, dear; but eat, Arabella, and talk afterwards. All the carts for the sick and wounded have come, and time is precious."

Let us look around while they are taking their simple meal. The garrison are bustling about, preparing for their departure. A number are employed in placing the sick and wounded on the elephants and carts which have been sent for them; some are wiping out their muskets; while others are cramming, by stealth, as much ammunition as they can stow away into their pouches.

An enormous number of the rebels wait outside to accompany the garrison down to the boats; why, does not appear, unless they are fearful of treachery, and suppose the Europeans might dash into the batteries and seize the guns.

"Depend on it, that's the reason," said Mr. Blank, the old civilian, to Peters (as they stood by the entrance, watching the wounded being placed on the carts and elephants): "they are so slippery themselves, they suspect everybody else."

"Yes; but I do hope they'll keep faith this time, and let us depart in peace," remarked Peters. "They ought to be satisfied with the way they've thinned our numbers; but four hundred and fifty left out of the seven hundred we numbered when we came in."

"A dreadful sacrifice of life certainly," said Mr. Blank; "and is it not really wonderful the way we have held out? Only look at those riddled barracks, at those insignificant earthworks, at our few guns, at the mass of women and children who have hampered our movements;—let any stranger look at them, I say, and he would scarcely believe we had kept that enormous multitude outside (eight thousand men) at bay for three weeks and upwards."

"No, really it is scarcely credible. It will be something to say hereafter that one was in the Cawnpore garrison."

Poor Peters! you are right; it will be something to say!!

"Ah! there's the call for the men to fall in," remarked Mr. Blank. "Now I suppose we shall be off."

"It will take us some time to get down to the river, all the same," Peters replied: "we shall accompany the carts, and they go slowly."

Everything was now ready. The men had formed up, each with his bundle; the boxes, bags, &c., had been placed on the carts. The women in a crowd, with their children at their sides, were already in advance of the soldiers, and the order to march was alone wanting ere the garrison left the intrenchments where they had suffered so much.

A sowar* at this moment rode in, and spoke to the general, who, with the others, was ready to start. He brought a message from the rajah—a short one—to the effect that the boats would not contain all the baggage prepared, and that the garrison must therefore leave as they were, taking nothing but what they could carry in their hands.

Murmurings were heard on every side when this was made known; but what could be done? The garrison were at the mercy of the Nana and his followers, and obliged to do as he wished.

"And the box is really not to go, Arthur?" said Marion. "Oh, how cruel! There are some things I shall want so *very* much; I could easily have taken a few in my hands."

"It's too late, dear Marion. The box is already on one of the carts. Never mind, my poor girl; I have money with me, and can buy you a few necessaries at the first village we stop at on our way down the river."

The garrison left the intrenchments. It was sad to see that long line of sick and wounded, that crowd of women and children, that jaded body of soldiers, that straggling mass of civilians, merchants, and shopkeepers, and compare them to what they had all been but three short weeks before. Sad was it also to trace the lines of suffering on every face; to note the starved aspect of each individual; to watch the whole body, one mass of dirt, disease, and suffering, totter onwards to the riverside, to the boats which they hoped would bear them away from the hell upon earth they had lately endured.

"Dear Arthur, I would rather walk than sit on this cart, it jolts me so dreadfully," said Marion, as she held out her hand to Edgington, to help her down.

* A horseman.

"Very good, dear. Take care how you jump off. That's right. But the road is stony, and you'll hurt your poor feet, your shoes are nearly worn out."

"I cannot stand the jolting, though. Mrs. Merton, remember you come in the same boat that we go in."

"Certainly," replied her olive-complexioned friend. "I wonder how many we shall be in a boat."

"We shall be crowded, I have no doubt," said Edgington; "but anything to get away from this horrible place."

"What an immense number of the rebels are with us,—they completely surround us," remarked Merton. "Do they suppose we shall run away on the road?"

"Alas! where could we run to?" said Marion with a sigh, as she put her hand on Edginton's shoulder, and tottered onwards.

The pace was slow. From the intrenchments to the river-side was but little more than a mile, and it took nearly an hour to accomplish. It was eight o'clock when they reached the bank; the boats were all moored in one long line, and the embarkation at once commenced.

The sick and wounded were first cared for, and put on board, or rather an attempt was made to do so, but there was such an immense crowd of the Nana's army around that great confusion existed. In the midst of this, Edgington, who had hold of Marion's hand, while Merton and his wife kept close to them, was addressed by a native officer of his late regiment, who, while he spoke, seemed to our hero to try and get between him and his charge, while others, who, Edgington thought, were acting in concert, pressed upon them, and tried to surround Marion.

"Don't let go my hand, Marion. Merton, do you get on the other side of her. I think these men want to separate us," said Edgington, speaking hurriedly.

"Here, jump on board this boat; it will do as well

as any other," said Merton, taking Marion's other hand, and pulling her through the crowd.

A little struggling, for the crowd around them seemed to increase, and all four gained the deck of the country boat, which had a thatched covering over the whole of the after-part, and was only open in front. The boat was full, more than full, when they got on board; the covered part was filled with women and children, while a few soldiers stood on the small fore-deck. Mrs. Merton and Marion retired among the women, leaving our hero and Merton standing on the open space.

"We may as well shove off, sir; we can hold no more," said a sergeant standing on the bamboo platform constructed above the thatch, and who recognized Edgington; "there are two boats loose already."

"Yes, let go," replied our hero; "but where's the boat's crew?"

"They jumped out as we jumped in, sir," said the sergeant, looking anxiously around; "and I saw them do it in the other boats. I don't like the look of it, sir, and think we'd better shove out as soon as we can."

"By all means," replied Edgington quickly, who, some distance from the river-side, recognized the Nana, who appeared to be pointing at their boat, and giving some orders.

The boat was not easily cast off from her moorings. She seemed to have been drawn up on the bank, and did not readily float.

"Come, give a hand, all of you," called out Edgington, laying hold of a long bamboo pole, and trying to shove off the boat with it,—"we've no time to lose; here are more poles—clap on, clap on, my men."

Those on the upper bamboo platform mentioned, as also those on the open fore-deck, did as our hero directed; but while they try to move the boat, let us note a few features in the scene which hitherto we have had no time to mention.

Whether treachery at this last moment was expected by some is uncertain; but certain it is, that once arrived at the river-side, a rush was made for the boats. All order, all military discipline was lost, and the first-comers, with their wives and families, scrambled into the nearest boat they fell across. No less hurry was apparent in the general desire to loosen the moorings and get off, but in most cases was this a work of time. The boats all appeared to be in the same state as the one Edgington was in, namely, drawn up unnecessarily high on the bank; and the heavy human freight now in each of course much increased the difficulty. The singular fact of the native crews leaving their boats as the Europeans got in, was observed by others besides the sergeant, and very likely prompted the quick and urgent efforts now discernible in all to get out into the stream. As stated, however, these efforts were not quickly crowned with success; the greater part of the boats seemed fast, and resisted all attempts to move them. Three—and only three—at the time of which we write had got off, and were hurriedly punting their way into deep water, while the Europeans on board of them laid aside their muskets and took off their coats, to work easier at the oars.

"Why, she'll not move," cried out Edgington, who had carefully seen that all the moorings were loose. "Her head 's still fast on the bank. Here—quick, all inside, get back close to the stern, and perhaps she'll float in front. Marion! Marion! make them move quick; quick, I say, all of you."

"Now she moves," cried out Merton, as he and every one else hung on the thick bamboo poles thrust against the banks, and strove might and main to shove the boat off.

"Yes, a little," cried out Edgington. "Now, a good shove, and all together. One—two—three; sh-o-ve away! With a will, boys—with a will. Damn it! I expect treachery."

Three reports of cannon, in quick succession, from the Nana's camp, while the crowd of natives about the boats gave way on all sides, called forth Edgington's last exclamation.

"Great God help us!—treachery it is!" roared out Merton, as he saw two guns, previously hid, run out at top of the bank, while the port-fires burnt ready in the hands of the gunners. "We've still a chance. Shove away men, its a case of life and death; she's moved a little already; another shove, and she's off!"

Whether the next attempt would have floated her cannot be known, for it was never made. As Merton finished speaking, even as the men on board, fully alive to the danger, collected their strength for a good trial, a volley of musketry was heard, and Merton sprang off the deck with a stifled scream, still keeping his hold on the bamboo. The only two others who had been exerting their power on the same pole, thus startled, let go their hold, and as it swung on one side, while Merton convulsively grasped it in the air, it precipitated him into the water, a lifeless corpse, for the bullet had traversed his brain.

Many others, both afloat and ashore, fell at the same moment; and a wild cry of despair rent the air, as the women heard the treacherous fire, and knew it portended death to all.

Mrs. Merton, transfixed for an instant with horror when she heard her husband's cry, rushed out the next from under the covered portion of the boat, and, with one long terrific scream, in which the name she so dearly loved was distinguished, plunged into the water after the sinking body, and disappeared with it.

A scene too horrible for words faithfully to portray then commenced. Volleys upon volleys of musketry were poured into the boats, the two guns on the bank belched forth grape on that hapless multitude, while those who had not yet embarked were cut down where they stood, or hunted from side to side—a hundred sabres, flashing in the morning sun, testifying to the number and animosity of their enemies.

But man was not the only prey of the treacherous and cowardly rebels, for the sand on the river's bank drank in also the blood of gentle woman, while little children were trampled under foot, or flung in the air and caught on the sword's point, their mothers, if still alive, rending the air with screams. Nor were those in the boats safer, for, crowded and huddled together under the useless covering described, the grape and the bullets entered and struck down many.

It is a horrible scene enacting,—it has no parallel on history's page,—but it will continue; for though the shriek of woman, the low-muttered curse of betrayed manhood, the cry of childhood, rise on high, they awake no pity in that arch-fiend the Nana, who, having organized the plot, now quietly looks on as his myrmidons work out his bloody ends.

All fell not, however, as sheep under the butcher's knife. The bold-hearted Englishman, the now desperate Eurasian, saw that hope there was none, and they fought like lions, selling their lives as dearly as they could. A few, on the first discharge of musketry, had jumped overboard, and attempted to swim to the three boats already loose, which had now reached the centre of the river, but most of them were drowned or shot by the sepoys as they swam. The greater number, however, remained where they were, true to their posts, guarding the women and children with them, and falling at last on the bloody boat-decks, monuments of the courage, the devotion, of the Anglo-Saxon, and the base treachery of the Asiatic!

Oh, how Edgington, in those fearful moments, envied those of his comrades who had no female charge to attend to. How his brain swam, as he realized how utterly all hope was gone, and the dark promise made to Marion flashed across his mind.

"Arthur," said a tremulous voice, "Arthur, I will be

shot by your side." Edgington turned, and there, as an angel of light amidst the dark scenes enacting, stood Marion Paris, still beautiful, with a wild light in her eyes, and her partly-untramelled golden hair, blown out by the hot blasts, brushing against his cheek.

But it was not Edgington alone who remarked the young girl and her wild beauty; the rajah, on the bank, did so too, and shrieked out,—

"Cease firing on that boat. There is the prize—the girl in white. A hundred gold mohurs to whoever brings her to me."

The Nana was not near, but Edgington heard those loud and fearful words, and trembled as he did so.

Marion heard them not, but she saw the rajah pointing at her, while some men left his side and approached the boat.

In an instant the recollection of her dream was revived, with all its horrors. "Arthur, Arthur! save me! save me!" she cried, as she clutched his arm, and, with a wild light in her eyes, looked up to heaven.

"There is but one way," whispered Edgington, as he bent his head to hers, while a frightful pallor overspread his face.

"I *choose* that way! It is that way I mean. Your promise — remember! Quick, 'twill be too late directly."

"God bless thee then in death, my Marion!" exclaimed Edgington, as he imprinted one long and ardent kiss on the lips of the young girl. It was the first and last kiss he ever gave her. She shut her eyes, for she could not look on the instant death which she knew awaited her. One instant more, as, with a trembling hand, the pistol was cocked, and the next the brains of Marion Paris bespattered the chest of her guardian.

"Now, hell-hound!" shrieked Edgington, as he leapt from the boat, all tremor, all fear past, and rushed up the bank towards the Nana. "Alas! I cannot reach him!" he added, with a despairing tone, as he was met by the rajah's emissaries; "but my bullet may. One chance remains, — if successful, I die happy."

With steady nerves, in the wild tumult raging, he rested his revolver on his left arm, and fired the last charge it contained at his—at England's deadly foe; but the Nana was reserved for a later fate, and the bullet touched him not.

Another moment and the spirit of Edgington, freed from its corporal tenement by the sabres of the rebels, winged its way, in goodly company, to that abode where treachery and cruelty exist not.

# POSTSCRIPT.

THE following, lately received from India, which appeared in the London papers last December, details at greater length, and perhaps more exactly than any other account, the final act of the Cawnpore tragedy, and is not, therefore, out of place here. The women and children, mentioned as two hundred and five, were composed of such as were not killed during the boat massacre, and such as escaped in the boats that succeeded in getting off that morning, but were pursued and brought back to Cawnpore, together with a portion of the fugitives from Futtehghur.

"Some time ago a half-caste Christian, named Fitchett, presented himself for admission into the police levy before the local authorities at Meerut. The usual inquiries into his character led to the development of his tale, which is as follows:—

"When the mutiny broke out, he was a musician in the band of one of the native infantry regiments at Cawnpore, and in the general massacre he saved his life by proclaiming that he would become a Mahometan, which he did by an easy process almost on the spot. He remained in Cawnpore, and was enrolled in the Nana's force, with which he did duty. On the afternoon of the 15th of July, when it became known that the British were advancing, a council of war, or of deliberation, was held by the Nana, at which it was resolved that the women and children at the Beebeeghur, numbering about two hundred and five, were to be murdered. The news went rapidly through the town, and the men of the mutinous 6th native infantry, entering the enclosure, proceeded to take from our unfortunate countrywomen any articles of value or any trinkets which they retained on their persons. When the Nana heard of this, he was very much displeased, and he also sent down a body of sowars with strict orders to surround the house and permit no one to enter but the executioners. It so happened that, by some means not clearly ascertained, four English gentlemen were at this time living with the women and children in the enclosure. Three have been identified beyond doubt; namely, Mr. Thornhill, magistrate and collector of Futtehghur; Colonel Smith, 10th native infantry; and Brigadier Goldie, of the clothing department. The identity of the fourth has not been established, but it is probable he was one of the Greenways. Shortly before half-past four o'clock, a message was brought to these gentlemen that Brigadier Jeekin, a native officer of the mutineers, desired to see them, and they left the house to repair to his quarters. They walked quietly along the road, suspecting nothing, in the direction indicated to them, and when they had got as far as the Assembly Rooms, they were suddenly attacked from behind, cut down, and murdered on the spot.

"Meanwhile preparations were being made for the execution of the orders of the Nana and his council. There was some difficulty about getting instruments for this butchery. The sowars wished to save themselves from the defilement of blood—the infantry were equally averse to the task—but at last some soldiers of the 6th native infantry were compelled to go inside, with orders to fire on the poor helpless crowd. They fired in the air, or did so little harm that it was evident the views of the assassins could not be accomplished in that manner. They sent into the town, therefore, and the sowars brought out two of the common butchers of the bazaar—two Bhooreeas, a man of wild, miserable, gipsy-like caste, and a vilaiytee—who were armed with hatchets and tulwars, and ordered to go in and kill every soul in the house and enclosure, while all egress was strictly watched by the sowars outside. It was a long and dreadful butchery. Fitchett, who was near the place, declares that the assassins entered the enclosure about half-past five p.m. and that it was ten p.m. before they came out to announce that their work were accomplished. Once, he says, a butcher appeared, with his sword broken in two, received a sabre from one of the sowars, and returned to continue his hellish labours. The Nana was in the hotel close at hand, and when he heard that all were dead, he gave orders that the doors should be closed for the night, and guards put over the place. That night the Nana gave a nautch—a kind of dance and ball—to his friends.

"Early in the morning of the 16th, the Nana gave orders that the doors should be opened, and that all the bodies should be flung into the well within the compound; but as it was far too small to contain so many bodies, it is probable that some were dragged away to other places, or were thrown into the Ganges."

It will not be forgotten, by those who take an interest in Indian matters, that one of the boats which got off on the morning of the boat massacre was never brought back to Cawnpore, and that one or two individuals in that boat escaped with life through the further dangers they then underwent.

THE END.

CPSIA information can be obtained
at www.ICGtesting.com
Printed in the USA
LVHW110346140123
737131LV00001B/192

9 783375 130664